T0304871

# The Trials of Marjorie Crowe

Also by C.S. Robertson

*The Undiscovered Deaths of Grace McGill*

C. S. ROBERTSON

# The Trials of Marjorie Crowe

HODDER &
STOUGHTON

First published in Great Britain in 2024 by Hodder & Stoughton
An Hachette UK company

1

Copyright © C.S. Robertson 2024

The right of C.S. Robertson to be identified as the Author of the Work has been
asserted by him in accordance with the Copyright,
Designs and Patents Act 1988.

Extract from *Grimoire: New Scottish Folk Tales* (Picador, 2020).
Copyright © 2020 by Robin Roberton.

A CIP catalogue record for this title is available from the British Library

Hardback ISBN 978 1 529 36769 0
Trade Paperback ISBN 978 1 529 36770 6
ebook ISBN 978 1 529 36771 3

Typeset in Plantin by Manipal Technologies Limited

Printed and bound in Great Britain by Clays Ltd, Elcograf S.p.A.

Hodder & Stoughton policy is to use papers that are natural, renewable
and recyclable products and made from wood grown in sustainable forests.
The logging and manufacturing processes are expected to conform to the
environmental regulations of the country of origin.

Hodder & Stoughton Ltd
Carmelite House
50 Victoria Embankment
London EC4Y 0DZ

www.hodder.co.uk

*To my dad, Allan Robertson. Still in our hearts.*

# CHAPTER 1

I close the front door of my cottage at precisely 11.30 a.m. Four seconds later, I pass through my garden gate, and click it firmly shut behind me.

After eighteen paces, I turn left onto Drymen Road, and begin the four-minute and twenty-second walk into the village of Kilgoyne.

It's a walk I make twice a day, every day. 11.30 a.m. and 6.30 p.m. Rain or shine, hail or wind or snow, never deviating from my chosen route.

The loop takes me east to west, through and round the village, and back. I always walk *widdershins*. That is to say, anticlockwise.

Kilgoyne sits in the flat carse of West Central Scotland, wedged between the lush green hills of the Campsie Fells to the east, the deep blue expanse of Loch Lomond to the west, and the trees and trails of Queen Elizabeth Forest to the north. South – twenty-five miles and a thousand light years away – is Glasgow.

The village is not so small that everyone knows everyone else, not quite, but there's no more than one degree of separation to those that do. I've no doubt that I'm a familiar face to everyone in Kilgoyne. A handful are well enough acquainted to swap passing remarks on the weather. A few are close enough to indulge in brief conversation, although they're all well enough informed as to not interrupt my walk in order to do so.

My timekeeping, if I may say so, is impeccable. The people of the village are fully aware where I'll be and when. They say that they can set their watches by me.

It's one of the few things they seem to be sure of in my regard.

I've heard that the wagging tongues put my age at somewhere between sixty and a less flattering seventy. They think me to be divorced or a lifelong spinster, that I used to be a librarian, a pharmacist, a teacher or a witch. Some even think I might be autistic or have had a stroke; others think I'm simply rude.

Kilgoyne has never been able to work me out, and I've never thought to make it any easier for them.

In a city I'd have disappeared, swallowed up by a mass of humanity, one oddity among thousands of other oddities. Seldom spotted, rarely noticed. In a village of just eight hundred people, I'm always seen, always talked about. I'm not comfortable with that but nor do I particularly care. I am who I am.

I'm aware that, in the context of Kilgoyne, I look … different. I walk taller than my five foot seven because of the way I carry myself – upright, head high, not so much sure of myself, more defying anyone to think otherwise. My grey hair tied behind me, unkempt but controlled, my cheeks a careless, weather-beaten rose, my skin taut. Clothes are not something I give much thought to and others seem to find this amusing. I wear them as I find them, with much more consideration given to the prevailing weather than prevailing fashion.

Today, my attire consists of a blood red, ankle-length woollen skirt, a heavy blue and yellow man's checked shirt buttoned to the neck, and a pair of sturdy brown walking boots. Practicalities take precedence over all else.

The people of Kilgoyne don't know much about me, but I'm considerably better informed about them. I walk and I see, and I remember. And I walk.

One minute in and I pass the war memorial on my right, its sombre stone blackened by a hundred years of rain, wreaths of poppies decaying at its feet. Soon after, the scruffy walls of Fletcher's Tyre Services are on my left. Old Mr Fletcher was a decent man but the son who now runs the business is too fond of racehorses and other men's wives.

It's warm for April and barely a whisper of wind disturbs the huddles of daffodils in Bell Park. Two young mothers keep a wary eye on their preschoolers, watching them race from swing to roundabout to slide.

Kilgoyne's red sandstone terraces are glowing in the spring sunshine, while the whitewashed houses and cottages are sparkling. Many are dressed in swathes of mature ivy and hanging baskets overflowing with primulas, pansies and lobelia. Hedges are neatly trimmed, and lawns are well tended. The street is still and quiet, picture-perfect.

At the corner of Croftburn Road stands what everyone still calls the old Moncur house, owned for generations by a tobacco baron and his descendants, owned for the past forty years by incomers from Glasgow. It's easily the largest and grandest house in the village, and now home to their son, businessman Rowan Haldane, and his young Filipino wife.

The Moncur house rises three storeys tall, topped by turrets and a roof of black Spanish slate. The building stands twenty-five yards back from the road behind wrought-iron gates, its entrance heralded by a large, imposing black front door of solid oak and dark metal studs. I've always found the house bothersome, finding something sinister in its intent, something threatening in the blackness of its grandeur.

I hurry on, past the taxi office and the new florist, and onto Main Street with its collection of small, locally owned shops and two of the village's three public houses. The shopfronts are painted in differing pastel shades; baby blues, soft yellows, mauves and minty greens; a twenty-first century innovation designed to look good on postcards. I don't much care for it.

At the end of Main Street, on the corner with the A81, is the Endrick Arms, Kilgoyne's oldest pub. The gaudy signage declares that it has been serving ale since 1787. It lies directly on my route, and so I treat it as such. I open the door and walk inside, barely sidestepping a couple of early drinkers as I march through the bar, giving a sharp nod in response to the landlord's sarcastic greeting, and out the far door onto Gartness Road.

I am not so strange as not to be aware that this habit of mine causes consternation among some, but that is their concern and not mine. I know that the landlord, the irritant peacock that is Mr Adam Cummings, likes to remark that his pub has many regulars, but none as regular as Marjorie Crowe. Which is me. *Marjorie Crowe has been to the bar twice a day every day for twenty-five years*, he likes to tell them, *and has never yet bought a drink*. And nor am I likely to when the landlord is in possession of such an attitude.

I veer right across Gartness Road, moving north, only a few paces needed to leave the heart of the village behind and bring hedgerows back into sight. The side of the road is dotted with clumps of cuckooflowers, or Lady's Smock as I prefer. The row of beech trees behind the hedge hangs thick with the pendulous catkins known as lamb's tails, and the wood beyond will soon be carpeted in a violet mist of bluebells. All around, the fields are a lush, flat patchwork of greens and beiges, cut through by the meandering wiles of the Endrick Water.

I walk on. On past the red telephone box, seeing stacks of paperback books inside, left for the villagers to read and swap. On past the Willow Bed and Breakfast and the turn to Geir's Farm, the village to my left. On Bodach Lane, I walk between tall, leafy elms, my ankles brushing past white dead-nettles and cow parsley, the air sweet and spicy with hyacinths.

Up ahead in Spittal's Clearing, but still just out of sight, is the Witching Tree. It's an ancient elm broken into two sections, much of the fallen upper half eaten up by the peaty earth. The bottom half is uprooted but still standing after a fashion, its trunk studded with iron pegs, each hammered in over a hundred years ago.

The tree itself is a stranger, an elm among beeches. I've always felt a particular kinship with it.

The Witching Tree marks the spot where I swing south and return east, the village still, as ever, to my left. *Widdershins*. The tree and the clearing are the turning point.

As I get closer, the clearing opening up before me, I sense something is wrong. It's still a hundred yards away but the picture isn't as it should be. I can't tell you if I see it or sense it, I can't say

4

whether it's coming slowly into focus or whether something inside is screaming out to me. But I know. I *know*.

At 11.58 on an unseasonably warm Tuesday in April, I reach the Witching Tree.

I stand and stare.

And, for the first time in twenty-five years, I stop walking.

# CHAPTER 2

The planet spins at around one thousand miles an hour. The speed is constant and that's the only thing that stops people from falling over or falling off.

They're racing around at more than the speed of sound and going too fast to notice. It's the way the world works. Until it stops.

When it comes to a halt, everything is thrown off.

Birds fall from the sky. Teacups shatter. Babies scream. Trains leave the rails.

It has happened to me twice.

The first was twenty-six years ago. A Tuesday. The Spice Girls had been playing on the car radio. It was hot once the sun burned off the cloud. The Olympics were on and Britain had won the rowing during the night before. I'd made a tuna salad. I'd had to go to the shop for eggs.

Then my world stopped spinning. A thousand miles an hour to zero in the blink of an eye. It was carnage. Everything stopped and everything broke.

And whatever anyone tells you, broken things can't be fixed.

It takes a lot to make the world stop spinning. It needs something huge, something overwhelming, to defy physics or astronomy or order or whatever it is.

It's happening again now by the tree on Bodach Lane.

World stopped. Brakes on.

It strikes me that hanging must be a hard way to die. The poor soul might believe it's a good idea. Right up to the point where it isn't. And then it's too late.

Then you're weighed down. Weighed down with all the worries and woes that drove you to it in the first place. Dragged down

6

towards the ground and the grave by the devils hanging from your ankles.

Too late then.

Hands grabbing at the rope. Knuckles whitening. Fingers scrambling. Fingernails breaking. Eyes bulging. Legs swinging.

All too late.

The world has stopped.

# CHAPTER 3

I back away from Spittal's Clearing, my mind doing somersaults. I take four unsteady steps backwards with my eyes closed. At first all I can hear is the crack of dry twigs under my boots but then I stop, stand still and listen carefully.

Behind me on the lane, a charm of goldfinches squabbles excitedly on the hedgerow. From my right comes a mournful ballad from a broken-hearted song thrush. From my left and up, I hear the thunderclap of a hovering carrion crow, its aggressive, gravelly bark echoing as it hangs on the breeze.

There's more. The rushing of blood in my ears. The rapid thump of my heart. The rustle of a growing wind stealing through the beeches. In the distance, I can hear teacups shattering, babies screaming and the death rattle of a train leaving the rails.

I take two more steps backwards, eyes screwed firmly shut, taking in a lungful of air before spinning on my right foot and turning through 180 degrees. I stand long enough to be sure I've regained my balance before I slowly open my eyes. In front of me is the way home. The path as it always has been.

I walk.

Across Bodach Lane, along the beaten path that leads to Blane Bridge, purple dog violets lining the way. A pair of beech trees stand like silent sentries to the bridge. I pause briefly in front of them, the river before me and the usual words of caution running through my head. As ever, I dismiss them. Two hundred years of stone are beneath my feet as I cross Endrick Water.

I know I'm walking like a drunk pretending to be sober. The forced, self-conscious gait of someone determined not to give anything away. Concentrating hard, making sure my legs keep me upright, never straying from the path.

I walk as the spire of Kilgoyne Parish Church looms into view on my left, the wind whipping up and dark clouds encroaching. I stare ahead fiercely, trying to shut out all the thoughts that are laying siege to me. On past the glamping cabins, past the rear of the primary school and its playing fields, the village growing larger, closer. I walk the line, closer to humanity, further from the truth.

When I open the door to the Endrick Arms from Gartness Road, noise attacks and envelops me, heads turn to look for me. People like routine and they're easily unsettled by a departure from it. I'm eleven minutes late, and they've all noticed.

Adam Cummings is watching me intently, scowling. Not only do I have the cheek to walk through his pub but I'm late in doing so. He's mouthing off to me but I've shut my ears to the words.

I can't help but stare at the couple sitting at a table facing the door, lunch menus in front of them along with a pint of lager and a glass of Chardonnay. Sandy and Evelyn McKee. Both in their early forties. Him in jeans and a blue polo shirt, stomach spreading, her a bottle redhead with a spray tan and red lipstick. Mr McKee nudges his wife with his elbow. *Here she is.* She looks up, amusement spreading across her face.

'You're late today, Marjorie. Miss your bus?'

I don't reply. Can't reply. I might vomit.

Mrs McKee is still processing the look on my face and her brain can't keep up with the pace of her mouth.

'We thought the sky must have fallen in. Oh come on hen, it's just a wee joke. Lighten up.'

I need to get out. I need to get back onto the High Street, the gossip and sniggers trailing in my wake.

'Did you see her face?' I can hear Sandy McKee asking his wife as I walk away. 'There's something no right there.'

'She looked like she'd seen a ghost, right enough,' the wife is saying. 'Oh Christ, I wish I hadn't said anything now. Me and my big mouth. She's a weirdo but I hope she's okay.'

9

'Sure as hell didn't look it,' he says.

And he's right.

I make my way haphazardly back down the high street and head for home, twice stopping to look behind as if the Devil might be on my tail. I'm aware of everyone on the street like never before, self-conscious of the vibes I'm giving off, looking anxiously at shoppers, neighbours, families, worrying at what they see on my face.

Mrs Leitch, nice Mrs Leitch from Carnock Crescent, is standing outside the butchers with her spaniel by her side. Mrs Leitch always says hello, always comments on the weather, always cheery. I don't have time for chat or cheery.

'Good afternoon, Ms Crowe. Such a warm day. Lovely, isn't it?'

I try to fight any rudeness, offer a tight smile and nod my head more times than is strictly necessary.

'Is everything okay, Ms Crowe?'

Everything is not okay. I stare straight ahead and walk quicker.

Past the shops, past the taxi office and the florist, hurrying by the Moncur house, by Bell Park with its fresh bloom of spring, past the blackened war memorial with its dead tributes to the dead.

My stride lengthens as I turn right off Drymen Road until I'm almost running towards my cottage at Stillwater Field, anxious to get inside before the world catches up. I push the gate shut behind me and it closes with a fearsome click. I race down the garden path and hurry inside.

I stand with my back to the front door, breathing hard and deliberating, my mind scrambled, my heart thumping against my ribcage. My eyes itch as if they can't decide whether to bleed tears.

Finally, I push myself off the door, hurry upstairs and into my bedroom. Drawing the curtains closed, I kick off my walking boots and fall back on the bed, staring at the ceiling and lying motionless, trying not to let myself think. I'm shaking like a leaf in a storm.

# CHAPTER 4

I know that a quarter of a mile away, in the Endrick Arms, chat is buzzing with gossip about me, has been for the last hour or so, bouncing back and forth between jokes at my expense and worries about why I seemed the way I was. I know this village; I know how they think.

*She's weird.*

*Did you see the colour of her face?*

*She freaks me out.*

*What do you think freaked her out?*

They'll get fed up with talking about me soon enough. The chatter will fizzle, the gossip will fade and they'll move on to someone else, something else. Sandy and Evelyn McKee will still be there, that's their way, lunch inside them, drinks too, their faces flushed. If Mrs McKee feels any guilt at having made fun of me then she'll have swallowed it.

She and her husband will have another drink, and all will be well until someone tells them. Until the alarm is raised that their son Charlie is missing.

That will sober them up sharpish.

They won't believe it much at first. It's not the kind of thing you think can be real.

They know Charlie's trouble. Has been for a few years now. Only seventeen but got into bother drinking a few times. A mouth of cheek on him. Sometimes runs with a bad crowd in Killearn.

They'll call his mobile but won't get an answer. That's probably not so unusual.

So they'll think it's just Charlie being Charlie. Until they get the text messages from his school. And the phone calls.

They'll phone the head teacher or the deputy. They'll be told that Charlie left the school premises and there will have to be disciplinary action, but the first priority is to establish where he is.

The school football team was playing this afternoon. No way he'd have missed that. Except he has.

The McKees will check at home. And with his friends. Calm will turn to fear will turn to panic. Someone will doubtless mention young Jenni Horsburgh and how she went missing from the village years ago, sparking fears Charlie has done the same.

Sandy will call Charlie's pals, insist that they call other pals. No one will know where he is.

The police will be sympathetic but say they can't do anything. The boy is seventeen. He's only been missing for a few hours. If he's missing at all.

Sandy McKee will argue and shout and maybe they'll send a constable over. Sandy will recruit help. He'll go to his friends, his neighbours, Charlie's pals. He'll get everyone he can to look for his son.

Doors will be knocked, phones will be called, streets searched. Someone will go Killearn to talk to his friends there. People will go to the newsagents, the chippie, the village store and the taxi office. They'll go to the sports hall, the playing fields and the park. And they'll ask in all three of the pubs – the Endrick, the Foresters Arms and the Lamb – just in case.

And they won't find him.

I know Sandy McKee well enough to know that he'll have spent time thinking about the look on my face when I walked back through the Endrick this afternoon. It will have been unmissable, I'm sure. And from the moment when he's sure Charlie is missing, it will be imprinted on the front of his brain.

He'll be sure that I saw something, and before long he'll have to know what it was.

He'll be coming to Stillwater Field to look for me.

My cottage is a small, two-storey building with exposed rough-hewn stone. The weathered slated roof is only a few shades darker than the light-grey walls, with two dormer windows giving it charm. At head height, there are latticed windows either side of an ancient wooden door, and flowers spring from the walls. A round chimney, shaped in dark grey brick, tops off the building and the look.

To the side is a mature cottage garden, borders stuffed with my plants, encroaching on a small lawn. The house is known locally as the Hansel and Gretel house. It had been called that by some long before I moved in, but the name stuck firm after I took up ownership.

I hear his boots ringing on the path before he knocks on the door, and before he then bangs on it.

'Ms Crowe. *Ms Crowe.*'

I lie as still as I can, fearful that he'll hear my breathing or the pounding of my heart.

'It's Sandy McKee. From Birchwood Avenue.'

He's standing still and listening but surely all he can hear is his own fear ratcheting up another notch.

'I need to speak to you. About my son. Charlie. I need to know if you saw him today.'

I can't miss the fear in his voice. I try to find the courage to get off the bed and talk to him, to tell him what he needs to hear and the last thing he wants to know, but I don't get anywhere near it.

I'm paralysed. Traumatised. Terrified.

Instead, I put my arms over my head and try to block my ears. Try to block out thoughts and memories.

He's pleading for help, and I'm just lying there. Thinking of the boy. And the rope.

He's shouting now. Top of his voice shouting. The emotion in it is raw. Heartbreakingly so. But I still don't answer him.

He's flattened the palm of his hand against the old wooden door and hammered it two, three, four times. He's pressing his face against both windows but sees no sign of me in my living room or my tiny kitchen.

'I need to talk to you. He's missing. My Charlie's missing.'

The last sentence passes through me like a stake to my heart.

He belts the door one last time with a clenched fist and I hear it shudder. His knuckles are surely bruising, the skin peeling back. I hear him swear in frustration and lurch back from the doorstep before he storms down the path and slams the gate closed behind him.

When I hear it shut, I get up and tiptoe to the window, hiding behind the curtain and peeking out. He sees me, catches me. Knows me for the coward I am. Maybe he doesn't know the source of my spinelessness, but he recognises it just the same.

'I know you're in there,' I hear him roar.

I shrink back and hide, standing with my back to the wall until I'm sure he's gone.

Time passes. I wait for the inevitable while pretending it isn't going to happen. I make tea that I don't drink. I make food that I barely pick at.

Six thirty comes and goes. I don't go on my walk. For the first time in twenty-five years.

Instead, I sit at my kitchen table watching the hands on the clock. Watch them tick over to thirty minutes after six and stare at them for a full five minutes after that.

The world doesn't stop, but I wonder if that's because maybe it already has.

I go back upstairs and lie on my bed once more, stare at the ceiling and do my best to neither move nor think.

With no response from me, Sandy McKee will call in more friends and favours. Other kids' parents, pals from the golf club, cousins from Drymen and Killearn, and anyone he can drag from the Endrick, the Foresters and The Lamb.

Sooner or later, it will occur to him to get someone to follow my route to see what I saw. Fraser Kinnaird and Geordie Dunbar are the most likely, golf and drinking buddies of Sandy's. If he gets them, they'll be a few drinks to the good by the time they are recruited from the Endrick and tumble out onto Gartness Road in my footsteps.

Doubtless, leaving the warmth of the pub for the chill of the night in pursuit of Mr McKee's wayward son won't make them happy. They've heard enough stories from Sandy himself about Charlie's antics that they'll have plenty of doubts about how serious it is. But a pal is a pal is a pal.

They'll head north out of the village as I do, probably arguing about whether Sandy McKee is sending them on a wild goose chase. They'll hurry past the red phone box, on past the Willow B&B and Geir's Farm. They all know my route.

They'll come to the two long lines of elms, the part of the lane that the locals know as Midnight Alley. The last of the day will probably have been swallowed up by the night and given way to dusk. The full moon hanging low in the sky will be blocked by the trees and they'll walk two hundred yards in darkness.

They'll see nothing and hear nothing but their own thoughts and, likely, somewhere high above them, the cawing of a murder of crows.

When they emerge from the trees and into moonlight, it will be like someone has flicked a switch, a soft glow bathing the track to Spittal's Clearing. Another couple of hundred yards, then they'll know.

Another couple of hundred yards, then then they'll see what I saw.

The silhouette will be unmistakeable, yet so shocking that they'll doubt the truth of their own eyes.

The boy's body hanging from the branch of a beech tree. His neck stretched on the end of a rope.

They'll run until they stand a couple of yards away, the body limp and lifeless above them. They'll silently hope things might somehow be different up close, that by some miracle they've got there in time. One look will tell them otherwise.

They'll see what I saw. Except that by then it will be even worse.

Charlie McKee's fingers, dark purple where the blood has pooled from hanging so long. His head bloated and discoloured.

The air will sting with the stench of death and urine. His black school uniform hanging from him like a cloak, his shoes pointing to the dirt.

It will be dark enough that they'll have to use torches. The light will pick out the horror.

The boy's fair hair will lie dank against his forehead, mottled with ugly dark stains, blotches of dried blood. His skin torn, cheeks scratched at and bitten, chunks of them gone, holes where flesh had been.

They'll know the birds have been at him. That the things have pecked at his skull.

The carrion crows have done what carrion crows do. There will be only two dark holes where Charlie McKee's eyes had been. Two sunken crevices. Absences with a thousand-yard stare.

Maybe a couple of lines from an old Scots song will come to mind, as it does to mine. From 'The Twa Corbies'.

*'Ye'll sit on his white hause-bane, And I'll pike oot his bonny blue een.'*

They will have to call 999, asking for the police and an ambulance that can do no more than help take the boy's body away.

Then one of them will need to phone Sandy McKee. The hardest phone call he's ever had to make.

# CHAPTER 5

Time passes. Slowly.

When I peer through the window, I see the full moon has cast a yellow haze over my hedge and fence, and dappled my plants in a buttery glow. So easy to believe nothing has changed, nothing has happened after all.

As I cower in my armchair, my back to the world, feet off the floor and knees to my chest, I hide from the reality that taps at my forehead for attention. I hide until hope is shattered by the first sounds in what must be hours.

When I hear the click of the garden gate and footsteps on the path, I feel sure he's back. Righteous and rightfully furious, demanding answers. I'll face him this time, empty-handed, answerless, and take what is coming.

I ease the front door open, my left hand on the handle, my right braced against the frame, ready to slam it shut if courage deserts me. But it isn't Sandy McKee standing on my doorstep. Instead it's a tall, gaunt man, wearing a black raincoat like a shroud, and tiredness like it's an old friend. Behind him and to his right is a young Asian woman, dark hair tied back tightly, brown eyes staring intently at me.

'Ms Crowe, I'm Detective Sergeant Tom Deacon from Forth Valley Division in Stirling. This is DC Misha Sharma. May we come in?'

I blink at him, barely taking in a word of it. I hold the door open wider, letting hope disappear into the garden, and the police officers and reality into the sanctuary of my cottage.

The man is in his early or maybe late forties, his lined face giving the impression of being older than whatever his birth certificate says. However, there's a quietness about him that is tolerable in the circumstances. His companion is in her early twenties, pretty and smooth-skinned, not worn down by a half-lifetime of worries like the sergeant.

'Ms Crowe, do you know why we're here?'

I look up at him, seeing him stretch a few inches over six feet, and wonder if I know anything at all. When he doesn't get an answer from me, he changes tack.

'Why don't you sit down, Ms Crowe. Would you mind if I called you Marjorie?'

I manage the slightest shrug of my shoulders.

'Or do you prefer Marj?' the young woman asks me.

I scrunch my eyes and eyebrows together in a manner that I hope conveys the fact that I very much do not prefer being called Marj.

The sergeant gestures with his arm, encouraging me towards the armchair, but I stand. Even if I'm not sure why.

'Why don't I make us a cup of tea?' the young woman suggests. 'You sit and chat. Let me do it.'

It takes a few moments for me to take it in but finally I nod dumbly and fall reluctantly into my chair, my fingers entwined.

The tall detective sergeant pulls a chair from the table and positions it in front of me, sitting low so his head is nearer to being level with mine.

'A boy went missing today from the village,' he tells me. 'A boy named Charlie McKee.'

He's watching my eyes but I'm sure there's nothing to be seen.

'That's why people were out looking for him today. You might have seen them? Heard them maybe.'

I say nothing.

'Mr McKee came to your door, wondering if you might have seen the boy. Perhaps when you were on your walk this morning.'

*How does this stranger know about my walks?*

'Marjorie, did you see Charlie McKee when you took your morning walk?'

I hold his gaze for as long as I can, finally giving in with a sigh and a nod.

'Okay, good. Do you know what time this was?'

I want to nod or shrug or sigh or look away. But this question demands words.

I hear my voice sounding weak. Out of practice. '11.58. It was 11.58.'

'Thank you. You're sure of the time?'

I nod again. Firmer.

He's studying me, wondering what to believe and what not.

'And where was Charlie when you saw him?'

'In Spittal's Clearing.'

'And he was standing? Walking?'

I can't look at him and say the words. I stare at the far wall.

'Hanging.'

'Charlie McKee was hanging from the tree? A rope around his neck?'

I flinch as if he's slapped me. My head bobs.

'And he was dead?'

I glare at him. Anger rising. Indignation at being forced to revisit this step by step.

'Yes.'

The policeman sits back in his chair and crosses his arms, his left thumb toying with his lips as he ponders. I'm sure it's for effect.

'There's a problem, Marjorie. I'm not doubting anything you're telling me, but I must tell you, not everything adds up.'

I'm confused. He's letting his words hang in the air, hoping I'll give him something more. I don't.

He leans forward, his forearms on his thighs, his head closer to mine. He speaks softly and earnestly.

'I need you to describe to me what you saw, and when you saw it. In your own words. This is very important, Marjorie.'

I need to find words. And find courage to go with them. I need to find my voice and hope it's strong enough to be heard.

'I walked to Spittal's Clearing where the tree is. The one they call the Witching Tree. I walk there twice a day, every day. I left my house at the same time I always do. I got to the tree at the same time I always do. 11.58.

'I saw something hanging from the tree. From the tall beech. I knew what it looked like from a distance. But it was only when I got closer that I was certain. It was a body. It was the McKee boy.'

'You've no doubt it was him?'

'No. None. I've known him since he was a child. Back when he was a nice lad. It was him.'

'What did you do?'

'Nothing. I couldn't move. I was … stuck. In shock.'

'You didn't try to help him down?'

I look at my feet. My head swings from side to side in shame.

'I couldn't. Couldn't move. Couldn't bear it. Someone else was there. I told myself he'd help. Though I knew he wouldn't.'

The policeman sits up, his lips parting as he takes a moment to process it and control himself.

'Someone else was there, Marjorie?'

I feel a tear roll down my cheek and clasp my bony hands tightly together.

'There was someone standing below the body,' I tell him. 'Below and a few feet to the side.'

My words echo. I see the constable's eyes widen behind him.

Not the sergeant, though. His features are expressionless but for the lines which knot above his brows.

'And did you recognise the man who was standing there?'

I breathe out slowly and close my eyes. 'Yes.'

'Who was it?'

I have to take a few moments, have to find the strength to say the words I want to keep inside me. But I do. I open my eyes and look straight at him.

'The Devil.'

# CHAPTER 6

I know what I saw. And I know I couldn't have seen what I saw. I don't believe there is a Devil. Not as such. Or maybe I do.

I can see the policeman doesn't believe me. He surely thinks I'm crazy. I see his eyes widen when I say the word.

*Devil.*

My grandmother, Granny Begg, had different names for him. Old Nick. The deil. Black Donald. Most often she called him Auld Hangie.

Hangie is an old Scots word for a hangman. And for his noose.

The man at the tree was in black from top to toe. He seemed to grow from the trunk of the beech, and it seemed to grow from him. Branches, twigs, leaves, flesh and bone. He was well over six feet tall, nearer to seven, and as broad as the trunk he stood in front of. A beast of a man. Or a beast.

The man-beast saw me looking at him and didn't flinch, didn't blink. He'd no fear of me, or of me seeing him there.

The boy's body hung in the breeze. His head limp to the side.

Charlie McKee. The wee smiley lad that grew into the vandal with a mouthful of cheek and bad language.

It broke my heart to see him. Broke my mind too.

I'd had to shut it down. I listened to the birds and the wind and the sound of my own fear. I turned to look at the crow, hovering, waiting, plumage shining, black eyes glistening, its wings beating furiously just to keep it in one place.

When I looked back, the boy's body hung alone. Auld Hangie had become one with the tree, or had never been there at all.

So I closed my eyes and wished it all away, despite a chorus of carnage telling me different. I heard the trains derail, and the babies scream. I heard the windows break, the oceans roar and a boy crying for his mammy.

I ignored it all and walked away.

# CHAPTER 7

'Are you sure someone else was there, Marjorie?' The policeman's voice brings me back into the room.

'No.'

Sergeant Deacon sits back in the chair, a grim smile on his face. 'And yet you said you saw someone. The Devil.'

'I was in shock. The boy ...'

The policeman says nothing, letting me find the words. It takes a while.

'Seeing the boy threw me. I couldn't think.'

He nods slowly. 'But you did think you saw someone? Even if you're not sure. You thought someone else was there?'

'Yes,' I tell him. 'I think so. I don't know.'

The policeman considers those three options. One hand across his chest and his chin resting on the other hand, he studies me some more. I can almost hear him thinking.

People think me both frail and strong, with my arms thin but muscular, my skin taut and mottled. They think me an odd old bird, and I understand why.

The young woman, the detective constable, returns carrying a tray bearing a teapot and three cups. She places a cup in front of me, carefully pours the tea, and steps back.

I wrap two hands round the cup, cradling it for warmth and comfort. Sergeant Deacon lets me sip at it and lets me think. I'm sure it's his way of buying himself time to look around the room, looking for clues to help him get a sense of me.

My cottage is my own. He'll see me in it if he looks.

It's something of a floral overdose. The working fireplace is housed in a mahogany mantelpiece with inset floral tiles. Three white wooden frames are side by side on one wall, each with a pressed flower on a white mount. The plump cushions on the couch are decorated with bluebells and cornflowers.

The mantlepiece is topped by four thick white candles in stubby iron holders, two on either side. In between is an ornate, five-pronged black candelabra with a mermaid writhing around the central stalk.

Above the fireplace, a five-piece mirror set shows the phases of the moon. The glass waxes and wanes either side of a glistening, reflective full moon in the middle.

A third wall is dominated by a large tapestry, a five foot by six mandala which features an eight-pointed star that spirals to its centre in different colours and patterns, including striking whorls of peacock eyespots in burgundies and blues.

Shelves and furniture tops are littered with trinkets. He'll see crystals and painted cabochon stones, carved Celtic bowls and a small white statue of a featureless woman with hands clasped above her head.

I let him look and fill my own time by staring into my teacup in search of answers.

'Are you a religious woman, Marjorie?'

I fail to prevent the ghost of a smile play on my lips as I look up at him. 'After a fashion, I suppose.'

'How do you imagine the Devil looks?'

The question doesn't please me much and I wonder if I'm being made fun of.

'It's not something I give much thought to.'

'Yet when you saw someone, or something, in Spittal's Clearing, that's who you thought it was?'

'I said I'm not sure.'

'What did he look like?'

I sigh and reluctantly tell him about the man and the tree, the flesh and leaves, the bones and twigs. I know it makes me sound crazy, but I tell it anyway.

I tell him of the man's height and of my confusion over whether it was a man at all. Man or tree or trunk or beast. Or imagination or madness. Or Auld Hangie.

The policeman gives open house to every word, his face offering neither consent nor censure. He takes notes and when I'm
finished, he simply nods to accept that I'm done.

'Marjorie, why didn't you call the police? Or an ambulance?'

The question takes me by surprise, as I'm sure it was intended
to. I feel my mouth fall open wordlessly.

'You knew the boy was dead, or most likely was. Why wouldn't
you phone for help? You surely knew the police had to be informed.
And the boy's family.'

I know my mouth is twitching and my eyes redden, tears running down my face, but still no explanation comes.

Sergeant Deacon is no fool. He knows I have none, not tonight
at least. He stands and gazes out of the window, seeing the darkness press itself against the glass.

'It's late, Marjorie, and you've had a difficult day. You should
get some sleep and we can talk again tomorrow.'

It's tempting to let him go and that be an end to it. But I know
it would only be an end for now.

I shake my head, more violently than I intend, and find my
voice.

'The boy will still be dead tomorrow, Sergeant. Sleep won't
change that.'

'No. No it won't.'

He's halfway to the cottage door when I call out to him.

'Sergeant, you said earlier that not everything added up. But
you haven't told me what the discrepancy is. Would you do me the
kindness of telling me?'

It's his turn to adopt a lengthy silence, his face troubled by
deliberation. The pause bothers me greatly.

'I'm not sure it would do your chances of sleep any good,' he
says. 'We can talk tomorrow.'

'I'm certainly not going to get any sleep wondering what it
might be. Please.'

He nods.

'Okay. You're quite sure that you saw Charlie McKee hanging
from the tree at 11.58?'

'I've said so. And I am.'

The policeman purses his lips. His face grave.

'My problem, Marjorie, is that I have a witness who saw Charlie on Dalnair Place in the village at ten past one this afternoon. Over an hour later. Alive and well.'

# CHAPTER 8

I can still hear the policeman's words an age after he said them. They're ringing in my head like church bells, rattling from one side of my skull to the other, echoing on and on.

A witness. A witness who says he saw Charlie McKee alive over an hour after I saw him hanging from that tree. Over an hour later. But it wouldn't matter if it was five minutes or five hours. *Alive*.

I haven't had a full night's sleep in twenty-six years.

I've had good nights and bad nights, long nights and fitful ones. I've had nights filled with dreams and nightmares, but all were punctured, for better or worse, by wakefulness.

This night is going to be long. To sleep, perchance to dream.

To dream of boys and ropes and Auld Hangie. To be awake and question my grasp of reality. To dream and see it slip away.

I try. I get into bed, turn off the light and do my best to find some sleep. I move, I turn, I kick off the bedclothes and pull them to me again. Try as I might, I'm kept awake by questions and worries and images that I can't bear to see.

The two police officers are going back onto the streets of Kilgoyne in search of answers. In search of more sense than I've offered them.

I told them the boy swung at 11.58. I *saw* that. Someone else told them different. They're believing the someone else. Of course, they're not believing me. Even I'm not sure if I believe me. And I *saw* it.

Yanking back the covers, I swing my legs out of bed and begin to pull on clothes. My intention is to grab whatever's nearest, whatever's warmest. At the last moment, I change my mind and put on a pair of jeans that I usually wear for the garden, a thick jumper, and then reach back into the closet and pull out a long, hooded coat that I haven't worn in a while. It will serve a purpose this night.

Ten minutes later, I'm on Main Street. There's a stillness in the village and my boots echo on the pavement. Up ahead, I see two men coming my way, a slight weave on them. I pull the hood up over my head and continue walking towards them.

They're talking louder than they mean to, their words carrying easily in the night. *Poor Sandy. He and Evelyn must be going through hell.*

I keep my head low, but they've got a drink in them and are not paying me much attention. I get a grunted 'awrite' and I tip my head in return. As they pass, they're still chatting. *Can't believe that old witch didn't call the cops. Aye, I think she's got something to hide.*

We've all got something to hide. I'm no different.

I'm not sure what I'm looking for, or even if I'm looking for anything other than a distraction. But I know I won't sleep and that I want to hear what these streets are saying.

Ahead, the Endrick Arms is shut but lights still burn inside. The glow is warm and welcoming, even if my usual route through it is barred. I go up to the door, as far as I'm allowed, and am just about to walk on when I catch sight of movement through the window.

Curiosity gets the better of me. I flatten myself against the wall and peer inside.

They're sitting side on to me. Adam Cummings is on one side of a round table in the corner, ringed by four wooden chairs. The landlord is sitting with his back to the wall. Deacon and Sharma are facing him.

Cummings is a tall, well-built man in his mid-forties with fussy fair hair. He doesn't look or act his age. His third wife will doubtless testify to that. Divorced at twenty-one, divorced again before he was thirty. A ladies' man who doesn't seem to be very good at it.

His face is creased now as he listens to the police, and his eyebrows bunched. Either concentrating or irritated. Possibly both.

Deacon and Sharma will be asking him about the McKees being in there at lunch. Asking about their timings, their reactions, how they were when they heard their son was missing. I can hear some of it, but it's more sounds and the occasional word than much that makes sense.

They'll be asking him about me too. Whatever Mr Cummings says about me, it won't be complimentary, that's for sure. He's always objected to my shortcut through his premises.

Whatever he's just said, it's made Deacon nod and glance at Sharma. They come back with another question and Cummings' face scrunches unhappily. He won't be taking kindly to being questioned. He's not the sort who enjoys anyone disagreeing with him.

Cummings is shaking his head forcefully, emphasising whatever point he's making. I hear him say no, loudly and clearly. Deacon makes a note in the book in front of him then asks something else. As he does so, he glances up and I pull back from the window in a fright.

I stand stock-still, my back against the pub wall, and wait for the door to fly open and a furious, curious policeman to rush out demanding to know what I'm doing there. I hold my breath, not daring to let even a stream of it fog the air and give me away. Seconds pass, maybe minutes, and I ease back to the window, convinced I wasn't seen.

Cummings is listening, a question being asked of him. He seems okay with this one, though, as a grim smile puts a fold in his face. He points to the front door, then to the door onto Gartness Road, his arm swinging from one to the other. No prizes for guessing who Deacon has just asked him about.

Then Cummings puts on a shocked expression, exaggerating it for effect. I assume this is meant to be me on my return. *After*. He finishes his mime with a rapid arm movement to show how quickly I left his bar.

It continues. Questions, notes, faces, gestures. A lot of shrugging. Then I see them all look up, their heads turning towards something further inside the bar. I follow their gaze and see a door opening inside the pub and someone emerging from the toilets.

He's a big man, drying his hands on a black woollen overcoat that is too big even for his generous frame, his eyes widening at seeing strangers in the closed pub. He's an odd figure and doesn't have the air of a late straggler among the drinkers.

I don't know him, but I know who he is. The locals, especially the kids, call him Soapy Moary. He stands around six foot two and is broad-shouldered, with a large, dark and straggly beard flecked with grey. His face is weathered and smudged with grime, his light blue eyes startling against his dark, tired features.

The oversized coat is tied tight above his waist, and he has a dirty yellow beanie hat pulled down low over his brows. Below, he is dressed in faded army fatigue trousers and heavy, muddy boots. Under the mass of facial hair, the streaks of dirt, and a set of deeply ingrained worry lines, the man could be anywhere from thirty to fifty.

I've seen him occasionally on my walks, usually in the distance. He lives rough somewhere locally, then drifts off elsewhere for a while, maybe as long as a year, then turns up again. Harmless enough, is what they say. The kids make fun of him, as kids do, and it was they who named him Soapy Moary.

Adam Cummings calls him his potman.

He says the man is down on his luck and he lets him clear up the glasses and sweep the floor after closing. Anything that's left in a glass that takes his fancy he can help himself to, along with any pies that go unsold that day.

I watch and see him turn his back to Cummings and the police, shuffling round the room, picking up glasses, wedging his fingers in them so that he can lift four in each hand and return them to the counter, his eyes occasionally sideflicking warily towards the police. At every other table he stops, glasses chinking against the-wood, raising one towards his mouth, shielding it from view with his body.

Deacon doesn't look impressed and makes a show of looking at the clock on the wall. He says something to Cummings, who sighs heavily but talks to Soapy Moary. The man looks confused and crestfallen, gazing forlornly at the pint glass in his hand that holds three inches of flat amber liquid. The landlord looks questioningly at Deacon, who gives a reluctant nod.

The pint glass is at the man's neck before anyone can change their mind. Head back and mouth wide, the lager disappears in a single swallow. Wiping his beard with the back of his hand, he mumbles at them and begins to leave. Halfway to the door, he stops, remembering something and returns to the bar where he picks up a white paper bag, wedging it and its contents into a pocket of his overcoat before turning away with a last cagey glance towards Deacon and Sharma. I hear the rusty creak of a bolt being pulled back, then the door opening.

I'm frozen with fear and hope he doesn't turn in my direction. He doesn't. As I resume my position with my back to the wall, I hear heavy boots walking away from me and allow myself a small sigh of relief before keeking through the window again.

The police and Cummings are talking again, and I guess that Deacon has plenty of questions to ask about the potman. Whatever answer Cummings gives causes the detectives to look at each other sharply. Deacon gestures with a tilt of his head and Sharma jumps from her seat and hurries towards the door. It flies open so quickly that I've no time or need to hide. The detective's feet are quick over the ground and soon out of earshot.

I dare a look and see her haring down Rutherford Street, the beginning of Bodach Woods up ahead. There is no chance of my old legs keeping up, so I stand and wait. It's five minutes before I hear her return, breathing heavily and swearing lightly. She isn't happy.

She's back inside. I'm not looking, only listening, wary of my foolishness and of pushing my luck any further. A few words come clearly through the glass. *Goodnight. Thanks.*

I heed the warning and hide best as I can in a slight recess off the corner. The door opens, closes and is bolted. They walk away a few steps from the pub. Far enough that they can't be heard inside. Close enough that they can be heard by me.

'Well, that wasn't much use,' she says.

There's a pause. 'Are you sure? Want to try again?'

31

A longer hesitation before she replies. 'We have a potential witness in the Soapy Moary character, if we can find him again.'

'And?'

'*And* we got confirmation that Marjorie Crowe went through here at the time she said. And that customers confirm she looked like she'd seen something that shocked her.'

He doesn't speak. He leaves the gap so that she has to fill it.

'So that would all fit with her having seen Charlie McKee like she said. But Councillor Dryden swears he saw Charlie alive an hour later.'

*Dryden.* The windbag on the council.

'So ...'

So, either someone's wrong or someone's lying. They can't both be right.'

'No.' I hear something change in Deacon's tone. 'They can't. But maybe they can both be wrong.'

They move off, talking as they go, and the rest is lost to me but I'm still struggling to make sense of what I *have* heard. Lewis Dryden is their witness. The local councillor. And I'm either wrong or a liar.

# CHAPTER 9

I'm back in the cottage and back in bed. And I'm staring at the ceiling.

I know sleep won't come without help. I'll either be awake or dreaming I'm awake, and one is as tiring as the other. It's a cruel trick, but then my mind hasn't been my friend for a long time. The only things worse, of course, are the other dreams. The dreams of him.

I've tried valerian root. I've tried chamomile. I've tried passion-flower, hops and lemon balm. I've even tried cannabis. It's probably the one that makes me sleep best, but also the one that lights a flame under the other dreams, magnifying them, igniting them.

So I've largely settled for broken nights, for tossing and turning, and for thinking deep into the part of the night when thinking shouldn't be done.

Four in the morning is the wrong time to question your sanity. It's the wrong time to doubt your memory or your ability to tell reality from fantasy.

I eventually sleep. Fitfully. Behind my eyes I see the boy on the rope. Every time I wake, my first thought is the policeman's words.

A witness. Councillor Dryden. Dalnair Place. Over an hour later. Alive and well.

*Either someone's wrong or someone's lying.*

Or mad. And I know the mad one might be me.

I saw Auld Hangie. And I saw something I've been told I couldn't have seen.

There is no sense to be made of it. No explanation that can calm my sleeping mind or satisfy my consciousness.

Thinking doesn't help. Nor does crying, but I do it anyway. Cry till my pillow is wet and I finally drown in sleep and blackened dreams for an hour or so.

When I wake it's still dark, the policeman's words still come to me, and the McKee boy is still dead. It is the only thing that's not in doubt.

# CHAPTER 10

*June 1998*
The Devil's Pulpit, Finnich Glen

*The sunlight's last was draining; a golden farewell filtering through the trees above. The air in the glen still simmered warm from the heat of the day and the shapeshifting red-and-green walls of the gorge were baked, radiating energy onto the semi-naked figures who were circling the rock in the fading light.*

*They waded shin-deep through the blood-coloured waters, chanting, incanting, then back onto the land, and around, and around. Five of them, hand in hand, a breathing pentagram. Three young men, two young women. Flesh taut, skin smooth, eyes hazy.*

*The pentagram split and one of them clambered up onto the rock, stripped to the waist, carefully guarding the bottle in his left hand. He turned slowly on the flat top, eyes closed in defiance of the risk of falling.*

*The rest of the group clapped in rhythm, working up a feverish beat and he turned quicker. His bare, muscular chest was glistening with sweat, his lean torso daubed with blood. He brandished the bottle by its neck, holding it high above his head, the amber liquid swilling as he danced, a joint in his other hand. Sweat plastered his hair to his forehead and a wide, pot-fuelled grin cracked his face. He took a vigorous gulp at the whisky before bending low to hand the bottle on.*

*It was passed around, each of the revellers supping on its nectar, some grimacing, others gasping. Their faces beamed and flushed. They too were smeared in blood, some to their forehead, some on either cheek.*

*Their own blood was rising, growing hotter in their veins, enflamed by alcohol and drugs, and the nearness of each other's flesh.*

*The clapping rose to a crescendo, the spaces between beats almost disappeared, until it was all sound and no rhythm, just a manic ovation that sustained the man whirling on the stone, his bare feet clinging nimbly to the surface of the rock. Then, at a signal, the clapping stopped.*

*The man dropped to one knee, his head lowered and arms outstretched. Another male voice shouted out.*

*'Thelema.'*

*The rest took up the call. 'Thelema. Thelema.'*

*From the far bank waded a giant.*

*A man and a half tall, broad and dark, as if a tree had uprooted itself and was marching through the crimson water to the pulpit. Branches jutted out, twigs sprouted, leaves shook. It was tree and trunk, and flesh and bone.*

*All eyes were now averted, all heads bowed.*

*'We bend to thee, Darklord,' said the man on the rock. 'We serve thee.'*

*'We serve thee,' intoned the others.*

*'Your desire is our desire, Darklord. We serve thee.'*

*'We serve thee.'*

*'Your command is our command, Darklord. We serve thee.'*

*'We serve thee.'*

*'We bring you sacrifice, Darklord. We bring you blood. We bring you life that you might eat. We serve thee.'*

*'We serve thee.'*

*One of the two young women was pushed forward from the group. Fair hair tumbled onto bare shoulders. She hesitated, fear halting her stride, but hands found her back and propelled her forward.*

*'We bring you sacrifice, Darklord. We serve thee.'*

*'We serve thee.'*

*The great beast, the living tree, extended itself wide till the girl shrank in its shadow, then it bent and engulfed her.*

*'We serve thee, Darklord. We serve thee.'*

# CHAPTER 11

A blanket of cloud hangs over the village as the sun comes up. It's the morning after the night before. The day broke wet with rain which moved over us from the Campsies, and doesn't look like it will let up until noon.

Pavements are black, the park is in gloom, trees drip melancholy, and the mood is sinking deeper and darker with every conversation, every sighting of a police officer, every piece of gossip, and every thought and mention of the tree, the rope and the boy.

In somewhere like Kilgoyne, where everyone knows someone who knows someone, you're only one separation from being neighbour or family. There are uniformed officers moving from door to door, and a communal sense of loss and confusion moves with them.

There's fear too. This isn't a place accustomed to being visited by such awful tragedy. People die in their beds of old age. It's a place where emergency sirens are limited to the occasional heart attack or chasing a boy racer. The village has known nothing like this since the Horsburgh girl and that was over twenty years ago.

Word of the hanging at Spittal's Clearing has spread like a sickness. People are catching it from their neighbours, it's passing between business owners and customers, it's raging in the cafe and flourishing on street corners. And like a virus, it's spreading with variants.

The Youngs gave it to the McFarlanes. Peter Lamont caught it in the chippy and passed it on to his family and the Symes next door. By the time Malky Syme told his brother on Boquhan Road, there was gossip about drugs. When Malky's brother told his pals in the Foresters Arms, it became gospel.

Charlie's schoolmates and friends heard it from Instagram and Snapchat, the news changing with almost every telling. The talk in The Lamb was of depression, in the Endrick it was of a girl and a pregnancy. In a village where everyone knows everyone, no one knew anything.

On Croftamie Crescent, they heard it mainly from Geordie Dunbar. He'd clattered back into the street last night, full of drink and fear, and noisily told his story to anyone who'd listen. He said how he couldn't tell them about the sorry state of the boy's face after being eaten by the birds, then told them anyway.

Birchwood Avenue buzzed at the sight of police cars outside the McKee house and the lights on into the wee hours. Word spread from there, in sympathy and hearsay, until the whole village was infected.

Most people in Kilgoyne knew of Charlie McKee's death before they went to bed last night, the rest knew before they'd finished breakfast this morning.

And house after house heard from person after person how I saw the boy hanging and did nothing.

I've been giving much thought as to whether to make my walk. The easy thing to do would be to lock myself behind my cottage door and hide. I could use the rain as an excuse, but I've never let weather put me off before and I can't pretend that it's a problem now. I'm not going to hide because I've got nothing to hide.

It's 11.29 and I'm standing with my back against the inside of the cottage door and drawing in as deep a breath as I can manage. With my eyes closed, I puff it back out again. Good energy in, anxiety out. That's the plan.

Staring back into the room, I fix the last of the buttons on my coat, hug myself and turn. I open the door, step through it and, with just a moment's hesitation, close it behind me at precisely 11.30. Four seconds later, I pass through my garden gate, walk eighteen paces, turn left onto Drymen Road, and begin the four-minute and twenty-second walk into Kilgoyne.

There are mothers and children in Bell Park. The Watsons' daughter, with her wee boy, and the young blonde woman who is married to the lawyer, with their son and daughter. The young woman who works in the Spar at nights, and has a wee boy with the fellow from the garage.

It's the lawyer's wife who looks up above her daughter's head and, seeing me walk past, says something under her breath to the mother who is nearest to her. Quickly, three heads turn to stare. I attempt a smile but get no smile in return. Just looks of confusion and disapproval. I snap my head forward again in embarrassment, telling myself that it's nothing. I'm used to being looked at, comfortable with being talked about. I walk on.

Passing the old Moncur House, I look up at its dark façade and I'm sure I see a shadow pressed against a second-floor window watching me walk by. I think it's probably the owner, the businessman Rowan Haldane, but I can't be sure. The face seems to follow me like the eyes of a painting, forcing me to look away and hurry on.

A police car passes, the blue and yellow livery making me jump. It's heading towards Main Street, doubtless going to Bodach Lane and on to Spittal's Clearing. Images flash through my mind, boys and ropes, and I have to blink furiously to rid myself of them.

There are heavy footsteps behind me and in a moment, they've fallen into step with mine. I look up to see the Reverend Graeme Jarvie walking alongside. He's a tall, dark-haired man, dressed today in a navy-blue parka over an open-necked white shirt, and a pair of faded denims. He's in his mid forties, chisel-jawed and dark-eyed with an uncompromising stare. He looks more like a boxer than a man of the church.

'Good morning, Ms Crowe. I won't hold you up as I know you don't like to stop on your walk. But it seemed rude to just walk past, today of all days. I hope you're okay after the terrible shock you must have endured yesterday.'

Mr Jarvie likes to say he's minister to all of Kilgoyne, including those who don't attend church and those who don't believe in his god. He knows I fall into the latter category.

'I wouldn't say okay, Mr Jarvie. But I'm sure I'm faring better than the McKees. My heart goes out to them. It's an unspeakable thing they're going through.'

He nods gravely. 'I'm on my way to Birchwood Avenue now. I spoke briefly to Sandy and Evelyn last night to pass on my condolences and to offer my services. I'm told the police are speaking with them now and I want to be there.'

'I'm sure they will be grateful for your help.'

'Ms Crowe,' his tone has changed, and I know he's about to come at me with something different. 'What would be useful is if I can tell Sandy and Evelyn why you didn't raise the alarm when you saw Charlie yesterday. They're having great difficulty understanding that.'

His walking beside me isn't a coincidence. It's not accidental. And I don't have an answer for him.

'Surely you realise that if you'd told them right away it would have saved much heartbreak. They've got to think that it might even have saved Charlie's life. Ms Crowe?'

We've reached Birchwood Avenue. His stop to turn off in the direction of number 4 with the stationary police car outside. The house full of broken dreams.

He's still talking to me as I walk on.

'Give them that at least. Let them understand why you didn't tell anyone.'

I can't. Not that I won't. *I can't.*

On the corner of Main Street, I pull back the door of the Endrick Arms and take a breath before plunging inside. I manage all of two steps before the pub falls into silence. I keep my head up, look straight ahead, concentrating on getting to the door onto Gartness Road. I almost make it.

I can hear Adam Cummings calling to me.

'You've got some cheek. Strolling through my pub like nothing's happened. Are you *listening* to me, Marjorie?'

Then there are other voices. Other shouts. My ears are burning and I'm sure my face is reddening.

*'Get out of here.'*

*'Who does she think she is?'*

*'You're not wanted in here, you old witch.'*

There's a final shout but, mercifully, it's muffled by the door closing behind me.

It seems colder on the Gartness Road side, like a new chill has descended. The village is damp and cold, and it's sad and angry. Angry at me, it seems.

I walk quickly, trying to get onto the lane before I meet anyone else. *Head down, walk faster, don't look. Don't look.*

I hear feet on the other side of the road. Low voices too. I don't look up or over. Not even when I hear a loud, disapproving tut. I don't want to know who it is.

It's different, thankfully, once I get onto Bodach Lane. There is a handful of teenagers walking back into the village, all giving me the side-eye, some whispering to those nearest. There is also a handful of memories going the same way as me. It's impossible not to think about walking here yesterday, when the sun shone, birds sang, and the hopeful scent of spring filled the air. Just before the lights went out and hope died.

The long walk through Midnight Alley chimes with the sense of impending gloom. Every step nearer to Spittal's Clearing is darker than the one before, every yard my footsteps grow heavier.

There's something that has been playing on my mind since last night, a quiet voice calling to me from the edge of my memory. A half-forgotten thing that's urging me to revisit it. I'm almost there and I still haven't decided. It would mean me deviating from my route and, today of all days, that seems like a bad idea.

I finally emerge into the clearing and see it's maddeningly busy, a mess of police and locals. Of course it is. How else could it be?

I'm used to it being empty, being my place, my turning point. The clearing has its own energy, a vibe that I've always tapped into. On the rare occasions there has been someone else here I'd sigh, be as polite as I had to be and move on. This though, this makes it almost like a different location. The energy is something else entirely.

It's the police and people in white suits like a TV drama. It's the children in school uniforms and anoraks milling around a large pile of flowers and other objects. It's the tree. It's everything I've seen. It all whirls round me, dizzying me, making my head light and my breath ragged.

I try to stop myself looking at the tree where the boy swung, but I'd be as well trying to stop the sun coming up in the morning. It looms large across the clearing and floods my mind with images. For a moment, everyone else has disappeared, it's just me and the tree and him, and I think my heart has stopped.

I soon realise my feet have stopped too, and then I find myself wandering from my route. I'm edging off my usual path to take in the mound that has the schoolchildren so enraptured. I see that it's an impromptu shrine in front of the crime-scene tape.

It looks like some have bought bouquets from the florist on Main Street, probably some from the petrol station, while others have plucked their own, bundled together violas or daffodils and placed them within sight of the tall beech and the witching elm. Red-white-and-blue Rangers scarves are knotted on branches or laid among the posies, some green-and-white Celtic scarves lie side by side.

The expressions on the faces of the young people tell their own story. I see disbelief, confusion, distress and plain old nosiness. They're here to pay their respects, but also because they don't know what else to do.

One looks up: young Derek Cummings, the landlord's son. He's a stocky lad, always brimming with some grievance or other, and quick to anger. In an instant I see his eyebrows knot and a moment later I hear my name. *Old Marjorie*. Next to young Cummings is the Cairneys' daughter, Hannah, and the tall Harris Henderson, the boy with the high mop of red hair. A malicious grin spreads across the Henderson boy's face and he elbows those next to him, his mouth working fast.

Heads turn. I hear teenagers swearing. Eyes unashamedly upon me.

Agitated, I look away, pretending I haven't noticed. But I can still hear. Gossipy, hurtful words being aimed at me. *The Crowe. Bitch. Crazy. Old witch.*

I'm ready to flee but two uniformed officers have heard the ruckus and step in between me and the teenagers, quelling them.

I take the chance to slip into Bodach Woods, the decision made about whether I should investigate the voice that had been calling to me with its blurred reminiscence. I've already drifted from my path, I may as well stray from it.

I hurry into the thicket of birches in search of this memory. It's been over twenty years since I first saw it and probably half that since I last did, but I'm hopeful I can find the spot without too much trouble.

It should be about twenty, maybe thirty, paces in from the clearing, on a tree facing the scuffed-out path. I let my hand drift from beech trunk to beech trunk, crossing them off one by one.

Maybe I'm not on the correct line of trees at all. Maybe the entry point from the clearing was different. Maybe ...

There it is.

A cross carved into the trunk at head height.

Not a simple scratch of vertical and horizontal bars but a carefully crafted cross, perhaps six inches high and three inches wide, the crossing point two-thirds of the way up the vertical. Each of the four arms widened at the end.

Christianity is not my thing, but I know this to be the cross of St John. It's been carved with a chisel or a gouge.

I run my finger lightly over the cross, feeling the grain against my skin. It's changed since I first saw it, weathered over and grimy. When I first came across it, in the months after Jenni Horsburgh disappeared, it was a fresh, lemony white, untouched by the seasons.

Seeing the carving scratches one part of my memory itch. The second part is what has been troubling me. *The what if.*

I move on with a last lingering caress of the beech trunk. I walk a few paces to my right, my skin tingling, and stop again. My stomach lurches.

At eye level, there is another cross cut into the trunk.

The same cross of St John. Same dimensions, same design.

But rather than the worn brown cross on the first tree, this one is shining white with fresh inner bark exposed to the world.

I can only stare at it. It's a few days old at the most.

43

# CHAPTER 12

I stagger away from the tree, a final look back at the new cross, seeing it almost glow in the rain-darkened thicket.

On past the old carving, aware that I'm now walking on the far edge of the footpath, as far from the cross as I can manage. In seconds, I'm back in the clearing. My return is greeted with jeering from the school crowd but this time I can barely hear them. I don't know what to think or say or do.

Looking around for an escape route, I see the two detectives who came to the cottage, DS Deacon and DC Sharma. He's stopped just before the tree. Charlie McKee's beech. He's a tall man, around six feet three, yet even as he extends his right arm, the branch is still four or five feet out of his reach.

He's talking to Sharma, who is gesturing with her arms and looking flustered. Perhaps he's asking her one of the many questions that are fighting for space in my head. Like, if you were of a mind to hang yourself, why would you do it out here?

Maybe to have time. Not many people come out here, so less chance of being interrupted. Less chance of being rescued if you don't want to be. Or else this place meant something to him. It's not convenient, wouldn't suggest an impulsive action, so he came here for a reason. There are plenty of trees between here and the village. So why here?

I slow as I watch Deacon march a few paces till he's standing before the Witching Tree that I know so well. He's waving an arm towards the ancient, broken elm studded with iron as if to say, 'What do you make of this?'

I love that strange old, damaged tree, and realise I'm defensive about any forthcoming judgements.

Sharma studies its metal steps and the raised green welts that writhe like snakes. I watch her eyes widen as she stares at its broken centuries-old trunk with metal jutting out at seemingly random points. The other half lies in the dirt, a large, severed limb with five identical pieces of iron protruding from it, each a foot or so long and forming an L-shape at the end. Man and nature in collision. Or collusion. Sharma turns from this remarkable thing, looks at Deacon and shrugs. I like that she's wise enough not to offer an opinion on what she makes of it.

Deacon hears my footsteps and turns, curiosity creasing his face on seeing me. He nods, politely, expectantly, perhaps thinking I'm there to talk to them. *Am I?*

Do I tell them about the strange crosses in the wood? In my head I realise I'm thinking of them as Jenni's cross and Charlie's cross. They may not be any such thing. In the last couple of days, I've learned that my head perhaps isn't to be trusted.

I hear footsteps behind me and turn to find myself face to face with Hannah Cairney. She's chewing nervously on her bottom lip and struggling to find words.

'I'm sorry,' she says at last. 'About my friends. The names they were calling you.'

'Hm.' I can't find it in myself to absolve her completely. They were *her* friends. I just make the noise.

'They were being mean,' she continues. '*We* were being mean. I'm sorry. Everyone's in shock. Charlie's friends, that is. It's not right though. Not right at all.'

I'm confused. She's talking in riddles.

'Is there something you want to tell me, Hannah?'

There is. I can see it in her face. But I can also see something else. I think it's fear.

'We're all in the youth group. Charlie was too. It's terrible what happened. Awful. And I know you saw it. I'm so sorry.'

If she's trying to tell me something, the girl isn't doing a very good job of it. Just as she looks like she's going to try again, she doesn't. She's on the verge of tears as she turns and goes back to her friends.

I need to keep walking. I'm back on my path. I'm not going to stop now.

Other police are active, fussing around the part of the clearing marked off by tape. Little yellow numbered markers dot the ground, white ghosts flit hither and thither, and dampness is enveloping it all.

I skirt the cordon, not daring to look back, yet knowing that the two detectives are staring at my retreat, the teenage gang doubtless doing the same. I think I hear my name being called but I let it drift over my head and escape from the clearing.

I make my turn and head back to the village. Along the beaten path and across Blane Bridge, past the church and the school until I'm back on Gartness Road, steeling myself to go through the Endrick Arms again. Going round the pub would be the easy way but it isn't *my* way. I have to stick to my route.

Easing back the door, I step inside, head high, refusing to bow to them. The reaction is immediate. They've been waiting for me.

'*Here she is.*'

'*Late again.*'

'*Ding dong, the witch is here.*'

People are booing. It's horrendous.

'*Why didn't you call an ambulance? Or the police?*'

'*Why did you do nothing?*'

The door on the far side can't come quick enough, and when it does, I slam it behind me, cutting out the shouts apart from the ones that still reverberate in my head. Main Street is the way home and I'm aching for it. Yet halfway along, another obstacle looms large.

They must have come back the other way, the shorter route. They're blocking the pavement, all watching my approach. I can't take any more, not today, and I cross the street to avoid them. It isn't enough.

'Hey Marjorie.'

I stare ahead and keep walking.

'*Hey Marjorie.*' Louder now.

I look, despite myself. There are five of them, the three boys and two girls, all staring, shouting, jeering.

Derek Cummings, eyes blazing. Next to him is Kai McHarg, Katie Wallace and Hannah Cairney. Most unnerving of all is the tall, red-haired figure of Harris Henderson. He's standing with his legs wide, his arm outstretched, his hand in a fist and a single finger pointing at me. He is staring, unflinching, not moving.

The Cummings boy is talking, cursing, bristling, a bundle of bad temper. All movement compared to the stillness of his friend. Henderson doesn't even blink.

The rest are jeering, angrily calling my name, demanding that I listen and look. I can't make out much of it though, thankfully. Two words do come across loud and clear, though. *Charlie. Witch.*

Whatever possessed Hannah to talk to me kindly earlier seems to have deserted her now that she is back in the company of wolves. A pack mentality is a dangerous, mind-shifting experience.

My cheeks are flushed and my mouth is tight, my throat dry. I think I sense rather than see the object that flies by my ear.

All I catch is a blur after it passes within an inch or two of my face. It's followed by a slapping sound, and I look down to see an egg splattered on the pavement just a few feet away. Laughs and whoops fly up from the gang opposite.

I feel a hot anger rising in me, humiliation too. I'm swithering as to whether to break my walk and confront them, but before I can, someone else does.

A tall man clad in a navy-blue parka and denims marches across and barks at them, gesticulating angrily. Even from the back, I know it's the Reverend Graeme Jarvie. He's pointing at them, then pointing at me. Most of the teenagers are now looking at the ground, like guilty schoolkids. Not the Henderson boy, though. He's dropped his arm but still stares unblinkingly at me.

Reverend Jarvie continues to berate them, giving me the opportunity to walk away without suffering any more abuse.

I cry all the way home.

# CHAPTER 13

His office is one floor up on Main Street, above the newsagent. I climb the stairs warily, not quite sure of the wisdom of confronting him, but knowing that it's something I have to do for my own peace of mind.

I knock on the oak-veneered office door and turn the handle to enter just as a loud voice from inside invites me to do so. With as much outward confidence as I can muster, I walk into the office of Councillor Lewis Dryden.

Behind a broad, heavy desk sits a broad, heavy man. Dryden is 20 stones of shirt and tie and a suit that has to stretch in various directions to accommodate his bulk. A thick reddish beard does its best to disguise his second, or third, chin and his long hair gives him the air of a security guard for a heavy metal band, dressed for his day in court after beating up a fan.

I glance round the room. The white walls are adorned with a series of black frames, all hanging in a neat single row. Two hold certificates, industry qualifications I assume, while the others show Dryden in a series of grandiose poses, cutting ribbons and shaking hands, opening businesses and presenting prizes.

Seeing me enter, his face knits with surprise, and he quietly closes the lid on his laptop with what I take to be practised ease.

'Ms Crowe. How can I help you?'

I stand in front of his desk, awkwardly, as if I've been summoned to the headmaster's office. I wonder how long it might take before he offers me a seat.

'I was hoping to speak to you, Mr Dryden.'

He looks confused, and it's obvious I'm not the only one who's feeling awkward about this.

'Is it a constituency matter?' he asks me.

It isn't, but now that he mentions it, it's as good an excuse as any. Dryden is one of three councillors for the Forth and Endrick ward on Stirling Council along with one SNP councillor and one Tory. He's an Independent, and he's the only one of the three who's ever lived in the village. He's lived here his whole life so he's the one that people go to. In practice, he might not be *the* councillor for Forth and Endrick but he's *the* councillor for Kilgoyne.

'Yes,' I tell him. 'Constituency matter. Yes.'

He does an odd thing with his mouth and nose, causing both to twist to the left side of his face. It's not a happy expression. Either he doesn't quite believe me, which would be reasonable, or he'd just rather this wasn't happening. Also reasonable.

'Are you busy, Mr Dryden?

He spreads his arms wide to encompass his office. 'Financial advisor by day and local councillor by an overwhelming majority. Proud to serve and never too busy for a constituent.'

I wonder how many times he's used a version of that line. Probably almost as often as he's had free dinners.

'So, what can I do for you, Ms Crowe?'

My mouth is dry, and I can feel the initial words sticking in my throat.

'I'd like to talk to you about Charlie McKee.'

His eyebrows rise and his jaw wobbles. 'I'm not sure that's appropriate. I thought you said this was a constituency matter.'

'It is. I'm a constituent. Charlie McKee was a constituent. Mr and Mrs McKee are constituents. I'd like to talk to you about what happened and the events around it.'

He takes a hard look at me, twists his mouth again, sighs heavily, and reluctantly gestures towards the chair in front of his desk.

'You better take a seat.'

I work my way into the padded leather chair, feeling my left knee groan in protest as I sit.

Dryden sighs again. 'What is it you think I can help you with, Ms Crowe?'

49

*Deep breath.* 'I've been experiencing some antagonism from people in Kilgoyne since yesterday and I feel that, in your position as local representative, you can do something about it.'

This seems to amuse him. 'Antagonism?'

'I've been name-called in the street. I've been verbally abused. And I've had an object thrown at me. All supposedly because I was a witness to the tragic event at Spittal's Clearing yesterday.'

He scratches at his beard. 'Well, I'm sorry to hear you've suffered some … unpleasantness. But I'm sure you understand that, in the circumstances, emotions are running high.'

'You think that excuses it, Mr Dryden? Because I don't.'

He clearly does think it excuses it but won't say so. It's writ large on his face.

He coughs. 'I'm not saying it excuses it, Ms Crowe. But it might help explain it.'

'Hm. It strikes me I'm being blamed in some quarters for Charlie McKee's death when my only crime is witnessing it. Do you think that's fair, Mr Dryden?'

I see him flinch at the word witnessing. His face is disagreeing with me and there's more he wants to say. I'm aiming to make him say it.

'Ms Crowe, people in the village are incredibly upset at what's happened. I'm sure you understand that.'

'I understand it more than most, Mr Dryden. And more than you think. I also saw that boy hanging from the tree. Am *I* not entitled to be upset? Have you any idea of how distressing it is to see something like that?'

He draws himself up in his seat, his mouth twitching at the corners as if he's found the last remnants of his lunch.

'I'm sure anyone seeing such a thing would be affected by it.'

'*I* saw it.'

He just looks back at me. It seems I'll have to do it the hard way.

'Another thing that's upsetting me, Mr Dryden, is that my word is being challenged. Either me or my eyesight, or my sanity.'

He says nothing and continues to nibble on his imaginary food.

'Are you aware that the police say they have a witness who claims to have seen Charlie McKee alive some time after I saw him hanging in Spittal's Clearing?'

He swallows.

'If the police have such a witness, then I'm sure that he or she would be kept anonymous as part of an ongoing investigation,' he says. 'Is there anything else, Ms Crowe? Because I have a lot to do.'

'Councillor Dryden, I know it's you that's the witness. I know it's you who says you saw Charlie alive an hour later.'

My words have lit a fire somewhere behind his eyes. He's angry.

'I don't *say* I saw him alive later. I *saw* him. Alive and well. Who told you this? It should be confidential.'

'Your son Kyle was good pals with Charlie McKee, wasn't he? I used to see them running around together quite a lot.'

'*What?* I don't see what that's ... I asked you who told you I saw the boy?'

'But I haven't seen them together so often for a while now. Did they have a falling out?'

My questions are doing nothing to ease his anger. The reddish beard parts as if to complain before sliding into a reluctant grimace.

'They just drifted apart. Kyle got more into music and Charlie got more involved with that group at the youth club. What the hell are you suggesting?'

'I'm not suggesting anything. I'm just asking. I know what it's like when people indulge in idle speculation.'

'Who told you I saw Charlie yesterday? If it's the police, I'll be demanding answers from them.'

He stares at me, and I stare back. I lean forward, hands on his desk.

'Councillor ... I need to ask you this. How sure are you of what you saw? Both that it was Charlie and when you saw him.'

He shuffles in his seat and settles his weight where it's most comfortable. He finishes the reorganisation with an irritated sigh.

'I'm sure of both. I know what I saw.'

'So do I. And I know when I was there. I make that walk at the same time every day.'

He issues a nasty little laugh. 'Aye, and doesn't the whole village know it. Ms Crowe, I've no doubt I saw Charlie yesterday. And I've no doubt about the time.'

'How can you be so sure of the time?'

He huffs. 'I don't need to explain myself to you. But, for your information, I'd been working here, restructuring financial plans for a client. I phoned Angus Dow to tell him I was leaving as we were meeting for lunch.'

'Mr Dow that runs the taxis?'

'The same. I left here at five past and I was in The Lamb by ten past. Steak pie and chips, apple crumble and a pint of Deuchars, in case you're wondering.'

'I wasn't. And you're sure you saw the McKee boy on your way there?'

He's really irritated now. His mask is slipping.

'*Yes*. Halfway there, I was going along Dalnair Place, heading to Main Street, when I saw him.'

'Did he have his school uniform on?'

'Yes.'

'Like all the schoolchildren in the village.'

'For Christ's sake, Marjorie. I've known the boy all his life. It was him!'

'And *I* know what *I* saw. And when I saw it. And we know what was found in Spittal's Clearing.'

He sneers. 'Well maybe you saw into the future. Again.'

'Are you making fun of me, Councillor Dryden?'

'Yeah, maybe I am. I'm sure you've heard the joke. If you want the winner of the Grand National, then ask Marjorie Crowe because she can tell the future.'

'I've never claimed any such thing.'

'Maybe not. But people think what they think. And who do you think the police are going to believe? The local councillor with all his marbles intact, or the old woman who lives in a shoe?'

I can feel my cheeks flushing with embarrassment. I'm furious and on my feet.

'I know what I saw.'

'Me too. And I've told the police that. Don't let the door skelp your arse on the way out.'

I can't find my voice or words to fill it. I need to get out of here before I cry in front of this man. I back away, mortified, and fumble for the door handle.

As I scurry through it, I hear him calling after me.

'I know what I saw. And the police know it too.'

# CHAPTER 14

Dryden's words are still ringing in my ears when I get home. They're making louder noises than my own protestations that I know what I saw.

I have doubts. Misgivings that are whispering to me, old insecurities that know just where to target for maximum effect.

*Did you really see what you think you saw? The man is a councillor. And he's very sure of himself. You think you saw Auld Hangie. How could you have seen the Devil? How stupid are you? How sane are you?*

I make myself a cup of tea, shakily filling a mug, and open my laptop. I need the escape of a trip through my historical searches or maybe to find an email from my niece Jessica in New Zealand. Some new photographs of her young sons, Ellis and Archie, at their little slice of paradise in Broad Bay near Dunedin are what I need to make this day a little better.

It was Jessica who talked me into buying the computer, finally convincing me of the benefits of it over the time it took airmail to fly around the world. The boys would be at high school by the time I got another six letters, she told me. I let the internet into my life. Initially tolerating this slice of technology, then slowly embracing it.

My heart lifts when I see Jessica's name in bold at the top of my inbox. It was always the most likely to be there, as apart from my cousin Katherine in Canada, a few suppliers for crystals and candles, and what I've learned is called 'spam', no one else is likely to mail me.

I eagerly click on the email and read. And can barely believe what I see.

*Hi Auntie M. I was so sorry to hear about what happened in Kilgoyne yesterday. A friend in Scotland read about it and knew it was where my aunt lived, so told me. It's so sad.*

*I'm sorry to bring more bad news at a time like this – and I wasn't going to – but decided you had to know. When my friend Lizzie told me about the boy, I went on Twitter to see what I could find out. There's quite a bit of talk about it there. But, and I'm REALLY sorry to tell you this, but there's talk about you too.*

*It's village gossip stuff and best ignored but I felt you had to know about it. It's nasty stuff, Auntie M. But at the end of the day it's just name-calling. I hope I've done the right thing in telling you.*

*It's better not to go on Twitter to see this, but if you do, don't engage. Don't feed the trolls. I know it's awful Auntie M but arguing back will make things ten times worse.*

*Lots of Love*

*Jess*

I'm staggered. And flustered. She's 12,000 miles away in New Zealand and telling me what the village is saying about me. I'm struggling to get my head round that.

I've heard of Twitter, but haven't heard anything that has ever encouraged me to visit it, far less join it. I'm completely perplexed. How can anyone on Twitter possibly know who I am?

This is all too strange. I know that I shouldn't look. That the dark door to that world should be kept firmly locked. Once it's open, I fear what devils might fly through it.

I look. And my eyes widen.

I've learned a bit about the internet through my searches into my particular area of history. The librarians at Drymen taught me how to do it. I'd worked my way through their stock and the books they could order so one of them, Christine, patiently explained how to use the internet to search for what I needed. I never thought I'd need her kind teachings for the depths of Twitter, yet here I am.

I make searches for Kilgoyne, for Charlie McKee, and for my own name. I'm not sure what to expect, but nothing could have prepared me for what's here.

Our little village is being talked about, so is the boy. Both are understandable, I suppose, particularly as much of the talking is being done by the villagers themselves. But so much of the conversation is about me. Me.

Someone calling themselves StuH is typical.

Can't believe wee Chaz is gone. Kilgoyne won't be the same without him. RIP wee man. Why the hell did the old Crowe no take the chance to phone for help when she could?

There are strings of anonymous accounts. People too cowardly or too smart to put their real names to their bile.

Something no right here. Cannae believe Charlie McKee would do this. Questions got to be asked. Ask the witch.

That old witch should be jailed. Even if she had nothin to do with it she should have phoned the polis

I'm hearing Marjorie Crowe made Charlie McKee do it. Somebody close to the family told me and they wouldn't lie

RIP Charlie McKee

What does old Marjorie know? More than she's saying. Bet ur life on it

My mouth is dry. This is horrible. Horrendous. And then it gets worse. As I watch, this awful Twitter narrative grows.

What's happnin to Kilgoyne? Place is going to pot. Strange things goin on there.

RIP Charlie McK. Kilgoyne no safe right now. The polis need to be looking in the right place. All I'm saying #CrazyCrowe

The auld bitch is dangerous I'm telling u #KilgoyneWitch #BurnTheWitch #MarjorieCrowe

I read with my heart in my mouth, a cold, clammy fear picking at my skin.

One post jumps out, this time with no attempt to hide the user's name. Harris Henderson.

> God bless my blood brother Charlie. And Hell mend that Crowe woman. Hell mend her #hellfire

That one has a lot of replies. Most of them taking the Henderson boy's lead, some from names I recognise.

> She deserves all she get. Do as thou wilt

> Kai McHarg: Charlie will always be with us. We'll always be with him #bloodbros #hellfire

> Hell mend the Crowe #RIPCharlie

> Hannah Cairney: God bless Charlie

> Katie Wallace: Your right Harris. Hell mend the bitch. Gods no gonna save her thats for sure

> Derek Cummings: RIP Charlie. The Crowe can burn in hell

So many people talking about me, the village and the boys. It's overwhelming. Some people know facts, others invent their own. Everyone has an opinion.

> I heard the Crowe gave Charlie a potion. Forced it on him. He went out of his mind and topped himself

> RIP McKee. Burn in Hell old Marj

> That old witch knows more than she's saying. She's to blame for what happened to Charlie McKee. Bet your life on it

The abuse is coming from far beyond Kilgoyne. And it's coming from far beyond my comprehension. There's a level of hatred and harassment that is taking my breath away.

There are people in America posting messages of hate about me. How do they even know I exist?

Scotland is surely an ungodly place. Thoughts and prayers from Savannah, Georgia. Purge yourselves of the evil amongst you.

I don't know what happened with Charlie but I know old Marjorie knows. How is she no behind bars? Get the witch locked up before it happens again.

These posts are horrifying. So many untruths. Surely they'd never speak to someone face to face the way they do on this site? The boy is dead. Is nothing sacred to these people?

As I ask myself the question, the answer leaps off the screen in tweet after tweet. Nothing is sacred anymore. Nothing.

There are outlandish theories about what 'really' happened to Charlie McKee, how I drove him to do it or summoned up spirits to do my bidding. There are amateur detectives offering advice and information to the police. There are strangers chatting together, discussing theories, trading misinformation.

All before my eyes. And I'm helpless to stop it.

I thought the internet was a place where I could learn things and interact with family so far away. I thought the internet was okay. And I guess it is.

Until it isn't.

# CHAPTER 15

I'm still shaking when I hear a knock at the door. I close the laptop, somehow hoping that doing so will shut out the chattering gossips that lurk within it.

Opening the front door, I find DS Deacon and DC Sharma standing there. The sergeant's face suggests he hasn't come to my door with good news. This is becoming a habit of his.

'May we come in, Marjorie?'

I don't bother to even try to stifle the sigh that slips out of me.

'I suppose you better.'

I show them inside and they both take a seat facing me, one in front to my left and one to my right. I wonder if this is a strategy that they're taught. If it's intended to intimidate, to leave me feeling trapped by them, then it works.

'We were surprised to see you at Spittal's Clearing today,' she says. 'Can you tell us why you were there?'

'I walk there every day. You know this.'

She smiles tightly. 'I thought you might give it a miss today. Not everyone in the village seemed pleased to see you. After yesterday.'

*After yesterday.* A phrase without context. Left hanging to see if I'll bite. I won't.

'I make that walk every day. I saw no reason not to.'

'There was a group of teenagers there. Shouting towards you. If they're abusive, you should let us know. Were they?'

'I'm used to nasty comments. It's nothing new and nothing I can't handle. It's not easy being young and they don't always know how to express themselves. I don't hold it against them.'

Another tight smile. 'They called you a witch.'

'I've heard it before.'

It seems DC Sharma is doing all the talking this time. She's harsher than Deacon, more direct. Maybe this is what they call good cop, bad cop. If so, I'm wondering what I've done to deserve the bad cop today.

'Marjorie, where did you go after you left the clearing?'

There's something in the way she says it. She's asking a question she knows the answer to. I see Deacon is watching me carefully, gauging my reaction. Perhaps that's why she's doing the talking.

'I went to talk to Councillor Dryden.'

'Why?'

I see no reason to pretend it's anything other than it was.

'Because he's your witness. Because he claims he saw Charlie McKee alive after I saw him dead.'

Deacon is still silent, but I can see him thinking. Sharma pares her lips back and comes after me.

'How did you know it was him who'd seen Charlie? We didn't tell you that. We didn't tell *anyone* that.'

I get the feeling Sharma likes confrontation in a way that Deacon doesn't. A young woman prepared to fight to get on. Because she has to. Despite her tone, I like her for it.

'This is a village, DC Sharma. I can know most of what anyone is saying as soon as I walk on Main Street. How many people do you think Councillor Dryden has told? Even if you instructed him not to.'

This catches her. It's a question she can't know the answer to. And she doesn't know Dryden well enough to even hazard a guess. She has to change tack.

'Councillor Dryden has an interesting theory,' she says. 'Not one that I can buy into, but I'd still like to run it past you.'

I sense trouble. I say nothing.

'He wonders if you somehow foresaw what was going to happen when you made your walk. That you had some sense of what was going to happen. He says you've done that before. Silly, I know. But then those teenagers called you a witch. And you have these things on your walls. The candles and the mandala, the crystals and the stones.'

I remain silent.

'You do know what the people in the village say about you, Marjorie?'

I've had enough. If her intent is to push me into talking then she's succeeded.

'DC Sharma, do you have any idea what it's like to be mistrusted for simply being yourself? To be mocked, laughed at, a figure of fun just because you're different? Just because people are afraid of things they can't understand.'

She's surprised at my tone, not ready for the anger in it. But she pushes back as I thought she might.

'I do have an idea what it's like, yes. I was brought up in Falkirk, where there's not many faces the same colour as mine. Was I mocked for it? You better believe it. Was I attacked for it? Yes, I was. So I do understand what it's like to be treated differently. I sympathise. And I want to listen if you want to talk.'

I do, now.

'I believe you do understand,' I tell her. 'Some of it at least. And I'm sorry you've had to learn it the hard way. That's so wrong.'

'It's just name-calling,' she says, her voice softer now. 'Sticks and stones. They can't hurt me with that any more.'

I nod. 'People can do a lot more harm than call others names. People like me have had to put up with much worse in years gone by. I'm getting attacked on the internet, but it's only words. They are judging me but they don't know me.'

Deacon's brows knot and he leans forward.

'Attacked on the internet?'

'On Twitter. All sorts are being said. People who don't know what they're talking about. Using words they don't understand.'

His face darkens with anger. 'I'll be looking at it. There are laws against hate speech and if anyone is identifiable and breaking those laws then I'll be knocking on their doors.'

'Marjorie, you said "people like you" have had to put up with a lot worse,' Sharma says. 'What did you mean by that?'

Is it time to go there? I guess it is.

'They call me a witch. And I am. Not in a way they'd understand, but I am. They use it as an insult, but that word bounces off me because it's accurate enough. The word isn't a pejorative. I *own* that word. I'm proud of who I am, what I am, and those that have gone before me. They can't insult me by telling me I'm me.'

Sharma's face is a picture of concentration. She's listening.

'My grandmother, Granny Begg, was a wonderful woman. She was what they'd call a witch. She taught me and she taught me well. Her grandmother did the same for her. It goes back generations and for generations women like me have been mocked, ostracised and persecuted for being different. I know my history. Do you?'

'Tell me.'

'We've always been misunderstood, either by accident or wilfully so. You'll know of Shakespeare's witches, the three old hags who met on that blasted heath? And you'll know their rhyme. *Eye of newt and toe of frog. Wool of bat and tongue of dog, Adder's fork and blind-worm's sting, Lizard's leg and howlet's wing.*

'Shakespeare knew how grotesque these things sounded and used them to make the brew appear something horrid, but the truth is none of these ingredients are what they seem.'

'So, what are they?'

'They're ancient names for herbs, flowers and plants. The kind of things that people like me have used for centuries. Eye of newt is another name for mustard seeds. Toe of frog is a buttercup. Wool of bat is just holly leaves. Tongue of dog is houndstongue, a herbaceous plant. Adders fork is adders tongue, a fern. Blind-worm's sting is knotweed, lizard's leg is ivy, and Howlet's wing is garlic.'

'I didn't know that,' Sharma says.

'Few people do. Instead, they they're happy believing the stereotype. But the problem is that ignorance breeds fear and fear breeds oppression. There were 2,558 people executed for witchcraft in Scotland. Eighty-four per cent of those were women.

Scotland executed five times as many people per capita than any-where else in Europe. Most were strangled by hand, then burned.'

They don't reply and I can see the enormity of the numbers sinking in.

'I learned much of it at my granny's knee, but I've read and studied every book I could find on witchcraft and witch trials in Scotland. Online too.

'Do you want names? Beigis Tod. The records show she was *wirriet and burnt.* Wirriet means strangled. Burnt meant burned at the stake. Grissell Gairdner was wirriet and burnt. Marious Peebles was burnt. Alison Balfour's husband, son and daughter were tortured. Meg Dow was burnt.

'Another woman, Jean Pennant, cured a merchant in Thurso of his boils when the man's doctor couldn't. She had him hold a chicken's foot, said some words, and wrapped the affected area in a poultice of sliced potatoes and potato extract. She wouldn't have known she was treating the boils by way of B6 vitamins, vitamin C, magnesium, iron, phosphorus, calcium, potassium, niacin and copper. She would only have known that it worked.

'When she tried and failed to cure the same merchant of gout, he accused her of practising witchery. It was magic when it worked and witchcraft when it didn't. She was found guilty and executed in 1726, strangled and burned alive in front of a watch-ing mob, many of whom she'd healed. She was thirty-three years old with two children, a son aged nine and a daughter aged five. Her daughter, Helen, made sure her own daughter knew Jean's story. Helen told her daughter, and so on.

'Jean Pennant was my Granny Begg's granny's granny's granny. My six times great-grandmother. My maternal line. My blood.'

'I'm sorry, Marjorie,' Deacon says. 'I knew some of that but not the extent of it. Those were terrible times of ignorance, and the consequences were horrendous.'

He means well enough but he's patronising me. And the irony of that means a fury is soaring in me.

'Don't you see? Nothing's changed. Nothing except the means of persecution. I'm on trial right now. I'm being tried by people hundreds, thousands of miles from here. People who don't know either me or the truth. Yes, it's just words. But what's next? Does it stop before I'm wirriet and burnt?'

He doesn't have an answer. Nor does Sharma. There's a long, uncomfortable silence only broken when his phone begins ringing in his jacket pocket.

'Deacon. Hi Fraser, what's happening?'

I see his face shift as he listens. And I can feel tension pulsing from him. A foreboding rises in me too.

'And he wasn't there? Uh huh. Uh huh. Okay, we'll go speak to them. Let me know as soon as you hear anything.'

A troubled smile has settled on Deacon's lips. He shakes his head.

'What's up?' Sharma asks. She can feel it, just as I can.

'That was Christie. He went to speak to the kid who last saw Charlie McKee. Jason Doak.'

'The boy who saw him sneak out of school?'

'Right. But we have a problem. Jason Doak has disappeared.'

# CHAPTER 16

'The parents say Jason came home from school last night as normal. He got agitated in the evening after hearing Charlie McKee was missing. Then this morning he heard what had happened and was in shock. They said he could take the day off school, but he insisted he was going in. He left on his bike, same time as usual. But he didn't get there.'

I think they've forgotten I'm in the room. Or somehow imagine that I'm not listening. I'm hanging on every word and flooded with dread.

'The school called the parents, Martin and Beth, when Jason was a no-show. They say there's no way he wouldn't just not go. It's completely out of character. He's been missing for six hours.'

'I take it they called his mobile?' Sharma asks.

'First thing they did. The number is unobtainable. The service provider says there's no signal coming from it. So it's either switched off or the battery has been removed.'

Sharma's face darkens and I know what she's thinking, know what she's going to ask.

'Has anyone checked out Spittal's Clearing?'

My heart stops until he nods and answers.

'Yes, and he's not there. That's the good news. But the bad news is that we've found his bike. It has one of those Apple AirTags on it and it pinged near somewhere called Duntroon Farm.'

'It's south of the village,' I tell them. 'The opposite direction from the school.'

Deacon looks at me as if remembering I'm there, then turns back to face Sharma.

'They've searched the area and there's no sign of Jason. He's vanished. Let's go.'

He stops as they're halfway to the front door and glances back over his shoulder.

'Marjorie, we'll be back.'

And with that, they're gone. The door closes behind them with a hurried, careless bang that echoes like a full stop on the conversation. A brooding silence is left in its wake.

I sit, mouth open, stunned.

Jason Doak. Missing. Charlie McKee dead.

These are things that happen in other places. Cities and towns. They're things that happen in newspapers and on television. Not here. Not Kilgoyne.

I know Jason as well as I know any of the young people in the village. He's not like Charlie, not constantly full of lip. He's a better boy than most, especially when he's on his own. When he's with his pals, in a pack, then he can be cheeky, but I've always felt his heart wasn't in that. The likes of Charlie McKee egg him on and lead him astray, but he's not wild like the others can be.

Alone, he's chatty more often than he is cheeky. I often bump into him in the library at Drymen and we sometimes walk back to Kilgoyne together, even if he hurries ahead as we near the village in case he's mocked for being seen with me. He talks about local history and his love for horror movies and the supernatural. I suspect that's what draws him to me, a wonder if I am who, and what, people say I am. He's a big fan of Stephen King and *Stranger Things*, reeling off references that mean little to me but that obviously fascinate him.

And he's gone.

Sometimes he talks, rather shyly, about how he wants to go to university and study film-making, perhaps even make his own movie or documentary one day. I've asked him why he's so coy about it and he says it's because his pals like Charlie just laugh at him and say that no one from Kilgoyne gets to do things like that. He's in Rowan Haldane's youth project though, and he says he's hoping that will be his way out, maybe get him on a course.

And he's gone.

He told me once how he believed anything was possible, something that had struck me as being a very un-Scottish thing to say. I remember thinking how I doubted he'd offer that kind of optimism with his pals around. But he pressed the point, saying too many people had closed minds, and that there was much more possible that we simply didn't understand. I took it as an invitation to tell him of the things I knew that were beyond the ken of others, but I declined the opportunity to explain.

And he's gone.

Jason's parents, Martin and Beth, are good people. He's an accountant and she's a classroom assistant at the primary school. He organises the local 10k run and she volunteers in the charity shop. They'll be imagining the worst. As that thought crosses my mind, so does an image of what the worst looks like. A memory swinging on the end of a rope.

He could have just headed off on his bike. Maybe distraught at what happened to Charlie and just cycled off to be by himself. He might come home when he's hungry.

It doesn't feel that way. Doesn't feel that way at all.

It feels all sorts of bad.

Duntroon Farm is about a mile and a half away. South and west of the village, near a bend in Endrick Water. It's not on the way to anywhere. The road stops just after the farm and there's nothing but a stony track trodden into the river bank.

There's no reason for Jason to have gone to the farm either. The McPhersons own it, two brothers in their sixties with no kids. No one of Jason's age that he might be friends with.

If Deacon and Sharma had waited, I'd have told them this.

And, maybe, I'd have told them that I think I know where to look for him.

# CHAPTER 17

I put on a pair of hiking socks and pull on my boots, tucking the bottoms of my moleskin trousers into the socks. It's going to be cold and probably wet so I wrap up in my waxed jacket, a thick jumper beneath it, and wedge a torch into one of the pockets.

I'm as ready as I'll ever be. Closing the front door behind me, I stop and take a breath, and wonder what the hell I'm doing. Going out in falling light, on no more than a hunch, on a feeling. Chasing shadows.

I have to, though. I owe it to the boy. To all of them.

If the police are there, near where the boy's bike was found, then I'll tell them and go home. I promise it, to myself and to them and to whoever might be listening to the thoughts running through my head.

'I promise,' I say out loud. Then I start to walk.

There are enough people out that I get stares and glares. Some nudge each other. Some point. I'll turn away from them soon enough, turn south onto Craighat Road and out of the village. Away from their judgemental whispers and their sanctimonious opinions.

As I make the turning, allowing myself a quiet sigh of relief, I see there's someone coming towards me on the other side of the road. A tall, dark figure, half hidden in shadow until he walks under the orange glow of the streetlamp. Then I see the bushy beard and the straggly hair, the yellow beanie, the greatcoat tied at the waist.

It's the one they call Soapy Moary. The man who cleans up in Adam Cummings' pub and sleeps rough somewhere around the village. He sees me but doesn't react like the others. Instead, he half turns his head away, seemingly reluctant to be seen. He's an odd one, this.

I'm trying not to look at him, and he's trying not to look at me. After we pass each other, I take another five paces then look over my shoulder. He's doing the same. It startles me and I wonder if it's doing the same to him.

The times that Jason Doak and I walked back from Drymen Library together, he'd talk about his love for exploring the countryside around the village. He'd mention places that he thought would be great locations when he got round to making his first movie.

The one place he talked about more than any other was Endrick Islands.

They lie in the middle of the river at one of its widest points. Although there are many little islands, at least a dozen of them I'm told, they are so close together that they're like one land mass with the river running through it. People have told me that you can step easily from one island to the next, sometimes by way of planks of wood sunk into the earth as makeshift bridges, others because the gap is so small.

I've viewed the islands from the riverbank but never had a reason to consider venturing across. I've always been aware, though, that the few folk who've mentioned them to me, have done so curiously. They talked obliquely and in whisper, as if there was local lore about the islands that they couldn't share. I've lived in Kilgoyne for twenty-five years which means I'm still regarded as an incomer, and always will be.

Jason was obsessed with the place. It was his number-one location choice, even ahead of the Devil's Pulpit. I'd ask why and he'd never tell me. He'd joke that if I knew then I'd steal his idea and make my own movie there. All he'd say was that it was spooky.

It's getting dark fast. There are no streetlights out here and I'll soon need to use my torch to see the road ahead. The clouds have closed in, and the moon above is flitting in and out of them as it pleases.

I've been walking for 15 minutes, the malicious murmurings of Kilgoyne fading into the distance, and the lights of Duntroon Farm are up ahead. There's no sign of any police. No hi-vis uniforms, sniffer dogs or helicopters, or whatever else I'd imagined might be out here. Just me and the road. And maybe Jason Doak.

*Amazing.* That's how he described Endrick Islands. His favourite place.

That funny, awkward, slightly strange boy. One of the increasingly few who'd spend time in conversation with me. Maybe the only one under 25 who'd give me the time of day rather than relentless cheek.

Missing. Disappeared. Run away. The last of those is the one I'm hoping for, but I don't believe it. There are other options that I don't even want to consider.

I'm deep in thought about Jason and his wellbeing when a dark figure steps seemingly from the hedgerow and blocks my path, a torch beam now shining in my eyes.

'Can I help you?'

My breath stalls in my throat and it takes a moment before the moon catches the hi-vis on his jacket, and before my brain catches up with the light. It's a policeman, a tall, dark-haired constable with a fierce glare.

'I … I'm just …' I can't find the words.

'What's your name and why are you out here?' he demands.

'I'm … I'm Marjorie Crowe.'

I can see that he's familiar with my name.

'I'm just taking my nightly walk and …' I hesitate. 'I thought I'd help look for Jason.'

His eyes narrow. 'There's been no public announcement made yet. How do you know about this?'

I can tell the truth. Even if it doesn't feel like the whole truth.

'Sergeant Deacon and DC Sharma told me. I was with them when they got the news about Jason's bicycle. Was it found near here?'

The constable is eyeing me up suspiciously. I think he knows of me by reputation, and I'd just as rather not know what he's been told.

'Not far,' he says guardedly.

I decide I don't like this policeman. He's not someone I can share my hunch with. I'm telling him nothing.

'Well, I'll just walk a bit further then head home,' I tell him.

'There's nothing out here,' he insists. 'Nothing to be seen.'

'I know. I live here.'

He frowns sceptically. He's thinking that anyone who chooses to live here must be a little bit crazy. He can't wait to get home to whichever town or city he comes from.

'Okay,' he says. 'But don't touch anything you shouldn't and if you see anything of Jason Doak then contact the police immediately.'

His tone suggests he's sure there's no chance I'll see any sign of Jason. He thinks it's a waste of time him being out here guarding grass, and he couldn't care less if I waste mine.

He may be right. But this spot, about two hundred yards from the entrance to the McPhersons' farm, is less than a of a quarter mile from Endrick Islands.

The path is rough from here, stony and bumpy and generally not somewhere you'd want to cycle. If you were going on from the farm, whether on your own or with someone else, you'd leave the bike behind with the intention of getting it later.

Five minutes' walk. That's all it is.

I round the final bend, the path opens up and the river is in front of me.

Fishing into in my coat pocket, I pull out my torch, casting the beam across the black sheet of the Endrick, my heart in my mouth. I can see the dark shadow of the islands, the tops of tall trees dappled in moonlight. I know the islands are only thirty or forty yards across the river, but they seem miles away in the dark.

Then the torchlight also picks out a thick rope that leads across the river at about head height, disappearing as it's swallowed up by the darkness. I turn and run my hand along the rope in the other direction, following it until it slips into a large clump of bracken. I wade in warily, reaching through the ferns, until I find something large and wooden hidden there. A boat.

I assume this is my way across if I choose to take it, but there's no way I can shift it by myself. I glance back at the river and briefly wonder if I can wade across, but I know that's way too dangerous and stupid. I'm stuck, and maybe that's for the best.

Then I see the rails. The boat is propped up on two long wooden poles that descend down the slope towards the water. Breathing out hard, I know I've got to try.

I clamber in, lifting my old legs over the boat's side, and take a seat facing the darkness where I know the islands to be. The rope is above my head now. I grab it with both hands, brace myself, and pull. For a moment, nothing shifts then, with another tug, the boat starts to slide. It's easier than I'd thought, and the system must be a good one. My scrawny arms are enough to have it glide slowly down the rails and in less than a minute we're in the Endrick.

If I want to do this, good idea or bad, then there's now nothing stopping me other than common sense.

The rope is a bit above waist height now, and I can see there are metal rings front and back through it to stop the boat from drifting with the tide. All I have to do is pull. It's tougher than getting it into the water but, pull by pull, the islands get closer.

Finally, there's a mooring post and I lash the shorter rope at the front of the boat to it as best I can. Testing it with a couple of hard tugs, I decide I can put my trust in it. Or that I have to.

Swinging my legs over the side, I land on a dirt path, inhale hard, ease aside overhanging branches and make my way between the trees. The tall pines are so close together that they snuff out the moonlight as though it's a candle in the wind. This is not feeling like a good choice.

My torch strobes the path ahead and the trees, showing them stretch high into the air, a seemingly impenetrable barrier. I pause at the sound of rushing water and the torchlight picks out the edge of one island and beginning of the next. There's what looks like a natural land bridge connecting them and I walk across.

The light picks out trunks and branches and hollows in the dark. I follow the light, the path and my nose.

And then I have to stifle a scream.

There are eyes looking back at me. A face inches from mine.

I instinctively step back, my hand over my mouth. My brain racing to make sense of it, but there's no sense to be had.

At eye level there's a baby. Blue eyes staring into the torch beam. A dirt-streaked face. And a rope round its neck.

It's a doll. A plastic child's doll with chubby cheeks and out-stretched hands, snub nose and a soulless smile. It swings from the tree, stripped of clothes and gently moving in the breeze.

My brain shrieks and races to other times and other places, other ropes and boys. It feels like my heart is going to explode.

I shine the torch on the grubby, creepy doll and it makes the eyes sparkle and the smile gleam. All I can do is shake my head and walk on. I turn the next corner. And gasp.

Dolls. Maybe a dozen of them. All hanging from trees.

Some are clothed, some naked. Some with hair, some baby bald. Some look haunted, others frighteningly cheerful. Some are missing an arm or a leg, some are beheaded. Most are dirty, weathered and decayed. All are shocking to see.

I don't scare easily, but I'm scared right now.

Jason Doak's words drift back to me. *Amazing. The place is so spooky. Nothing like it.*

Shaking, I stand in front of a girl doll, the thing staring down at me with empty eyes. Its face is grimy, the mouth stuck in a tight pout. The doll's hair, four red braids of it, has been separated from its scalp and hangs to the side of its face. Its clothes are dirty and damp, as if it's been dug from a grave.

All these dolls. All hanging. All dead.

I know how stupid it sounds. But dead is how they're showing themselves to me. My head is full of lost boys and I have to won-der if there's one more hanging here.

Turning slowly, I take in the spectacle and the horror of it. There a girl doll, her blonde hair darkened by rain and dirt, her gaze eternal. There a furious-looking baby boy with fierce blue eyes and dirt-dappled head, cherubic and chilling. There a burned doll, cheeks charred, eyes gone, mouth wide open in a silent scream.

The dolls are hung at random heights, some in pairs, most dangling individually. A few have their heads at odd angles from their necks, as if snapped by the fall from the rope, making me shiver and remember.

I can't stand here, not with them. I need to move on.

Two broad planks of wood lead from one small island to the next, their ends now embedded in the earth and part of the archipelago. I cross the bridge, two blank-eyed doll sentries guarding the way, and the islands offer up the true extent of their secrets and the sheer number of dolls suddenly becomes apparent.

A single short tree, no more than six feet high, bears fifteen dolls from its leafless branches. They hang like strange fruit, the words of the Nina Simone song playing in my head. *Here is fruit for the crows to pluck.*

A toddler boy dressed in faded blue dungarees hangs, eyes closed as if sleeping, his chin slumped onto his chest. Part of me thinks a gentle nudge and a whispered word would wake him. Near him, a naked boy hangs, a rope around his neck, his eyes looking up, the whites of them visible, his once fair hair now a grimy shade of hellish brown. A severed head is stuck on a branch, its tubular neck grieving for its plastic body, its expression mournful, its eyes missing.

*What the hell is this place?*

I hop to the next island, feet heavier. The trees are thinner here, the dolls ever-present. I duck under a low-hanging baby boy who's wearing a gruesomely gleeful expression. When I rise again, I'm in a small clearing ringed with dolls and the torch beam picks out a circle of stones, each about a foot high. In the middle is the remains of a fire.

Crouching, I place my hand close to the coals, feeling some residual heat. It's recent. My nerves are shredded and I'm regretting ever coming out here.

There's nothing else to be seen around the stone circle. Whoever made the fire has taken away everything except the ashes. I move on again, shaking.

Four small baby dolls are hung together, as if for comfort and company, each in once-white baby grows, all smiling cutely, disturbingly. A smiley girl in a gingham and lace dress has a mop of golden hair, its colour having survived the storm. Next to it a doll that could be its sister but stripped bare of the weathered clothing, its chest bearing a series of small, regimented holes in the plastic. A talker, I guess. One with no more tales to tell.

Another severed head. An older girl with long, incongruous grey hair and chubby cheeks. Round another turn and a washing line of dolls, strung out together to dry or to die, pink babies and brown babies, wigged and bald, naked and dressed, arms missing, legs missing.

The gloom thickens and the dolls keep coming.

A bride, her painted face fading, her veil a dirty grey, once-red lips now a lurid smudge as if kissed too often or too hard. A baby boy stares at me through glassy blue eyes, but his mouth is burned and now a dark grey streak blurs his lower face from ear to ear.

A bird, a crow I think, bursts from a tree and whistles overhead, doing nothing for my state of mind.

The path turns right past an ancient pine and as I lift my head, I see a figure standing in the gloom.

I stop. So does my heart.

It's only when I shine the torch beam over it that I see that the figure isn't standing. He or she is too high off the ground for that. It's hanging in mid-air. It's hanging from a rope from a tree.

I see the shape of the body. I see the head and the odd angle that the head hangs at.

Hangs. *Hanged.*

# CHAPTER 18

'No. No.'

My whisper snakes across the small clearing and I can hear the two short words crackling with electricity.

I'm stuck for a few moments, then I rush forward towards the body, my comprehension changing with every step, my eyes making sense of it through the gloom, my brain slow to catch up. The torchlight picks out a black school blazer, the white badge shining on the breast.

I thrust my torch up into the hanging figure's face.

The dead eyes of a doll stare glassily back at me.

Now I can see that what I thought were legs below the school blazer are two tree trunks a few feet behind it, their perspective lost in the dark. The doll is wearing the blazer like a shroud, a broken branch supporting the shoulders. But as I look closer, I see a streak of vivid red smeared against the black and across the white badge.

Above it, the cherubic face of the boy doll hangs from a branch of a pine tree, smiling cheerfully at me, as if this is the most natural thing in the world. I don't need this level of insanity. I can't afford to question my own reality any more than I'm already doing.

Warily, I reach inside the blazer and look for clues as to its owner. A white label is stitched behind the breast pocket with a name printed on it. I shine the torch onto the dark letters.

JASON DOAK

My heart sinks. Of course it's the name I expected to see, but it's still shocked me, still disheartened me and sent my mind racing to places I'd far rather it didn't go. What has he done. What's been done to him?

My hands are trembling now. Closing the blazer over again, I point the torch at the front badge.

The red flash and spatter is blood. Definitely blood. And I think it's recent.

My head is spinning. The doll's face is demonic in the half light. The blood is glistening against the white. Maybe if there is a hell then I'm in it.

I need to do something to sort this. Something to help. I need to keep this village safe.

Reaching up, I ease the blazer off the branch and away from the doll's head. Folding it carefully in half, I put it under my arm. I'm taking it back to Kilgoyne with me.

There are two more mini-islands, more dolls, and no sign of Jason before I turn back through the trees and the darkness, back towards the boat. My load is heavier now. Not just the blazer under my arm but the weight in my heart and on my back.

I realise I'm walking faster than I was on the way in. The dead dolls are at my back and in front of me, but I want away from them. I want a river between me and them. I want a village between me and them.

They follow me. Bleak stares following my every step, as I wind my way back to the boat that will rescue me from this island cemetery. It's there, thankfully, still tied to the mooring post as I left it.

I'm cold now and it's harder to swing my legs over the side of the boat than it had been earlier. Pain shoots through my hip and my knee complains, but I manage. Placing Jason's folded blazer next to me on the narrow seat, I begin to pull on the rope.

I'm weary, and my arms are tired, but the boat does its job, and we glide back towards land, a raw nervousness gnawing away at me. It's like having a small, anxious animal living inside me.

I'm going to go the police. I'm not sure what I make of DS Deacon but I know he's the only person I can take the blazer to. It's the right thing to do.

I'm halfway across when I hear the shouts. They're indistinct at first, lost on the wind, but then I make out words. My name.

'Marjorie. Ms Crowe.'

There are figures on the bank, four or five of them huddled together. Police.

'Marjorie. What the hell are you doing?'

Sergeant Deacon. His voice for sure.

'Why are you here, Marjorie?'

I look at the blazer on the seat beside me and realise what they're going to think. Now I'm asking myself the same questions that Deacon is. I consider pulling the boat back to the islands or quietly dropping Jason's blazer over the side. Either move would be madness and I'm not there. Not yet.

I pull on the rope and the boat glides towards them. As I near, torches shine in my face and into the boat. Jason's blazer is in the spotlight. Unmissable.

# CHAPTER 19

Hands grab the prow of the boat and pull it the final few yards till it's out of the water. It bumps onto the land, shaking as it's rocked side to side and forward. I need to hold onto the seat, my fingers gripping the wood just inches from Jason's school blazer.

As they manoeuvre the boat onto the rails and place it at rest, I see there's seven of them in all. Deacon and Sharma are standing in the middle of four officers in uniform, three men and a woman. To the side stands the tall, dark-haired constable who'd spoken to me when I walked down the path near where Jason's bicycle was found. He must be the one who called them in. Told Deacon the crazy woman was walking here.

Deacon is standing right next to the boat, his head shaking hard enough that I think it might slip from his shoulders.

'Why are you out here?'

I glance at the fierce policeman and remember what I told him. 'I was out for a walk. And I was looking for Jason.'

He shakes his head harder than before, frustration boiling in him, flushing his face. 'Why here?'

I shrug. 'I heard you say Jason's bicycle was found in this area. I thought I'd take my walk here.'

He breathes deeply, keeping his temper in check. 'That's not your job, Marjorie. You should *not* be anywhere near here. You've already been at one scene too many.'

He looks at the black cloth at my side and I know he recognises it for what it is. He stretches out an arm and points at the blazer.

'It's his.' I answer the question before he can ask it. 'Jason's.'

He blinks, long and hard, and bites at his lip. 'Are you sure?'

'It's got his name stitched into the lining.'

I begin to reach for it, but Deacon stops me, his voice sharp and harsh.

'*Don't* touch it. That's evidence.'

'I already have.' I realise how stupid it sounds as soon as the words are out of my mouth.

'I guessed that,' Deacon says dryly. 'But I don't want it contaminated any more than it already is.'

Sharma walks forward, pulling on a pair of blue latex gloves as she does so. She lifts the blazer carefully from the seat, making sure to hold it by the edges, and unfolds it. I wait, knowing she's going to see the blood smeared across the badge and find the name inside.

I'm not looking at her but I hear the short explosion of breath, and I know. Deacon begins moving towards her and I know too that she's signalled to him to check it out. I watch him stand over the blazer and see his shoulders slump.

When he turns slowly, almost reluctantly, to face me, the anger is obvious on his face.

'Where did you get this, Marjorie?'

'I found it.' I realise how weak that sounds. 'On the island.'

He sighs heavily. 'Specifically.'

I point. 'If you work your way left to right, there's a clearing with a ring of stones with the remains of a fire in the middle. Not the next island, but the one after that. It was hanging there, the blazer over a broken branch and below the head of a doll.'

'*A doll?*'

I explain, as best I can, and watch their eyebrows rise. Deacon has the look of a man whose bad day has just got a whole lot worse, and he can't believe it. He and Sharma look at each other and she can only shrug.

'Maxwell,' Deacon shouts. A tall, slim female officer ambles over, blonde hair peeking out from under her hat.

'Take Ms Crowe to the car and wait with her. Call this in ...' he points at the blazer, Sharma holding it up, a single finger under the collar, '... and get forensic services over here to collect it, then get them onto the islands. Marjorie, I'm going to want to talk to you when I get back. I've got a *lot* of questions.'

'And what if I don't want to sit in a cold police car in the dark?'

Deacon's smile is grim.

'I can offer you alternative accommodation. If you'd rather go directly to the police station and wait in a cell, then I can arrange that quite easily.'

'I've done nothing wrong.'

He stares at me hard. 'Car or cell?

'I'll wait in the car.'

It's dark and quiet at the end of the lane. PC Maxwell is in the front seat and I'm in the back. I can hear the wind picking up outside, gusting across the McPhersons' field and heading for the river.

The constable tried to make some small talk for a little while, but I didn't offer much encouragement for her to continue. So we sit in silence, her doubtless bored, me busy torturing myself with my thoughts.

I need to know where Jason Doak is. If he's well. If he's alive.

I'm tired but I don't dare close my eyes for fear of seeing boys and ropes and dolls and ropes. The hellish horrors of the islands have me jumpy, nervous and questioning everything.

I realise that part of me is anxious for Deacon and Sharma to return so that they can confirm what I saw. Sitting here in the dark, the sights of the islands seem increasingly surreal, increasingly unlikely. I'd like to be told I'm not crazy. It would mean a strange, terrifying reality, but better that than another suggestion that I'm losing my mind.

Occasionally, I catch the constable studying me in the rear-view mirror. I'm sure she's wondering about my sanity too. Why wouldn't she? Sitting in the dark of night in the middle of nowhere, with this strange woman and all the talk of dead dolls and the supernatural.

If only she knew what I know. That there's no supernatural. It's *all* natural.

My mind jumps to a line from Shakespeare that Granny Begg used to quote when my mother wasn't around. Hamlet says,

'There are more things in Heaven and Earth, Horatio, than are dreamt of in your philosophy.'

*All natural.*

There's a cough and my eyes flick back to the mirror, where I see Maxwell staring at me.

I pull my coat tighter to my body, unconsciously wrapping up my doubts in waxed cotton and tartan lining, making myself smaller in the back seat, and wonder if I'd said the words aloud.

'I can put the heating on for a bit, if you want,' she says.

'No, thank you.'

I'd rather be cold. Cold and miserable suits my mood right now. I've no right to be warm when Jason is out there somewhere, bleeding and hurt. At best. The thought that he might no longer be out there, alive, is stabbing at me like a hundred tiny knives. I deserve to suffer.

There's a sudden click and a rush of cold air, and I nearly jump out of my skin. The car door opens wide and Deacon slides into the seat next to me. I can feel an icy blast emanating from him, and I know it's not all because of the outside temperature. Seconds later, Sharma gets into the front beside Maxwell, twisting so that she's facing me. She doesn't seem happy either.

Deacon holds my gaze for an age before he speaks. He's trying to read my mind.

'Why were you here, Marjorie? The truth, please.'

My eyes close wearily and I shake my head in protest at having to explain myself.

'Jason told me he liked going to the islands. He'd talk about them a lot. It was his favourite place around here. When you said his bike might be near Duntroon Farm, I knew how close it was to Endrick Islands.'

'So you *knew* this was where he'd gone?'

'No.' I hesitate. 'I felt it.'

Deacon sighs and turns his head away. I suspect he's swearing under his breath. He turns back.

'And you didn't think to tell us that instead of going yourself?'

I lie a little. 'It didn't occur to me until you'd gone. You left in a hurry.'

Sharma makes a little noise. It's a laugh. Or a scoff. I look at her and she stares back defiantly.

'You could have told us this before we left,' she says. 'Couldn't you?'

'Perhaps.'

I know she's trying to needle me. Deacon is annoyed enough that he's not going to stop her.

'Marjorie.' She leans over the seat towards me. 'Why didn't you tell us what you knew? Is there a reason you wanted to come here rather than us?'

'No.'

She tries again. 'Is there something you aren't telling us? Do you know where Jason is?'

'No.'

She mocks me. 'Do you have a *feeling* where he is?'

'*No.*'

She stares, challenging me. I refuse to blink, and it stays that way until Deacon's voice takes me away from her again.

'Marjorie, what do you know about those damned dolls?'

'Nothing. All I've ever heard are half whispers, snippets about the islands, people hinting but not saying about things that happened there many years ago. That's it.'

He's studying me, doubting me.

'We made some phone calls. Asked the people in the village about the dolls. You're telling me you've no idea what they might have said?'

'None.'

So he tells me. He does so watching me closely, looking for any and all reactions. I know that's his game, but I still can't help myself. Within moments, he sees my eyes widen in shock.

# CHAPTER 20

Deacon's sources told him that it was a long story. Two long stories, in fact.

They told him that it wasn't a secret as such, it's just that it was decided not to talk about it. Most people in the village don't know anything about it. But the older ones do.

It began in the mid 1960s, that was the first surprise.

There was a local character named Johnny Lyle, a name with which I was vaguely familiar but couldn't have told you anything about. It seems Johnny basically lived on Endrick Islands and knew them like the back of his hand. He'd catch rabbits and fish, shoot pheasants, he'd even get himself the odd deer who'd waded across the current at low tide. He'd eat some, sell the rest. Hunting and drinking, that was Johnny's life. Folk in the village at the time used to say if you wanted Johnny Lyle then you'd find him on the Endrick or in the Endrick. The islands or the pub.

It was Johnny that found Mary Cochrane's body. The wee girl had been swimming with her cousin, Annie Kerr. The current took her down and she drowned. Annie ran screaming for the village when Mary didn't surface. Johnny knew where she'd most likely pop up and he was right.

He pulled the girl's body out, but she was long gone. Eyes like fish, Johnny told people. Poor wee thing was just seven years old. Buried in the kirkyard.

Three days later, Johnny found the doll. A little plastic baby with glass eyes. Stood to reason it was Mary's. Her cousin said she'd had the doll with her. Johnny believed in spirits, in ghosts, and in bad luck. He believed people and places could be cursed. It seemed the right thing to Johnny to hang the doll on a tree.

It was his way of showing respect and keeping the girl's ghost onside.

It didn't work out that way, though. Johnny hit the drink hard. A lot of people said that messed with his mind, but Johnny said it was the girl. Or more to the point, the girl's ghost. She came to him in his sleep, he said. She couldn't rest and neither could he. He couldn't catch a fish, the rabbits and the deer outran him, and he couldn't hit a pheasant.

So Johnny decided that if one doll wasn't enough to please the girl's spirit then he'd hang more. He got hold of eight other dolls and hung them around the islands. It became an obsession. He told some people that he was convinced the dolls themselves were possessed by the spirits of other dead girls. So he got more. And more. He raked in bins, he asked people in the village, he bought some for himself.

For seven years, Johnny sourced dolls and hung them from the trees. They got weathered and decayed, blackened and dirty. They lost arms, eyes, and heads. Endrick Islands became this awful cemetery for scary dead dolls.

Then, seven years after Mary Cochrane drowned, after hanging hundreds of dolls on the islands, Johnny Lyle died of a heart attack. He dropped dead right on the spot where he found the wee girl's body.

The story spread, grew arms and wings. All sorts about how he was possessed or how the girl's ghost had appeared and frightened him to death. Or worse, that the dolls did it. The more likely truth is the poor man's heart just gave out after years of hard drinking and obsession.

But it meant more people knew about the islands and the dolls. Word spread. People came from all over to see the place. Some brought dolls of their own and hung them. Others would come as a dare, bringing alcohol, leaving litter, and basically disrespecting the place. It stopped being about Mary Cochrane. It became an ugly tourist attraction.

So in June 1973, it's said that a group of local men got together and decided to put an end to it. Mary's dad, Laurence, was one of them, so was Sandy McKee's dad, old Alec. It was June 21, the summer solstice, the longest night of the year. Four of them took a boat over to the islands and took all the dolls away.

They cleaned the place out. Except for one doll. The original one that belonged to Mary Cochrane. They left that where Johnny Lyle had hung it, a final mark of respect to wee Mary.

It's thought that they loaded the dolls into hessian sacks and buried them. But only the four of them knew where.

Deacon's calls hadn't been able to discover who the other two men were who had buried the dolls. The village either never knew or had forgotten.

They did turn up another nugget, however. Some people in the village were aware that the dolls were back and had been for quite a few years now. They were first noticed a few months after Jenni Horsburgh disappeared in 1999.

They didn't appear all at once. Instead, it was thought they'd grown in number over time. Someone had been adding new ones. No one knew who. Or why. And this time no one wanted to take them away. It was like once was enough. It was decided they were best left alone.

No one wanted a repeat of what happened the first time round so it was decided best not to let the world know. Or even the rest of the village.

I listen to all of this with as straight a face as I can manage, while also asking myself why I feel the need to give nothing away. I doubt that I manage it well.

Deacon is watching every raised eyebrow, every twitch of my mouth, every change in my pupils. He's spoon-feeding me the story of the dolls to gauge how truthful I've been. His suspicion is obvious. And natural.

I give nothing away but surprise and sadness. It's all I have to give.

Deacon says he'd asked who'd made the decision to keep secret the reappearance of the dolls but didn't get an answer.

I don't have much doubt who it would have been. *The high heid yins.* The village leaders. Some elected, some ordained, some self-appointed. All men.

Councillor Dryden. Reverend Jarvie. Rowan Haldane. Adam Cummings.

I suspect they too are behind the final piece of information Deacon gives me before having PC Maxwell drive me home. There's to be a meeting in the village hall tonight. Everyone who can be there has been asked to attend.

I don't know if he's told me this with an eye to me going or if he's warning me to keep away. His words are ambiguous. I think deliberately so.

'Be careful, Marjorie. Some people the village aren't well disposed towards you right now. And I can't say I blame them.'

I say nothing, but in my heart, I can't entirely blame them either. Those who don't know any better, at least.

It's said that knowledge is power, but my belief is that sometimes it can leave you feeling powerless too. The truth is that I *know* two boys have hung dead from ropes. And I'm terrified what will happen next.

Whether Deacon's intention was for me to attend the village meeting or not, I'm going.

# CHAPTER 21

*March 1999*
The Devil's Pulpit, Finnich Glen

*It was snowing. A soft white blanket settling on the gorge, accentuating the beauty and otherworldliness of the place. The Pulpit itself was a beguiling patchwork of sandstone red, lichen green and snow white.*

*The glen somehow contrived to be even more surreal under the falling flakes. It was a primordial wonderland, a place of strangeness, beauty and possibilities.*

*They all knew spring snow was an ephemeral visitor. Temperatures would rise the next day, and winter's lingering would be no more than a memory, perhaps they'd doubt it had ever been there at all. But in that moment, it was magical.*

*There were six of them in the heart of Finnich Glen, still young enough to be excited by snowfall, and momentarily distracted from their purpose. The balmy, reckless nights of the previous summer seemed a world away, but they were here, and nature had laid on a show. Together, they would seek out darkness under the falling white.*

*One of the man-boys found a stick by the edge of the bloody waters and choose a large patch of ground which the snow had claimed for its own. He traced a circle and then an inner ring within that. Between the two rings, he marked five points, then used the stick to connect those and so create a pentagram. At its heart, he drew the face of a goat.*

*The others gathered round, an unspoken understanding, and stood behind each point of the pentagram, their heads bowed. He circled them, like a lion staking prey. Three times he walked around them, harnessing the power of repetition.*

*He fetched a bottle from a backpack, twisting off the lid and throwing it aside, then positioned himself behind the first of the group. Putting his head near the girl in front of him, he leaned in close and whispered, 'Thelema.'*

*She cupped her right hand in front of her and he tipped the bottle towards it, pouring blood into her palm. Her pale skin washed crimson. She dipped a forefinger from her left hand into the blood and smeared both her cheeks and her forehead.*

*The man-boy worked his way round the circle and the points of the pentagram, whispering to each and giving them the blood they required to anoint themselves. One after the other, they daubed their faces in fresh red. All the while, the snow fell.*

*As they stood there, he slipped off his jacket, then tore off his sweater and the T-shirt below it in one movement, throwing both to the ground. Picking up the bottle again, he daubed his own cheeks and drew a bloody line down the middle of his chest.*

*The others stayed in position as he climbed, half-naked, onto the Pulpit. From there, he commanded them.*

*'I call on thee to make a sacrifice. For Thelema. Give blood.'*

*As one, they cast the remaining blood cupped in their hands into the air and watched it spatter the snowy pentagram.*

*'Thelema. Thelema. Thelema.'*

*The man-boy on the Pulpit looked to the sky, arched his back and caught a mouthful of snowflakes, his arms outstretched, and palms turned up. With a wide grin on his face, he unleashed a scream of delight.*

*She watched from the edge of the circle, liking the way flakes clung to his bare chest before slowly melting from his body heat. If the others weren't there, she'd have taken some of that heat for herself. Wrapped herself in it. Shared it. That would have to wait, though.*

*He'd whispered in her ear as he'd done to the others before dispensing her share of the blood. But with her, he'd let his lips brush against her ear, sending a shiver through her body. He'd also added an extra word. 'Later.'*

*She observed his dance on the rock with a longing that ached within her. She saw that he must be cold but knew he'd never admit it.*

He was too full of bravado for that, too full of the show. He was three years her elder but sometimes she felt like she was the older one. He had a lot of boy still in him, a lot of growing to do. And he'd do the growing here in Kilgoyne, she was sure of that. She'd spread her wings and see the world, but the village would be enough for him. He'd be big in the small place; she'd be as big as she could be in the world that was waiting for her.

He'd do for now, though. He was fit and he was funny. And it all being a big, bad secret made it more of a turn-on. She liked that they were all out here and none of the others knew the two of them had their own thing going on. No one knew, and that was the way it had to be because of his situation. His poor, pretty, boring wife. She knew she should feel bad about it, but she couldn't quite bring herself to do so. Life was too short for regrets or guilt.

She stood back to look around the group and smiled to herself. She was the youngest in this second tier of theirs and the most recent to be admitted. They were all so serious about this Thelema nonsense, but she didn't buy into it the way they did. She was here for the thrill and the fun, and that was it.

When she'd had her fill, she'd be off. For London and beyond.

This village couldn't keep her.

# CHAPTER 22

Kilgoyne village hall is home to carol concerts and children's art sessions, a food distribution hub and yoga classes, Boy Scouts and Girl Guides, election counts and kiddies' playgroups. It's a draughty old barn of a place, one hundred and twenty-three years old, held together by layers of paint and goodwill.

With a large main hall complete with a stage, and another large room upstairs, it's available for hire by all the groups and organisations that make a small community like ours work. This dark Thursday night is different from most, though.

I know I'm not welcome. I probably wouldn't be at the best of times, and this is far from that. The meeting is about to start so most of them are already inside but I know that the side door will be open as it always is, short of a snowstorm or a torrential downpour. I stand as tight to the wall as I can, getting a better line of sight to the stage, and being out of sight to those in audience. I'll only be seen if someone turns round, and if that happens, I'll leave.

From what I can see of it, the old hall looks to be full to the rafters, and if the faces I can see are anything to go by then emotions are raw. They're all staring at the stage, hanging on every word. I recognise Councillor Dryden's voice although I can't see him.

'Thank you for coming out tonight. I'm heartened to see that so many of you are concerned enough to turn out and discuss it as a community.'

I squeeze closer to the wall and edge forward. Now I can see him. He's at the front of the stage, resting his arms on a lectern. Behind him and to the right, I can make out the Reverend Jarvie and Mr Haldane. All three are grim-faced.

'First of all, I want to send love and condolences, on behalf of everyone in Kilgoyne, to Evelyn and Sandy McKee, who have suffered a terrible tragedy with the loss of their son Charlie. They are our friends and our neighbours ... our family. And it's at times like this that we have to look after our family, to look after each other. It's at times like this that Kilgoyne can show its true worth.'

*If I wasn't so scared that someone might hear me, I'd consider vomiting.*

'However ...' he lowers his voice, '... and I can scarcely believe that I'm saying this, as if Charlie's loss wasn't enough, there's another reason that we need to pull together and look after our own. Most of you will know by now that Martin and Beth Doak's son Jason has gone missing.'

From the noise that rises around the hall it's obvious some of them are hearing the news for the first time. Dryden gestures with his hands for them to settle down again.

'This is why I've called this meeting. Jason left for school this morning, never arrived, and hasn't been seen since. This is really out of character and we're going to need all the help we can get to find him. We pray he's going to be found safe and well, and as soon as possible. Martin, Beth, we're all thinking of you, and we'll do anything we can to find Jason.

'This is a terrible time for Kilgoyne. We had a search party yesterday for Charlie McKee and we need to do the same again today. We do *not* want the same ending. Some of you have been out searching already but we need as many of you that can help to do so. Spread the word, talk to your children, look anywhere you think he could be.'

Dryden has paused and I think he's trying to avoid looking at Mr and Mrs Doak.

'Look in the places you hope he won't be. We need people to look in the river, on Bodach Lane, in the clearing. Everywhere. We need to find this boy.'

*I want to shout out that I've already been looking. That I've found his school blazer. But I don't.*

92

A murmur ripples round the hall. Sandy McKee is on his feet, drawing all eyes to him. His face is flushed, eyes red and wide, voice creaking.

'Martin. Beth. My heart's breaking for you. I've been where you are, and I know exactly what you're going through. I wouldn't wish this feeling on my worst enemy. I'm devasted. Evelyn's devastated.'

He looks around him. 'The whole village is, I know. So whatever we can do, even now, we will. We tried yesterday. We had people out looking but it was too late. And it was too late because of one person.'

He's shouting now. And I'm pressing myself so hard against the wall that I might push it over.

'If you ask me, if you want to find out where Jason is, then go ask that old witch Marjorie Crowe. Get yourself, or the police, down to that cottage at Stillwater Field and ask her what's going on.'

*His words make the blood rush in my ears.* Dryden tries to calm him. 'Sandy this isn't …'

'No. *No.* My boy was fine until she got involved. She's key to finding Jason.'

'Sandy's right.' Another man's voice roars. The one who owns the chip shop. 'She had the chance to let us know where Charlie was. Maybe the chance to save his life. And she did nothing. *Nothing.* I don't know how she's got the nerve to keep living here. In fact, I think she should be told to get out.'

*I've no breath and feel like I've been slapped in the face.* Voices, mostly the ladies of the village, try to shout him down, but Mr McKee is still standing, still holding court.

'That old witch has messed with my Charlie's head somehow. Made him do it. She's got something to do with this. I know she has.'

A woman's voice pipes up from the audience. 'Oh Sandy, she couldn't have. And she wouldn't.'

'Wouldn't she? Then you tell me this. How is that she claims she saw my Charlie hanging from that tree when Councillor Dryden himself saw Charlie alive a whole hour later?'

There's a moment's lull while they process that information. A moment that stretches and resonates until they all seem to be shouting at once. Many of them are looking at the stage. Dryden doesn't seem to mind the attention being back on him.

'It's true. This is part of the police investigation, but I've always been truthful with the people of Kilgoyne and I'm not going to change now. Marjorie Crowe insisted to the police that she saw Charlie hanging from the tree when she was on that walk of hers at noon. Well, I'm not one to speak ill of people but you can't believe what she says.'

*My ears are burning and I'm sure they're scarlet. My cheeks too.*

'I saw Charlie with my own eyes, crossing Dalnair Place at ten past one yesterday afternoon. I'm not going to speculate on what she saw, or what she did, or what she knew was going to happen, but these are the facts, and you all deserve to hear them.'

*He's so sure of himself. So sure.*

The chip shop owner is on his feet again, face red. 'The woman's a liar. A complete liar. She's making stuff up for attention. Either that or she really is a witch. Either way, something should be done about her.'

'Hang on there.' The Reverend Jarvie has moved to the front of the stage. 'One minute you want Marjorie kicked out of the village because she saw Charlie hanging and did nothing about it, the next you want her burned at the stake because she lied about seeing him. Make your mind up because you can't have it both ways.'

The chip shop owner doesn't like that much. He's spluttering. 'That's not the point. Point is she's a danger. And a … a …'

'A witch.' Sandy McKee finishes the sentence for him. 'If you knew what I do then you'd think she was.'

McKee has them in the palm of his hand now and I'm scared as to where he's going.

'Those of you who're defending her, tell me this. How is it that she told my boy *three weeks ago* that he'd die?'

*I think my heart has stopped beating.*

The hall is an explosion of noise. There's an outrage of shock and shouts and questions and denials and arguments. I'm not sure if time has stopped or accelerated. It could be both.

Sandy raises his hand for silence and continues.

'Aye. You heard right. She said my boy would be *hanged* and here we are. She's got what she wanted.'

'Sandy …' Evelyn McKee's voice is despairing and half-hearted, and quickly drowned out.

*'She should be locked up.'*

*'She's a bloody witch.'*

*'She should have been kicked out of the village years ago.'*

*'She wanted the boy to hang. Then did nothing when she saw it happen.'*

*'This is all on her.'*

I'm shaking. Trembling. I'm afraid my chattering will give me away. But I'm also not sure I care. I'm at least as furious as I am scared. It's all too much like being a fly on the wall at your own funeral.

Councillor Dryden has both hands raised for quiet and for his voice to be heard.

'Sandy, are you *sure* she said this? How do you know?'

'My other boy, Zak, said it when the police interviewed us this morning. It was the first I'd heard of it. He told the police sergeant that old Marjorie was always on Charlie's case. Always giving him a hard time. Zak called her an old witch and when Evelyn told him off for it, he said the woman has special powers.'

*My mouth is dry. All I can do is stand and wait.*

'Of course, I told him no one's got special power. That's she can't do magic. She's just a crazy old woman. He tells me how she does spells and can tell the future. She did that with Charlie. That's when he said it. He told us how the witch said Charlie would die. That he'd be hanged.'

I'm vaguely aware that there's gasps and shouting but all I can really hear is Sandy McKee.

'Zak said that three weeks ago he was out with Charlie on their bikes. The two of them and another pal of Charlie's. They were cycling on Bodach Lane when the Crowe woman was coming the other way. Seems Charlie was messing a bit, nothing bad, and old Marjorie went crazy. She started saying how Charlie was wicked, that he was a vile boy. Zak's fifteen, he's old enough to remember what he heard. And he swears he remembers it word for word.

'*You'll swing from a rope one day. See if I'm wrong. You'll swing from a rope.* That's what that old witch said. And here we are.'

# CHAPTER 23

*I didn't. I didn't. I swear I didn't.*
*I don't think I did.*

Mr McKee's words are still reverberating round the hall. They've whipped the crowd into a frenzy of shouts and gasps.

Those words. I don't know which are true and which aren't. But I wouldn't say something like that. I wouldn't.

Councillor Dryden is trying to quieten them but he's fighting a losing battle. They're consumed by my supposed prophesy and all sense has been lost. There's lots of shouting and finger pointing, mostly by the men. Some of the women have their heads close together in quieter but still fervent discussion.

'It's bloody witchcraft,' the chip shop owner roars, his arms outstretched. 'Why's no one just calling it what it is? It's witchcraft.'

That gets noisy approval from some parts of the hall, drowning out the objections.

'We all know the kind of stuff she does,' he yells. 'And it's not right. Not natural.'

'Now hang on there,' someone calls out. 'Some of what Ms Crowe does is *completely* natural. I was struggling after our Kevin was born, a really bad dose of the baby blues. She treated me with a mix of St John's wort and other herbs, and I was sorted in a week.'

'Yes,' agreement comes from somewhere across the room. 'My mother had heart problems for years because of anxiety. The doctor couldn't help. Marjorie gave her a tincture of motherwort and it helped her no end. Wouldn't take a penny for it. She may be strange but she's kind.'

'You've always been against her,' someone else shouts. 'From the minute she arrived in the village, you all took against her just because she's different. Not because of anything she's done, just because she's not the same as everyone else. She's a kind old lady, not this monster you're making her out to be.'

'They're right,' another calls out. 'I've been using her sleep potion for years because I'd rather take herbs and flowers than some chemicals that a pharmaceutical company dreams up. It's natural and harmless and it actually works.'

'A potion? *A potion?*' The chip shop owner is mocking her. 'Is that we're talking about here? A witch that makes potions, and makes prophesies that drive kids to hang themselves? It's witchcraft and she's dangerous.'

I want to scream. Burst into the middle of the room and scream at the top of my lungs.

'All right, everyone cool it.' Dryden is trying to regain some control. 'There's no such thing as witchcraft and we need to concentrate on finding Jason. Everyone sit down and stay quiet. I said, sit down.'

Behind Dryden, I can see Mr Haldane, standing still with his arms crossed in front of him. I don't think he's said a word the whole time.

'Sandy …' Dryden has the quiet now that he wanted. 'When your Zak told you and the police about what Ms Crowe said to Charlie – about how he'd swing – did he say who else was with them so they can back this up?'

McKee is getting to his feet again. He looks worried, perhaps nervous.

His head slowly turns, and I can see he's looking at the Doaks. My heart sinks.

'Yeah. Jason was with them. My Charlie and Zak, and Jason.'

Martin Doak's jaw drops. His wife seizes his arm.

'I'm sorry, Martin.'

He's quieter now. Some of the fire gone from his voice. 'Really sorry. Zak says Charlie and Jason had both taken the piss out of her. She threatened both of them. We need to find Jason fast.'

*No. No. No.*

I can see Mrs Doak. She's burying her head into her husband's shoulder. Mr Doak looks shell-shocked.

Sandy McKee looks shaken but he's still ready to stick the knife in. 'For those of you saying she's not a witch, how do you explain it? How could she have said what she did?'

'She did the same with Jenni Horsburgh.'

My skin is tingling and my breath has disappeared.

I can't be sure who spoke as they're out of sight. The same with the person who answers.

'That's right. She said Jenni would run away to London and it happened. Never heard of again. She prophesised it. Maybe put the idea in Jenni's head too. Like she did with Sandy and Evelyn's boy. Sometimes I think people here prefer to forget that ever happened.'

*I don't forget it,* I want to say. Never, but certainly not now. Not after seeing the cross on the tree by the clearing, not after learning about the dolls on the islands.

Something moves on the edge of my vison and my eyes are drawn to the stage. Rowan Haldane is standing behind the Reverend Jarvie, whispering something in his ear. Now Jarvie is moving quickly to the front of the stage and in seconds he's beside Dryden at the lectern.

'No one here has forgotten about Jenni,' he says. 'We're all still praying she'll return to us one day. I can only imagine her mother's heartbreak of never having heard from her since that day. But she's not forgotten.'

'Isn't she?' It's the first voice again. 'She was as dead to this village the day she walked out as she would have been if she'd been hit by a bus. Even now, we're only talking about her because Marjorie Crowe said it would happen.'

People are on their feet. I can see Harris Henderson and Derek Cummings now, banging their hands together, grins on their faces, whipping up the mob.

Derek's father, Adam, is shouting above them all.

'Kids are hanging themselves and disappearing,' Cummings screeches. 'She's *telling* them they'll disappear, and they're never seen alive again. We're not putting up with this. She's got to leave the village. Enough is enough.'

'Adam's right,' roars another voice out of sight. 'We should go back to her cottage and pack her bags for her.'

*I need to get away from here. Now.*

'We need to find Jason,' Dryden is shouting. 'Get organised into groups and search everywhere you can. We need to find him tonight.'

I'm not sure they're all listening.

The meeting is breaking up. There's a commotion of scraping chairs and raised voices as people begin to leave.

I hurry away from the hall door, seeking the blackness of the night, anger and fear burning holes inside me.

# CHAPTER 24

*1662*

Margaret Wallace from Glasgow, thought to be 34 years old, was accused of plotting to cause the destruction of men, women and children 'through witchcraft, charming, incantation, and using devilish and unlawful means to do so, expressly prohibited and forbidden by the laws of God and the laws of the kingdom.'

Margaret's principal crime was being quarrelsome. She'd cursed at a man named Cuthbert Greg. She'd threatened a burgess named Robert Mure, saying to him 'thou shall go home to thy house, and shall bleed at thy nose one quart of blood but shall not die until thou send for me and ask me for forgiveness'. She also said that her acquaintance Christiane Graham had powers similar to God.

Her trial ran from 19 February to 22 March 1662. She was found guilty and sentenced to be strangled then burned at the stake. Her execution took place at Castlehill, Edinburgh.

She was *wirriet* and *burnt*.

*2024*

Twitter

> Charlie McKee was in Marjorie Crowe's cottage the night before he hanged himself. Coincidence? No chance. She made it happen. Bet your life on it.

> The old Crowe is pure evil. She's to blame for everything bad that's happened in Kilgoyne. She's cursed the village. Or worse. Her time is up and we should drive her out.

The cops have got to be asking serious questions about Marjorie Crowe. She swears she saw Chaz McKee dead before it happened. CCTV proves she was wrong. So was she lying or seeing the future? Either way she has to answer for what she's done.

That ugly old witch in Kilgoyne has no right to live. She's messing with stuff beyond human understanding. She must be punished.

The old Crowe is involved in all of this. Can't believe what's going on in Kilgoyne. One deid and one missing? This is all her doing.

Burn her!

# CHAPTER 25

I've never made the walk from the centre of the village to home as quickly as I've just done. It was more of a run than a walk. I got back to the cottage as fast as my legs could carry me.

Closing the front door behind me, cursing my shaking hands, I make straight for the larder. My nerves are raw and my head is a jumble of thoughts and fears. Doubts and contradictions are tumbling over each other and I'm struggling with it all. And I know I can't do this unaided.

My medicine cabinet is my treasure chest. A well-stocked cupboard in the pantry that holds bottles of potions, tinctures and remedies for all times of need. There are bottles for sleeping, bottles for anxiety, bottles for energy, bottles for tiredness and for confidence. There are recipes I inherited from Granny Begg and some of my own design. Lifetimes of experience distilled into flasks of green and brown.

There's something solid and comforting seeing them huddled together on the shelves. Something for all occasions. Tonight however, my need is not for the green bottle of foxglove for my pounding heart, or the brown one filled with my mix of ginseng and saffron as a mood pick-me-up. Not even my special tincture for anxiety made from lavender, passionflower and lemon balm. No, at times like this, only one bottle will do and I ease aside a tiredness remedy to pull it out.

It's an Islay single malt whisky. A bottle of Ardbeg that has served me well in times of trouble. I've had this particular bottle for five years and I'd thought it good for another few yet, but if things go on as they are then its end will be hastened.

I pour a decent measure, hesitate a polite second or two, then slip in some more. I can't resist a sniff and immediately get an intense noseful of bonfires and dark chocolate, and a big hit of peat.

I resist the urge to drink it all immediately, placing it on the small table while I set about lighting the fire. It's a task I've done a thousand times and in minutes it's in good heart. I scrape a chair closer to it, feeling its burgeoning warmth reach out to me. I need the comfort of the flames more than ever.

As a girl, I loved sitting in front of the fireplace. I'd soak up the warmth until someone would finally pull me away, my bare legs marked with the heat. Lazy tartan, my mother used to call it.

Like then, the flames are hypnotic now. I look at them through the glass, seeing them dance through the dual prisms of the whisky and the crystal. Orange and amber and gold, subtle shades shimmering. I'm making myself wait for the first taste while I give room to the voices shouting in my head.

They're chattering, arguing, about trees and crosses, about islands and blazers, about mothers and lost boys. The first carving on the tree in Bodach Woods had always disturbed me, but I'm not sure I could have said why. It was a nebulous thing, a hazy distraction more than anything ostensibly sinister. It was probably all about the timing but even then, there was perhaps two months between Jenni Horsburgh going missing and when I first saw that cross. It could have been nothing more than coincidence. It could have.

I sip at the Ardbeg and let the heat of it fill my mouth. All pepper and smoke and salty tang. It slides down my throat, fire burning.

It was May 1999 when Jenni left the village. I'd only been living in Kilgoyne for a year or so, and was still getting to know the place, and the people.

She was just sixteen. A bit of a wild child, I suppose. It was none of my business, though, and I'd have left it alone, except she'd speak to me. She wasn't exactly cheeky. More that she didn't seem to have any boundaries, no concept of distance or respect.

Her father had been out of the picture for five years, her brother Billy had left home to join the army after falling out with his new stepdad, and it certainly seemed that Jenni wanted away too. One evening I was walking out past Stuarton Farm and she was sitting on a wall, drinking from a bottle in a brown paper bag. She called to me and asked me if I wanted some. I guess I was supposed to be shocked or outraged. I said no thank you and kept walking.

She began walking after me, chatting and swigging from the bottle, asking me why I'd moved to such a boring place as Kilgoyne. It wasn't meant to be insulting, just what she saw as a statement of fact. She said if she had the choice of the world then this was the last place she'd choose.

I said something like she should be careful what she wished for. That she'd run from here but never get to the place she was looking for because it didn't exist. I told her she might think the streets there were paved with gold but they were only for those who could afford them.

That was it. Nothing more.

A week later she'd gone. Run off. Packed a bag and vanished into the night.

I take a mouthful of the Ardbeg and it stings the roof of my mouth. There's a sudden numbness to my tongue that I like. When it washes away, I'm left with a lingering warmth just as great as that coming from the fire.

A couple of weeks after Jenni disappeared came the news of the postcard sent from London. A confirmation that she'd done what she said she would. Kilgoyne tutted. Kilgoyne disapproved. Kilgoyne looked the other way and slowly forgot.

I've never forgotten. The person who carved the cross of St John has never forgotten.

And now there's a cross for Charlie McKee too.

I let the whisky warm my tongue again. I'm aware that it's working its magic, for good and for bad, freeing my mind and taking me places I'd rather not go. I'm scared to look at the fire through the glass for fear of what I'll see.

I don't need golden-hued visions of boys and ropes. I can't bear to see faces, shapeshifted and lost. I drink the next drop with my eyes closed.

They're still there though. Dancing behind my eyelids. Swinging. Dying. Dead.

I raise my glass, say a silent toast to my boy, and drink the last of it.

It's nearly midnight and the fire is fading. I need to choose between putting on more logs or letting it die. If I thought I'd sleep then I'd make for bed but I'm not sure that's likely to happen. I might be better being plagued with waking thoughts than sleeping ones.

Another whisky is tempting but I won't. I'm not a drinker. I don't go to pubs unless they're standing in my way. The occasional dram is my lot. I'll put the kettle on for tea instead.

Holding the kettle under the running tap, I drift off in thoughts of Jenni, Charlie and Jason, the whisky fuelling my imagination, and not for the better. Then, from somewhere on the edge of my consciousness, I hear noises.

Turning the tap off, I listen.

There's shouting out there in the darkness. It's a way off, the other side of the garden gate for sure, but I'm still startled. Being startled is easy when your nerves are razor-blade raw.

My brain is scrambling. Is it Sergeant Deacon? But there's more than one voice. A few of them.

They're getting closer, and now I can make out words.

*'Open your door.'*

*'Tell us what you know.'*

*'Why didn't you do anything?'*

They've come.

# CHAPTER 26

I knew they would. It was only a matter of when.

When I dare look out of the window it seems half the village is standing outside demanding answers. I can see McKee, cast in the glow from my living room, looking haunted and throbbing with rage. Two men are next to him, flushed with drink or anger or both. Just behind them is Adam Cummings, his face dark and brows furrowed, standing next to his young wife, who looks embarrassed to be here.

There are three teenage lads, probably similar ages with Charlie McKee. They're wild-eyed, frothing at the mouth and so furious that I can barely understand what they're shouting. I get the message though. And I can hear the word witch.

My head switches right and left, hurriedly, trying to take it all in. People everywhere.

The chip shop owner is there and his wife from the florist. He's waving his arms about, fit to burst, and roaring at the top of his voice. She's holding him back by the shoulders.

More teenagers. My five tormentors from this morning. Together, gleefully relishing the uproar. Harris Henderson. Derek Cummings, the landlord's son. Hannah Cairney, who I'd thought better of. Kai McHarg and Katie Wallace.

The man from the taxi office is there and so is the red-haired man who works in the garage. Rowan Haldane is standing behind them, not screaming like the others but staring and glaring, half hidden by the gloom. Sandy McKee's sister-in-in-law is there, tears streaming down her face, shouting *Why?* over and over.

The noise is coming from all sides. I'm surrounded in my own home.

The worst thing is the look in their eyes. Hatred. It's a wild, frenzied loathing, a mob hysteria.

I don't have the courage to face them or the words to answer them. So they're just getting angrier.

I want to scream but I don't think I have any voice to do so.

A hand slaps hard against the window and the glass rattles till I'm sure it's going to shatter. A face is pushed up against the pane, the mechanic fogging it with breath; his features are contorted, his cheeks an angry red. Adam Cummings is behind him, urging him on.

The chip shop owner is bellowing so hard I can barely make him out. One phrase comes through. *Get out of our village.*

There's shouting from left and right. Someone is hammering on the door. The kitchen window is being clattered. Hysterical voices tripping over each other. The handle on the front door is being tried. They're trying to get inside.

I drop to the floor, my knees scraping, and scramble to the furthest corner of the room, as far from the window and the people and the shouting as I can get. They can still see me though, and I can still hear them.

*'Let us in.'*

*'What do you know?'*

*'What happened to Charlie?'*

*'What did you do to Charlie, you old witch?'*

*'Where's Jason Doak?'*

*'Witch!'*

*'Open the door.'*

*'What have you done to Jason?'*

It's as if Twitter has marched on my front door and is trying to break it down.

My hands are shaking. My breathing is rapid and ragged. And I think my heart is going to explode. I can hear the most awful shouts. The stuff of my worst nightmares.

*'Burn the witch.'*

*'Burn her.'*

There's no way out. Not through the front door or the back. The cottage is surrounded.

*'Get out of our village.'*

*'No one wants you here.'*

*'Tell us where Jason is.'*

*'Burn her out.'*

I can hear Sandy McKee amongst the tumult too. His voice cutting through the mob. The rest are shouting at me, he's shouting TO me. Asking the questions that I've asked myself for two days.

*'You saw my son. I know you did. Why didn't you call the police? Why didn't you tell me?'*

I know the questions. It's the answers I'm struggling with.

There's pounding at the door. They're actually trying to knock it down. The door is solid, it will hold. I hope it will hold.

Then I hear myself screaming as if it's someone else I'm listening to.

Glass has smashed. Something crashed into a wall near my head. A thud. My heart has stopped, and my senses are tangled.

It takes seconds to make any sense of it. A rock has been thrown through the right-hand window. The stone hitting the wall to my right.

I look across and see a hand reaching through the hole in the window, grasping for the latch and trying to lever it open. I'm frozen, can't move. Don't know whether to run to try to close it or to flee the room.

I do neither. Instead, I stay in the corner and cower. And shake.

There are more voices. More shouting. More anger. The commotion surges and the mob throw themselves at my cottage. The door rattles and I hear scrapings of metal on metal.

My heart drops into my stomach as the realisation strikes.

The door is opening.

# CHAPTER 27

The door flies open and three dark figures hustle through. I take one anxious glance towards them before twisting my head to the wall again, curling into a tighter ball.

Footsteps echo across the wooden floor, charging straight towards me. My hands clasp tighter to my head, and I have to swallow a scream as fear courses through me.

The clatter stops a yard or so away as a voice cuts through the uproar, commanding the others to a halt. Floorboards squeak softly as the invaders choose their play.

I can only hold my breath, tremble and wait.

I'm slowly aware of words, their meaning lost between my arms being over my ears and the fog of fear that's swirling in my head. The words are repeated.

'Ms Crowe. *Marjorie?*'

The voice is calm, less angry than I'd expected, but it takes time for that to trickle through to my frightened, scrambled brain. It takes time, too, for me to recognise it.

Detective Sergeant Deacon.

I dare a glance to the window and see only darkness. The villagers have disappeared into the night. Maybe they were never there.

I slowly uncoil, shuffling round till my back is against the wall, my knees pulled up to my chest, my arms wrapped around them, my eyes red and wary.

Deacon has knelt down so he's level with me.

'I apologise for unlocking your door, Marjorie. We knocked but you couldn't have known it was us. Not with all that noise. All those people have gone home now. There's a constable here with us and he's going to stay outside till the early hours, to make sure they don't come back.'

I look back at him blankly. Aware now that DC Sharma and a young man in uniform are also here.

'And we'll be talking to them tomorrow. Are you okay?'

His voice is calm enough that it helps cushion my heart as it crashes against my ribcage but not calm enough to let me answer. Not yet. I hold my voice inside me, afraid it will break if I set it free.

'Marjorie, there was a meeting in the village hall tonight. It got out of control and that's why those people acted the way they did. We'll make sure it's calmed down.'

I nod. Not wanting to tell him that I know. That I'd heard.

'I'm told there was a lot of loose talk. Some accusations thrown around. About you. There has also been a lot of ... activity on Twitter like you told us. We think that also contributed to what just happened. When you're ready, I need to talk to you about what was said at the village meeting. Is that okay?'

I lift my head to look at him, anger taking over from fear. I find my voice. 'You're asking me if it's okay but you're telling me that you're going to ask regardless.'

He concedes as much with a smile. 'I need to understand what was said. And only you can do that.'

'I'm not sure that I can. But I'll try.'

'Thank you. I want to ask you about some things that were said about Jenni Horsburgh.'

I flinch at the name, and he sees it.

'People said you prophesised that Jenni would run away to London. Is that true?'

'No.'

'They say that you planted the idea of running away in Jenni's head. That you engineered it.'

'That's just not true.'

I bury my head in my hands. My flushed arthritic fingers, all bone and puckered skin, are clinging to my skull and twisted through my grey hair. When I show my face again, I know it's streaked with tears.

'I don't properly remember what I said to Jenni Horsburgh. It was over twenty years ago. *If* I did say that then it wasn't how I meant it. I can't … '

'Do you think you said something like that to the girl?'

I close my eyes and exhale hard. 'I've been thinking about this recently. I said something like you'll end up running from here but you'll never get to the place you're looking for because although you might think the streets there are paved with gold, they aren't. A week later she'd gone. Run off. Packed a bag and disappeared into the night.'

Deacon paces the room until he turns and stands in front of me, bending at the waist so his head is near to mine.

'*You'll end up running from here?* I can see how that might be taken as a prophecy. Especially when it came true. And streets paved with gold? Where's that if not London?'

'Maybe.' I'm annoyed and my chin is jutting out. 'People will see things how they want.'

Deacon shakes his head. 'And how do you see it, Marjorie? Coincidence? There seem to be a lot of those.'

I scowl at him. 'What is it that you're trying to trap me into saying? I know you're not the kind of man who believes in anything he can't prove or touch or measure. You know my family history. You know what I am, but you don't believe in any of it. So, what is it that you think I can do?'

He stares. Hard.

'Did you tell Charlie McKee that he'd swing from a rope?'

I should have seen the question coming. From the moment I heard it said in the village hall, I should have been waiting for him to ask me it. But it's caught me by surprise, and I know the shock is showing on my face.

'What?' I can hear the shake in my voice.

'I'm told that you spoke to Charlie McKee a few weeks ago. That he and another boy made fun of you and that you responded angrily. That you said, and I quote, *You'll swing from a rope one day. See if I'm wrong. You'll swing from a rope.* Is that correct?'

I can't speak. I've no words.

'Did you say that, Marjorie?'

I claw at my hair in thought.

'I don't know. I was angry at the boy, I remember that. And I think maybe I said he'd come to no good. I can't remember exactly what I said. I can't.'

'So you *might* have told Charlie McKee he'd swing from a rope?'

'I might have. Yes. It might have been a warning.' Words are running ahead of my brain.

'A warning that you'd make it happen? Same as with Jenni?'

'No! You're baiting me, Sergeant. Whatever it was, it was not that. Nor was it a *prophecy*. If it was anything, it was a warning that they'd get into trouble if they carried on the same way. I'd seen it before, and I didn't want it to end badly for him.'

That's given him pause. I can see cogs turning; connections being made. His voice softens and lowers.

'I guess having seen it before would make you worry.'

He says it like he can see inside me. Like he knows. I feel a shiver running down my spine, but I say nothing.

'We've something else we need to discuss with you, Marjorie. On a similar vein.'

I'm not sure how much more of this I can take.

'As you're aware, there's a discrepancy between what you saw, and when you saw it, and when Charlie McKee was last seen.'

I laugh, almost incredulous. As if this hasn't dominated my every walking thought since I'd been told of it.

'I'm aware, Sergeant. Are you here to tell me that I can believe my own eyes or to tell me something different?'

He puffs out his cheeks. 'DC Sharma has been trying to determine a timeline on what happened and when. I've never doubted your sincerity on this, Marjorie. And I'm still not doing so. But I'd like you to hear from her.'

Sharma clears her throat nervously. It makes me nervous too.

'I wanted to find CCTV footage that could prove things one way or another,' she starts.

I interrupt. 'DC Sharma, I get that you could find video that proves Charlie was alive later as Councillor Dryden says. But I don't see how you could find video that proves he wasn't. So not really one way or another, is it?'

She sighs. 'Perhaps a bad choice of words. I'm just trying to get whatever proof there is. Can I continue?'

I nod my permission.

'There isn't an abundance of cameras in the village. There's only one shop on Dalnair Place, Robbie's Rolls, but it does have a security camera visible from the street. The manager allowed me to view his recording from around the time Charlie was said to have been seen.'

She pauses as if expecting me to interrupt again. I don't.

'I worked my way through it, frame by frame, but the camera didn't have any recording of Charlie McKee.'

Relief and reassurance floods through me. It lasts as long as it takes Sharma to say one more word.

'However …'

*No.*

'There are three shops on Main Street with cameras but I was fairly sure if he'd walked there then more people would have seen him. So I tried one of the roads off Dalnair Place, Chisholm Avenue. Paterson's Chemist is there and has a camera. The owner was initially reluctant to let me view the recording, but the threat of a warrant changed her mind.

'The recording shows Charlie McKee walking past the shop at 13.13 the day before yesterday. More than an hour after you say you saw him hanging at Spittal's Clearing.'

The world has stopped spinning.

'There is no doubt it's him,' Sharma is saying. 'He was dressed in his school uniform, just as he was found last night.

Teacups are shattering. Babies screaming. Trains leaving the rails. Everything is broken.

'The CCTV was time and date stamped,' she says. 'There's no doubt about it.'

# CHAPTER 28

My sleep is fractured at best. Too much of the night is spent staring at the ceiling, agonising over how I saw what I couldn't have seen. What has been proven not to have been true. If I had any kind of explanation, I'd have offered it to the police but I've none.

*I know what I saw. I thought I knew what I saw.*

At least my insomnia spares me from dreams for a while. The waking night is long, the sleeping night torturous.

I am plagued by nightmares of devils and boys and ropes. Auld Hangie sprouts more branches and leaves and merges with trees, a giant of a beast that roars at me till the forest shakes and the earth trembles. I twice wake to the shock of that, bursting from sleep to flee it. When I fall asleep again, Auld Hangie is waiting for me. So, too, is the boy on the rope, spinning slowly, faces turning away from me and toward me. Face slumped, lifeless, then screaming silently at me for help.

When I lie awake, the attack on my cottage weighs heavily upon me. All those people, my neighbours supposedly, shouting and screaming, blaming me for everything. I can still see their faces in the dark, see the anger and the hate.

All the while, I think.

I get out of bed before six, cold and tired, my legs aching as my feet hit the floor. Those first few steps get harder each day and it takes longer for the night to unwind from my body.

It's a dank and chilly morning and the old cottage feels like a freezer; cold brick after cold brick. Peering outside, I see a low mist hanging over Stillwater Field, fresh daylight struggling in its fight against what remains of the night. I light a fire in the living room to bring some heat to the cottage, turn on the radio, and resolve to face whatever the day brings.

I want to walk. I want to do *my* walk. But I'm not sure that I can.

Maybe I'll stay at home, make some tinctures, perhaps write some poetry. I'll do whatever I can to tear my mind away from the McKee boy. And Jason Doak. And the other thing. The thing that plagues me most. That I can no longer believe what my own eyes tell me.

Something else is nagging away at me too. Twitter. Perhaps if I have just one look I'll be able to get on with my day. Just one scratch at the itch. Just one.

My trawls through the site's dark ditch have become obsessive. This must be how addicts feel. Knowing that the thing I most want to do is the last thing I should do. Even with the laptop closed, the site calls to me, promising nothing but heartache, beckoning me onto its rocks.

When I give in, as I always do, lines and sentences jump out at me from the screen.

Justice for Charlie

What really happened to Charlie McKee? And where is Jason Doak?

Has anyone looked in the Crowe's cottage for Jason Doak? Try the cooking pot #KilgoyneWitch

omg off the scale in Kilgoyne. Hope they find Jason. And no hanging from a tree

She lives at Stillwater Field. She's a witch. Burn the witch.

On and on. Digital graffiti. My name plastered all over invisible walls.

I've heard auld Marjorie said Charlie would hang himself and he did. Said same about Jason and noo he's missing. Probably deid.

There's another tweet from Harris Henderson.

116

God help Jason Doak wherever he is.

The hashtags have largely coalesced into two that seem to have found favour with the trolls above others. #BurnTheWitch and #CroweOfKilgoyne

I know that if I'm foolish enough to click on either – and I am and I do – then they'll guarantee a litany of misery.

> Jason left for school on his bike and nobodys seen him since. Except maybe the Crowe #WitchVillage

> My brother's pal was there when the Crowe said Charlie McKee would hang himself. Was like she was going to make it happen. Scary stuff. Don't go near her #Kilgoyne #StaySafe #KilgoyneWitch

> The kids of Kilgoyne aren't safe. Get rid of the wicked witch.

> Marjorie Crowe is an evil old witch. She made Charlie McKee hang himself.

Then I see the post that stops me in my tracks. A tweet by @Marjorie_Crowe. A tweet accompanied by my profile picture.

> I made Charlie McKee sway. I made Jason Doak go away. Pray you're not my next prey.

I stare at the screen, momentarily incredulous. *That's not me,* I think, before scolding myself for being stupid. *Of course* it isn't me.

It's my photograph, taken from the local newspaper I think, perhaps at the opening of a summer fete. It's my name, used by someone else. It's words coming supposedly from my mouth.

I'm flooded with indignation and rage. How *dare* someone do this? *Why* would someone do this?

I click on the fake Marjorie's profile and see that 'she' has posted seven other tweets. All of them have been 'liked' by dozens of other people.

> Double double toil and trouble. Fire burn and cauldron bubble. Get in my way and you'll be in the pot. I keep my cauldron hellish hot.

Charlie McKee RIP. That's what you get for being cheeky to me

Marjorie and Charlie sitting in a tree. H-A-N-G-I-N-G. First comes a spell then comes a potion, then comes a rope and a swinging motion

I'm Marjorie, I'm a wicked witch. I'm Marjorie, I'm a fucking bitch.

Where's Jason Doak? Is he in heaven or is he in Hell? I'm the only one who knows, and I'll never tell.

Before my eyes, I see the likes against the fake profile's tweets grow and grow. People are liking them and replying to them as I watch. The replies and retweets are just as awful, including some from people who seem to think they're really talking to me.

Dunk her in Endrick Water. If she drowns, she's not a witch. If she survives, she's a witch and we burn her at the stake! lol

Have u seen this @policescotland? Arrest this bitch

Hey Marjorie. Do everyone a favour and kill yourself

Let Jason Doak go. Ur gonna get raped u old bitch

Tears are rolling down my cheeks, salty and stinging as my face burns with humiliation and anger. Whoever it is taunting me this way knows the power of rhyme and what it means to me. This person, this *troll*, knows how to get under my skin.

I can hear Jessica's words ringing in my ears as my fingers hammer at the keyboard. *Don't engage.*

It takes me just a few frantic minutes to set up an account. @TheRealMarjorieCrowe. *Don't feed the trolls.*

I'm in. Or on. Whatever. I'm part of it, for better or worse. Almost certainly worse. *Whatever you do, don't reply to them, Auntie M.*

I will send just one reply. Something short, sharp and to the point, making it clear that the other account isn't real, isn't me. One reply, then it will be done, and I'll never have to deal with this Twitter again.

I sit with my fingers poised above the keys, deliberating. Nothing too confrontational. But not timid either, I've no reason to be contrite or cowed. This person is impersonating me, something the site clearly hasn't checked and should have strictly forbidden. It just needs a simple statement of fact.

@Marjorie_Crowe You are perpetrating a fraud. Please desist now. I do not appreciate this parody of me or the lies you are telling. Please have some respect for what has happened.

I sit back and look at it. Satisfied that it's neither aggressive nor apologetic, I press Tweet.

Nothing happens. The world doesn't stop. I feel I've done the right thing. Made my point. They'll see sense and that will hopefully be the end of it.

I look at my post, my first tweet. It sits on the screen in front of me, like a fledgling bird barely believing it has flown. Now what?

Below the tweet and to the right, there are four vertical lines, the second one longer than the others. I click on it and it reveals itself to be 'Analytics'.

My reply has made 322 impressions. There have been 207 engagements. The word engagement brings Jessica's warning racing to the front of my mind. There have been 98 visits to my profile. I have 64 new followers.

This isn't what I wanted. How can this be happening, and so quickly?

As I watch, the numbers climb. And climb.

I hover around some other symbols, trying to make sense of them. My reply has 46 likes. That is good, surely? It has been retweeted 59 times. No, 65. And, I swallow, I have 27 replies.

I want an end to it, not a continuation. This isn't a conversation. This isn't a starting point to anything.

I definitely should not look at the replies. I do.

omg I think your actually the Crowe. No one else would be daft enough to post that

A fraud!?! Sake that's hilarious. Welcome to the 21st century ya loony

You talk about lies! What about the lies you told the police? You said you saw Charlie dead when he was still alive! And you didn't phone for help. What's wrong with you???

You really the real Crowe? If you are then hand yourself into the police. Or hang yourself.

Then a reply directly from Fake Marjorie.

You say you're really Marjorie Crowe? How are we supposed to know? How do we know if you're friend or faux?

I type. My fingers betraying my brain, beating it to the punch.

I'm real. I don't have to prove it to you. Leave me alone and stop pretending to be me. This has gone too far.

I look at the analytics, seeing the figures soar. Over 5,000 impressions. Over 2,500 engagements. Over 400 followers. More and more and more replies. I don't dare to look. Then another reply from Fake Marjorie.

Leave you alone? I don't like your tone, old crone. Your cover's been blown, the seeds have been sown. God I love hearing you moan.

As I wade through the filth and insults that make up the now hundreds of replies to my tweet, I'm astonished to see where some of them have come from. Much as I try to avoid reading the replies themselves, just seeing key words leap out – *witch, liar, murderer, crazy* – I click on profiles and see their locations. Glasgow, Edinburgh, Glasgow, London, New York, Kilgoyne, Las Vegas, Hamburg, Glasgow, London, London, St Petersburg.

This is madness. my post has been seen over 12,000 times and is still on the rise. I can't comprehend the scale of what's happening. There are now over 500 replies to it.

Jeez ur crazy lady. Off the scale crazy

Do unto others as they do unto you. Remember that and cower

They're using the language of satanists now. Threatening me and insulting me by confusing the craft with the Devil.

Fake Marjorie again.

Real Marjorie are you feeling the heat? Can you feel the flames of the stake burning your feet? Are you getting more scared with every tweet?

I want to throw up.

My email flashes. Jessica. Normally the sight of an email from Otago fills my heart with joy but now I shrink from it in fear. I've little hope that it brings good news.

*Auntie M, I've seen what's been happening on Twitter. I am SO sorry. I wish I'd never mentioned it. You have to realise that it's not really about you. It's just how these people are. They're bullies who run in packs, like wild dogs. They love nothing more than a pile on. Most of them couldn't care less about the McKee boy, or you come to that. They just want to be mean and cause as much hurt as they can.*

*Please stop engaging with them, Auntie M. No good can come of it. You have to let it go. This is what these cowards thrive on. I know how awful it must be, but you have to try to ignore them. Please. And I know you're probably going to say no to this but think about coming out to visit us for a month or two. I'll pay for your flights. Please think about it.*

Fake Marjorie pokes at me once more.

Oh Marjorie when will you ever learn? Is all this making your stomach churn? Listen to the flames and burn baby burn. Burn baby burn.

# CHAPTER 29

I have to do something, be active, do anything except be at that laptop. I'll make a potion. A much-needed tincture. I need freshly picked lavender to go with, passionflower and lemon balm, and it isn't going to pick itself. I'll brave the chill of the morning and head into the garden.

Pulling on my boots and my heavy coat, I make for the front door, opening it just enough that I can sneak through the gap and stop the wind from invading the cottage to attack my fire. As I make a half step through the opening, I look towards the garden and stop in my tracks.

My breath catches in my throat and my feet forget how to move. Hanging in the middle of the doorway, facing me, is a doll.

The thing twirls slowly on the rope around its neck.

At my feet is a pentagram scratched into the dirt. It has a sigil – a symbol – drawn into the middle where none should be. My tormentors still can't tell witchcraft from satanism.

The doll isn't like the ones on the island, not quite. It's a Barbie doll – or it was. It's an altered, mutilated Barbie. Rather than a glamorous dress, it's wearing a shapeless skirt and a man's shirt. There are lines painted on its face to make it look older. Its eyes have been hacked out, leaving just two ragged holes. And its hair has been painted grey and pulled back into a ponytail.

It's an effigy. It's me. Part Barbie, part voodoo doll. Hanged.

As it slowly turns, my mind flashes to my dream of the boy on the rope. His face turning away from me and towards me. His face lifeless, then silently screaming.

The doll spins gently on the rope.

I stare at it, scared of it, shocked at the power of it. I take a step back, away from the thing, and slam the door shut again, banishing it from sight.

I stand, my breathing ragged, my eyes wet, brimming with indignation, and continue to look at the back of the door, seeing what's behind it large in my mind's eye. It's still there, taunting me, frightening me.

I look at my bony hands, seeing them shaking with fury or fear, and clasp them together, trying to hold them still but failing. This won't do, won't do at all. I refuse to be trapped in my own home by a doll or by whoever put it there.

Marching angrily across the room, I yank the door open and rip the rope from where it hangs on the frame, stepping out and stamping the pentagram into the dust. I hold the doll for a moment, feeling it hot in my hand, staring into its empty, soulless eyes, ready to throw it as far away as I can, but I have a better idea.

The fireplace is one of my favourite parts of the cottage. The grain of the mahogany mantle, the charm of the floral tiles either side of the intricate wrought iron hood, all fill my heart with joy. I love my thick white candles in their short iron holders, and the ornate black candelabra. I adore my moon mirrors which wax and wane. But above all, I love the flames of the fire itself. I can sit for hours watching them dance in their oranges and yellows, their golds and whites, beguiling and bewitching.

I lit the fire this cold morning to fill the cottage with heat and the smell of heat. Now it can serve another purpose.

Barbie Marjorie lands flat on her back, flames nibbling at her rough brown skirt and her painted grey hair. Fire eats at her plastic legs and begin to devour her body inch by inch. The acrid odour of burning plastic spirals up towards me, then too the tang of scorched hair and smouldering rope.

I watch, fascinated and appalled, as my own effigy curls and melts, the plastic singed then enflamed. I've never used likenesses, never had the need or desire to do so, but I know their power. I know that it's me on the fire, that it's me that's blackening before my eyes, that it's me I can see slowly disappearing. My innards tighten, my teeth clench, fighting against the thoughts that percolate into my brain like the foul smells snaking into my nostrils.

The words of the villagers come back to me from the night before. *Burn the witch.* The taunts from Twitter come at me too. *Burn the witch.*

My mind twists and turns with thoughts of Jean Pennant. Granny Begg's granny's granny's granny. Strangled and burned alive. *Wirriet and burnt.*

I'm owning it. Not running from it. That's what I keep telling myself as I watch in horror.

The doll's face is the last to go. The fire eats all around it, the empty eye sockets staring into a void, the smile still beaming, until they too are swallowed up, turn black then liquidise.

I blink hard as the empty eyes vanish and feel the heat on my lips as the doll's mouth surrenders to the flames. It's done. It's not without price, but I've rid myself of it.

Now I just have to rid myself of whoever hung the thing at my door.

# CHAPTER 30

*1607*

Isobel Griersoune from Prestonpans in the presbytery of Haddington had caused trouble in her community for years. She'd consistently fallen out with her neighbours, taking offence and vowing vengeance.

Robert Pedan and William Burnet were amongst those subject to Isobel's outbursts of swearing and blasphemous words in public. When Margaret Donaldson called her a witch, Isobel responded by declaring, 'The faggot of hell light on thee, and the hell's cauldron may throw seethe in!'.

Her record of misbehaviour and public discord, particularly in yelling at men, was anathema to the church and seen as signs of witchcraft. The prosecutors at her trial, which began on 10 March, were her supposed victims. She was found guilty and sentenced to be strangled and burned.

Her execution took place at Castlehill, Edinburgh.

She was *wirriet* and *burnt*.

*2024*

Twitter

Marjorie Crowe deserves all that's coming to her

She's to blame for Jason disappearing. It's all on her. Burn her

I hear she was talking to Jason the morning he went missing. She made him disappear. 100%

The old Crowe has children's bones buried in her garden

Burn the witch!

# CHAPTER 31

It's not yet 8.00 a.m. but I'm going to take my walk now, rather than wait till 11.30. I don't need to be walking through Kilgoyne when it's busy with people, and Kilgoyne doesn't need it either.

The morning is still damp and I feel the chill of the road through my boots. The fields are wet, plants drip morning, and menacing clouds hang low over the long shoulder of the Campsies. This day is the dictionary definition of *dreich*. The hills, the weather and my mood are in sync.

I want Jason Doak to turn up safe and well and to have just been messing around. I want the island of the dead dolls to be a bad dream and *nothing* to do with any of this. I want to be left in peace, to be just the strange old woman this village thinks I am. And, terrible, tragic as it is, I want poor Charlie McKee to have taken his own life, and it not to be anything more sinister than that. Every instinct tells me otherwise, though.

I'm nervous as I turn onto Main Street. Nervous for who might be there. Nervous for how they might react.

There's someone coming out of the newsagent's up ahead on the other side, the old man from Birchwood Avenue, just a few doors down from the McKees. He stops briefly when he sees me, then drops his gaze to the pavement and carries on walking without another glance. I watch as he walks towards home and see him bump into someone walking the other way. It's the lady from the bakery.

They stop and chat and, of course, she turns her head and looks across at me. I'm the talk of the steamie, right enough.

There's someone coming towards me, head down. I gasp when I see it's the chip shop owner's wife, the one who works in the florist. *Damn.* It's the kind of confrontation I'm out early to avoid.

She lifts her head when I'm about ten yards from her. There's no surprise on her face; she'd seen me from far off, I'm sure. She's chewing on her bottom lip, seemingly thinking what to say. I'm not going to make it easy for her and I'm not going to back down. I'm nervous, though, not going to deny it. As she passes, her mouth is twisted to one side and she's looking a mile away, but I hear a single, muffled word. 'Sorry.'

I'm not sure what I expected to hear, but not that. I look over my shoulder, but she is walking on as if she'd said nothing at all.

I turn, slightly shaken, and resume my route. The Endrick Arms looms large in front of me. Doors locked at this early hour. I hadn't considered this. I'll need to walk round it even though it breaks all my rules. No choice.

As I go to the left of the pub, I see there's a light on inside.

Steam is rising from cups of tea or coffee at a table near the bar, where four men sit talking. I slow out of curiosity and stop when I see who's sitting there.

Maybe it's because it's his pub, but Adam Cummings is holding court, gesturing with his arms and thumping the table. Next to him, the Reverend Jarvie has his head in his hands, studying the contents of his cup or the stains on the table. Rowan Haldane has his hands clasped behind his head, seemingly perfectly relaxed. The fourth man has his back to me, but his girth and long hair leave no doubt that it's Councillor Lewis Dryden.

An early morning council of war? An emergency meeting?

A blonde-haired woman walks into the room and the men stop talking as if a switch has been thrown. It's Cummings' latest wife, her name might be Katrina, who's a good few years younger than him. She picks up some cups then leaves again, and the talking – maybe arguing – resumes.

Cummings notices me. His face adopts the same angry, flushed expression I saw at my own window last night. He mouths an obvious obscenity at me, and Jarvie seems to chide him for it. Haldane slowly swings round and looks at me blankly. Someone

127

says something and Dryden gets to his feet, stomping across towards me. I'm already moving away as he pulls the curtains closed, his face twitching in annoyance.

The four of them were in the village hall, stuffed with self-importance and either stoking hatred against me or failing to stop it. I'm calling them guilty either way. They've held sway in Kilgoyne for too long, men with their own interests at heart.

I hurry away from Cummings' damn pub, my mind churning with questions, but anxious to get back onto my route as quickly as I can. I want out of the village and onto Bodach Lane. I want to see fields and trees, no more people.

At last I can breathe in bluebells and hedgerows, lady's smock and lamb's tails, leaves and trees and water and air. Life. I'm smelling life. And filling my lungs with it.

Spittal's Clearing is getting nearer, though, and that's already messing with my thoughts. I can feel tension rising in me as I pass the turn to Geir's Farm, and hate myself for it. As I walk through Midnight Alley, between the long lines of elms with the low morning light snuffed out by the trees, I know my heart rate is climbing at the expectation of what might be awaiting me when I re-emerge into the lingering grey. The last fifty yards of elmy blackness and my mind is racing, filled with images I can't bear to see. If Jason is there, hanging there, it will be the end of me. I know I won't be able to survive that again.

Almost there. Moment of truth. *Deep breath.*

Nothing.

Nothing more than a tall beech with an outstretched arm. Just the Witching Tree and the shrine to Charlie McKee. No rope. No boy.

I'm flooded with relief. And something else. A strange, shameful sense of anti-climax that I have to forgive myself for. Wherever Jason is, I hope he's safe. Everything I know makes me fear that he isn't.

I walk into the heart of Spittal's Clearing, making my way along the path marked out by the police to preserve the scene. The ground squelches slightly beneath my feet and a bird is singing in a distant tree. Otherwise, the only sound is my own breathing.

I'm going to leave my route again. It's the wrong time and I've already skirted round the pub, so this won't change anything. I walk back down the police path and make my way into Bodach Woods, curiosity and trepidation biting at me. This is my second reason for coming out.

Twenty feet into the thicket, I find the first tree. The beech with the cross of Saint John carved into it. The ornate six-inch vertical, three-inch horizontal cross with the widened arms.

I walk on a few feet, seeing the fresh carving that, probably, coincided with the death of Charlie McKee. Another deep breath. Another step.

*No.*

Facing me, at eye level, is the exposed yellowy flesh of live bark.

*No. No.*

My eyes and brain take it in together, fighting to make sense of what I see. There's a new cross. A freshly carved emblem of St John chiselled into the beech.

*No. No. No.*


I need to get out of here and get to Sergeant Deacon as quickly as I can. He has to know about this, all of it.

The quickest way back to the village is to turn and retrace my steps down Bodach Lane but I know I can't do it. It may be crazy, it may mean *I'm* crazy, but I need to complete the rest of the route. Now more than ever, it has to be widdershins.

I hurry as best I can. Puffing and huffing, shuffling quickly from path to path, across the bridge and on until the school is on my left, the village so close and so far away.

I know Sergeant Deacon thinks I'm strange, thinks I can't tell reality from my own imagination. I'm the woman who saw the boy dead when he was still alive. I'm the one who said Jenni would run and Charlie would hang. He wants to believe me, but he can't.

Well, he can now. I have evidence.

# CHAPTER 32

It's busier when I get back to the village. More people, more stares, some catcalls from a distance. There's no sign of Deacon or Sharma. I'm heading home. Head down and ignoring everyone. I have a phone number in the cottage for Deacon and I'm going to call him.

With the door closed behind me, I search for the card he gave me and find it on the kitchen table. *Sergeant Thomas Deacon.* A mobile number. My fingers are trembling as I make the call.

He answers immediately.

'Deacon'.

'It's Ms Crowe. Marjorie. I need to speak to you.'

'Marjorie. Has something else happened?'

'No. I mean, yes. I've found something. Something you should see.'

'What is it?'

'I … It's easier if I show you. You'll need to know where to find it. It's in Bodach Woods near the clearing.'

I can hear him thinking. Deliberating.

'Where are you?'

'Home. My cottage.'

'Stay there. I'm sending a car to pick you up.'

'I can walk. It's only …'

'I'm sending a car. Sharma will come too.'

On the short drive back through the village, I can't help but feel entirely uncomfortable. Two uniformed constables in the front, one of them PC Maxwell who babysat me in the car last night, and me in the back alongside DC Sharma. The car is all blue and white and yellow and conspicuous.

People have become used to seeing patrol cars snaking through the village the last few days, but they still look. And they see me.

Helen Lawrence from the Spar sees me. Robbie Hepburn from the rolls shop sees me. Derek Cummings sees me. Mrs Liddell sees me. Mrs Kinnaird and her son see me.

Tongues will be wagging. Again. Twitter will be full of it. Again. I've no desire whatsoever to be talked about, never have had. But to be talked about in a spiral of misinformation and lies is the worst possible of outcomes.

Sharma's voice breaks my dwam, surprising me.

'Marjorie, what do you know about the man they call Soapy Moary? The one who helps out in Adam Cummings' pub.'

My paranoia tugs at me and I wonder if she knows I earwigged on them when they were in the Endrick Arms and Soapy Moary was helping collect glasses.

'Not much,' I answer warily. 'I've seen him around the village but usually from a distance. He keeps himself to himself. Why?'

'I saw him in the village today, on Chisholm Avenue. I called on him to stop so I could ask him some questions but he took off, belting along Main Street as fast as he could. He recognised me from the pub, I'm sure. I got tangled up in shoppers and lost some ground. By the time I got closer again he was on the edge of the village, vaulted a hedge and ran into the trees. I climbed over to look for him but he'd vanished somehow.'

'Those woods are a mystery to anyone who doesn't know them,' I tell her, 'and a haven for those who do.'

'I learned that,' Sharma concedes. 'But why would he run?'

'I don't know. He's a strange one. Maybe he ran because he was being chased.'

The police car has driven as far up Bodach Lane as it can, and we walk the final short stretch. Deacon is waiting expectantly.

'Thanks for coming out, Marjorie. What is it you want to show us?'

I lead them into the trees without another word and they follow on obediently. For the first time I begin to doubt the significance of what I've found, aware of trepidation creeping over me.

When I stand in front of the first tree, my nerve has nearly gone. I wave a hand in front of it as if they aren't going to notice it.

I see Deacon's eyes narrow as he studies it. Sharma doesn't seem to be sure what she's looking at.

He runs his finger lightly over the cross, feeling the grain against his skin.

'The cross of St John,' he pronounces. 'This has been done with a chisel or a gouge. It's neat work. And it's interesting, Marjorie, I give you that, but it was carved years ago. I take it there's more to it than this?'

I swallow hard and nod.

'This was first seen in 1999. A few months after Jenni Horsburgh disappeared from the village. At the time, there probably wasn't much reason to think the two were connected. But I still did.'

'And now?'

I lead them to the next tree.

They stare at the second cross, seeing yellow inner bark exposed to the world.

'A few days old at the most.' Sharma says it aloud even though the newness of the carving speaks for itself, filling in time while Deacon processes what he sees.

'When did you find this, Marjorie?

'I came here yesterday. I had a feeling, nothing more. I'd always wondered about the first cross and … I can't explain it. You can call it what you want, Sergeant, but something drew me here to see if it had happened again.'

Deacon looks perturbed, a man unhappy with things he can't easily explain. I'm going to make him unhappier still.

'Get someone to photograph this, Misha. Both of them. And see what forensics can find. Marjorie, thank you for bringing this to our attention. It's very useful.'

'Sergeant, there's more.'

They follow me as I take two paces to the third tree.

Deacon has a face like a disappointed undertaker as he looks at the new cross. He stares at it for long enough that I'm convinced he's willing it to change, to disappear or grow over in front of his eyes.

He prowls round the girth of the tree, carefully giving it a wide berth, looking for anything that might help. When he finishes his hopeful circumnavigation, he stops and looks at me.

'And you're sure this wasn't here yesterday?' he asked. 'Not when you saw the second cross?'

'No. I looked at the trees around these ones. This wasn't here. I came back this morning to look and here it is. A cross for Jenni. A cross for Charlie. And now a cross for Jason.'

'We don't know that, Marjorie,' he says. He doesn't sound convinced at all.

He turns to Sharma. 'Misha, find someone who knows what they're talking about when it comes to trees. An arborist? A tree surgeon? Whatever you call them. Get them to age the three crosses, put some dates and times on them for us. Then maybe we should talk to someone who can tell us about any significance of this cross. An expert on emblems or the like.'

'I'm on it,' she tells him.

He studies me, like he's seen me for the first time.

'You're a wonder, Marjorie.'

'And what do you wonder, Sergeant?'

He considers the question, then grimaces. 'Everything.'

'Fair enough. I can walk home.'

'Are you sure that's a good idea after last night?'

'I still live here, Sergeant. And I'm not going away, whatever they say.'

He nods. 'Then be careful. I'll have a constable show face near your cottage to be on the safe side.'

I consider arguing but don't. 'Thank you.'

Deacon walks ahead as we emerge from the trees. Sharma is on the phone trying to rouse the experts they need. Spittal's Clearing is in sight and there are groups of teenagers standing in front of

Charlie McKee's memorial. The numbers have eased but it seems Jason's disappearance has brought them out again in search of solace or salvation.

As we get near, I realise who one of the groups of teens are. Harris Henderson. Derek Cummings. Hannah Cairney. Kai McHarg, Katie Wallace. Their little gang. They're standing in a line of five. Some with arms linked, some with heads on the shoulders of the one next to them.

Deacon has seen them too and I watch him approach as quietly as he can, keen to speak to them and wary of spooking the herd. Even from where I am, ten yards further away, I can hear soft crying coming from at least one of them. I listen long enough to be sure it's from Hannah Cairney.

'It must be a tough time for you all,' Deacon calls to them.

Heads turn, some slowly, some quickly. The red hair of Harris Henderson turns last and slowest, not even registering mild surprise at seeing Deacon there.

One look at Hannah Cairney confirms it had been her who'd been crying. Katie Wallace looks upset too, but it's Hannah's face that is streaked with tears. She wanders off in distress and no one seeks to stop her.

'It's a tough time for the whole village,' Henderson replies to Deacon. 'We've lost a friend. Now another one. And the village is full of strangers sticking their noses in but not helping.'

Young Cummings grins at that, revelling in his pal's cheek. 'Are you not supposed to be out looking for Jason?' he asked.

'We're looking,' Deacon tells him. 'We're looking right now.'

'Well, he's not here,' Henderson retorts. 'Don't let us keep you.'

Sharma has finished her call and has joined Deacon.

'I want to talk to you two,' he glares at Henderson and Cummings. 'No walking away this time.'

'We haven't done anything wrong,' Henderson objects, coolly. 'We don't *have* to talk to you. Either of you.'

Deacon takes a single step closer. 'You don't. But it would make me wonder why you don't want to help find your friend. And I'm pretty sure it would make me want to talk to your parents and find out why that is.'

The two boys look at each other, cheeks flushing, silently weighing their options. As they do, they see me beyond Deacon's shoulder. Cummings glares and Henderson stares. It's the latter who nods at Deacon and ends it.

'Okay, what do you want to know?' he asks.

The DS gestures with his head. 'Over here. DC Sharma will chat with your pals.'

Henderson and Cummings posture but relent, following Deacon to the side of the clearing. Sharma takes McHarg in the opposite direction, leaving the two girls to wander off.

I'm left unsure what to do. I can't deny an interest in what's being said, but they've been taken far enough away, deliberately I'm sure, that they're out of earshot. My nosiness is frustrated and I linger, trying to decide whether to walk home or wait. I decide that the sergeant hasn't said I can go, so I'll stay.

I can see the anger on Derek Cummings' face, his default position, and I can't help but be struck by how much he looks like his father in the moment. Memories of that florid face at my window last night and at his own this morning. Harris Henderson is almost unnaturally calm. He's sneering at Deacon like he hasn't got a care in the world and it's all a game.

McHarg is more subdued, staring glumly at the ground as DC Sharma quizzes him. Over their shoulders, I see Hannah Cairney standing under Charlie McKee's beech, or as close as the police cordon lets her. No one else seems to be paying her any attention.

I sidle up, hoping she's too deep in thought to hear me coming and run off. I'm standing almost next to her before she realises that I'm there. When she sees me, her jaw drops.

'It's such a terrible thing, isn't it?' I ask.

It's much more of a statement than a question and it takes her by surprise. I'm hoping that its truth is so obvious that she's left with no option but to agree. To my relief, she simply nods her head, tears close again.

'A young life should never end like that,' I tell her. 'My heart is breaking for his parents. For Mr and Mrs Doak too. They must be sick with worry.'

Hannah is shaking. I'm sure she needs a hug but I'm not confident she'd accept one from me, so I keep my distance.

'It's awful,' she says. 'All of it. Everything's so messed up. Just wrong. All wrong.'

She's a different girl from the one who jeered at me from across the street alongside her pals. The brashness has gone, the rudeness too. But she's also lost her confidence and the security that comes with thinking everything's okay in the world. She's suddenly a little girl lost.

'I know it feels like nothing will be the same again, but it will. It'll get better.'

'Not for Charlie it won't. And maybe Jason too.'

I curse myself for my fake, paper-thin optimism. I try again.

'No, you're right. I shouldn't have said that.'

She looks at me awkwardly. 'People think you had something to do with it. With Charlie. And Jason going missing.'

'I didn't. Nothing whatsoever to do with it. I couldn't and I wouldn't. I've seen what's being said on Twitter. None of it is true.'

Hannah looks embarrassed. 'I'm sorry. And I'm sorry we shouted at you in the street. I didn't feel good about that.'

I nod, accepting the apology.

'Hannah, I want Jason to be found safe as much as anyone does. I know what a parent goes through when they lose a child, and I wouldn't wish it on anyone.'

She blinks hard. The tears roll down her cheeks again. 'I'm sorry, Ms Crowe. Really sorry.'

I have the feeling she's apologising for more than Twitter, for more than the shouting, but I don't know what.

'It's all such a mess,' she says. 'All so wrong.'

She knows something. I can feel it.

'What's going on in the village, Hannah? You know, don't you?'

Her brows furrow and her mouth drops open. She shakes her head in lots of little nervous movements.

She's struggling for the answer. Any answer. Her breathing is deep then shallow. She's troubled, but trying to find the words. A yell from behind ends the search abruptly.

'Hey Hannah. You all right?'

The other girl, Katie Wallace, has seen us and is shouting over. She's alarmed at seeing Hannah with me. The others will know soon enough if the police have finished with them.

I lower my voice to make sure the watching Katie can't hear me. In the background, I can also see Henderson and Cummings walking away from Deacon. I don't have much time.

I reach into my pocket and pull out a sprig of a plant; three slender tendrils of tiny green leaves and small white flowers off a long purple stem.

'Hold out your hand.'

She's startled. 'Why?'

'Just do it. Please.'

The girl warily stretches out her arm, the palm of her hand facing upwards. I lay the sprig on her palm.

'That's eyebright,' I tell her. 'Do you know what it is?'

She shakes her head, bewildered.

'Its botanical name is Euphrasia. It's a truthteller. People … people like me … have been using it in Scotland for centuries. You carry eyebright if you want to increase your psychic powers, or to know if someone is telling the truth.'

Hannah stammers. 'I need to go. My friends …'

I place my hand on hers, slowly folding her fingers over the sprig of eyebright and closing her hand into a fist.

'Hannah, tell me about what's going on. You must.'

She closes her eyes. Resisting.

'One of your friends is dead, Hannah. We can't let it happen to another.'

She opens her eyes. And her mouth.

Then another shout from behind her. She looks over her shoulder and sees Henderson and Cummings approaching.

'Hannah. Come on. Get away from her. She's mental.'

The girl opens her fist as if electrocuted and lets the sprig of eyebright fall to the floor.

'I don't know anything, and I've got to go.'

She turns quickly and slips in between the two boys. Henderson smiles at me and Cummings scowls. McHarg and Wallace quickly join them and all five form a chorus line as they walk away.

Deacon and Sharma catch up with me, neither looking like they'd enjoyed their chat with the other teenagers.

'We've spoken to them about their Twitter posts and told them it's unacceptable,' Deacon tells me. 'And that some of the stuff that's been posted about you falls under the category of hate crime and is punishable by law.'

I blanch at that. 'They're just children. They don't know what they're doing.'

Deacon frowns. 'I'm not so sure about that. I think you're being very generous, Marjorie. They've taken the time to type that bile out. I've told them we'll be watching what they post, and we will.'

'I'm sure they took that well.'

He grimaces. 'Young Mr Henderson told me it was free speech. I put him right on that. He said that no one should be on Twitter if they can't "handle a bit of shade".'

I must look confused, as he laughs. 'I didn't know either and had to ask Sharma. Apparently it means disrespect.'

'I see. Well, that sounds accurate.'

'It does. The cheeky bandit informed me how easy it is for social media users to post anonymously and hide their addresses using ... what was it, Sharma?'

'VPNs.'

'Right. But we have people working on it. We *do* take it seriously and we will prosecute if we can.'

I sigh. 'It's just words. I told you before, it's actions that worry me more.'

Sharma's eyes narrow and I know she hears something more behind what I've said.

'Has something else happened?' she asks. 'Something more than words?'

I tell them about the doll hanging at my cottage door. The voodoo Marjorie.

Deacon curses under his breath. 'I had a constable posted there until daylight after the attack on your home. No one could have hung that thing without him seeing.'

'He couldn't have stood there all night,' Sharma counters. 'If he went for a pee or even the moment he left, someone could have seen him go and taken their chance.'

'I suppose so,' Deacon grumbles. 'Do you still have the doll, Marjorie?'

My heart sinks.

'I burned it.'

'Why?' He's clearly unhappy. 'It's evidence.'

'I wanted rid of it. It got to me, just like it was supposed to. I threw it in the fire.'

He grimaces and I'm not sure he believes me. He stares at me before changing direction.

'Marjorie, what do you know about the local youth group?'

'It's not exactly my age group, Sergeant. But then it's not exactly a youth group either. As I understand it, it's a ... an initiative. Mr Haldane runs it. The fund picks local youngsters and gives them a helping hand with training, travel expenses, job placements, things like that. I think they select youths who've been trouble and those with talent to go far. Why do you ask?'

He and Sharma exchange glances. 'Charlie McKee was in it. And so were, are, the four that we've just spoken to. And so is Jason Doak.'

I'm not convinced. 'It's a small village.'

'Yes. With lots of youngsters who *aren't* in this youth set-up. Haldane runs it, you say. That's Rowan Haldane, right? The businessman?'

'That's him. I've always had a bad feeling about him.'

Sharma's eyes widen and I see a sly smile creep onto her lips.

'Is this a sense you have, Ms Crowe?'

She says it without inflection in her voice, but I see the glint in her eyes. I don't appreciate it. Neither, it seems, does Deacon.

'That's enough. Sharma. No more *shade*. From them or you.'

She purses her lips but there's no remorse. She looks down. 'Sorry, Ms Crowe.'

As she says it, something catches her eye on the ground at my feet. She looks confused.

'What's that?' she asks.

'What?'

'*That*. This area has been swept and that wasn't here before.'

I make a pretence of at looking at the eyebright sprig and, ironically, lie.

'I've no idea. No sense of what it is or why it's there.'

I *know* she doesn't believe me. And I don't care.

# CHAPTER 33

*June 2023*
The Devil's Pulpit, Finnich Glen

*Midsummer is a night like no other. A time for ritual, for play, for magic and fire. Nocturnal hours featuring no more than twilight and dusk, and when true darkness only comes if summoned.*

*The solstice is a time when everything is in balance, and nothing is.*

*As the clock turned towards midnight, a grey gloom finally descended to the floor of the glen, but there was still light enough to see the youths who frolicked there. Their bodies were lithe, writhing effortlessly as they danced and chanted. Smooth skin shimmered, glowing slick with sweat, smeared in flashes of red. Eyes were wild, dilated, lacking focus.*

*A fire roared on the bank, crackling and snapping as reds and oranges danced on the wind. The blaze spat angrily at the world, coming alive as the daylight died, like a demon rising. The man-boys took it in turn to leap over the flames, the heat licking at the soles of their feet. Again and again they jumped, urged on by whoops of encouragement from the watching girls.*

*The air around them was thick with the scent of clover and moss, of charred wood, booze and weed, and the earthy aromas of lust and rising excitement.*

*This was their place and their time. They were the chosen.*

*The broadest of the youths climbed onto the rock, stripped to the waist, dusk dappling his shoulders as he stretched into the last of the light. His companions passed him his instruments of need: a wooden staff, a glass phial and an old, leather-bound book.*

*He faced east, opened the bottle and cast frankincense into the waters. He held his left arm out wide and, holding the grimoire in his right, he read aloud.*

'O ye Spirits, ye I conjure by the Holy Name of God Eheieh, which is the root, trunk, source and origin of all the other Divine Names, whence they all draw their life and their virtue, which Adam having invoked, he acquired the knowledge of all created things.

'I conjure ye by the Name Tetragrammaton Elohim, which expresseth and signifieth the Grandeur of so lofty a Majesty, that Noah having pronounced it, saved himself, and protected himself with his whole household from the Waters of the Deluge.

'I conjure ye by the most powerful Name of Elohim Gibor, who punisheth the crimes of the wicked, who seeketh out and chastiseth the iniquities of the fathers upon the children unto the third and fourth generation; which Isaac having invoked, he was found worthy to escape from the Sword of Abraham his father.'

As the man-boy read the conjuration, a wind picked up and scurried through the gorge, leaves rustled on the trees, birds took to the air, and ripples swept across the blood-red river. Nature was on the move.

'I conjure ye anew, O Spirits, by the sun and by the stars; by the waters and by the seas, and all which they contain; by the winds, the whirlwinds, and the tempests; by the virtue of all herbs, plants and stones; by all which is in the heavens, upon the earth, and in all the Abysses of the Shades.

'I call on thy Name, the greatest among Gods. If I say it complete, there will be an earthquake, the Sun will stop and the Moon will be afraid and the rocks and the mountains and the sea and the rivers and every liquid will be petrified, the whole Cosmos will be thrown into confusion. I call on thee.'

Swapping the grimoire for the wooden staff, he began to bang it on the top of the rock, sounding out a battery of six knocks, sacrificing frankincense as he did so. Then he turned to his right until he was facing south.

'I call on thee as the south.'

He sounded a further battery of six knocks and cast out more frankincense before turning to face west, east, and then the north, repeating the procedure.

'I call on thee as the west.'

'I call on thee as the east.'

142

*'I call on thee as the north.'*

*He stared into the air and then to the heavens.*

*'I call on thee as the air.'*

*'I call on thee as the Cosmos.'*

*He hammered the staff against the flat top of the Pulpit, sounding the final battery of six, and made a last offering of frankincense to the waters.*

*'I conjure ye, and I command ye absolutely, O Demons, that ye come quickly and without any delay into our presence from every quarter and every climate of the world wherein ye may be, to execute all that we shall command ye in the Great Name of God.'*

*The other youths began chanting, their voices climbing the gnarled walls of the gorge.*

*'We call on thee. We call on thee.'*

*When the Devil strode through the crimson waters of the Carnock Burn, the entire glen shook beneath his feet. All heads turned away. The youths bowed and the vast beast soon towered over them, his darkness blocking out the light.*

*He was the world and the other world, nature and supernatural. His appetite was great, and his great appetite was depraved.*

*They tried to appease him with words and offerings despite knowing that eventually he would eat them all.*

*'Thelema. We welcome you.'*

*'Thelema. We offer you sacrifice.'*

# CHAPTER 34

The afternoon stretches in the confines of my cottage. I've fretted and tried to busy myself. I've tried but failed to avoid Twitter, seeing the bile and misinformation grow.

Find Jason ASAP

Burn that witch. She's behind all of this

Marjorie Crowe killed Charlie and Jason. FACT

The old Crowe was arrested. I saw her in a cop car. They're trying to make her tell them where Jason's body is

I've made tinctures and read poetry, I've pottered about in the garden, but none of it has come close to shutting my mind to everything that has happened. Too many things are preying on my mind and I have itchy feet.

I have to get out again. I refuse to be trapped here by effigies or insults or the mob mentality of my so-called neighbours. I want air and I want to walk.

Not my walk, I haven't the stomach for that for now, but I need the fresh air and to get miles into my legs. I need to try to clear my head and to think straight. No loop, no Bodach Lane, no widdershins, and definitely no clearing. I know where I have to go instead. My special place.

I'm on Marshall Street, soon to turn out of the village, when I see someone coming towards me on the other side of the road. Dressed in a long black wool coat, black suit trousers and a black turtleneck sweater, is Rowan Haldane.

I can perhaps pretend I haven't seen him. He calls my name.
'Ms Crowe.'

He's crossing the street towards me. No getting away from this.
I don't think I've shared more than two words with the man. And
now, of all times, he wants to speak to me.

Up close, I see everything about him is expensive. My coat
is second-hand and has been for ten years. His looks like it cost
more than a second-hand car. They say he goes to Glasgow to get
his hair cut and it certainly bears the signs of it. This is a man who
takes care of things.

'I think the village owes you an apology, Ms Crowe. Things got
out of hand last night and they shouldn't have done. I'm sure you
understand, though, that emotions were running high.'

He's smooth. Makes it sound like a little misunderstanding.
Rather than a lynching. Or a witch hunt.

'Emotions?' I ask. 'That's what caused people to act like that?'

He tilts his head to the side and grimaces. 'A poor choice of
words, perhaps. But this is a very difficult, a very stressful time for
many in Kilgoyne. And stress causes people to act irrationally and
out of character.'

'That excuses what happened?'

'No. But it might help explain it.'

'You were there, Mr Haldane. You could have stopped them.
You could have tried.'

I see a flash of annoyance in his eyes, but he acknowledges what
I said with a small bow of his head.

'You're right, of course. But I thought they'd blow themselves
out, and any attempt to have reasoned with them might just have
caused more arguments and brought more heat to the situation.'

'*More* heat. *More?* People wanted to break my door down,
Mr Haldane. I'm not sure more heat could have been brought.
Nothing justified what happened last night. Nothing. And I hope
you're not attempting to do that.'

'I'm perhaps trying to explain. There's a young man dead and a
young man missing. People are seeking answers to that.'

I feel the anger rising in me.

145

'I had nothing to do with what happened to Charlie McKee and I have nothing to do with Jason Doak going missing.'

'People are finding that difficult to believe right now, Ms Crowe. You'll understand the confusion at what you say you saw and when you saw it, and what others have seen.'

'I know what I saw.'

'Perhaps you were confused.'

'I wasn't.'

*Was I?*

'Ms Crowe, I think it might help to defuse the situation if you weren't a visible reminder to people here of what you say you saw. That would allow things to cool off, and avoid a repeat of what happened last night.'

*Is he threatening me? Is he telling me to leave Kilgoyne?*

'I'm going nowhere, Mr Haldane. I've done nothing wrong and I've no need to hide.'

He just looks back at me.

'Nowhere,' I repeat. 'And with that I wish you good day.'

I turn on my heel and walk away.

It's little more than a brisk half-hour walk due south across Endrick Water to where Station Road meets the road to Croftamie at Finnich Toll, then through a gap in the stone wall at the end of the bridge. Finnich Glen, also known to many as the Devil's Pulpit, is one of the most beautiful, and beautifully haunting, places in Scotland.

It's around a hundred feet from the top to the bottom of the glen and even from above, the first glimpse of the water never fails to surprise me. Each new sighting is a revelation, a fresh shock to the senses. The Carnock Burn, the stream that gushes through the glen, is red. Not a tinge of red, not a hint, but rather a lurid crimson red, like a severed bloody artery winding its way through the gorge.

Of course, I know the waters take their startling shade from the red sandstone that lies at the bottom of the stream. That knowledge doesn't dull my imagination, though.

It thrills me to see it. I stand and stare down from on high, wondering at the dark majesty of it. This red river snaking its way through the surreal and ancient green rock formations. It's magical. And it's just what I need right now.

The descent to the burn is treacherous, especially on wet days. The 150-year-old rough-hewn steps known as Zaine's Ladder or, more usually, the Devil's Steps, are often slippery and I'm glad of my boots and the rope banister that I cling to as I edge my way down. My neck is old enough to break easily if I take a tumble.

When I've navigated my way to the bottom rung, I step into the stream and feel the chill of the spring water through the fabric of my boots. I stand, letting the red run over me and round me, taking comfort in the sensation of nature. With my eyes closed, I'm as one with the glen.

With them open again I marvel, as I always do, at the beauty and the otherworldliness of the place. Towering green rock formations are all around. There, Edvard Munch's *The Scream*, next to it a giant hog slurping at the water, then the long, elegant neck of a woman, face raised to the heavens, mouth open in ecstasy or agony. Every side of the gorge holds a face, if you have the mind to see. The shapes are sinister, the tops often out of sight. Rocks jut, ferns thrive, every angle of rock seems an impossibility, every hollow a portal.

I walk on, but turn to take another look at the rock face I think of as *The Scream*, the ghoulish open mouth mimicking the agonised horror of the painting. My mind flashes to Charlie McKee. The boy hanging, his mouth hanging open. Had the boy screamed? Had the noose let him do so? I twist my head away, forcing myself to look forward, and to walk.

I let the sights of the gorge flow through my mind, washing away the unwanted images, remembering that the glen was carved into these weird and wonderful shapes by the water, by the sheer force of its being. Nature painted these twisting walls in greens and purples and gave the stream its vivid red. It took an eternity, but it was work well done.

I love it here. I usually come at first light to best avoid the tourists, the ones drawn by the movies and TV programmes filmed in the glen. It didn't work out that way today but without the presence of others, it's still mine. My place. My pulpit.

How still it is. How serene and how strangely sinister. How quiet. Visits to Finnich Glen are my paradise.

As if nature is reading my thoughts, the silence is broken. A loud noise startles me from way above and echoes through the canyon. My head twists as I crane to see what's disturbed the calm. Can it be tourists, or an animal strayed from its usual habitat?

Whatever it is, there's no follow-up sound. Then, in a delayed reaction, two crows burst from the highest ridge, seemingly spooked, and hurry across to the far side and out of sight. Did the birds make the noise I'd heard, or did they take flight at the sound of it?

I stand still and listen, but hear nothing. But there, on the edge above, someone emerges into view, then just as quickly steps back and disappears. Did I see that? Imagine it?

I stare, waiting for the shadow to reappear or more noise to be made, but there's nothing. The moment bothers me, but I shake my head and move on.

There hasn't been too much rain apart from the last couple of days so the red burn is shallower and easier to walk through, even upstream as I'm going. I wade past the huge, flat sandstone rocks that form a natural landing area, their red-orange surfaces glistening in the light from above. Most of the glen is claustrophobic, but I like it that way, the sides of the gorge leaning in, the huge fronds of ferns filling the few gaps and often keeping the upper ridge out of sight.

A few paces later, as I splash past the remains of an enormous fallen tree, the canopy opens again, and I can't resist looking up. There's someone on the ridge, close to the edge, and walking in pace with me. I stop and the shadow stops. I raise a hand to block out the sunlight in the hope of a better look, but can only make out a dark figure silhouetted by the sun, seemingly dressed all in black. As I stare, frightened, the man – I'm sure it's a man by the size of him – steps back and is gone.

My mind betrays me and fills in the gaps. It reminds me of the tall, broad creature all in black that stood by the hanging boy and seemed half-man, half-tree, all branches, twigs, leaves, flesh and bone. My mind tells my it's Auld Hangie.

My mind, though, isn't to be trusted.

My mind saw the hanging boy when the boy still walked, still breathed. It saw men who weren't there. It saw devils when there were none. It keeps me awake at night and dashes my dreams with memories of lost boys. The people of Kilgoyne think I'm out of my mind and maybe I am.

Shooting regular glances skyward, I wade on, the glen darker than before, the green walls closer. I see no one, and maybe there was no one to see. That thought both calms me and scares me.

A few minutes later, I wind my way through a narrow gap between two rock faces and when the stream widens again, there it is. I stop in my tracks at the sight of the large, mossy, mushroom-shaped rock that takes centre stage at the edge of the burn. Although people sometimes refer to the whole gorge by the name, *this* is the actual Devil's Pulpit. It rises from the water looking like a giant cloven hoof, most of it covered in rich green moss and lichen except for a grey-brown section at the front, which separates into what seems for all the world like four thick toes.

Its flat top offers a naturally elevated vantage point to hold court from and it was here that the Devil was said to stand to address his band of followers, the blood red waters swirling below him. The flat top of the pulpit was where druids would stand to preach, where they would make merry or make sacrifice.

And that ancient lump of stone is where witches would be executed hundreds of years later.

I come here by way of pilgrimage.

I reach into the pocket of my skirt and produce a single sprig of rosemary. It's the herb of remembrance, often tossed into open graves to help the dead find their way. I place it reverentially on the flat top of the pulpit, close my eyes, and incant.

*I will wash thy palms in showers of wine,*
*In the juice of rasps and in honied milk.*

*I will put the nine graces in thy white cheeks.*
*Black is yonder house and black are its inmates;*
*Thou art the brown swan going in among them.*

When I open my eyes again, the rosemary has gone. The breeze has whispered to the sprig, convinced it to fly from the flat stone and into the crimson swirl below. I watch it drift slowly downstream, spiralling on the current until it slips from view.

I don't know for sure that this had been the stone of devils, druids or executions, but I believe it might be. I believe the latter most of all. For me it's all too easy to imagine that the bloody water that runs over my ankles and tests my hiking boots once ran with the blood of those that have gone before. The stories are carved onto my heart.

Clasping my hands in front of me, I bow my head and stand in silence. I let the red river run over my feet and the quiet of the glen fill my mind as I commune with my martyred ancestors.

I stand until the cold waters of the Carnock eat into my bones and I know it's time to go. I leave with a lingering caress of the ancient stone, feeling the centuries under my palm; my blood and its blood separated by only a film of flesh.

As I paddle to shore, my eye is taken by a dark patch some twenty feet back from the water's edge next to two low, flat stones. Getting nearer, I can make out rubbish lying on the ground and see that the dark area has been caused by a fire. Anger rises in me at the sight.

This a place of natural beauty and, for me and others, a sacred haven. To see it scorched and littered with bottles and cans is upsetting.

There's an empty vodka bottle, the smashed remains of another bottle and four squashed beer cans. Crouching, I see a handful of white-wrapped dowts, the short, unsmoked remains of cigarettes. Bringing one to my nose, I recoil at the herbal earthiness of it. I'm not so naïve that I don't know those cigarettes weren't rolled with tobacco.

There were stories, a couple of decades old now, of a group of younger locals using this place for wild nights under the moon.

I heard talk of sex and drugs, of cult-like activity and devil wor-ship. No individual names were ever mentioned, but the group were known as Thelema, supposedly a nod to the cultist Aleister Crowley, the so-called 'Wickedest Man in the World'. The Pulpit's history doubtless drew them, but hardly excused it.

The suggestion was that a full moon was the signal for the group to descend on the glen and play out their games. It was grist to the gossip mill, of course, and the village devoured stories of nudity and satanism, depravity and drugs. The police supposedly started to patrol when the moon was full and maybe it worked because the rumours petered out and it seemed the practice stopped. Or hadn't happened in the first place.

A few marijuana roll-ups and some alcohol are some way short of satanic rituals, but they're still bad enough. I've a carrier bag in my pocket and I'll clear their mess away for them. Any remnants will only encourage others to follow suit.

There's something else too, a couple of yards beyond the burnt area. Walking over, I can see it more clearly. A symbol drawn in the earth, probably with the end of a stick. I stand and stare, shaking my head in disbelief. And I remember the pentagram scratched into the dirt outside my cottage.

This is more than upsetting, this is sacrilege.

I can't leave like this. For me, a trip to Devil's Pulpit is a means to a spiritual cleansing, a way to recentre myself. I'm not going to achieve that with my mind upset by this desecration. I'm going back to the rock.

Wading into the burn, I take my place next to the Pulpit again and close my eyes. I take in a lungful of air and breathe out my anxieties, letting a renewed calm slowly descend upon me. I reach out with my right hand and place it on the stone, making the con-nection physical as well as mental.

My reverence lasts for almost a minute before it is shattered by a roar from somewhere above me accompanied by a crashing sound that my waking brain struggles to comprehend. My head has barely begun to turn in the direction of the noise when some-thing hurtles into the river just a few feet from where I stand, the ground beneath my feet reverberating, my ears rattled by the sound of something hitting water then hitting solid earth, a wave of ice-cold water leaping at me and soaking me head to toe.

I instinctively scramble backwards, blood pumping, fear and adrenaline coursing through me, stumbling on the small stones under my boots. As I half fall, half crouch, I see a heavy boulder, maybe two feet in diameter, protruding from the water where there was none just seconds before.

Eyes wide and breathing ragged, I look up the cliff face to the top of the gorge.

There he stands. The tall, broad, dark man. Auld Hangie. Staring down, silhouetted by the morning sun, a flash of yellow at his head. As I stare, shaking, the man-beast pauses for a moment longer then turns away.

'Who are you?'

I know I'm most likely shouting at the wind, but the words come from me anyway. They come from panic and resentment, and from deep within me.

'*Who are you?*'

Nothing comes in reply. The gorge is silent but for the rippling waters, a murmured gust, and the haunting echoes of my shouts. The steep green rise of the gorge seems to tilt towards me, all sides leaning in closer even than before.

I stay on the riverbed, knees bent, hunkered low, hands in the water, flat against the floor, my eyes scanning the clifftop for an age. Finally, I push myself to my feet, shaking off the water's chill, slowly spinning to look above me. There's nothing, no one to be seen or heard.

Leaving this place with any sense of calm is now a forlorn hope. The question is in my head now, but the words are the same. *Who are you?*

# CHAPTER 35

Sunday service at Kilgoyne Parish Church has become much as it is across the rest of Scotland. A diminished and ageing congregation occasionally supplemented by those celebrating christenings or fulfilling a couple of pre-wedding visits to get their credit rating up.

This Sunday is different.

This Sunday the village has lost two of its young. The service is a funeral in all but name and the people of Kilgoyne know where they have to be.

There's been a steady drizzle from six in the morning and it rises to a downpour by ten. Clouds hover over the Campsies like carrion crows, with barely a breath of wind to push them away. The rain is coming down in stair rods.

I am not what you might call a believer, and I'm far from being a member of Reverend Jarvie's congregation, but I know my way to the church. And I'm going. My attendance won't be appreciated by many, perhaps by none, but I mourn recent events as much any of them and I believe I am entitled to register my sadness by being there.

I'm clad in black walking boots, black trousers and a long black waterproof coat, ready to brave the lion's den. I'm determined that I will appear oblivious to whatever glares and stares descend upon me. I shall turn the other cheek.

As I begin my walk, I see that the villagers have piled into cars, the deluge forcing all but the most foolhardy to abandon the idea of making the half-mile walk to the church. In Birchwood Avenue, Evelyn McKee takes a firm grip on her husband's arm as he leads her to the car, tottering on high heels and grief. She sits in the back, shaking, their son Zak sitting quietly beside her as Sandy drives.

Martin and Beth Doak are making a similar journey, a man that I think is Beth's brother at the wheel. As their black Volvo turns onto Main Street, the driver glances in his rear-view mirror and sees the McKee's Citroën immediately behind them. He instinctively slows out of surprise or respect for the situation. Before they reach Killearn Road, they've been joined by three other cars heading for the church and they're at the head of an accidental cortege.

The procession has grown two dozen strong by the time it reaches the black metal gates that guard the small, whitewashed church and its ancient graveyard. There's barely a car park to speak of and the drivers seek space on the grass verge by the low, weather-beaten dyke. As more arrive, some have to park almost as far from the church than if they'd stayed at home and walked.

I'm not far behind them, but by the time I enter almost every one of the white wooden pews in the old church is taken, bodies squeezed close together, family and friends and neighbours, a hubbub of condolences and quiet rumour rising to the roof.

As I settle myself into the final space in the rear pew, I see Sergeant Deacon further along the row, dripping wet in a black raincoat. He nods at me politely, seemingly unsurprised to see me there. Others react differently.

Villagers elbow their partners, people tut, there are furious glances in my direction and open-mouthed surprise. I look straight ahead.

When they stand, I'll stand. When they pray, I'll bow my head respectfully, eyes open. When they sing, I'll stand silently. The agitation I seem to be causing will be only through my presence rather than my actions. I shall be entirely respectful of their religion and their choices.

The church falls silent and as I look up, I see the reason. Reverend Jarvie has appeared, face grim.

When he's in and around the village, he's usually dressed casually, like one of the kids, in jeans and an open-necked shirt. The kind of minister that looks like he's walked off a TV programme where's tried too hard to be *cool*. Today, he's in regulation black suit and dog collar, weighed down by solemnity.

He climbs the steps of his pulpit and stares down at a full church, his upraised palms commanding all to stand, his eyes searching the room. 'Let us pray.'

'Our Father in heaven, we open this service acknowledging your presence in our midst. Nothing is hidden from you, O Lord. You know each and every person who has gathered here today.

'I commit every person in this room. We release all feelings of sorrow, pain, longing and even guilt. We commit our young people to your hand. We come to you this morning, O Lord, with heavy hearts but with full knowledge and trust that we are in your care and that we are truly loved. Amen.'

The final word echoes round the church in mumbles and affirmations.

I've heard tell that often when the church is busy with day-tourists, Jarvie makes mention of seeing unfamiliar faces and tries to lay some guilt on them for their hijacking of his service. It seems this isn't the day for that.

'Please sit. I'm going to read from Psalm 139. *Thou art before me Lord, thou art behind.*'

Mr and Mrs McKee are towards the front with Zak sat between them, tucked under his mother's arm, his head on her shoulder. Sandy McKee is staring at the light coming through the stained-glass arch in the middle of the wall, his gaze never shifting.

One row behind, the Doaks are sitting tight together, his arm around her. Even from several rows back, I can hear the fractured snuffling coming from Mrs Doak as she fights a losing battle to keep her composure. My heart breaks a little more at the sound.

The men who found Charlie's body are both in the fourth row, sitting next to their wives. One sits with his head bowed, the other is busy looking around, head twitching.

Councillor Lewis Dryden is up front, taking up space for two. He sits tall, back straight, making regular eye contact with those around him. A man of the people, there for his constituents, and making sure they're aware of it.

Adam Cummings, the pub landlord, is there with his wife, the young one. I get a glare as he turns and sees me. Rowan Haldane is there too. So is the chip shop owner and his wife, the mechanic and his wife, the man from the taxi business, the McHargs, the Irvines and more. It's like a reunion of the mob that assaulted my cottage. I hope that their God is looking down and judging them.

There are teenagers, presumably classmates and friends of Charlie and Jason, most with protective parents by their side. In the third row are five familiar bodies. The tall, slim red-haired boy and his stocky pal with the dark wavy mop. Harris Henderson and Derek Cummings. They're huddled together with Hannah Cairney, Katie Wallace and Kai McHarg. My tormentors suffering torment of their own. There isn't an inch of space between them; shoulder to shoulder, arm in arm, tears flowing.

In the oak pulpit, the Reverend Jarvie is in complete control. He's finished the reading and is trying to make sense of the situation for those gathered before him. He acknowledges confusion and doubt, recognises anger at the unfairness of life, and is urging the community to come together to support the families and each other.

I can hear an underlying ferocity in the man's tone, even if it's at odds with his words. The anger is unmissable.

'Lord,' Jarvie raises his head and looks down upon us, 'embrace our young people and give them strength. As they grieve, give them succour. As they doubt the meaning of life, show them its value. Light their path, Lord. Show them the way.'

I follow the minister's gaze and see that it has settled on the group of five. Three of them bow their heads, two others seem to shake theirs. If Jarvie had been seeking a reaction he's had the satisfaction of it, and moves on.

He is relishing the opportunity to have such a large captive audience, but I get the impression that he's now improvising. It seems he's stopped speaking from the Bible and is now speaking from the heart.

'We need to pull together, now more than ever. If we lose our young people, then we have nothing. They're our future and without them we may as well all move to the cities. Close the shops and the businesses, sell the houses, go our separate ways. Without our young people there will be no Kilgoyne. So hold them close. Listen to them. Cherish them. Educate them. Above all, protect them.'

Jarvie looks around his congregation, pausing to linger on one individual then another. Some hold his gaze, some shrink from it. I see two of the teens look away, and I see Rowan Haldane stare right back.

A final prayer. One last hymn. And closing words of instruction.

'Go now. Go home and look after each other. Go home and look for Jason Doak. Go home and look for that which divides us and strike it out. Go home and look within yourself. Ask if you're part of the problem or part of the solution. Go now and go with God.'

The rain has eased to something short of torrential when we emerge from the sanctuary of the church. Most make a run for their cars, but enough linger that they spill off the asphalt path and onto the lush, wet lawns of the graveyard where a solitary tree offers little shelter from nature's wrath. They stand among the dead of the village and chatter.

I spot Sergeant Deacon stage left, standing quietly under a black umbrella, watching.

Adam Cummings and Lewis Dryden are huddled close together, raincoat collars upturned, voices low. Dryden is forcefully making a point with his index finger, jabbing it repeatedly. Cummings clearly disagrees and looks unhappy at whatever's being suggested.

The McKees and the Doaks are deep in conversation, swapping hugs and condolences. Teenagers are pressed against the church walls, seeking protection from the eaves above. Dunbar and Kinnaird, the two men who found Charlie are puffing on cigarettes, plumes of smoke spiralling, as their wives stand a few feet away, gossiping. Other couples are a whirl of pointing, jabbing and head shaking, most of it seemingly for my benefit.

'You shouldn't be here,' hisses the mechanic's wife. 'You're not welcome.'

'Go,' the chip shop owner mouths, a violently gesturing thumb reinforcing the message.

'I'm paying my respects, the same as everyone else,' I tell them. 'I've done nothing wrong.'

'Nothing?' laughs the mechanic. 'Try telling that to Sandy and Evelyn. Doing nothing was at least one of the things you did that was wrong.'

Two of the teenagers, Henderson and Cummings, jump down from the church wall and are suddenly just a few feet from me. Instinctively, I take a step back in fright but then hold my ground. Cummings moves towards me, closing the distance between us again, a scowl on his face. He's intent on coming closer but the taller one grabs his arm and holds him back.

I'm not sure whether to stay or run when a figure steps out from the crowd, stands in front of the two and talks quietly to them.

Rowan Haldane is wearing another expensive black suit, this time with black shirt and tie, the rain running off his black raincoat as if it were made of glass. He's undoubtedly a handsome man, dark-haired and clean cut with those startling blue eyes, but there remains a coldness about him which I've never taken to. He seems to be in complete control of the situation. Derek Cummings nods meekly before falling back into line. Henderson continues to hold his glare until Haldane leans in again, and that too disappears.

The man in black turns and nods politely towards me, seemingly sure he's done me a service, before he walks away. I'm shaken and wondering quite what happened when Sergeant Deacon approaches.

'You're ruffling a few feathers here, Marjorie. Is that your intention?'

I look at him wearily. 'My intention is to show that I won't be scared off. I have done nothing other than be myself, Sergeant. I don't intend to give in to ignorance and bigotry. Do you think that I should?'

He gives the faintest of smiles. 'I'd never be in favour of giving in to either of those. But the situation here is tense enough without making it worse. Don't go winding them up. Please.'

I stare back defiantly. 'These people came to my house. They threatened me. They broke the law. Who is the victim here, Sergeant? Who is doing the winding up?'

He sighs and nods. 'I know. You're right. But ...'

He gets no further. A fresh commotion rises from the crowd and we turn in time to see Mrs McKee striding, almost running, across the sodden grass and heading straight towards the group of five teenagers.

She's on them in seconds, her outstretched right arm reaching for Hannah Cairney. Evelyn's hand closes round her throat. She rears back, trying to free herself from the assault, but Mrs McKee grabs her blonde hair with her left hand and yanks it towards her.

Bedlam erupts. Girls scream, men shout and the four remaining teens try to lever Mrs McKee from their friend. Sandy McKee has been caught on his heels and by the time he realises what's happening, a crowd has filled the gap between him, his wife and the shrieking girl.

The voice of the Reverend Jarvie comes from somewhere across the graveyard, demanding respect, calling for decorum. The minister is furious but he doesn't know how loud to shout, caught between making it better and making it worse.

Hannah is yelling at Evelyn McKee to get off her, that she's crazy, that she doesn't know what she's talking about. Evelyn is screeching in her face, 'My son. What happened to my son?' over and over.

Deacon lets it play out. I'm guessing he's here to observe, not intervene, and the drama is intriguing him. Me too.

Harris Henderson is tugging at Evelyn's arms but can't budge her. Derek Cummings seems to find it all hilarious, laughing like he can't believe his eyes. The other two teenagers look either horrified or terrified, possibly both. And all the while, the rain continues to fall.

From my left, Rowan Haldane and Adam Cummings step into the middle of the fight. Haldane doesn't grab at anyone, doesn't push or pull, but he cuts a swathe through the bodies by his presence and some quietly spoken words that I can't hear. Cummings is less subtle, shoving people aside and then grabbing at Hannah's arms, trying to pull her free.

Haldane leans in close to Evelyn, speaking into her ear. Within moments, she lets go of the girl's throat, springing back from her, her breathing as ragged as if she'd been the one choked. Cummings pulls Hannah clear, holding her firmly in case she launches an attack of her own.

Hannah's friends close in, rushing to console her, getting between the girl and Cummings, and she collapses into Harris Henderson's arms, tears bursting from her.

Sandy McKee has reached his wife, his eyes wide. She shrugs off his attempt to put his arm around her and instead walks off to the side of the church, standing there as if nothing had happened.

Cummings shouts at the teenagers. 'Go home. All five of you. Now.'

'We're not the ones that did anything.' Henderson speaks for the group, venom in his voice. 'That woman's crazy. She attacked Hannah. You saw it. She can't get away with that.'

Haldane is calmer. 'Yes, I saw it. I'm sure the sergeant over there did too. Should we ask him if he wants to charge her? The woman whose son just killed himself?'

Henderson's head rocks back, the veins in his neck stretching until he's staring at the sky, mouth wide open in a silent scream. When his face comes back to them, an exaggerated picture of calm has returned.

'Okay. Okay. Let's go, you guys. Too many crazy people round here for us.'

'Not so fast.' Deacon is next to them. 'I want to know what that was all about.'

All five of them face up to him. Henderson speaks. 'We don't have to talk to you.'

'You don't have to worry about it, Harris. Because I don't want to talk to you. Not this time. I want to talk to Hannah.'

'She doesn't have to talk to you either,' Henderson persists. 'Not without a parent or a solicitor.'

Deacon laughs. 'Maybe I should wonder why you're so clued up on Police Scotland guidance, Harris. However, this isn't an interview, I just want to ask Hannah some questions. If she'd rather her parents were present, then we can do that.'

'No.' The girl rushed the answer out. 'No, I'll talk to you. There's nothing to tell, but I'll talk to you.'

'Good. Stay there. I'm going to talk to Mrs McKee, then I'll be back.'

Evelyn McKee is deep in discussion with her husband. Sandy has his hands on her shoulders, his head close, his eyes furiously focused on hers. There's no missing how unhappy Evelyn is.

'Mrs McKee?'

Her head turns on hearing Deacon's voice. 'I'd like to speak to you, please.'

Sandy keeps his eyes fixed on his wife. He tightens his grip on her shoulders, turning her back to face him, a confirmation of whatever message he'd been sending. He slowly takes his hands away, freeing her to speak to the sergeant.

I'm close enough to hear.

'I need to ask you why you attacked that girl,' Deacon asks. 'What did you think she could tell you?'

Evelyn's trembling, her hands closed into fists, and she's either just been crying or about to. Or both. Her voice is a timid cousin of the roar she unleashed on Hannah Cairney.

'I just wanted to know what she could tell me about Charlie,' she replied, 'about why he'd do what he did.'

'So you grabbed her by the throat and hair?'

'None of us are thinking straight,' Sandy jumps in. 'How would you cope with what we're going through? Evelyn doesn't have to explain herself to you.'

'I'm afraid she does. That was assault. Mrs McKee, why *that* girl? Why was it Hannah Cairney that you wanted answers from?'

'I just wanted answers.' The words seep out, slow and low.

'Why from Hannah?'

'She knew Charlie. They went out together. That's all.'

'Hannah Cairney was Charlie's girlfriend?'

Evelyn scowls. 'She wasn't good enough for him. He could have done much better.'

'Mrs McKee, you grabbed her by the hair and made her scream. Why did you do that?'

The woman stares at the ground and shrugs her shoulders like a sulky teenager. Her husband moves in front of her, shielding her from Deacon.

'She just lost it. That's all it was. We're going through hell. Now leave us alone.'

Deacon holds McKee's stare before nodding.

'I'll let you go. But I'll be in touch.'

The teenage five are still standing together, whispering conspiratorially. Deacon walks Hannah away from the group. I edge nearer, my all-black disguise working in my favour.

'Why did Mrs McKee attack you, Hannah?'

'I don't know. Ask her.'

'I did. And now I'm asking you. Why would she think you'd know what happened to Charlie?'

'I've no idea. She's crazy.'

'No, I don't think she is. She's distraught. She's grieving. But she's not crazy. She seemed sure you would have some information about Charlie. Why would she think that?'

'Charlie hung about with us sometimes. I suppose she thought we'd know what was wrong with him. But we don't.'

She looks over at her friends. Deacon steps across her and blocks the view.

'Why you, Hannah? Why you and not the others? Why was it *you* that she grabbed, and *you* that she asked?'

'Charlie and I were … seeing each other for a bit. That's it. Knowing him, he probably made it out to be more than it was. He was so immature. We didn't even … we … we were just hanging out. His mum's blown it up into something it wasn't.'

'Did you and Charlie break up?'

'No. There wasn't really anything to break up from. It wasn't heavy like that. I told him I needed someone older. But that wasn't why he …'

Hannah dissolves into tears and Sergeant Deacon lets her go. She has no more to give him for now.

She's left, lonely and lost, when Deacon goes to talk to Henderson and the others. I sense an opportunity and move towards her. As I do so, I see Adam Cummings had the same thought but I've beaten him to it and he turns away. Hannah sees me coming but doesn't move, and I let myself find that encouraging.

'I'm sorry about Charlie, Hannah. It must be even worse for you as you and he dated.'

Her eyes go big. 'You were listening?'

I have the good grace to look embarrassed. 'I heard. Yes.'

She looks around, worried about talking to me, but her friends are being grilled by Sergeant Deacon. I can't tell if she's happy about that or not.

I've known Hannah since she was five. Our handful of conversations have been about the weather or her new dress or how she was looking forward to going to secondary school. I remember one year around Halloween, when she was about seven, she stood and stared at me as her mother and I spoke. Mrs Cairney looked horribly embarrassed and mouthed 'sorry' but I recall being quite comfortable with it, thinking it showed awareness in the girl.

She was always such a pleasant and polite child, bright and enthusiastic. I'd put the change in her attitude down to nothing more than becoming a teenager and all that that brings. Now I'm wondering if there's something more.

'Are you okay?' I ask.

She shrugs a bit. 'Yeah. I'm fine.'

163

'I hope so, Hannah. It must be so difficult. One friend dead, and another missing. I don't know how you and the others are coping.'

She glances back at her friends, seeing them still talking to Deacon. When she answers, there's an edge of anger in her voice.

'Some are coping better than others.'

'Harris and Derek?' I ask.

She's said more than she wanted to. I can see it on her face. Her guard is going back up, but I can't let this go.

'What's happening, Hannah? Do you know?'

Her lower lip trembles as she tries to speak, then hesitates. This should be an easy question. If the answer is no.

'I don't know why Charlie did what he did. And I don't know where Jason is.'

Careful words, not answering the question. I'm left to wonder what she *does* know.

'Are you afraid, Hannah?'

'Yes.'

I say nothing and wait. All other noise has disappeared. I can hear nothing but her breathing.

'I'm afraid for Jason,' she says. 'I'm afraid of what might happen next.'

'Are you afraid to talk about what you know?'

Tears are close again. I can see them forming in the corners of her eyes.

'I need to go. They're waiting on me.'

My brain is scrambling to think of something to make her stay. To make her talk. I blurt it out.

'Hannah, do you think Charlie took his own life?'

Her jaw drops. 'Yes. Didn't he?'

'I'm not sure. Do you know of any reason why he would?'

She manages an open-mouthed shake of her head before she dissolves into tears.

'Will you talk to the police, Hannah? Talk to Sergeant Deacon.'

'I can't.'

'Then talk to me.'

Her mouth tries to form words, but she's struggling to find the courage to push them out. But I'm sure she wants to.

'Hannah!'

The shout comes from behind her. I look over to see her friends standing together close by. Harris Henderson shouts again.

'Hans. Are you coming? Let's get out of here.'

Hannah stares hard at me, wiping her eyes, then calls back to her friends.

'Yeah. Coming. If this old witch will let me go.'

I take a step back, but my eyes never leave hers until she turns and walks away. Without looking back, she puts her arm in the air, her middle finger sending a clear message.

Henderson and the others laugh and swallow her up into the middle of their group. Jeering at me, they wander off.

I watch them go, my spirits sinking. My fears for all of them overwhelming me. I try to will my thoughts into Hannah's head.

*Please, Hannah. Will you talk to me? Will you tell me what's going on?*

As I watch, she turns her head over her right shoulder and looks back at me. And nods.

# CHAPTER 36

M y cottage seems smaller than it used to. The four walls of the living room have closed in by a foot or so, the ceiling even lower than before, everything over-familiar and claustrophobic.

All I have are my thoughts and my doubts. I've filled the room with them.

Lewis Dryden's sighting of the McKee boy has been confirmed, according to DS Sharma. The CCTV can't be wrong, so I have to be.

I'm sitting in my armchair and questioning everything. My timing, my eyesight, my beliefs, my entire lifestyle these past thirty years. My reason for being. My sanity.

Doubting everything you know and everything you are is as self-defeating as it gets. For hours on end, I stare at the walls and try to make sense of it all. But can't.

A knock on my front door shatters the silence and my heart jumps. The sound of the hammering on the door reverberates round the cottage and once I get over the initial fright, the reality of it scares me even more.

I freeze in my chair and wonder who it is. None of the few people who might occasionally visit are expected, and none of them would bang on the door with such ferocity. It isn't the policeman's knock, I recognise that by now. His is a rap-rap-rap.

Again. A single thump. I see the door frame rattle at the impact.

No one calls out. I can hear no one talking, no feet moving. Just the echo from the fearsome strike on the door.

If the villagers who mobbed at my window are back and they're trying to scare me, it's working. If they're hoping I'll open the door, they're going to be disappointed. There's no way I'll answer it without knowing who's there.

I push myself quietly from the armchair and steal across to the window, flattening myself against the wall, half expecting to see a face glaring back at me through the glass. There's no one to be seen. The front door is just out of sight and whoever's there must be standing close to it.

The door is hammered for a third time.

I catch my breath, afraid to make a sound, aware that my hands are shaking and my chattering teeth feel alien in my mouth.

My mind is scrambled, and maybe that's why it takes so long for me to realise. This isn't knocking. People don't knock like this. People knock in twos, threes or fours. *Rap rap rap.*

Each one of these is a singular, determined bang. Each one sounds like someone trying to knock the door down with a single blow.

Staring hard at the pentagram on the wall, I try to summon up courage and inner strength and a *sain*, a charm against danger that Granny Begg passed down to me, comes to mind.

*Thou will be the friend of God*
*And God will be thy friend;*
*Iron will be your two soles*
*And twelve hands shall clasp thy head.*

The fourth bang on the door shrivels the little bravery I can muster. My inner strength shrinks. The noise booms in the silence.

I need to get help. I need to phone the police. I need to call Sergeant Deacon. I'm halfway to the telephone when I smell the smoke.

I sniff again. Then twice more in rapid succession. It's undoubtedly smoke. The charred wisps tickle my nose and turn my stomach. I follow the smell to the front door, sensing the tang grow stronger as I get closer to it.

Then I see it too. Sinister grey-brown whirls, squirreling under the door and spiralling into the cottage. Drifts of smoke invading my home.

I have to get out. In a panic, I rush at the door and grab at the brass handle, regretting it immediately as my hand is scalded at the touch. Even when I try with a tea cloth wrapped round it, the heat is fierce and the handle won't turn, forcing me to give up and retreat from the door.

The smoke is flooding under the frame now and I have to close my mouth against it. A hand over my face, breath held, smoke sneaking into my nostrils all the same. And there isn't just smoke. Dancing orange flames light the gap below the door.

Spluttering, eyes watering, I stumble to the back door and try to make my escape into the garden. It takes me two attempts to turn the key in the lock, trembling hands and fraying nerves hindering me. When it finally turns, I grab at the handle, twisting it and pulling in one frantic motion, but the door won't budge. I yank at it again, desperately, but can't make it move.

The room is getting hotter, flames are licking beneath the door and trying to sneak inside. The sense of terror grows inside me as my worst nightmare threatens to become reality.

I shout an almost forgotten charm in desperation.

*Fire will not burn thee.*
*Seas will not drown thee,*
*A rock at sea art thou,*
*Fairer than the swans on Loch Lathaich*
*And the seagull on the white stream.*
*You will rise above them*
*As the wave rises.*

I snatch at the telephone, punching in 999 and feeling the handset hot to the touch, unable to tell if it's real or imagined, if the receiver is warmed by fire or fear. Someone asks which service I require.

'Fire.'

I cough out answers as demanded, giving my name and address, praying I'll hear sirens before the call is over.

'Hold the line, please.'

I can't hold, I can't wait. I'm in the grip of dread, and I need to hear sirens. An age drags by, smoke swirls round me and the roar of fire is deafening.

'Marjorie, the retained crew at Balfron Community Fire Station isn't available right now. I'm calling in units from Aberfoyle and Stirling. They will be with you as soon as possible. Please vacate the property. Marjorie? Ms Crowe?'

'I can't get out. I can't.'

I end the call, tearing at my hair in fear and frustration. I try to banish the thoughts of Jean Pennant from my head. Granny Begg's granny's granny's granny. My blood. Jean Pennant who was burned alive.

This nightmare has ruined many a sleep. Of the woman I never knew, have never seen, my maternal line being destroyed by flame, her flesh eaten by fire, consumed in a blaze of patriarchal hate. Countless nights I've seen this play out in horrific detail somewhere in my mind. Now it's taken form and is about to devour me.

*Fire will not burn thee.*

*Seas will not drown thee,*

I pull at the garden door again but fail to move it. I advance on the front door but am beaten back. Fat red and orange flames now grow out of the back of the door and rear up like monsters.

*Fire will not burn thee.*

I fill a pan full of water, run at the door and throw the contents over the burgeoning flames. It douses them, sends them back but they come again just as strong. I repeat the effort, stalling the advance but not quelling it.

*Fire will not burn thee.*

I retreat to the back of the room, now with a head full of smoke. Two lungs full of smoke. Everything rational is riddled with dread. Dropping to my knees, I seek clearer air and find the relative cool of the floor against my face. Sleep seems a good idea. Seems a terrible idea. I want it but fight it but feel myself drifting.

The heat is above me. Separate from me. The darkness engulfs me, wraps me up like a comfort blanket and I fall deeper and deeper into its arms. Even the choking seems to be coming from someone else.

In the dark, I hear Granny Begg calling me to safety. I hear Jean Pennant calling me to her side. There are lots of words in the dark.

169

A different kind of siren. Calling me onto the rocks. I'm waving, drowning, sinking deeper.

Names run through my head. Beigis Tod. Marious Peebles. Grissel Gairdner. Meg Dow. Alison Balfour. All burnt. All calling me to them. The easy thing is to give in. To embrace a forever sleep.

And then I'm moving. The carpet rough against my skin. Fast, bumpy, uncomfortable, stirring me. Hands on my hands. Pulling me. I swim in the dark like a drunken fish.

Heat sears me, near me, past me. Fresh air slaps my face. I open my eyes just long enough to see blue sky above and a pair of black, thick-soled boots by my face. Outside. I'm outside.

Water is being offered to my lips and I drink at it greedily, choking and choking.

*Fire will not burn thee.*

I cough and splutter as the darkness began to take me again. A look back at the cottage, seeing the door wide and wet, broken at the lock. Smoke and steam and flickering flames. And something on my door that shouldn't be there.

In the distance, I can hear sirens wailing. Sleep and relief and exhaustion and smoke overwhelm me. The black boots are walking away.

The something on the door. It's a cross. A wooden cross. Nailed to my door. And set on fire.

# CHAPTER 37

I turn my head slowly and see Detective Sergeant Deacon sitting in a chair by my bed, dressed all in black and momentarily causing me to think he is an undertaker measuring me up.

Deacon uncrosses his long legs and moves his head closer. 'Here, drink this.'

I take the glass of water he offers and gratefully sip on it. The liquid stings the back of my throat but it feels good and I savour its descent.

'You suffered some smoke inhalation, Marjorie. But otherwise, you're in good shape. Thankfully you got out in time, or it could have been a lot worse.'

I take a second drink, gulping at it this time, and drain the glass. 'My cottage?'

'It will be fine. Like you, it suffered only minor damage. The worst of it is just the first few feet inside the door. Scorched tiles, some wood damage and some ornaments. You need a new door, but one is being put on as we speak. Some of your neighbours clubbed together and the joiner is giving his time for free. There's a lot of people concerned and angry about what happened. Do you feel well enough to talk about it?'

'You don't have to, Marjorie. It can wait.' The woman's voice comes from behind Deacon. A dark-haired nurse. 'It can wait till you're feeling stronger.'

'I'm fine. I can talk.'

Deacon shuffles closer in his seat.

'What do you remember about what happened, Marjorie?'

'There was a knock at the door. No,' I correct myself. 'A banging. I thought someone was knocking on the cottage door, but it wasn't that, not quite. I was frightened by it, with everything else that's been going on. So I didn't answer. I think there were four bangs on the door in all. Then I smelled the smoke.'

'The four bangs you heard would have been the cross being nailed to the door before it was set alight. Go on.'

A burning cross. History repeating. More persecution.

'I tried to get out, but I couldn't. I phoned 999 but they said ...' the memory nearly has me in tears, '... that they'd have to send a fire engine from somewhere else. There was so much smoke. I think I passed out. I lay down below the worst of it and tried to stay awake, but I couldn't.'

I see the confusion on Deacon's face.

'You couldn't get out?'

'No. The handle was too hot, and the garden door wouldn't budge.'

'Then how ...'

I share his confusion. 'I thought ... Someone dragged me out. I thought it was the fire brigade or the police. Or maybe you.'

Deacon shakes his head. 'DC Sharma got there just after the Balfron community crew. She said you were lying on the lawn in front of the cottage when they got there. The door was smashed at the lock, but she thought the fire crew had done it to get in. Someone else must have broken the lock to get you out of there.'

Distress surges through me. 'The person who set the fire? It was set deliberately, wasn't it?'

He frowns. 'It certainly looks that way. There's paper and branches shoved into the gap under the door. They were set alight as well as the cross. But I'm not sure I buy the idea that the same person who set it would then drag you to safety. And the fire crew were surprised there wasn't more damage. I think whoever pulled you out also doused the fire.'

It's all too much for me. Shock and confusion cause me to burst into tears. The nurse comes over to tend to me, scolding Deacon with a glare.

I see the look and correct it through my suffering. I wipe at my eyes, damming the flow. 'No, it's okay. I want him to ask. It needs to be done.'

The nurse concedes reluctantly.

'Marjorie, did you see anything of the person who rescued you?'

'Just boots. Black boots. Serious boots. Like police or fire brigade.'

'Did the person say anything?'

'No.'

'And you've no idea who it might have been?'

'If I had, I'd tell you. They saved my life. I want to go home.'

'Marjorie ...'

'You said the cottage was fine. A new door, you said.'

Deacon's expression is grim. 'Someone set fire to your cottage. We have to consider that it was attempted murder.'

'Not just words,' I say.

'What?'

'I told you that words couldn't hurt me, but that it never stops with just words. Words have consequences. All that hate on Twitter leads somewhere. It always does. People like me, people who are different, know that words become actions when the other people get scared. I asked you what would be next after the words. I asked you if it would stop before I was wirriet and burnt and here we are.'

His eyes close and I can see the tiredness in him. 'You're right,' he says. 'And I'm going to talk to Harris Henderson and his pals. I want to know where they were yesterday.'

'You think they did this?'

'I don't know, but they're top of my list. Unfortunately, there's not much chance of getting footprints from the scene that might help. The fire service's priority was putting out flames and saving the building, not preserving the scene for forensics. So they've almost certainly trampled all over any prints that were there.'

I'm suddenly engulfed in sadness, and I fear I'm going to cry again.

'Sergeant, can you stop me from going back home?'

'No. I can't.'

'Then that's what I'm doing.'

'Okay. Then I'm going to have to make sure your cottage is under surveillance as often as possible until I'm sure it's no longer required.'

'Can I stop you from doing that?'

'No. No you can't.'

'Okay then. I'm going home in the morning.'

# CHAPTER 38

*Early March 2024*
The Devil's Pulpit, Finnich Glen

*Five bodies. Five voices. Five senses. Five souls and spirits, five serv-*
*ants of the Darklord. A walking, breathing pentagram.*

*Each of them had one hand on the rock of millennia, so connecting*
*to each other and to the ages. Their words took them back to days of*
*death and sacrifice, to those who'd stood here before them. Bone to*
*blood to flesh to rock to history to rock to flesh to blood to bone. An*
*unbroken circle so strong it spoke to darkness and summoned it to*
*them.*

*She no longer believed a word of it.*

*The others were so caught up in the ritual, in the repetitions, incan-*
*tations and conjuration, that they couldn't see that she wasn't with*
*them. She made the movements and parroted the words, but her mind*
*was elsewhere.*

*All she could think about was her secret. About him.*

*The others wouldn't understand, and they could never know. Them*
*knowing about her and Charlie McKee had been bad enough. If they*
*became aware of this new thing, the world would end.*

*It was all kinds of wrong. Something she'd never thought she'd have*
*done. It was something other people do, people she'd judge badly. But*
*she'd found herself in it before she knew. She'd sort it, though. Get out*
*before anyone got hurt.*

*Charlie was the unknown factor. He was the one who worried her.*
*Charlie knew too much, and he was angry.*

*She'd made a mistake ending it with him the way she had. He wasn't*
*the kind of boy to take something like that well.*

It wasn't him; it was her. That's what she should have said. It just wasn't working out. That kind of thing. But she went with something nearer the truth instead.

She'd thought she was making it easier for him, telling him she wanted someone older. Of course, it turned out to be a slap in the face, an insult to what he thought was his manhood. Charlie had lost his shit.

He'd asked if she was seeing someone else. He'd demanded to know who it was. She hadn't said, but she knew Charlie, he'd stick his nose in. He'd find out. Maybe he'd already found out.

She looked at the others. At their blood-smeared faces, their manic expressions, their lazy, doped-up eyes. The new thing hadn't been her only poor decision. She'd only wanted to belong, to be a part of something, anything, to have a support mechanism to help her get through.

At first, the edginess of it had thrilled her. Now it scared her.

The rest seemed to have bought into Thelema with a passion that she couldn't understand. It was as if they believed it. Every crazy, frightening, out-of-control, cult-like moment of it. Thelema had taken over their lives. No, she corrected herself, it had become their lives.

From the moment that one of them had found out what his father had been part of years before, they'd seized upon the idea with a vengeance. The old guys were all out, but the blueprint was there. Aleister Crowley. Thelema. The Darklord. The costume. The conjurations. What they didn't know, they found online. They vowed they'd be darker, stronger and more dangerous than the previous incarnation. They weren't playing, they weren't messing about. It was for real.

She was scared to remain part of it, and she was scared to leave. Breaking the code of silence was the greatest sin. The penalty for betrayal was death.

So she stayed, and she played. She daubed her face; she spoke the words; she summoned the demons.

The blood made her cheeks itch. Her imagination filled in the dots so that she could feel it seeping into her pores, poisoning her skin. Would he still want her if he knew her baby-smooth face was contaminated like that? Would she still want him to want her if he did?

*The ferocity of the others' fervour unnerved her. They might end it with a laugh or a wink, but she could see them in the moment. She saw madness and knew it for what it was. And was she just as crazy as them? She didn't know any more.*

*Once you're not the person you were, how can you have the first idea of who you are?*

*Thelema.*

*Thelema.*

*Thelema.*

# CHAPTER 39

I don't go straight home from hospital. I have a visit to make first. One that fills me with dread, but which I'm not going to shirk from.

The old Moncur house on the corner of Croftburn Road has bothered me from the day I moved into Kilgoyne. I couldn't have necessarily said why, at least not in a way that most people would understand. I've walked past it at least twice a day, every day, for twenty-five years, and each time it has caused me to shudder.

The biggest, the grandest house in the village, and a sinister mausoleum of a place. It was built in the late 19th century by a tobacco baron, Hector Moncur, and therefore built on the blood and the bones of slaves. That's part of my loathing of the building.

I've always felt ominous vibes from it too. There's a story locally that the owner in the 1910s, the son of the original Moncur, killed a maid by throwing her downstairs, causing her to break her neck. I don't know if it's true or not, or if there was a terrible accident, but the legend has it that money changed hands to ensure a cover-up.

There's something visually, viscerally wrong with it too. I don't know if the blackness of the stone is an ironic or shameless nod to the source of the wealth that built it, but it rises like a tombstone and sits in stark contrast with Kilgoyne's whitewashed cottages and grey granite homes.

Its black wrought-iron gates, midnight Spanish slate roof, and giant, solid oak door that looks like the gateway to hell, all offer no invitation to the uninvited. Like me.

I stand before the gates now and consider just going home. I don't know what I hope to achieve, but I feel I have to make a stand. I've had enough of this.

There are twenty-five yards from the gate to that iron-studded front door. It looks a long walk from where I'm standing. I press the intercom at the side of the gate and wait.

'Yes?'

'I'd like to speak to Mr Haldane, please.'

'Do you have an appointment?'

'No, but I believe he'll see me. It's Ms Marjorie Crowe.'

'Wait there, please.'

Two minutes later, the gates swing open.

I'm greeted at the door by a young Asian woman who bobs her head politely and leads me inside the lair. The hallway seems to be carved ornately from a single piece of mahogany, like stepping into the trunk of a huge tree which will never breathe again.

The woman leads me into a drawing room where Rowan Haldane sits in a large brown leather armchair, reading a newspaper.

'Ms Crowe. This is a surprise. Can I get you some tea? Coffee maybe?'

*You wouldn't get me the tea* is my first thought. *You'd make sure she did.*

'No, thank you. I won't detain you long. I wanted to speak to you briefly if I could.'

'Of course. I heard about the fire at your cottage. What a terrible accident. I'm so glad you were unharmed. Please take a seat.'

'I'll stand. And it was no accident. Someone set fire to my cottage with me inside it.'

Haldane gets to his feet. I'm not sure if it's in a show of feigned surprise or misplaced chivalry, but he walks over and stands in front of me.

'If that's the case then I'm sorry to hear it. And hope the police are making progress in finding who's responsible. But what is it you want to speak to me about?'

Smooth. Like his clothes and his house and its furnishings. Like having your whole life smoothed out in front of you.

'Mr Haldane, I could have died in that fire. The hatred that's been fuelled against me in this village was poured onto the fire.

179

I said to you before that you could have stopped it. I'm asking you again now to do so.'

He spreads his arms wide in a show of mild confusion.

'What is it that you think I can do, Ms Crowe?'

'Anything you want to. I've seen the power you have over people here, Mr Haldane. You can break up fights with a single word, even get teenagers like Harris Henderson to stop, listen and obey. They dance to your tune. Well, I want you to change their tune.'

He smiles like a politician. Or Satan. 'You credit me with too much, Ms Crowe.'

'No, I don't. You own half this village. You own the Endrick Arms, the garage, the chip shop, the taxis. And those are only the ones I know about.'

His lip curls at the edge. 'You seem well informed, Ms Crowe. But not so well informed on my nature. I have a low threshold of tolerance for invasion of my privacy and your time is up. I'll get Anna to show you out.'

I stand my ground till I've had my say.

'Mr Haldane, you told me before that it might help to defuse the situation if I were less visible in the village. Did that include the idea of me going up in smoke? If it did or if it didn't, let me tell you now that I'm going nowhere. Kilgoyne is my home. I'm staying.'

With that, the conversation is over and I'm shown to the door.

The first sight of my cottage sinks my spirits.

My eyes are drawn to the new front door and my immediate thought is that it isn't mine. That it shouldn't be there. I miss the battered, trusted old door that had done its job since the cottage was built. It and the cottage were meant to stay together.

It's only a lump of wood but it's a slap in the face, a reminder of what happened, as if I needed another.

At the same time, I'm grateful. People in the village have gone out of their way to do this. To pay for it, to make it better. If ever I needed my faith in Kilgoyne restored, it's now. Being reminded that there are good folk in the village is exactly what I needed. A dark cloud with a sliver of silver lining.

I'm alive, the cottage is still standing, and kindness has revealed itself. I'll get used to this new lump of wood.

The smell of smoke reaches out to greet me as I get nearer to the cottage. I sigh and realise I'll probably have to put up with that for a while longer. I'll open every window, usher out the charred memories as well as I can.

In my hand I'm grasping what I'm regarding as insurance against further attack – a juniper plant I found in Bodach Woods. Teaching has it that no house with juniper in it will take fire. As tradition dictates, I pulled it out by the roots and made its branches into four bunches, taking them between the five fingers and making the incantation.

*I will pull thee bountiful yew, Through the five bent ribs of Christ, In the name of the Father, Son and Holy Ghost, Against drowning, danger and confusion.*

I repeat the words as I pass through the gate and draw near to the cottage. When I'm a few feet from the new door, I see that there's something pinned to it. A brown envelope. Setting the juniper on the doorstep, I pull the envelope from the door, wondering what's inside and who might have sent it. A well-wishing note from those who bought the door, perhaps. I'll need to pay them back as soon as I can, the joiner too.

Opening the envelope, I see there is indeed a note inside. I unfold it and my mouth drops open.

*This has gone too far. Here's my mobile number. Text me. Hannah.*
*07700 900728*

I'm flooded with shock and excitement in equal measure. With an anxious look over my shoulder, I fold the paper again and thrust it deep into my pocket, opening the door in a fluster and marching straight inside, barely noticing the tang of smoke or the blistering on the wood.

I have a mobile phone. A basic model made to do little more than make phone calls. But it can text. All I have to do is find it.

It's in the hall, I think. In the drawer of the telephone table. I use the mobile so rarely, and haven't done in months. I pull the drawer open and rummage. Spare keys. Gloves. Letters. Candles.

Batteries. I know I'm searching haphazardly because I'm in a hurry and I need to slow down and look properly. *There!*

I pull the phone out and press the button to bring it to life but of course it's out of power. I dig into the drawer again but there's no sign of the charger. Kitchen. It *must* be in the cupboard in the kitchen.

I hurry through, desperate to find the thing, get it charged and make contact with Hannah. There's a box of cords, plugs and chargers. It has to be in there. And it is.

I fiddle with it, forcing the connection, trying it the other way and going back to the one I first tried. I shove the plug into the socket and wait. And wait. It takes an eternity, but finally it flickers into life. As it does so, I realise how nervous I am.

What am I going to say? How am I going to say it?

I might only have one shot at this, and I have to get it right. The girl is scared, skittish, and if I don't say the right thing, she might not reply. The last thing I want is for her to change her mind about talking to me.

I type out five messages. I delete all five.

I agonise over the wording. I fret about the tone. More than that, I worry what might happen if someone else reads it.

I try again.

Hi Hannah. Thanks for getting in touch. I'd be grateful for any help. Can we meet?

I delete the last sentence. Then I delete all of it. It isn't saying anything I haven't said before and the request to meet runs the risk of scaring her off completely.

Hannah, it's Ms Crowe. Delete. Too formal.

Hannah, it's Marjorie. Delete. Too familiar.

Hannah, We're running out of time. Jason is in grave danger. Anything you know might be vital. Delete. Putting too much pressure on her.

Damn. I need to put pressure on. I type again.

Hannah, Anything you can tell the police might help save Jason's life. Please help. Ms Marjorie Crowe

I look at it. I read it again. Twice.

I push send.

The wait is agonising. I am staring at the phone, watching the numbers tick over. Five minutes. *Has she seen it?* Eight. *Has anyone else seen it?* Eleven. *Is she thinking what to say?* Fourteen. *Has she changed her mind?*

Sixteen minutes. The phone pings.

2 many bad things going on in the village. It has to end

Before I have a chance to reply, it pings again.

No police though. I'll talk to you but I can't talk to the police

I reply immediately, no time to waste on second-guessing myself.

Please think about talking to the police, Hannah. You can trust Sergeant Deacon.

No. I can't. No police. Just forget it

No, no. I type furiously. I can't let her drop this.

Okay. No police. Do you know where Jason is?

No. Scared that he's dead. Whole village has gone crazy. People just losing their minds.

Tell me what's going on. Let me help.

Want to. But scared

Hannah, you know how important this is.

No answer. I wait. And I wait some more.

No answer.

Another ten minutes. Then fifteen more.

A knock on my front door nearly makes me jump out of my skin. Is it her? Is it Hannah?

I look out the side window and see DS Deacon and DC Sharma standing on my doorstep. They're both studying the cottage, looking at the damage, no doubt. I don't have time for them. I'm just about to hide and pretend I'm not at home when Sharma looks up, sees me and waves.

I huff in frustration. I've no choice now but to let them in.

They follow me inside, looking round for signs of the fire, Sharma's nose twitching at the smell. I offer them seats and wonder when Hannah will reply.

'Is everything okay, Marjorie?' Deacon asks. 'You seem tense.'

'Everything? I'd be surprised if *everything* is okay, Sergeant. But I'm fine. Have you news about Jason Doak?'

He shakes his head, his expression grim. 'No sighting of him, no. And in one sense that's good news. But it doesn't make it any easier for his parents. But we have had DNA results back from the blood on the blazer you found. As we suspected, it's Jason's.'

Deacon looks hard at me as he tells me. He's looking for a reaction. The only one I can give him is the one that comes naturally. Sadness, mixed with fear for Jason.

'Tell me again how you found it, Marjorie. And why you went there.'

I sigh. And I tell them.

They're suspicious of me. I know that. They switch from friend to foe to keep me off balance, but I know they think I know more than I'm telling them. They don't like that I found Jason's blazer and I'm not sure they believe my story.

When I finish, Deacon stares at me for what feels like an age, then turns to look at Sharma. It's performative, I'm sure. I'm supposed to think *they* know more than they're saying.

'We spoke to Harris Henderson and his friends. Obviously they strenuously deny having anything to do with what happened to your cottage. Henderson was with his parents, they've both confirmed that. Katie Wallace and Kai McHarg were together in Bell Park. Derek Cummings was fishing with his father. We've not been able to talk to Hannah Cairney this morning. We don't know where she is.'

*I do. Or at least I know how to find out. If you'd just leave.*

'I'd like you to stay at home as much as you can for a while, Marjorie,' Deacon says. 'It would be for the best.'

'Am I under house arrest?'

'No. Nothing like that. It's for your own safety.'

'I didn't feel very safe at home when someone tried to set fire to it.'

He grimaces at that. 'Fair point, but there will be a regular patrol. It should keep away anyone with trouble in mind. How long have you lived here, Marjorie?

'Twenty-five years.'

'It's a nice cottage,' he says looking around. 'A relief that the fire didn't do any serious damage. Do you know who built the place?'

I do. But I'm wondering why he's asking. I let him speak till I see where he's going with it.

'I did a bit of research,' he continues. 'And took the liberty of looking up the cottage's history. It was built in 1923 for a man named Ronald Collinridge. I had to google him, but learned he was an antiquarian and photographer from southwest England, and a colleague and disciple of a man named Alfred Watkins.'

He's a clever man, this Deacon. Too clever.

'Alfred Watkins was the man who first came up with the theory of ley lines, the idea that they are straight lines that connect historic structures and landmarks, lots of them with spiritual significance. Watkins believed that ancient Britons were aware of these energy lines and built their most important buildings on their path.'

He's watching me closely, looking for signs again. I try to keep my face still.

'There are a number of ley lines running through Scotland, linking up places like Iona, Rosslyn Chapel and the Ring of Brodgar. They make up a pentagram, just like you have on the wall there, across Scotland. The pentagram's base is the southwest Scotland line and it goes straight through this area. It passes just north of Killearn and just south of Drymen. But straight through the heart of Kilgoyne. In fact, it goes straight through your house. Did you know that?'

My face, I hope, remains expressionless. This is none of his damn business.

'Now, obviously I don't know for sure, but I'd bet my life that Ronald Collinridge built his cottage on this very spot because it sat directly on the ley line. It's the only logical explanation.'

My phone pings. A text.

I turn my head and see the phone's screen has lit up where it sits on the worktop.

'Marjorie? Did you buy this cottage because Collinridge built it? Did you buy it because it sits on the ley line?'

'What?' I heard him, but I'm distracted. 'I … yes. Yes, but so what?'

'And your route through the village,' he continues, 'you know that your walking route through the village, along Main Street, through the Endrick Arms, onto Gartness Road, out to Bodach Lane, to Spittal's Clearing, and back, you know that your route directly follows the path of the ley line?'

The phone pings again. Either a new text or the same one repeating because it hasn't been read. It can't be anyone other than Hannah. I turn to look at it briefly, then swivel back to Deacon defiantly.

'Please don't talk to me as if I'm an idiot, Sergeant. It would be one almighty coincidence if I was walking that line without knowing it. However ridiculous you might find them, I'd ask you to respect my beliefs.'

'And what *are* your beliefs, Marjorie?'

'They're my own.'

'I'd like you to explain them to me.'

I bring my hands up to my head, index fingers nestling in the inner corner of my eyes. I breathe deeply under cover, then re-emerge.

'Belief is an interesting subject, don't you think, Sergeant? If I say I believe in ley lines, does that make me some kind of crank? Do you think you can only believe in something if it's been proven to be factual?'

'I wasn't saying that, but—'

'What about children who believe in Santa Claus? Are you going to tell them they shouldn't? Or people who believe in a god they can't see? Believing in something doesn't make it real, but it makes the belief real and that's a powerful thing.'

He nods acceptingly. 'I can see that.'

The phone beeps again. I manage not to look this time.

'Do you want to get that?' Sharma nods at the mobile.

'No. It won't be anything important. I'll get it when you're gone.'

I'm desperate to know what Hannah's reply is, but her words come back to me. *No police.*

186

'Marjorie …' Deacon won't let it go. 'Explain to me please why you walk the same route and at the same time every day.'

I need them out of here. I need to be able to see those texts.

'It's who I am,' I tell him. 'I'm a creature of habit, but I also believe in the power of repetition. I believe in the power of the line, so I walk it. Religiously, you might say. And I walk anticlockwise, widdershins as it's known, to create a ring of protection to keep the village safe.'

As soon as I say it, I see the look on his face, Sharma's too. I can almost hear what they're both thinking.

*Well, that didn't work too well, did it?*

'You say you believe in the power of the ley lines,' Sharma says. 'Do you believe *you* have powers?'

I'm tired of this. I need to finish it, and quickly.

'Do you believe in the notion of powers, DC Sharma? If not, there's little point in me trying to answer your question.'

I hope, perhaps expect, her to say no and that will be an end to it. But she takes her time, and I see she's weighing up her answer. She looks to Deacon, then back to me.

'I was raised as a Hindu. My mother was … zealous. My father less so. So I was brought up to believe in the power of many gods, all the divine representation of the cosmos. Krishna, Rama. Shiva, Ganesha. But as a girl, I was drawn to the goddesses. To Durga, Lakshmi, Kali, Parvati, Sita. I was taught to worship them, and I did so willingly.

'But as I grew up, I learned that although Lakshmi is the deity of domesticity, it was me who had to clean my parents' house. Durga is the protector of the righteous and the destroyer of evil, but she couldn't stop teenage boys from sticking their hands up my skirt or trying to rape me. And although Saraswati endows human beings with the power of speech and wisdom, it didn't stop me getting called every racist name under the sun. So I got sceptical.

'Now? Now I'd say that I believe in nothing, but in the possibility of everything. Does that answer your question?'

It does. It doesn't. But it probably buys her an answer to her original question. *Do I believe I have powers?*

187

My phone pings again. It seems more urgent than before.

'I am what I am, DC Sharma. We all have powers. Powers of reasoning, powers of deduction. My powers, if any, lie in age and experience, in my DNA, and in living the way my granny showed me, and her granny showed her. It's who I am.'

'Are you a witch, Marjorie?'

I shrug.

'I'd say that the term doesn't have much meaning. It's become conflated with so many different forms of practice that I don't think it's helpful to use it any more.'

'I see. Is there a word you'd rather use?'

'No. I don't feel the need for a label. It's just my way of life.'

She nods. 'Did you always live your life this way?'

'I did not. I had an awakening. It was always there, but it had been put under lock and key by my mother until it couldn't be kept locked away any longer.'

Deacon stirs at this. He knows. I'm sure he knows.

He leans forward. 'Was it what happened to Andrew?'

'What?'

The mobile pings and I can barely hear it. There's blood rushing in my ears. My heart is pounding. I feel nauseous.

Deacon perseveres. 'This change in your life, your awakening, was it because of what happened to your son?'

# CHAPTER 40

'I've done my homework, Marjorie,' Deacon is almost apologetic. 'It's my job to know who and what I'm dealing with. It must have been a very difficult time for you.'

'Of course it was.'

'Would you mind telling us about it? About what happened to Andrew.'

My mouth is dry and I'm struggling to swallow. This is no one else's business.

'I think I would mind. I'm sorry. I haven't spoken about this in the longest time.'

'I do understand, Marjorie.' Deacon's voice is like a comfort blanket now. 'But maybe you could start by telling me about Andrew himself.'

I hesitate for an age, then manage a weak smile. 'He was a good boy. My world. It had just been me and him almost since he was born, so we were as close as any mother and child could be.

'We lived on the south side of Glasgow, in Shawlands. For fifteen years, it was idyllic. Just the two of us. Then it wasn't.'

They're staying quiet, letting me speak. Letting me reveal myself.

'It wasn't that he fell in with a bad crowd, just teenagers being teenagers. At the time, I believed they were a bad influence and told him so. He pushed back, maybe for the first time in his life. He was just at an age when he had to make his own choices, find out who he was. I was a bit too stupid or mothering to see that. Instead, I saw him acting like someone he wasn't in order to impress his new pals. Pushing boundaries that he'd never felt the need to push before.

189

'I tried to rein him in when maybe I should have given him the trust and freedom that he craved. So, of course, he pushed back all the more. He started to dress all in black, dye his hair dark and spike it, use bad language, be louder, and like all those strange bands and singers.

'Looking back, that was all camouflage, disguising what was really going on. I should have known my boy well enough to see that, but I didn't. I was too busy being outraged, like a silly old woman. Too busy to notice that he was lonely, that he was struggling to fit in, that he was finding it difficult to grow in a world that he wasn't ready for.'

I stop, fighting tears, and stare into space for a few moments.

'I let him down. I failed him by not seeing what was going on inside. Under the black clothes and the make-up and the silly tough-guy act was a frightened wee boy. If his own mother couldn't see that, how was anyone else going to? He started spending hours in his room, not even coming out for meals. When he did emerge, he'd rush out to see his gang. It was like having a stranger living in my house. When I did see him, I'd only get a few words, but enough to know that his mood was getting darker and darker.

'Then, one Tuesday morning in July 1998, I couldn't get a word out of him. I could see it in his eyes, though. He was in a really bad place. Like he'd given up. I tried to make him stay, to talk, but he was having none of it. It was like he couldn't hear me. He left the house without having any breakfast, wandering off empty and angry.'

I'm not sure I can say what happened next. If I don't say it, it won't become real again.

The stillness stretches long enough that Deacon finally feels obliged to fill it. Clumsily.

'And that was the day Andrew committed suicide?'

I can feel the blood rushing to my cheeks. I'm furious.

'He didn't *commit* suicide, Sergeant. He *suffered* suicide. It's different and I'd appreciate it if you got it right.'

He swallows and gives a little bow of his head.

'You're right and I apologise. I should have known better. Let me rephrase that, I *do* know better, but I fell back on outdated phrasing. I'm sorry.'

I bob my head, eyes closed.

'Andrew suffered suicide on Tuesday July 21st, 1998. I'd been to the shops to get eggs to make a tuna salad for our dinner. When I got back there was a police officer standing outside our gate. I knew right away that it was about Andrew. That something had happened to him. Just as I always knew it would. I was in tears before the policeman spoke.

'I don't think I even heard what he said. Just bits of it. Just occasional words. He mentioned Queen's Park, and I started running. He was shouting at me not to go, that I shouldn't, but there was no way he could stop me. I was … possessed.

'There were two more police in the park. And Andrew, Andrew hanging from a tree. I ran towards him, they grabbed me and stopped me. I fought but they wouldn't let me past. So I howled and screamed until I'd no voice left.'

I stop and gulp in air. The silence in the room is a chasm. Sharma fishes a paper hanky from her pocket and offers it to me. I take it, gratefully, and dab at my eyes and cheeks.

'Sometimes I think I died that day too. I was 42 years old, and my life was over. I hope neither of you have ever felt, or ever feel, the emptiness that the loss of a child leaves in your heart. I've heard it said it's like losing a limb and I think that's right. A part of you is constantly missing, except it's not been surgically removed, it's been ripped from you and the wound is raw and exposed forever.'

Deacon clearly can't face another silence. He fills the gap before it's there.

'Is that when you left Glasgow and moved to Kilgoyne?'

'Yes. I couldn't stay there. Not without Andrew. I couldn't walk by that park, or clean his room, or wash his plates, or breathe the air that he breathed. I had to get away. So I moved here and bought this cottage.'

'Ronald Collinridge's cottage.'

'Yes.'

'And you made your walk round the village to keep it safe?'

'Yes. However crazy that sounds to you. I did. A widdershins walk wards off evil spirits. But, obviously, I failed.'

He pauses.

'Marjorie, do you think it's possible that this trauma contributed to you thinking you saw Charlie McKee hanging by that rope?'

I can't help but laugh. Scornfully.

'And that I coincidentally imagined this on the day that he hanged himself? Hardly believable is it, Sergeant? I saw him. I *saw* the boy hanging from that rope. I saw him and it took me back twenty-six years.

'It took me back to Queen's Park and to Andrew. It was as if I was seeing my own son hanging there. I shut down. I don't know how long I stood there looking. Just looking. The world had stopped. I couldn't hear anything, couldn't think anything. I could only *feel*. Physically I was paralysed, but my emotions were screaming.

'Then, and I've no idea how long it took, it was as if a seal had been broken, and the world poured in on me. I could hear the madness inside my own head. That's why I didn't call the police or an ambulance. That's why I didn't call the boy's parents. I couldn't accept what I saw. Not again. And I couldn't put someone through what I went through.'

Sharma has stretched out a hand and placed it on mine. It feels good. But I have to go on.

'I don't know if I lost my mind or whether I lost the courage to do the right thing, but I just couldn't. I walked home, numb, and I hid. Not just from telling anyone what I saw but hid from everything. The past, the present, the future, *everything*.'

My voice sounds like it's about to shatter into a million pieces.

Sharma looks into my eyes. 'Marjorie, you said you always knew something would happen to Andrew. Can you tell me what you meant by that?'

I can't bear this much longer. And my phone pings. Hannah is calling to me. Another child needs me.

'It's not what you're insinuating. Maybe most mothers have similar thoughts about their children. It's fear, not anything predictive. A mother's instinct borne out of knowing your child is born into a world of danger and predators. I'd always felt it. An inescapable worry. You can call it what you want. I just sometimes have feelings about things.'

'How would you describe this feeling, Marjorie?' she asks. 'Is it like a sixth sense?'

'I suppose that depends on what you think a sixth sense is. Is it a sixth sense or a seventh? My granny … Look, all I know is I sometimes have a feeling, good or bad, about things. And that I've grown to trust it.'

'Is that why you said what you did to Charlie McKee?'

'I don't know.'

Did I know? Was Andrew on my mind when I said it? Was that day and that rope ever far from my mind?

I answer the question the only way I can.

'I don't know. I don't know. *I don't know.*'

# CHAPTER 41

They've gone. The sound of the closing door is still echoing through the cottage, but I'm already on my feet and heading for the worktop and my mobile.

My hands fumble with the phone's buttons, my desperation slowing me down. Less haste, more speed, Granny Begg was fond of saying. All I have is haste.

Texts. Six of them. All from Hannah. I scroll through them with my heart in my mouth.

The first answers the last question I asked her.

Of course I know how important this is. Jason is in big danger. If he's not dead already

I need to know I can trust u.

Too many bad things going on in the village. Too many bad people.

There's a time gap till the next text. She's wondering why I haven't replied.

Are u there?

Ms Crowe???

Another gap. More time taken up by Deacon and Sharma.

I thought u wanted to help. Are u just messing with me?

It's over ten minutes since her last text. She's given up on me. I know it. I punch at the keys.

I'm here. I'm so sorry. I couldn't answer but can now. I promise you can trust me. I want to help. Please tell me what's happening in the village.

I send it. And wait.

It takes three minutes, and it seems like forever. I've put the phone down and picked it up again four times, but finally it lights up and pings, and I have an answer.

I can't tell you by text. Too risky

I answer as quickly as I can.

Then meet me. Today.

The reply comes immediately this time.

Needs to be somewhere am not seen. No one can know I spoke to u

This afternoon. In Bell Park?

No way. 2 many people could see me. Will meet u at Spittal's Clearing.

That way can say was at Charlie's memorial thing if anyone sees

Okay. Can you just tell me who's involved in this Hannah?

No, not on here. Will tell u when see u.

Meet me at Spittal's Clearing at 3. Come alone. Please. Tell no one.

# CHAPTER 42

The two hours waiting have crawled by. I made the grave mistake of filling part of them by looking on Twitter. The mob have been active.

Active and malignant, misinformed and cruel. They're up to date with events but their take on them is awful. Of course, I shouldn't have looked. And of course, I did.

> Yay! The witch has been burned out of her lair. Serves the old bag right

> I heard the Crowe had been keeping Jason Doak prisoner in her cottage and he set the fire to get out

> Someone should finish the job. Burn her cottage to the ground

Fake Marjorie has been posing messages too. The power of rhyme has gained 'her' over ten thousand followers.

> First they call me awful names, Then make all sorts of untrue claims, Now they've sent me up in burning flames

> Double, double toil and trouble; Fire burn, and caldron bubble

> I made Charlie choke. I made Kilgoyne a national joke. You'll never find Jason Doak. I've made him go up in smoke

I close the laptop, curse the day I bought the thing and try to distract myself as best I can by cleaning the inside of the cottage to try to rid it of the lingering smell of smoke. Finally, the clock confirms it is time to leave for Spittal's Clearing.

The walk through the village is harrowing. Eyes on me, chattering about me. Scorn and pity coming from those who I call neighbours. I hear words and phrases.

*Witch. Shame. Disgrace. Witch. All her fault. Poor Marjorie. Get her out.*

I was wrong, or perhaps not honest, in what I told Sergeant Deacon about words and how they couldn't hurt me. They're hurting me now. And words are the starting point. It's how they dehumanise people, how they then make it acceptable to abuse them, attack them, kill them.

I keep my head down and the tears from my eyes, walk briskly along Main Street until I'm faced with the Endrick Arms. This isn't really my walk, my widdershins route, so I can avoid the pub without risking further calamity. I could face them up, show them they can't beat me, but the truth is that they might have done. I walk around it.

My nerves are rattling, coursing through me like electricity. This is important, and it's weighing heavily on me. Turning onto Bodach Lane, I think of Granny Begg and ask her for the strength to see this through.

I stop a few yards before emerging from the two dark lines of elms that form Midnight Alley, a few yards before the clearing will come into view, and take a moment. I'm not entirely sure what I'm doing, or why, but I feel the need to stand and think. To pray? I've no one to pray to. To hope? Yes, maybe that. Maybe.

'Okay,' I say out loud. 'Let's go.'

Two paces and I see that the clearing is almost empty. Two teenagers, the Watsons' girl and Millie Harrison, are turning away from the pile of flowers and football shirts and seem to be leaving. They glance at me as they pass, and then at each other, a tale to tell their friends no doubt.

No police stand around, no forensics are working the scene. I look towards Charlie's tree and see a tall, broad man standing there. Lewis Dryden.

I curse the sight of him and hope he isn't going to spook Hannah and make her turn around. I glance at my watch and it's still just a quarter to three. Fifteen minutes to get rid of him.

He glances over his shoulder, perhaps sensing my presence, and sees me standing here. His shoulders slump and he's obviously as happy to see me as I am him. He turns slowly and shuffles over towards me.

I don't have time to engage him in conversation but I'm curious as to why he's here.

'Ms Crowe.'

'Councillor Dryden.'

'I just wanted to see the site for myself. Where it happened, I mean.'

He's explaining himself to me, which I find curious.

'You'll know by now that you were wrong,' he sneers. 'That you didn't see Charlie when you claim you did.'

'A young man lost his life hanging from that tree. And you think the right thing to do is score points?'

'I was just saying.'

'And I'm just saying you should be more concerned with what happened to Charlie McKee than trying to prove me wrong.'

'You were wrong.'

'No, the CCTV proves you were right. It doesn't necessarily prove that I was wrong.'

He laughs in my face. 'You're crazy.'

He's still laughing as he walks off. I watch him till he disappears from sight, the word crazy echoing in my head. I don't like the man nor his manner, and certainly didn't need this right now.

But he's gone, thankfully. I have the clearing to myself. For me and Hannah.

She isn't here, but I hadn't expected her to be. It's still ten minutes to three and I'm sure she'll be dragging her feet, reluctant to take the chance of being seen with me any more than necessary. If she turns up at all. She's obviously scared witless of something or someone, and I have to protect her after dragging her into this. She is afraid of the bad people.

*Too many bad things going on in the village. Too many bad people.*

Not just one person. People.

I take up a spot against one of the birches on the edge of Bodach Woods; no point in making myself any more obvious than I have to be, until I have to be. I have a view of the lane and the clearing, and one step will put me in the open and Hannah will see me.

*Has to stop.*

She didn't say what or who. But I'm desperately hoping that she will.

I look at my mobile phone, watch the time tick over to quarter past three, and look as far down the lane as the elms will let me. No one. Not yet.

I don't need anyone to tell me how bad things might be for Jason Doak. Every bit of experience, every bit of human instinct, every growl of my guts, tells me the boy is at huge risk. Hannah's confirmation hasn't made anything any easier.

*He is in big danger. If not dead already*

If. Not dead. Already.

I pace. I'm not naturally the nervous type, but neither am I the kind to happily stand and wait. I walk to the beech where Charlie had hung. And I walk back again. I march to the shrine, I count scarves, then I count football shirts, then teddy bears, then bunches of flowers. This isn't helping. This is just reminding me why Hannah has to turn up. I walk back to the Witching Tree and half hide behind it.

I glance at the time again, even though it's only been two minutes since I last did so. She's more than fifteen minutes late.

Has someone talked her out of it? Did she never intend to come in the first place? I remember the middle finger she flipped at me as she walked away at the church. Maybe she's flipping it again now.

I text her.

Hannah. Have you changed your mind? I'll wait if you're still coming.

There's no answer. I put the phone back in my pocket, fish it out and look at the text again. It has been delivered but not read.

I said I wouldn't phone her. Promised her I wouldn't. Text only.

'Damn.' I call her number.

It rings and rings. I wonder if she's with the group and can't take the call. Or if she's seeing my name and laughing. Or whether she's staring at it and trying to find the courage to answer.

It goes to voicemail and I hang up, not willing to take the risk of having my voice heard. I text again.

I'm leaving the clearing, Hannah. Text or call me if you still want to talk. You know how important this is.

With a final glance at the tree where Charlie McKee hung, I begin the walk back into the village. I go no more than twenty yards before I take another look at the last text that I've sent her.

Delivered. Not read.

# CHAPTER 43

I check my phone every few minutes on the walk home, as if somehow it has lost volume and texts have been delivered that I haven't heard. There's nothing.

It's dispiriting. Worse than if she'd never said she'd meet me in the first place. Maybe she never intended to. Why would she meet a crazy old woman to tell her something she'd no right to know?

She was my chance to make some things right. For Andrew, for Charlie, for Jason. Maybe she still can be. I'm holding out hope.

The gauntlet of Main Street feels like they all know I've been on a fool's errand and every one of them is laughing at me. Sniggers and pointing, whispered words and stares. Never have I felt more like a stranger in the place I call home.

When I'm greeted with the new door again, my spirits take another dive. Nothing is as it should be.

Inside, I still can't decide if the charred perfume I smell in the cottage is in my head or in the carpet and curtains. Either way, I can't get away from it.

The scent of smoke hangs in the air like a bad memory. The sight of singed wood, blackened tiles and scorched glass depresses me.

I busy myself, wiping down surfaces, washing windows, scrubbing thoughts. I catch occasional glimpses of the constable that Deacon promised, the man making himself visible enough to ward off any further threats. I hope.

In case anyone is watching, I put on a brave face, make out I'm undeterred and will be staying come what may. The reality is different. I am terrified. And in need of sustenance. The bottle of Ardbeg is tempting but I'm not going to give in to that. Instead,

I'll take my potion for easing anxiety and calming nerves, the one Granny Begg swore by.

She said the formula went back three hundred years and had passed down through the family. I tweaked it, modernised it. I start with a smoky quartz crystal in a glass jar, which I sit in a larger bowl filled with vodka. The crystal works its magic, infusing overnight under a full moon. Then I take the crystal away and the vodka is ready for use.

Lavender and passionflower are picked from my garden along with a handful of leaves of lemon balm. They are harvested mid-morning, when the dew has dried but before the sun has burned off any of the essential oil in the herbs. Granny Begg used to air-dry the herbs by tying them into bundles with twine, keeping the bundles small to avoid rot or mould, and hanging them upside down wrapped in muslin for two weeks until they were completely dry. I use a microwave. One minute at high power, then another 30 seconds, if needed, until all the moisture is gone. I say a silent apology to my granny every time.

I crumble the dried herbs with my fingers, then grind them finer with the mortar and pestle before placing them in a sterilised jar and pouring over the vodka. The lid goes on tight and the jar is left for six weeks, hidden away from sunlight, the alcohol topped up when needed. Finally, it is decanted and wrung through a fine mesh bag, pressing out the tincture from the dried roots and herbs, then funnelled into the amber bottles.

I've put five drops of tincture into a glass of water when I hear a commotion outside.

I freeze, holding the dropper. Not again. *Please.*

It's a shout, a raucous, angry voice. No, I think, two voices at least.

The voices rise again and I think I hear a muffled scream. I check the front door is locked and wonder if I should call the police. Deacon said not to hesitate if I'm under threat. Am I?

I pick up the phone, ready to dial or use it as a weapon. Amid the commotion, I hear a yelp of pain, then another. It's not me under threat, someone else is. I put the dropper back in the bottle, twist the lid tight and put it in my cardigan pocket. I'm out the door, fuelled by outrage. I follow the noise down the path and around the corner.

There's a fight in the middle of the road, teenagers either side of someone on the ground. Their legs are swinging violently, boots kicking the person.

I soon recognise them, Derek Cummings and Kai McHarg. My memory flashes back to my own protective curl when the cottage was under attack, and anger swells in me.

I shout at them to stop. They're surprised and stop kicking, but it doesn't last.

Cummings stares straight at me defiantly as he kicks savagely at the victim's ribs. He's enjoying it.

'Stop. Stop that.'

'Get stuffed, you old witch. He's getting what's coming to him. He chose your side.'

The violence is sickening me. I can't stand to watch this and need to do something.

Reaching into my cardigan pocket, I pull out the tincture bottle and hold it above my head. The boys' eyes are immediately drawn to it, and I see confusion spread across their faces.

I start a chant, moving the bottle slowly and pointing it at each of them in turn. My voice rises in volume and ferocity. They're puzzled and worried.

I repeat the same word over and over.

*Maleficium. Maleficium. Maleficium.*

I hold the bottle of potion high, my arm at full stretch, and their eyes follow. When I'm sure I have their attention, I hurl the bottle to the ground, shattering it.

The pungent aroma rises as the dark liquid stains the ground.

McHarg runs. Cummings stands his ground, eyes wide.

'I'm not scared of you,' he says. The edge in his voice says otherwise.

I begin to walk towards him, chanting *maleficium* while trying to look as crazy as possible. He hesitates, looks over his shoulder to see his pal disappearing, and slowly backs off before turning to run after him.

I watch them go and breathe out hard, my hands shaking. I need that anxiety potion more than ever, but it has served a different purpose.

'It's okay,' I tell the man on the ground. 'They've gone.'

As he warily uncoils, I realise who he is. The unkempt beard, the straggly hair, the yellow beanie and oversized greatcoat. It's the man they call Soapy Moary.

He slowly removes his hands from his head and stretches out his legs. As he rolls over, I gasp, seeing violent scarlet weals on his cheeks and forehead, torn skin, too, where the boots have caught him. He rubs at his lips, already swollen, and winces.

Sitting up, he immediately grabs at his ribs, his face contorting in pain.

'Wait. Let me help you.' I bend and put his arm over my shoulder. He's twice the size of me and I can barely budge him, but he tries to stand and I can help lever him the rest of the way.

It's only when he's upright, wincing in pain, that I notice his footwear. A pair of black, thick-soled boots. Serious boots. I stare at the battered and bruised man under my arm and remember what the Cummings boy had said. *'He chose your side.'*

# CHAPTER 44

I help the man along the path and through the cottage door. He tries not to show how much he's hurting, but I know that every step is causing him pain. I ease him into my armchair and fetch a glass of water from the sink. He swallows a mouthful then grimaces.

'You got anything stronger?'

'I'll call an ambulance,' I tell him. 'You need treatment. And I'm going to call the police.'

'No.'

He pushes himself up from the chair, clutching his ribs.

'You're hurt. You might have broken ribs. Sit down.'

He doesn't need much persuasion to slip back into the chair and sip more of the water after as I hand it to him.

'No ambulance. Please. And no police.'

'Why?' I sound harsher than I mean to. 'Those boys could have killed you.'

'I don't want the police involved. Those wee bastards would just deny it anyway. I've had worse.'

He sees me make a face at the swear word.

'Sorry. Sorry.'

'You need treatment.'

He sighs. 'Old Dr Reynolds used to look after me. Let me into his surgery after he was done for the day. Never needed me to be registered, knew I wouldn't. He saw me right. But since he's retired ...'

He finishes with a shrug. 'I try to stay healthy.'

'What's your name?' I ask.

He frowns with his eyes. 'Local kids call me Soapy Moary.'

'But that's not your name. Do you mind them calling you that?'

'I mind. But it will do.'

I'm a great believer in what you can see in a person's eyes. Truth and lies, joy and sorrow. A window to the soul, to the past and maybe even the future. I look and I see.

'I'm not a doctor but I know some medicine. I'll treat your wounds. If you'll let me.'

The man nods. And so do I.

'Let's get you cleaned first.'

I fetch a bowl of hot water and begin swabbing gently at his face, seeing him wince as I bathe the cuts to his cheek and the torn skin on his forehead. He winces but doesn't make a sound.

As I rub away the dirt from the road, and probably from the past month, I uncover a face slightly younger than the man normally presents. I wipe back time and look at him anew.

'Okay, you're clean enough that you won't die. Sit there and don't move. I'll be back as quickly as I can.'

As I work, my mind has time to drift to Hannah. I take the chance to check my phone for messages. Twice. There's nothing. I sigh heavily enough that Soapy Moary lifts his head to wonder what the problem is.

I return ten minutes later carrying a large white bowl which I place on the table beside him. When he peers into it, he sees it's three-quarters full of a vivid dark green mulch.

'What the hell is that?'

'It's a poultice made from comfrey, a shrub that grows on the riverbank.'

'A plant? That's going to help me?'

'It's very high in vitamin K and vitamin K2. They promote healing of fractures. It also has the protein allantoin which stimulates cell proliferation.'

His eyebrows lift in scepticism. 'Really?'

I give a hint of a smile. 'Yes. Comfrey comes from the Latin *confera*, meaning to knit together. Its botanical name is *Symphytum*, which comes from the Greek word *sympho*, meaning to unite.'

'Like symphony?'

'Yes, like symphony. The old name for it, the country name, is knitbone.'

His brows furrow. 'Are you like a witch doctor or something?'

'Or something. You need to take your shirt off.'

His eyes open wide. 'My shirt?'

'This isn't going to work if I put it on *over* your shirt. It needs to be against the skin. Against the bones. Don't worry, I've seen it all before.'

He huffs, but unbuttons his heavy plaid shirt and raises his arms so I can pull the grubby white T-shirt over his head. I stick my right hand into the bowl and scoop out a large handful of the green pulp, then begin to slather it over his ribs.

His nose wrinkles. 'It stinks.'

'It works. That's all you need to worry about. Do you know the boys that beat you up?'

'I'm getting old. Time was I'd have easily leathered them.'

'There were two of them. Do you know them?'

He shrugs. 'I know them by sight. Little … devils. Always full of cheek. They've been getting worse. I try to keep out of their way but today I wasn't so lucky.'

'Is it just luck? They said you chose my side.'

He looks away awkwardly. 'Life doesn't always have to be about sides. I just try to keep to myself. Kids like that don't need a reason to take against anyone. Today it was just my turn.'

'Is that all it is?'

As I ask the question, I pull the bandage roll tight, making him flinch again. When he doesn't answer, I pull the next roll tighter still.

'Okay, okay! I know those kids were here the other night, banging on your window with the others. I dug them up about it. Told them they were out of order. No way to treat anyone.'

I wind another roll around his chest, working my way up, the comfrey being slowly enveloped in the bandages.

'And what about yesterday?'

He hesitates.

'Were you here? When my cottage was set on fire.'

I see a lot going on in his eyes. Reluctance. Anguish. Pain.

'Yes.'

'It was you who pulled me out. Wasn't it?'

'Yes.'

'I remember your boots. About the only thing I can remember. That and being alive when I thought I wasn't going to be.'

He looks to the floor, embarrassed. 'Anyone would have done the same.'

I laugh scornfully. 'I doubt that. In this village? Anyway, not anyone did it, you did. Thank you.'

He nods awkwardly. 'Welcome.'

'Did you see who did it?'

'No. I saw the smoke and ran over here. I'd been nearby. Knew there might be trouble after the other night. There was no one there, though. Whoever it was had scarpered. Maybe heard me coming.'

I fix the last of the bandage in place with a safety pin.

'And you put out the fire?'

'The worst of it. Used the bucket out back and filled it from Stillwater pond. Soaked it till I heard the fire engine coming.'

I study him. 'You know the village well, then? To know the name of that old pond.'

'Well enough,' he says guardedly. 'That it done?'

'It's done. Keep the bandages on for a week if you can,' I tell him. 'I'll give you a shirt to put on for now.'

'I've got my own clothes,' he responds.

'You can take them with you if you want, but you're not putting them on. You've got cuts and they're filthy. You'll get infected.'

'Okay. Okay.'

'I can wash your shirt,' I say, 'and that too.' I nod at the yellow beanie on his head.

'No. I can wash them in the river.'

'Okay. Please yourself. Do you want to stay for dinner? I dare say you could do with a good meal,' I offer.

'I dare say I could, but I've got somewhere I need to be. Thanks though.'

I shake my head. 'It's me who should be thanking you. You saved my life. Let me feed you at least.'

He finally relents and I make a stew of lamb, beans and potatoes while three times fruitlessly checking my phone. The smell of cooking quickly fills the cottage and I set two places at the table. I watch as my patient eats heartily, as if he hasn't had a meal in a month.

'There's more in the pot if you want it,' I tell him. 'It's keeping warm on the stove.'

His eyes light up and he looks at me awkwardly. 'This is delicious. Best meal I've had in a long time. Can I maybe take some of this with me? If that's okay?'

I nod. 'Of course.'

'Thank you,' he says. 'Means a lot. Can't say how much.'

'You're welcome. The least I could do.'

He stares at me, making me self-conscious.

'You're like me,' he says quietly. 'An outsider. Different reasons but same result. Don't you think?'

'Yes. Suppose I am. Different though, like you say.'

He nods, agreeing with his own conclusion, and fidgeting furiously in his seat. He's rocking back and forward, with what looks like an internal argument raging.

'Are you okay?' I ask.

'Yes. Yes.'

'Is there … is there something you want to tell me?

The way his mouth drops convinces me I'm right.

'I … I can't. I don't …'

'You can trust me. Outsiders stick together.'

He looks pained and on the edge of bursting into tears. 'Can I?'
'Yes.'

'I've made a promise, though. Not to tell. But I can't do this by myself. Ms Crowe, I don't know what to do.'

I decide to say the one thing I feel sure could convince him.

'I know who you are.'

His eyes stretch and his lips tremble as if to speak, but he says nothing.

'I didn't know till this last hour. Any other time I've seen you round the village I didn't see it. You always had months of beard and you're a lot older and … well, you've not been the cleanest. But when I washed you, I saw. Maybe I should always have known. But I know now.'

I lean in close so that my head is inches from his.

'You're Billy Horsburgh. Aren't you?'

His face crumples in distress. His arms come up, crossing over and wrapping protectively round his head. He ducks towards the table, curling into a ball and tries to disappear from view. I wasn't sure what response I'd get, but it wasn't this.

Disturbing as his reaction is, I take it as confirmation that I'm right.

'Billy, it's okay. It's okay. I'm not going to tell anyone. If you don't want anyone to know then that's your choice. Okay?'

He unfurls slowly, a reluctant re-emergence. His face is tracked with tears and his eyes show all the signs of fright and flight.

'Years have been hard on you, Billy. I can see that. I guess living rough would do that. And your time in the army, I'm sure. And losing your sister like that.'

His arms come up again but only to the top of his head this time, clutching his skull as if he'd just heard of Jenni's disappearance for the first time.

'I can't talk about it. Can't. Got to go. Can't stay. Thanks but got to leave.'

'Wait. The food. You wanted more to take with you. I've a feeling you'll need it.'

He stops mid-stride, painfully torn between the need to go and the need for food.

'Aye. Please.'

He stands nervously, fidgeting like he's on a piece of elastic set to go snap as I fill a dish with stew, place a lid over it and wrap it all in a tea towel. He takes it from me with a nod and a broken smile. With that, he pushes past me, grabs his greatcoat and makes for the door.

'Billy,' I shout after him. 'Will you at least tell me where it is you're sleeping rough? In case I ever have the need to come looking for you.'

I can see him deliberating nervously. 'You won't tell anyone. You promise?'

'I promise.'

'Endrick Islands. I'm living out on Endrick Islands.'

# CHAPTER 45

*E*ndrick Islands.
    And with that he's gone. Gone as soon as he said it, giving me no chance to ask anything else. Almost certainly to make *sure* that I couldn't ask anything else.

My head is whirling. There's far too much to process and I'm not sure I understand any of this.

Billy Horsburgh. Jenni Horsburgh's brother. The one that left the village to join the army. Living on Endrick Islands. On the islands of the dead dolls.

The questions I would have asked, *still* want to ask, are lining up in my head, jostling each other to get to the front of the queue.

I don't have many answers, but at least now I have an idea why this man has lived on the edge of the village when he's been here. He's kept himself at a distance from anyone who might recognise him from old. It doesn't answer everything though, far from it.

A more recent memory comes back to me. Of seeing him as I turned onto Craighat Road on my way to look for Jason Doak. Three days ago; a lifetime ago. The sight of Billy emerging from the glow of the streetlamp. Where else could have he been coming from if not from the islands?

Thought tumbles onto thought. Jason's bloodied blazer. Those dolls. Jenni's disappearance. Billy rescuing me from the fire. Hannah Cairney.

I don't want to think he has anything to do with Jason going missing, hate to assume he's hurt the boy. He saved my life, pulled me from the fire. But did he start it too?

I promised him that I wouldn't tell anyone where he's living, and I won't renege on that. My word is important to me and I couldn't live with myself if I broke it. Although living with myself won't be any easier if something else happens because I've kept this information secret.

Another thought. A hidden memory. Of the shadow on the ridge at Finnich Glen when the rock nearly hit me by the Devil's Pulpit. Of the tall, broad, dark man that I thought was Auld Hangie. Of the flash of yellow at his head.

I'm bewildered and scared. This is unbearable. Jenni Horsburgh's brother. But it can't be right. Can't be. Nothing in this village makes sense any more.

I need that anxiety tincture, but it lies splashed across the path where I hurled it this afternoon. I'm tempted to have a glass of the Ardbeg instead, but I know it won't make my thoughts any clearer. It will muddle them further, pile paranoia upon doubt upon confusion. I'm enough of a mess.

I'll make tea. I'll clean the cottage. I'll stop thinking. I'll start making a fresh batch of tincture. I'll go for a walk.

I'll look on Twitter.

I do all of those things.

I potter around aimlessly and hopelessly for hours, my mind somersaulting. The Twitter mob are still in full flow, flinging hate at their screens and mine.

Burn the witch. Do it right this time.

Billy Horsburgh was said to be really close to his wee sister. Looked after her when their father left. I've heard it said he went to London and scoured the streets for her. Looked in hostels and bars, looked under railway arches, everywhere he thought she might be. I heard it drove him crazy.

I'm cradling a cup of tea, my third, and staring into the fire. Watching the flames and wondering if he was the only one who went crazy.

As I think it, my mobile phone signals two incoming texts and my heart nearly stops.

*Hannah.*

I hurry to the worktop and press the phone into life. The display shows 11.05 p.m.

Two new texts. From her. Of course from her.

I couldn't make it today. Sorry. It was too close to the village. Got scared.

I'll meet you at the Devil's Pulpit at 8am. Come alone.

Taking the phone, I fall back into my armchair, rereading the texts as if they might have changed. *Devil's Pulpit at 8am.*

I'm worried that she's scared. And worried about what she's scared of. The choice of the Devil's Pulpit concerns me too. But it makes sense, if my gut feeling is right.

At least she's responded, at least she wants to meet. If her choice of venue turns out to be the cause of a new problem, then so be it. I'll deal with that when it happens.

Morning is a long way off. It leaves hours to be filled, and thoughts and worries to fill them with. A deep pit of uncertainty echoes inside me. *Devil's Pulpit at 8 a.m.*

I remember the raw nervousness that gnawed at me on my return from the islands after finding Jason's blazer. The small, anxious animal turning inside me. It's there again, nibbling, chewing, biting at my guts.

*Devil's Pulpit at 8 a.m.*

# CHAPTER 46

I wake at 6.30 a.m. I might not have slept at all.

It usually takes me thirty-five minutes from my gate to the Finnich Glen, and another half hour through the gorge to the Devil's Pulpit itself. A look at my watch halfway there tells me I'm a few minutes ahead of schedule, despite conditions that should be slowing me down. It rained again overnight and the paths are heavy underfoot, mud clinging to the soles of my boots, and it feels like I'm trudging through regrets.

I know I might be reading too much into her texts. Know I might be getting ahead of myself. But I can't think she's asking me to come all the way out here just to tell me to get lost.

There are things to be told, things she can tell, and although I'm well aware that I'm being utterly selfish, I'm praying to all the gods that this is my chance of redemption. For all of it.

Taking a moment at the top of the glen, I stop and stare at the sight of the water a hundred yards below me, shrouded in a fine mist. Through the smirr, I see that the rains have turned the Carnock Burn the rusty, burgundy red of a bloodstain, and it's rushing through the gorge like there's somewhere it has to be.

I hesitate before starting the descent. The ancient stones that form the Devil's Steps are slippery at the best of times, and these are far from the best of times. I see them slick with mud, lying in wait to break my old bones.

Taking a fierce grip on the rope banister, I edge my way down, one stone at a time, steadying myself before daring to take the next. My heart's pounding and the steps seem steeper than they've ever been before.

When my right heel slides, I'm taken by more surprise than I should be. My leg shoots out across the front of the stone and the rope yanks hard on my arm and my shoulder. Pain races through me even before I hit the step but multiplies once I do.

I manage to keep hold of the banister, despite my weight and the slick mud trying to drag me down the steps. All breath has exploded from me, and I'm left gasping and gulping for air, hurting everywhere.

It takes all my strength and no little faith to pull myself first onto my knees and then back up onto my feet. It takes an age because the fear of slipping again is overwhelming. Finally, anxiously, I'm standing, gripping the rope for dear life. The remainder of the descent is painful, painfully slow, and terrifying. But I make it.

I'm wet and dirty but nothing's broken. I'll hurt like hell tomorrow, but for now I'm okay, more shaken than anything else, I think. I'm going on.

The blood-red water is deeper than usual and therefore fast, making another tumble a real possibility. I promise myself I'll tread carefully, but I've got a deadline to meet. Hannah is waiting.

The low mist lingering in the glen lends another layer of mysticism that this place barely needs, like seeing its strangeness through a fine mesh or a large glass of single malt.

I don't give the wonderous contours of the gorge walls the same consideration I'd normally do. Instead, I keep my eyes on my feet, watching every step and every stone, knowing that around me, the rock formations are winding, bending, shapeshifting as they choose. They'll be changing faster, being more sinister and more beautiful, safe from my prying human eyes.

All around me, rock faces smile and glower; ferns wave and hide; trees bend to look closer; and a breeze whispers through the gorge sounding for all the world like a young woman calling my name. I pick my way across the stones and through the water, and I do all I can to stay on my feet.

I know I've gone past *The Scream* and the giant hog, beyond the woman with the elegant neck and upraised face. I'm passing through the twisting walls in their greens and purples and their

216

feet of clay, wading by the large, flat landing area where people sunbathe in the summer months. I'm striding by the large fallen oak that looks like a calcified dragon, and up ahead is the narrowing gap which signals I'm almost there.

I've been giving plenty of thought to why she's asked to meet here. Speculating why she'd want to meet quite *so* far from the madding crowd. I understand her need not to be seen, but we live in a village surrounded by quiet places and hidden corners. Instead, we're meeting out here, with its mystical rock walls and places of prayer and sacrifice, with its scorched earth and litter of alcohol and drugs. It's no coincidence.

I'm sure the Devil's Pulpit isn't just a place to give me answers, but is part of the answer.

At the spot where the river narrows, I stop and lift my head, secure that I'm not at risk of slipping when my feet are planted. The lichen-green walls are close and magical, the vibrant colours bewitching and surreal.

Looking ahead, I can make out the Pulpit through the mist, appearing more ethereal than ever. There's no sign of Hannah, though, and my heart sinks at the thought she's changed her mind. *Be positive*, I tell myself, the way here is muddy and slow and she's probably just late. *Please just be late.*

The rock seems bigger through the prism of the smirr. The rock walls and the river are in shroud, but the Pulpit looms large as if it has emerged from another time and place, looking majestic in a wispy veil.

Something is wrong, though.

I can't say whether it's something I can see or something I can't, whether it's feeling or instinct or something more, but it bothers me. A coldness pricks my skin and a stranger's voice whispers in my ear, telling me to be ready.

The mossy rock of the druids is ever nearer. The ancient lump of execution stone just thirty or so yards away.

I've become aware of every sound. Every bird call; every ripple; every sigh of wind; every beat of my heart; every stone that moves beneath my feet. And my eyes never leave the rock.

Hannah *is* here.

I'm sure it's her. It must be her.

Someone is lying on top of the rock. I see the soles of her feet and the denim blue of sodden jeans. The voice that's whispering to me is getting louder, more anxious, like it's leading me off a cliff.

I know the truth before I get there. Maybe I knew it from the first moment I saw the rock and the fear rose within me. I hear the world putting its brakes on. It's all about to come to a screeching halt.

I see it all now. The blonde hair. The porcelain skin. The bloody mess on her cheeks and temple.

All those things swamp me. Recognition, realisation and horror drowning me as one.

Hannah Cairney. Splayed across the altar.

Hannah Cairney. Dead.

I scream.

# CHAPTER 47

I get as close as I dare, needing to be sure. Lean in closer than I want, seeing everything.

The side of her skull is a broken, bloody mess. She looks so young. *Is* so young. *Was* so young. The words and the corrections trip over each other as my brain scrambles in fear and confusion.

I turn and vomit. Shock and dread erupt from me in a retch that spills into the blood-red waters and swirls away downstream.

Bent at the waist, still heaving. Shaking. Terrified. I'm dizzy and it's like a thousand people are shouting inside my head.

I stand, catch my balance, and look again. It's horrific. Awful beyond belief.

If she'd been standing on the rock, she could easily have fallen, wet and treacherous as it is. If she'd slipped, if she'd hit her head on landing, that would explain the horror in front of me.

I don't think she fell. I don't think she slipped.

Stifling another scream with a hand over my mouth, I gawk at her and the Pulpit and the blood.

The rock, the old stone of preaching and execution, is stained with her blood. I stare at a large crimson spot of it and wonder how many others have had their blood spilled here in centuries past. And do they matter now? Now that Hannah's dead.

Her blonde hair is matted with blood and brain and pushed deep into her skull.

She didn't fall.

Am I the reason she's lying there with her head bashed in? I'm the one who pressed her to talk. The one who put her in danger. I *knew* she was scared to speak. I knew that, but still pressured her to tell what she knew. I did this.

She didn't slip.

I take the hand from my mouth, tilt my head back, and scream as loud as I can. The noise reverberates from the walls of the glen, rushing back at me like memories, like nightmares, like guilt.

Like a selfish, foolish old woman, I'd thought Hannah might be my chance at redemption, but the fates are laughing at such a notion now. I've made things worse, far worse, not better.

I reach out to touch her, to feel how cold or how warm her skin is, but stop halfway to her. A realisation kicks in. I have to call the police. I mustn't touch her, must not disturb the *scene*, must call the police.

Still standing in the Cannock Burn, blood and blood-red water swirling around me, I take my mobile phone from my pocket.

I call 999 and I find some words. Tell them who I am. Where I am. Who Hannah is.

I tell them they need to get Sergeant Deacon then I walk to the shore, sit down on a rock and wait. And I cry.

# CHAPTER 48

It's taking a while. An age.

I knew it would. They have to contact Deacon. He has to get to a car and find his way here. Then he has to make his way through the glen. He won't be dressed for it. Not prepared.

I could walk back through the burn and meet him, but I'm not prepared to leave the girl.

Instead, I fight the urge to take my coat off and cover her with it. I know I shouldn't, know that I can't, but all my instincts tell me to shield her, keep her warm, hide her. I won't. But it's hard.

It's quieter here now. And noisier too. Silence is loud when the world is a mile away. I can hear the nothingness, and the little bits of sound there are – birds, river, wind – are roaring.

She's just lying on that damn rock. Draped over it like a sacrifice, like a broken doll.

I remember when I bumped into her and her mother in the village. Hannah, aged seven, had lost her two front teeth and was grinning broadly. 'Five pounds each,' she told me excitedly. 'That's *ten* pounds. Ten pounds the tooth fairy will bring.'

Her hair was tied back in a ponytail. She wore a light blue dress and still believed in things she couldn't see.

Alison, her mother, is a lovely person. This will destroy her.

I hear voices. They're in the distance but the sound carries through the glen like gunfire. I stand but can see no one and nothing through the mist. I think about shouting to them, but it seems wrong. Disrespectful somehow. I sit again. Then stand.

When I see figures emerging, I get up, waving both arms, crossing them above my head. There are two constables in uniform, hi-vis flashes shining in the gloom. Behind them are Deacon and Sharma.

The constables reach the Pulpit first. One turns almost immediately to nod his head vigorously towards Deacon. Confirmation.
The old woman isn't completely crazy. Unfortunately.

The first of the constables speaks into a radio device clipped to
his shoulder. Making sure that help is on the way for the helpless.
Deacon and Sharma have reached the rock and are standing with
their backs to me. Deacon's hands rest on his head, his elbows out
wide. I let them look, give them time. They'll come to me.

I sit, physically and emotionally exhausted, and watch and listen. I'm far enough away that I only hear partial sentences.

*… two of her fingernails are chipped … could be the result of a fall …*

*… no obvious sign of skin under her nails … no defence wounds… no
grab marks at the wrists or throat …*

*… she's been dead for hours …*

*… maybe overnight …*

*… she could have fallen … it's credible … landing on the rock like this?
Less credible …*

*… the position of the body … could be the way she's landed … could
be ritualistic …*

I see Deacon's feet before I hear him. Wet shoes. Wet trouser legs.
He's standing over me, waiting for me to realise he's there. When I
look up, his face is grave. The sergeant is seriously troubled.

'Why are you here, Marjorie?'

'I came to talk to Hannah. I've been trying to get her to talk to
me. To tell me what's been going on.'

He closes his eyes and huffs out what feels like the last breath
he has in him. There's a rock a few feet from the one I'm sitting
on, and he perches himself on it.

'She's been missing since last night. Her mother called us at
midnight when she hadn't returned home after going to see a
friend. There have been searches ongoing, but no one would think
to look for her out here. No one except you.'

I say nothing.

'How did this arrangement to meet her come about?'

'I gave Hannah my mobile number and asked her to text me.
She did and said she'd meet me. She said she'd talk to me at

222

Spittal's Clearing but she didn't show up. Then last night, I got a text telling me to meet her here.'

He shakes his head, clearly unhappy.

'Do you have your phone with you?'

'Yes.'

He holds out his hand. 'Can you open it at the texts then give it to me, please?'

I do so and hand it over without argument.

Deacon scrolls through it, pausing twice to look over at me, his face darkening. I somehow hadn't expected him to be affected by her death as much I am. I perhaps thought he'd maintain a professional veneer or something. That seems unfair now. He's angry, and I know some of it, maybe a lot of it, maybe all of it, is directed at me.

'I need to keep this,' he says holding the phone up. 'You'll get a receipt.'

'I don't need one.'

'You'll get one. You'll get one because there's a way of doing things. A procedure. We put procedures in place because we know what we're doing. And one of the things we try to avoid is things like *this*. What the hell were you thinking?'

*I don't know.*

'Marjorie, the girl is *dead*. Charlie McKee is dead. Hannah Cairney is dead. And you were first on the scene at both. Jason Doak is missing and at the very least, he's hurt. You *found* his school blazer. Can you explain all that to me? Did you prophesise this one as well?'

'I didn't …'

I can't finish the sentence. No words, No point.

'Why here? Why would she ask to meet you out here?'

'I don't know for sure.'

'But you have an idea?'

'I think I do. Yes.'

'Then tell me. Please.'

*Deep breath.*

'About twenty years ago, there was talk of satanic parties out here. Alcohol, drugs, sex, rituals. There was a group called

Thelema. No one knew who was in it, but they supposedly met here. Well … I think maybe they've started again.'

This clearly isn't what he was expecting.

'Go on.'

'I came here just two days ago. There's a piece of burned earth over there which was clearly from a campfire. And there were remains of alcohol and drugs. Marijuana. Maybe more.'

He looks at me surprised.

'I wasn't born old, Sergeant. I was a teenager in the seventies. I know a joint when I see one, even if they don't call it that these days.'

'Booze and weed aren't unusual. A party by a river. It's what teenagers do. What makes you think there was more to it?'

I sigh inside. 'Come with me.'

He follows me, Sharma too. I lead them to the site of the fire, nothing more now than scorched earth and damp ashes.

'The fire, as you can see, was here. The bottles and cans and the smoked-down relics of the marijuana too. What I want to show you is just over here.'

Skirting the burnt patch of ground, I take another two steps and point at the earth. The rain has damaged it, but most of the shape of a circle scratched into the soil is still visible.

'You see the circle? Now, can you see the what's left of the five points drawn within it?'

He squints. 'A pentagram?'

'An inverted pentagram, yes. And you can probably make out the face drawn in the middle. Some of it has gone but the eyes are still there.'

'Yes. I think so.'

'That's supposed to be a goat's head. The whole symbol is known as the Sigil of Baphomet. It's the official insignia of the Church of Satan.'

'Oh for fu—'

'They're just children, Sergeant. Playing games that they don't understand. The same symbol was drawn outside my cottage when they hanged the voodoo doll there. I took it as a sign of ignorance, thinking someone thought witchcraft and satanism to be the same thing. Now I know different. They were sending me a message.'

He's staring at the remains of the symbol, his mouth tight and a quiet fury burning him.

'You think Hannah was part of this?'

'I've no real way of knowing. But I *do* know that there was a reason Hannah asked me out here. And I know the words she and her friends used on Twitter.'

'*Hellfire. Blood brothers. Darklord.*'

'Yes.'

'Oh for Christ's sake.'

'No, Sergeant. Not for his sake. Far from it.'

'Hang on a second,' Sharma interrupts. 'Can we back up a bit? Marjorie, you say this first happened about twenty years ago? Can you be more specific?'

*I can because I've been thinking it through.*

'1999.'

I can see by Deacon's face that he's caught up with Sharma's thinking.

'So around the time Jenni Horsburgh ran away?' she asks.

'Yes. Very much that time. The story was that it came to a stop soon after she disappeared.'

Deacon blows a stream of air from pursed lips. 'And no one connected the two things?'

I can only shrug. 'I've no idea what the police thought. It was accepted that Jenni had run away. There was a postcard from her sent from London. The stories of the cult were just that, stories. Only the people involved knew for sure.'

'And who were the people involved?'

'I don't know. I hadn't lived here that long and wasn't privy to the heart of the gossip. Anyway, by the nature of what they were doing, they'd have been doing their best not to be known.'

Deacon looks around, taking it all in. The Devil's Pulpit, the body and the remnants of the fire.

'Marjorie, you're *sure* that what you saw at the fire were marijuana smokes?'

'Yes, I'm sure. I …'

I stop and he looks at me quizzically.

'I have them.' The words come out of me louder than I intend because the realisation takes me by surprise. 'I picked up the rubbish and took it home in a bag. It's outside my cottage.'

Deacon and Sharma look at each other and there's a lot going on unspoken.

'You can use them, Sergeant, can't you? Test them for DNA or something?'

Deacon puffs out his cheeks. 'Maybe. It depends on the condition of them. But it won't be us, Marjorie.'

I'm confused. 'Why not?

'It will be out of our hands from here on in. We were called in to deal with a likely suicide. But this? I have to pass it higher up. The Major Investigation Team will take over. There will be a team sent in, probably from Edinburgh. And they'll want to talk to you at length. This is a murder investigation now.'

I don't know why the word shocks me, but it does. All the evidence I need is lying on the Devil's Pulpit.

Hannah Cairney. *Murdered.*

'Sergeant?' One of the uniformed constables is shouting to Deacon from where he's crouched by the bank about twenty feet away. 'You should see this.'

Deacon walks over to him and I follow uninvited, watching him crouch beside the constable and blocking my view.

'Misha,' he shouts. 'Get your phone. I need you to photograph this.'

My skin is tingling. There's a sense of foreboding growing quickly inside me, and I feel nauseous again.

I move to the side so that I can see past Deacon. As I do so, my mouth drops open and everything stops.

At the constable's feet is a dirty yellow beanie hat, streaked with blood.

I made him a promise not to say where he was living, and I'll keep that. But not this. I take a deep breath.

'Sergeant Deacon, I know whose hat that is.'

# CHAPTER 49

A mirror can be a curse.

An object of usefulness to most, a godsend to the vain, but a torment to the guilty.

I'm brushing my hair above the bathroom sink and in the reflection of the cabinet mirror I see myself in the harsh light of awakening. I see every blemish, every pore, every line and liver spot. I see an old woman. I see the bags under my eyes and the creases that will never unfold. The rough, thin skin you could poke a finger through, its flesh dull and tone uneven.

Worse than all that outer decay, I see inside myself.

I see an arrogant fool. Someone so wrapped up in her own hopes for redemption she couldn't see the perils on the path she lured a young woman down. At the fag end of her life, seeking forgiveness at the expense of one whose life had barely begun.

Hannah was seventeen.

A baby.

I persuaded her to take risks. She's dead because of that.

As I open the mirrored door to put the brush back on its shelf, I catch myself with half a face and pause to study it that way.

Half witch, half mother. Half right, half wrong. Insider and outsider.

It's Hannah's tragedy, not mine. Her death, her *murder*, and that trumps my guilt.

I place a finger on the sagging bag below the one eye I can see and pull down on the discoloured skin, stretching it until it's briefly smooth and vaguely youthful. When I release it, it puckers and snakes back into its place of custom.

As the door closes, just for a second, I think I see Hannah in the reflection of my eye. Then I blink, and she's gone.

# CHAPTER 50

*1591*

Agnes Sampsoune from Dalkeith was said to be a 'grace ma-tron-like woman of a rank and comprehension above the vulgar, a woman not of the base and ignorant sort of witches, but grave and settled in her answers.'

She was charged with trying to heal Partik Hepburn by prayer, for the charming to death of George Dikson's horse and cattle, and giving some cheese and butter to George's wife who died after consuming the food. Among the other charges against Agnes was that she quarrelled with a man named Straton, that she eased the pain of childbirth, and that she predicted a man's death.

Among her interrogators at trial was King James VI himself, who sought to blame Agnes and others for sending a great storm with the intention of sinking the King's ship with him on board. Her complex trial began on 22 October 1590, and ended on 21 January 1591. She was found guilty and sentenced to be strangled then burned at the stake. Her execution took place at Castlehill, Edinburgh on 28 January 1591.

She was *wirriet* and *burnt*.

*2024*

Twitter

Have you heard? Hannah Cairney? Omg

Hannah Cairney is dead! Murdered by Marjorie Crowe

The old Crowe found Hannah at the Devil's Pulpit. No way she just FOUND her

Why is that old bitch still allowed to walk around free???

Burn her!!

# CHAPTER 51

Kilgoyne has gone dark.

The village is in shock at the news of Hannah Cairney's murder, and I hear that neighbours can't look neighbours in the face.

A suicide is one thing, an obvious tragedy, but it could happen anywhere, particularly with the pressure young people are under today. A missing boy is a terrible worry, but missing boys can turn up. If you had a mind to, you could probably still convince yourself that the village was the place it has always been.

But now? This? This is a thing of nightmares.

This makes it all too easy to think that the place it has always been is not the place you want it to be. Darkness runs through Kilgoyne and is harboured in secrets. Now that it has revealed itself, nothing can be the same again.

I'm at a loss what to think or how to think. I've paced the room, going over it again and again in my head. Debating what I should have done differently. Blaming myself. Cursing my own damned selfishness. I was so consumed with trying to make amends that I didn't see the danger I was putting the girl in. I should have left it alone. I should have left *her* alone.

My head is a mess. A mess of my own making.

Twitter has exploded with the news about Hannah. I've tried to avoid the worst of it, but even in the small glimpse that I dared take, I could see outlandish theories beginning to take hold. Amateur sleuths are on the case, piecing together a jigsaw that has no picture on the box and several pieces missing. They don't seem to care that these are real people they're talking about, that a real person has died. It's all some sort of twisted game to them.

Their chief suspect is, of course, me. I'm the witch, the easy, obvious target. My trial had already begun, now the verdict is in. Guilty as charged. Sentenced to death. To be *wirriet* and *burnt*.

I want to reply. Tell them that I'm guilty, just not of the crime they think. I'm guilty of meddling. Of putting Hannah at risk. Blame me for that. Sentence me for that. I don't do it because I'm a coward, and because I know it will just make things worse. So I read as much as I can stomach as punishment. Twitter abuse as self-flagellation.

There's no mention on there of either Soapy Moary or Billy Horsburgh. I've searched for both names and there's nothing. Whether that's a good thing or not, I have no idea.

There are quotes from Hannah's mother on the news sites and I force myself to read them till I can't take it any more. The poor woman is devastated and my heart breaks for her.

Sergeant Deacon has arranged for a constable to stand guard round the clock at my garden gate. There are four of them on rotating sentry duty, although no one has been clear as to whether they're there to keep others out or me in. It seems I'm both victim and suspect.

I'm staring aimlessly out of the window, watching the tall policeman standing with his back to me, when I see DC Sharma approaching the gate. She's on her own, walking purposefully, face grim. I greet her at the door, and we go inside without a word.

'No Sergeant Deacon?' I ask as we settle into chairs near the fireplace.

She shakes her head. 'No, it's as we said yesterday. It's a murder investigation now, and a team under a DCI Maitland have taken over. Deacon has been reassigned.'

'Yet you're still here?'

'Sorry if that's a disappointment.' She smiles.

'No. I'm glad you are. Really. I'm just surprised.'

'Me too, a bit. Deacon managed to persuade them that the arson attack on your cottage is a separate investigation, so I've got that,

231

for now at least. Albeit with a heavy warning about not getting in their way.'

'How is he? Sergeant Deacon, I mean.'

Sharma pushes out her bottom lip and blows out air. 'He's taken it badly. Personally. He's blaming himself for Hannah's death.'

He can get in the queue. My own guilt will take some shifting.

'I'm glad you're still here,' I tell her. 'I've heard there's a lot more police in the village.'

'Yes. They've come mob-handed. DCI Maitland is the Senior Investigating Officer. His deputy is a DI Zebrauskas, who'll be running things on the ground. You'll meet him, unfortunately. There's a Detective Sergeant as Crime Scene Manager, crime scene and forensic staff, an attending forensic psychologist, and a squadron of detective constables as foot soldiers.'

'That sounds like a lot of people.'

'The murder of a pretty blonde girl always gets more space on the front pages, always gets more television time,' she explains. 'So, in turn, it gets more resources. Which is ridiculous, obviously, but it's the way it is. It's all about optics. Which is a fancy way of saying that the top brass are scared of looking bad. So, they've moved into the village like a conquering army. The Major Incident Team is a different animal.'

'Surely they're just police like you and Sergeant Deacon?'

She smiles. 'These are the elite. They have polished shoes, haircuts that cost more than my car, and more degrees than a compass. They've all been on courses and completed modules. They're like ninjas.'

'You're not a fan, then?'

'Ah, I'm just jealous. Listen, Marjorie, things have changed, it's not just MIT. There's been a couple of reporters nosing around the past few days, but now they've descended en masse. There are TV and radio people here too. BBC, ITV, Sky, all the big boys. So it might be better for you to stay at home, definitely avoid the centre of the village. And don't talk to any reporters.'

'I've no intention of doing so.'

The look on her face says she doesn't consider my lack of intention enough.

'Marjorie, people will want to know what you know. And why you were at the Devil's Pulpit. Say nothing, please. The timing of the text you received and the timing of Hannah's death is crucial. That information shouldn't be shared with anyone.'

'I wouldn't ...'

I stop mid-sentence. The truth of what she hasn't said is now obvious and should always have been. *Timing*.

'Hannah was already dead when that text was sent to me, wasn't she?'

Sharma doesn't flinch. 'I can't confirm anything, Marjorie.'

She just has.

'You've told these new officers about the satanic rituals and how they're being played out again twenty-odd years later?

Sharma looks troubled. I've likely asked about something else she shouldn't be telling me.

'Yes, and they're looking into that. If this group exists then they'll find out who is or was in it, whether it involved Hannah or any of her friends, and they'll investigate. It's not going to be ignored. But obviously finding the hat has changed things. They're very keen to find Soapy Moary but there's no sign of him. Adam Cummings says he hasn't been at the pub for a couple of days. If he's still in or around the village then they'll find him soon enough.'

I say nothing. A foolish promise binds my lips.

'Tell me what you know about Billy,' she says.

'That he saved my life.'

'Uh huh. Anything else?'

'Is this as part of your investigation of the fire, DC Sharma?'

She smiles again. 'Of course. And Billy Horsburgh pulled you from that fire. I think that makes him entirely relevant, don't you?'

I do. I'll tell her what I know. *Most* of what I know.

'Billy and Jenni were very close. Billy was four years older. Their dad had died when Billy was fourteen and he was determined to look after his mum and his little sister. Then his mother met Stevie Wright and remarried. They say Billy argued endlessly with his new stepdad, fight after fight, until Billy gave Wright what he wanted and left home. It was 1995, and Billy joined the army. He was just seventeen. Jenni had begged him not to go but he did it anyway.

'He promised Jenni that he'd come back and get her, take her out of the village once he could afford a place in Glasgow for them. When Billy heard Jenni had disappeared, he went AWOL and ran to London to look for her. The army found him before he could find Jenni. It's said he looked everywhere, asked in all the hostels, Salvation Army shelters, under bridges, asked anyone he could find. But nothing.

'People say he was never quite the same after that month. His mother, Alexis, said he went back to London the first official leave he got and began looking again. He spent the nights where the homeless slept so that he could speak to them without them getting too suspicious. No one had seen Jenni or heard of her. He walked miles every day, covered the whole city and never got close. I think the truth is he'd never be able to find her.

'Within a year, he was discharged from the army. He had PTSD but they say he was also a drunk, and he left without a penny. That was the last his mother heard of him, that was the last Kilgoyne heard of him. Or so we thought.'

'And no one knew that Soapy Moary was Billy?'

'I don't know if *no one* knew. I didn't know. His mother let out her cottage years ago and moved to Stirling to live with her sister, or she'd surely have recognised him. He mostly kept his distance from people and his appearance has changed a lot. And he would be away from here for months on end, in London probably. I'd seen him around but never made the connection.'

She swears under her breath, but I hear it.

'They'll find him. If he stays they'll find him soon enough, if he runs they'll catch him. Marjorie, I'm going to call back to speak to you from time to time. Is that okay?'

'As part of the fire investigation?'

She smiles with her eyes. 'Of course.'

234

'If I can help, in any way, I will,' I tell her. 'I feel I've got a lot of making up to do. I don't know if I can, but I'll try.'

'Oh, you can,' she says. 'You've been at the heart of this, Marjorie, and I know you have the answer to it. I'm not going to pretend I know how or you know how, and I'm not dwelling on what you know or what you feel or what your other sense tells you, but you have the answer to what's going on here.'

I'm stuck for words. And thoughts. But I know, somehow, that she's right.

Instead of something rational, which is beyond me, I blurt out something obvious.

'You're staying, aren't you? Whatever the other police unit do or say?'

'Oh yes. I'm going nowhere.'

Sharma makes for the front door and opens it. Just as she's about to leave, she turns and looks at me.

'Marjorie, why are you so sure Billy Horsburgh wouldn't have found his sister in London? You said he'd never be able to find her.'

The answer comes from deep inside me.

'Because I don't think she ever left the village.'

Sharma draws in the deepest of breaths, her eyes holding mine, her lip pursed tight. She nods and leaves.

# CHAPTER 52

I'm on my way to Drymen, and to 1999, in search of Jenni Horsburgh.

I know I'm a meddling old woman who can't leave well alone. The proof of that lay cold on the Devil's Pulpit. But I also know in my bones that Jenni Horsburgh's disappearance is connected to everything that's happened here this past week. To all of it.

My last words to DC Sharma were that I believed Jenni never left the village. She left without us discussing the implications of that statement, but we both knew what I meant. She'd nodded. She'd agreed.

What I'm unwilling to trust, twenty-five years on, is my memory of how things unfolded. I want contemporary proof, and I want it from a primary source.

The *Endrick Examiner* covered life in the villages of Drymen, Kilgoyne, Killearn and Balfron – as well as going as far west as Gartocharn and as far east as Fintry – since 1884. Its staples were births, deaths and marriages, court reports, council matters, farming and gossip, along with as much advertising as it could muster.

It has since gone the way of so many local papers, and the final edition rolled off the presses in 2004. Its footprints still exist, though, in the form of its back issues, all held on microfiche in Drymen Library.

I'm a familiar sight in the library, one of the few places I've never been judged, and a helpful member of staff soon directs me to the microfiche reader and talks me through how to use it. The machine is old but still perfectly functional, much like me.

I go straight to the edition from 12 May 1999, the first Wednesday after Jenni was last seen. The girl has the front page to herself.

## Concern For Missing Kilgoyne Teen
### Jenni (17) not seen for three days

Jenni's school photograph sits large at the right of the page; she is smiling bright-eyed at the camera but with an unmissable, rebellious glint in her eye. A glint I remember well.

I stare at the photo for a while. It's the first time I've seen Jenni's face in over a decade, probably since the tenth anniversary of her disappearing. Smart. Cheeky. Pretty. Confident.

Vulnerable too? I'm not sure if I'm seeing that, or assigning it with hindsight.

The story is peppered with phrases of shock from family and neighbours. *Out of character. Much-loved. Never done anything like this before. We're all worried sick.*

I read the continuing story inside, and scan through the remainder of that week's edition. In the following week's paper, 19 May, Jenni's disappearance has been demoted.

The front-page story is about planning permission being sought for a proposed housing development to the east of Killearn. Locals up in arms about disruption and loss of green belt, developers promised jobs and growth. In a single column down the right-hand side, runs the latest on Jenni.

By then, it had emerged that the rucksack was missing from her room, clothes and toiletries too. The narrative had changed. Anonymous locals were quoted, saying how Jenni had spoken about running away. How she'd tired of the village and dreamt of London.

It's all as I remember it. Fear and worry giving way to judgement and disdain. I felt it reflected badly on the village then, and it looks no better a quarter of a century on.

But there's more. As I read through the copies of the *Examiner* before and after Jenni's disappearance, I find something that, to the

237

best of my memory, I'd been unaware of at the time. Something or nothing, it could be either, but I'm keen to find out which.

And I know just where to go to do that.

I talk out loud to myself as I walk back to Kilgoyne. It's more an argument than a conversation, and inevitably I both win and lose the debate. By the time I get to the outskirts of the village, the decision has been made, and although I don't know what I'm going to say or what I hope to achieve by it, I'm going to speak to Reverend Jarvie. For better or for worse.

The road that leads to Kilgoyne kirk was built at the same time as the church, so is barely wide enough for today's traffic. After the turn off, the pavement disappears and pedestrians are left to fend for themselves.

I can see the church in the distance now, its whitewashed walls in stark contrast to the greenery behind, and I mentally prepare to question its caretaker.

There's a car coming from that direction, a large black one, and I move as close to one side of the road as I can. It's taking the bends quickly, and I'm hoping the driver is remembering how narrow this road is.

Thankfully I'm on a straight stretch now with a few hundred yards of tarmac ahead of me, and unmissable. The car hasn't slowed or shifted position, though. It's still barrelling straight down the road towards me.

It's a Land Rover or Range Rover, one of those. It's less than a hundred yards away. Surely the driver has seen me.

I move further to my left, almost on the narrow strip of grass verge. The car swerves so it's further over too, on the same side. I take another step left till I'm squashed hard against the farm fence.

The car is close enough that I can see the driver and his passenger. It's heading straight at me. Just a few feet away. I turn my head to the side, close my eyes and hope.

I feel it breeze past, almost touching me. I feel the heat of it and hear the roar of the engine. And I'm still standing. It missed me by inches.

I spin and see the car heading into the distance, rounding the next bend. On the correct side of the road again.

My breath is convulsive, fast and draining. I grab onto a fence post to steady myself and take a minute to recover. Did that really just happen?

It did. I turned my head away, but not before I saw who was in the car.

Councillor Lewis Dryden was driving. Adam Cummings in the passenger seat, laughing his head off.

Still shaken, still shaking, I pass between the black gates which split the low, two-hundred-year-old walls surrounding the church, I take in the weathered grey headstones on either side of the asphalt path. They stand proud on lush green lawns, age rendering the names and dates almost illegible.

Inside, the rows of white wooden pews lead to the dark oak altar and pulpit in front of ornate stained-glass windows. I might not be a believer, but there's a lingering sense of history and solemnity, one which is being rudely disturbed by a loud banging from the right-hand wall.

The Reverend Graeme Jarvie is perched on a stepladder, a hammer in hand, a screwdriver in his back pocket, doing a repair on an oak panel. He hasn't heard me come in.

'I'm no expert,' I call out, sounding braver than I feel. 'But I believe there were some notable carpenters in the Bible.'

Jarvie turns to put a face to the voice and there's no mistaking his surprise at seeing me standing here. He regains his composure quickly.

'Quite a few, yes. Noah was chief carpenter on the building of the ark, Bezalel made the ark of the covenant from acacia wood. There were those who built King David's palace and Solomon's temple. And Jesus, of course, was a carpenter like Joseph before him. But I wouldn't dare compare my skills with theirs. I'm just saving the church some cash with my basic handyman efforts. How can I help you, Ms Crowe?'

'I was hoping for a few moments of your time, Mr Jarvie.'

He doesn't look pleased at that prospect, but he climbs down from the ladder, places the hammer into an open toolbox, and approaches me.

'Take a seat, Ms Crowe, please. But I'm afraid I can't give you long. I have a funeral to prepare for.'

I realise with a jump that I can't be sure whose funeral it might be. Charlie McKee's. Hannah Cairney's. Someone else's entirely.

'It's a terrible time for the village, Mr Jarvie. I've lived here for twenty-five years and never known a time like it.'

The man looks like he hasn't slept for a week. His eyes are red and lined, and there's a weariness to his voice. I'm guessing his exhaustion is as much emotional as physical.

'I pray there's an end to it, Ms Crowe. I don't think the village can take much more of this. Every person here is feeling it. What do you want to speak to me about?'

I steady myself. I decide to be direct. I want to see his reaction. 'Jenni Horsburgh.'

He doesn't give much away. The corners of his mouth tighten ever so slightly. I think the pupils of his eyes dilate.

'Why? I mean, why do you want to talk about Jenni *now*?'

'Do you remember when she went missing? How things were here?'

He's exasperated at me not answering his question. I know the man's got a temper and I can see it beginning to emerge.

'Of course I do,' he snaps at me. 'It's not the kind of thing anyone would forget easily. People in the village were devastated.'

'Were they? I think most people seemed to get over it quick enough if the newspaper was anything to go by.'

'I think that's harsh. There's many people in Kilgoyne who knew Jenni well, who grew up with her, and were really upset at her running away. They haven't forgotten her. Again, why are you asking about her now? Isn't there enough heartache in the village?'

'More than enough, I'd say. Two young people dead. And I saw both of them.'

That stops him in his tracks, eats into his anger a little.

'Why are you here, Ms Crowe?'

240

'I told you. I want to talk to you about Jenni Horsburgh.' He is about to interrupt, but I press on before he can. 'And your part of the youth group. The Inner Circle.'

This time he reacts, eyes widening, jaw wobbling, but he says nothing. I've no doubt his mind is working overtime.

'I read the newspapers from 1999. At Drymen Library. That's how I can be so sure that the village forgot Jenni so quickly. She went from front page to page five within two weeks. Then to a smaller story further back. It read like people blamed her for running away. And that's how I remember it. If she ran away at all.'

'What?'

I ignore his question again.

'I found something else interesting in the editions of the newspaper around that time. In the same week that Jenni was reported missing, there was a photograph of the Inner Circle. Four young men holding a giant cheque for money they'd raised for CHAS, the Children's Hospice Association in Scotland. It was Adam Cummings, Rowan Haldane, Lewis Dryden and you.'

He laughs incredulously. 'Well, that's hardly a revelation. It wasn't a secret, Ms Crowe. We posed for photographs for the newspaper. That was the whole point of it. Publicity.'

'That wasn't the interesting part.'

His forced smile disappears.

'I kept looking through other issues of the *Examiner*. There were other photographs of charity fundraisers by the Inner Circle after that date. And you weren't in any of them.'

'*And?*'

'And you were in all the Inner Circle photographs until the week Jenni Horsburgh disappeared. I checked. You were in every one. But from that week, that moment, you were out. Why?'

He can't hide his shock now. He's angry.

'I'm not sure that's any business of yours.'

I'm not backing down. I've had my fill of lies and secrets from this village.

'It might not be my business, Mr Jarvie, but I think I have a right to know. I've been verbally abused, I've been attacked, my cottage was set on fire, and I barely escaped with my life. People are trying to drive me out of Kilgoyne, but I'm not going to be a victim any longer. So I want you to tell me why you quit the Inner Circle at the same time as Jenni went missing?'

'It …' He's flustered. 'Ms Crowe, I really don't have time for—'

'For the truth? I think the village needs the truth, Mr Jarvie. Don't you? I'd like to know why you left the Inner Circle at the time you did.'

He wants to tell me to get out. He wants to throw me out. But something is stopping him. Maybe he *does* want to tell the truth.

'I had a … falling out with the other members of the Inner Circle. It was time for me to move on.'

I hear the truth but not the whole truth. I wish I had a sprig of eyebright to push into his hand.

He opens his mouth to speak and closes it again. He looks as if he's ready to burst.

'Jenni running away was a very stressful time for the whole village, as I'm sure you remember. It gave me cause to re-evaluate my life and I decided to leave and study for the ministry.'

'That's why you left?'

'Yes. Now I really have to get on.'

'Or because you had a falling out with the other members of the Inner Circle?'

'I … It was a long time ago. A lifetime ago. Now, I devote my life to the church, to God and to this village. I prefer to look forward than back. I'm going to have to ask you to leave, Ms Crowe.'

He's on his feet. He's making me leave. One final question.

'What happened to Jenni Horsburgh, Mr Jarvie?'

'I don't know. You need to go, Ms Crowe. Now. I don't know why you came here today, or what you think you know. But I can assure you that I don't know what happened to Jenni.'

I hear the truth, but not the whole truth.

# CHAPTER 53

*1645*

Agnes Finnie was a shopkeeper in Potter Row in Edinburgh who was known to have had many disputes with customers and neighbours. She argued with Janet Grinton over two rotten herrings; threatened Beatrix Nisbet for refusing to pay her rent; was threatened by John Buchanan, whose wife had many fights with Agnes; and blasphemed regularly. When she was called a witch by Euphan Kincaid, she answered, 'If I be a witch you or yours shall have better cause to call me so'.

Her trial began on 8 July 1644, without the defence having even spoken with the accused, and ended on 6 March 1645. Agnes was charged with being in company with the Devil, and of consulting with him. She was also accused of taunting. The witnesses against her included two demonologists. She was found guilty and sentenced to be executed.

She was *wirriet* and *burnt*.

*2024*

Twitter

The Crowe. The Crowe did all of this. Charlie. Jason. Hannah. Arrest her!

Arrest her? Burn her!

I heard old Marjorie put a spell on Hannah

I heard Hannah knew what happened to Charlie and was going to the police

Burn her!

Burn her!

# CHAPTER 54

I'm picking lavender in my garden, a rushed anxiety tincture being better than none at all, when I hear a vehicle pull up beyond the gate. I look up to see two men emerging from a sleek and expensive-looking black car. They walk briskly towards the cottage, offering just the briefest of nods to the policeman on the gate.

By the time I collect myself and stand up, they're standing on my doorstep as if they own the place. The one nearest to me is a tall, slim man with fair hair swept back from his angular face. A half step behind, a squat, red-haired man glowers.

'Ms Crowe? I'm Detective Inspector Tom Zebrauskas of Police Scotland, from the Major Incident Team. This is Detective Sergeant Brodie. We'd like to ask you a few questions.'

The policeman's demeanour bothers me, and I take an instant dislike to him.

'May we come in, Ms Crowe?'

'If you must. I hope it won't take long.'

'It won't.'

His tone is curt, business-like and verging on rude. I wonder if I'm supposed to feel grateful that he's gifting some of his valuable time to speak to me. I instinctively resent his presence in my home, but I told Sharma that I'd help in any way I can.

Zebrauskas and Brodie look around my living room as if they've landed in another time dimension. There's a fine line between curiosity and disdain, and they've crossed it.

The inspector indulges in the bare minimum of introductory questions before getting to the point.

'Ms Crowe, you were the person who found the body of Hannah Cairney at the Devil's Pulpit. Is that correct?'

'Yes.'

'And you say you went to that spot because you received a text supposedly from Hannah asking you to meet her there?'

Why is he asking me questions that he clearly knows the answer to?

'Yes.'

He makes a noise that I think is designed to make me think I've just admitted to a crime.

'When the constable pointed out the yellow hat on the river-bank, you identified it immediately. Is that right?'

'Yes.'

'How did you know who it belonged to?'

'I've already told all of this to Sergeant Deacon and DC Sharma.'

He sniffs. 'I'm sure you have, but I'd rather hear it for myself. Sergeant Deacon isn't involved in the investigation any longer. It requires fresh eyes and fresh minds.'

The man's condescension is nauseating.

I explain. Again.

The interview continues in the same vein. A rapid recount of the events of the past week. A revisiting and retelling of the stuff of nightmares. Zebrauskas asks little that strikes me as being insightful or new. He makes clear his deep disapproval of my attempts to communicate with Hannah Cairney. The shorter man says nothing but takes copious notes.

Most of all he wants to know about my interactions with Soapy Moary. I tell him about my infrequent sightings of him around the village, and about me treating his injuries two days earlier.

'Did he tell you know his real name?'

Ah there it is. All the obvious questions leading to the one after this.

'Yes. And I've already told Sergeant Deacon and DC Sharma. It's Billy Horsburgh.'

'And yet he won't tell us. Why not?'

'You'll have to ask him that. There doesn't seem much point in me guessing.'

He doesn't like that much. 'What else do you know about him?'

246

'Nothing.'

Of course, I know one more thing. But I'm not keen to tell. The small inclination I have to do so is being wiped away by the man's manner.

Just when I think there's no more to be said, Zebrauskas finds something.

'Ms Crowe, I'd like to check one thing with you. You told DS Deacon that you saw Charles McKee hanging at Spittal's Clearing. Is that correct?'

My stomach lurches.

'It is, yes.'

'And you told Deacon that you saw this at ...' he pauses, as if making a show of recalling the time, '... 11.58 on the day of his death. Do you stand by that?'

'I do.'

'And yet that wasn't the time of Charles McKee's death, was it? A witness proved he was alive at least an hour later. CCTV proved it too. Is that correct?'

'You know it is.'

'How do you explain that?'

Any answer I may have isn't one I wish to share with this man.

'I don't explain it. I've only said what I saw. I do not dispute other versions of events. I do not dispute what they saw or when.'

Zebrauskas and Brodie share a look that is entirely readable. *She's crazy. We're wasting our time here.*

He smiles coldly at me. 'I see. Thanks for your time, Ms Crowe. We'll be in touch if we need to.'

They're leaving and he's dismissing me. Both in this instance and from his case.

I have the information he's looking for and he's not making it any easier for me to give it to him, even though my conscience is calling on me to do so. I'll give him one last chance.

'Inspector Zebrauskas,' I call after him. 'Mr Horsburgh. Do you know where he is?'

The man is already halfway to the gate. Beyond him, I see a young woman climbing out of a blue Mini.

'I'm afraid I can't discuss that with you,' he shouts without looking back. 'But I think you're about to find out.'

He and my latest visitor pass each other with polite nods as if they might know each other. I watch as she talks to the duty officer on the gate and introduces herself. He waves her on and she arrives on my doorstep, neatly dressed in a black skirt and white blouse, and a long, light grey raincoat belted at the waist, smiling professionally.

'Ms Crowe, I'm Angela Kerr. I'm the duty solicitor acting for the man calling himself Soapy Moary.'

'He's been arrested?'

'I'm afraid so. Last night. He's been arrested in connection with the disappearance of Jason Doak. He is also being held on suspicion of the murder of Hannah Cairney.'

I take an involuntary step back, my feet suddenly unsteady.

'Are you okay, Ms Crowe. Can I get you something? Water perhaps?'

'No, I … yes. I have tea in the pot. Come in. Please.'

The solicitor sits at my table while I pour two cups of tea, the noise of cup on saucer betraying my nerves. I place them, shakily, onto the table and slide into a chair.

'My client, who we're still officially referring to as Soapy Moary, has been taken into custody in Stirling, but hasn't been charged. I understand that you've met with him, Ms Crowe.'

'Two days ago. He sat on the very seat where you're sitting now.'

'And how did he seem to you?'

I want to tell her that my mind is trying to untangle the knots between how he seemed then and how he seems to me given what I know now. I give her the most honest answer I can.

'He seemed … nervous. He'd been beaten up by two local youths so was shaken up. But he was wary of taking any help. I think he's just wary of people in general.'

The solicitor smiles. 'That's certainly my experience of him. Please, go on.'

'There's not much more to say. I patched him up, made him some dinner. He took some with him. He was grateful.'

She takes some notes, glancing up at me a couple of times as she does so.

'Did he say much about the kids that attacked him?'

I shake my head. 'I asked if he knew them. He said he did by sight. That he usually kept out of their way, but this time he wasn't so lucky. The same boys, Kai McHarg and Derek Cummings, had been banging on my windows and he'd told them off for it.'

She scribbles again.

'He's being uncooperative,' she continues. 'Hasn't said a word to the police. About either Hannah Cairney or Jason Doak. He hasn't even told them his real name. Which isn't doing him any favours. It's just slowing them down and annoying them.'

'He's told you who he is though?'

The solicitor sighs heavily. 'No. He refuses to say.'

'How ... how did they get him? I mean, how did they know where he was?'

Ms Kerr looks me in the eye as she sets down her pen and I get the distinct feeling that I'm being tested.

'My client says he was on Endrick Islands last night when noises alerted him that there were other people there. This was about nine o'clock. He knew they were looking for him and he ran. He says he knows the islands like the back of his hand and led them a merry dance for a while.

'He was heavily outnumbered, though, and they had him surrounded. They caught him in a clearing with a fire, sur-rounded by dolls. He put up a fight but was ... subdued. At least that's how the police are describing it. He says they gave him a kicking.'

'He was already hurt.'

I'm not sure why I said that. She looks at me curiously.

'When he was caught, my client was wearing a yellow water-proof jacket that belonged to ...'

I know. I interrupt.

'... to Jason Doak.'

'Yes. And it had blood on it. As did Jason's school blazer when you found it. Was the yellow waterproof there when you discovered the blazer?'

'No.'

'Are you sure?'

'As sure as I can be. How did they know he was there? On the islands, I mean.'

She studies me closely and addresses the question this time. 'I have contacts within the police, and I'm led to believe that someone phoned them and told them my client could be found on Endrick Islands.'

*It wasn't me. He'll think it was me.*

'You're aware of the dolls on the islands, I believe, Ms Crowe?'

I nod and she shakes her shoulders theatrically. 'Very creepy. Do you know who put them there?'

'I think you should ask your client that.'

'Hm. Perhaps. Is there anything you can tell me that will help my client?'

'I'm not sure I can.'

'Are you sure? He seems to believe that you can. It's why he sent me here.'

I don't know how to react to that. I can only shrug, and I see it annoys her. She tries again.

'Why do you think he's being so uncooperative? It's my job to help him even if he won't help himself.'

I place my cup on the saucer with more force than I'd intended. The china's complaint rings round the room.

'I don't know. I really don't. I'd be guessing and I refuse to do that. All I know is that your client has made promises of silence. And that's he's trying to keep his word.'

Kerr leans forward intently. 'Keep his word to whom?'

'I don't know.'

She sits back in her chair again, obviously frustrated. She studies me for a few moments before reaching into her black leather handbag and handing me a sealed envelope.

'Ms Crowe, my client asked me to give you this.'

I take it warily.

'I know there's a note inside but I've no idea what it says. He asked me for a piece of paper and an envelope, and that I give it to you. Which I now have. If it's something that can help him, then I ask you to let me know. But it's up to you.'

I don't like this. At all. But I take the envelope from her.

I run a finger through the seal, tear the envelope open, and read. I look back into the expectant gaze of the solicitor as I slip the note deep into the pocket of my cardigan.

'I'm sorry. It's nothing that can help you. Or him. It just says he knows it won't have been me that told the police where he was. And that he thanks me for not doing so.'

I'm not sure if the look on Angela Kerr's face is doubt or disappointment but either way, after a few seconds, it merges into reluctant acceptance.

'Okay. Well, that's unfortunate. But if you learn of anything, or remember anything, that might help him, then please get in touch. Here's my card.'

I take the proffered business card, say goodbye and close the cottage door after watching the solicitor get into her blue Mini. Back inside, I sink into my armchair and rescue the note from my pocket.

*If you told the police where I was, I don't blame you. But I can prove to you that I didn't hurt the girl or the boy.*

*I trust you. Go to the Drover's Linn. Go behind it. Go in from the right. Take food. TELL NO ONE*

*Billy H*

# CHAPTER 55

There are a few stunning waterfalls along Endrick Water. The Pots of Gartness are a series of rocky pools, a romantic cascade that has prompted poems and songs. A few miles north of the village, the pots draw tourists, particularly in October and November when the river is swollen with autumn rains and salmon can be seen leaping up the falls on their way to spawn.

There's the Loup of Fintry, just beyond the Campsie Fells, where the river meanders gently before spectacularly crashing down over a series of mossy crags and giant boulders, a bubbling white torrent, until it settles again ninety-five feet below.

Then there's the Drover's Linn.

Linn is an old Scottish word for a waterfall, or for the pool below it. And this one is a beauty. Legend has it that Highland cattle drovers would stop there to wash and to water their beasts on their way to and from markets in central Scotland.

Anyone who lives in Kilgoyne is likely to know it. Certainly someone who was born here.

Of course, I wonder how sensible it is going there on the word of a man who might have done the most awful thing imaginable. And I know the answer is that there's none. But my gut tells me to go. Instinct, feeling, intuition, a sense beyond explanation, whatever it is, I've decided to follow it.

I first have to negotiate my way past the policeman on sentry duty just to get out of my own home. I insist that I'm going for a walk, and that he can choose to guard me or my house. He's unsure of what to do but opts not to follow me. He'll no doubt be calling his bosses, but I'm out of sight before they can pick up the phone.

I make my way along the north side of the river, crossing Blane Bridge and heading west, carrying a backpack on my shoulders and all the worries of the day on my mind. I'm heading towards a waterfall in the wild, going for reasons I don't know, going on the say-so of a troubled man arrested for murder. Sent by a ghost, searching for a ghost.

The road rises before me and soon I'm high above the river where the linn begins its tumble towards the Endrick. From a mountain to a stream, from a waterfall to a river, and on to the mighty Loch Lomond in the west.

It's a breathtaking sight and for a moment it makes me forget the blackness that's descended on the village.

The waterfall cascades down from the lush green above, cutting through a narrow crevice, gaining speed then opening wide, rushing over two terraces of exposed stone before crashing across a curved, jutting rock and creating a perfect arc of gushing white, thundering into Endrick Water below.

I take the moment, finding reassurance in Mother Nature's wonders, hoping that it is indeed a matriarchy, and trusting it's on my side. Surely the power of this waterfall could put out any fire made by man.

Across the river, so close and yet impossibly far, I can see Endrick Islands. The home of the dolls. The place where Billy Horsburgh was arrested. No more than twenty-five yards from shore, yet no way to cross from this side. My mind swirls, viewing the trees from above and envisaging the dolls hanging there. Thinking of all of them.

The descent is tricky. With wet rocks and a muddy track, it's a test for the young, never mind someone of my age with uncooperative knees. I use my hands where I have to, finding holds, gaining balance, wary of the weight of the backpack throwing me one way or the other, edging ever closer to the Endrick below.

Finally, breathlessly, I put both boots on solid ground, the sheet of water roaring past my ears, the noise deafening but thrilling. I look up and see the tonnes of silvery water crashing down from above. But is this the end of it?

I've got this far, a sight I've seen before, but the next step isn't so obvious. What did he intend me to do, or see? Is it all a wild goose chase?

I look around, seeking some kind of inspiration, any sign of where I'm supposed to go or what I'm supposed to do.

The rest of the words from Billy's note come to mind.

*Go behind it. Go in from the right.*

I back away, trying to get a better perspective of where any opening might be. All I can see is the blanket of water and the rock face behind. *Behind.*

I go as near to the right-hand edge as I dare and press myself against the rock.

There. Is it? A single step, likely carved by hand rather than nature, dropping down a foot or so. I step onto it and see it leads to another, then a third. From there, the rock wall falls back, and I've found it.

A cave. A huge, hidden cave.

My heart is pounding with the excitement of it, and with the fear of the unknown.

The light filters in, as if passing through a prism, shimmering against the limestone walls, accentuating the already vivid natural colours. The walls swirl in reds, pinks and greens. It's a magical, mysterious grotto.

The roof is a clear two feet above my head, stretching fifty feet across and a hundred feet to the back wall, where the light has lost its battle with darkness. My boots cause the cave to echo with every step, and I know there's no way my arrival has gone unnoticed if there's anyone here.

When I speak, my voice comes back to me in tremulous tones of anxiety.

'Hello?' I need to be louder to be heard above the waterfall. 'Billy sent me. The one they call Soapy Moary.'

Nothing.

'I've brought food.'

Ten seconds trickle past. Then movement. A scrape of feet. And a shadow steps out from behind a recess in the rock and into the murky half-light.

254

I'm uncomfortably aware that the figure standing in the gloom can see me, but I can make out little more than a shape.

'*You?*'

It's a teenage voice, crying out in surprise.

'I'm here to help,' I say.

I slip off my backpack and begin to unzip it. 'Do you want food?'

Another wait, more deliberation, then perhaps hunger wins out over fear, because the figure begins to edge forward into the light.

Dressed in a greatcoat two sizes too big for him, black school trousers and trainers, the curly, fair-haired teen looks like a little boy lost.

I look at Jason Doak and try not to cry.

# CHAPTER 56

Jason blinks furiously as he focuses, no doubt still barely believing he is seeing me standing before him. My shock might be greater than his and I'm struggling to contain it.

'Are you okay?'

No answer.

'Food?' I ask.

Jason nods quietly. 'Please.'

I pull out a package wrapped in tin foil and place it on a flat rock between us.

'Cheese and ham sandwiches. There's more in the bag. I've got some sausage rolls here too. A few apples and bananas, some pieces of chicken, a jar of honey, packet of chocolate biscuits for energy, some dried fruit. And a drink.'

He hesitates for a moment, disbelieving, as if it's an elaborate trap. Then he moves. He's limping badly, dragging his right foot, but he's still on the food in seconds. He rips the bundle of sandwiches open and tears into them ravenously.

Then he stops abruptly and stares at me.

'Why are you here?'

'Why are *you*?' I reply.

He decides not to answer and instead launches back into the sandwiches, taking huge bites, and biting again before he has a chance to swallow.

'Take your time. You'll choke. And don't eat it all.'

He finishes the first sandwich and half of a second before collapsing back onto the rock, breathing hard. I hand over a bottle of an energy drink and he gratefully guzzles on it, finishing with an exaggerated gasp.

'Better?' I ask.

He nods, eyes shut. 'Can I have an apple? Please.'

I hand one over and Jason crunches into it. I can see his nerves settling, energy returning. He's dishevelled, dirty and scared, and I'm sure he's lost weight, but otherwise seems well.

I nod towards his foot. 'What have you done to yourself?'

Jason looks down as if remembering his injury 'I tripped and turned it. And cut myself.'

'Let me see it.'

He pulls up his trouser leg to reveal an ugly tear to his skin that is swollen and festering in reds and yellows.

I frown at the wound. 'That looks like it's infected. Sit down and keep your trouser pulled up.'

The boy does as he's told, and I fetch the jar of honey from the backpack and twist it open.

'Honey?' he asks sceptically.

'Well, I could put a piece of chicken or a chocolate biscuit on it but that's not going to do you any good. The honey will dehydrate the bacteria and reduce the swelling.'

I slide a finger into the jar and smear the sticky honey across the wound. 'I'd like to add turmeric to it but that's not an option so this will have to do. How did you do this?'

'I was collecting wood for a fire and had my arms full of branches when I tripped over a log, did my ankle in and cut my neck as I fell.'

He pulls back the collar of his coat and shows me his neck. A ruddy, fresh scar stands proud of his skin.

'Did that bleed a lot?' I ask.

'Yeah. All over what I was wearing.'

'Hm.'

I make him hold still and apply honey to the cut, seeing him grimace at the touch.

'What are you doing out here, Jason? Half the village thinks you've been murdered. Or kidnapped by me. You know your parents are sick with worry, don't you?

He nods, ashamed. 'I didn't mean to worry them. But I thought they'd have more to worry about if I didn't run. I was scared. Terrified.'

'What of? Who of?'

He shakes his head anxiously. 'No. Sorry. Can't.'

'Okay, okay. I found your blazer. The police have it now.'

His eyes widen. 'That was *you*? We knew someone had come onto the islands but it was too dark to see who it was. I'd never have guessed it was you.'

I say nothing and he wonders why. Then I see him realise, remembering what he said.

'Who's *we*, Jason?'

He clamps shut. Scared and defiant. But I'm not having that.

'It's the man they call Soapy Moary, isn't it?' He remains tight-lipped. 'Or do you know him as Billy? Billy Horsburgh.'

He nods, reluctantly.

'Did you find him, or did he find you?'

'He found me. I just went to the islands to hide. After what happened to Charlie. I was sure no one would find me here. I'd no idea that's where Billy was living but he found me in two minutes flat. He said he heard me coming through the trees. He says the birds let him know when he has visitors.'

I look at him questioningly. Jason shakes his head.

'He wasn't saying they talk to him. He's not crazy. But they make a commotion and he's learned what it means. It's as good as a siren.

'Billy said he saw me long before I saw him. My bright yellow jacket was a dead giveaway for a start. He knew it wasn't my first visit because the dolls freak most people out, but not me because I'd seen them before.

'I walked as deep into the islands as I could, where I felt safe. I ended up sitting on a fallen tree and I ...' he looks embarrassed, 'I started crying.'

I make my voice soft. 'I'm not surprised. It's natural.'

'Anyway, that's when Billy came out of the trees. I think it was when he heard me crying that he decided to help me. I was petrified, all I knew about him was as scary Soapy Moary. I thought he'd kill me, but he told me it was okay. He sat me down, got me some food and tried to calm me.

'He looked after me. When I didn't want to talk about who I was hiding from, he was okay with that. He told me that he had plenty that he didn't want people to know, so he understood.'

I have plenty of questions about that and they can't keep any longer.

'Did he say what they were, these things he didn't want people to know?'

Jason nods but he's still wary of spilling Billy's secrets. 'That he used to live in the village. I didn't think he'd told anyone before.'

'It's okay, Jason. Only you and I know who he is.'

He sighs unhappily. 'I'd heard my mum and dad speaking about Jenni Horsburgh and how her brother spent years looking for her. And I knew about the dolls on the island. But I'd never connected the two of them.'

I'd put them together. In my head. Now I want to hear.

'Billy says he spent a lot of time in London, looking for his sister. When he had nowhere else to look, he came back to Kilgoyne, to make sure she wasn't here. He knew the story of Johnny Lyle hanging the dolls at Endrick Islands to protect the girls and ward off evil spirits, and he decided to do the same. He says he hung a doll. And hoped.

'He went back to the army, but then had to leave. So he went to London, living rough and looking for Jenni. He spent his time between there and here. He didn't go into the village for fear of meeting his mother or being recognised. The doll that he'd hung on the islands didn't work, so he hung another. And another. Over time he hung hundreds.

'He hung all of them?'

The boy nods, tears not far away. 'He said he had to do something.'

I lean across and place my hand on his.

'I probably understand it better than anyone in the village, Jason. Objects have power in ways most people don't appreciate.

259

Hanging those dolls made sense. It made sense to Billy and that's all that mattered.'

'You believe in it? Really? That sort of … magic?'

I lean back and breathe out hard. 'Not sure I'd call it magic. My granny, she knew about such things, and she called it power. And I do know that if you believe in it, then it has a power for you. Belief is most of what you need. Did Billy feel better for having hung all those dolls on the islands?'

Jason thinks about it. 'Yeah.'

'Then it worked for him. Maybe it wasn't magic, but it worked.'

'It didn't bring Jenni home.'

I choose my words carefully. 'Maybe she couldn't come home. Doesn't mean Billy's doings didn't help keep her safe.'

The boy looks sad and lost. I reach into the backpack for the chocolate biscuits and hand the packet to him. As he bites into one, I risk asking the big question.

'Jason, where were you and Billy two nights ago?

His eyes furrow. 'We were here. Here and on the islands.'

'Did Billy leave you for a while?'

'At night? No. Billy had been in the village in the afternoon but came back in the evening with some hot food. He didn't go to help out in the pub, so we were both there all night. Why are you asking?'

The boy is telling the truth.

I've little doubt about it. Billy Horsburgh was with him on Endrick Islands when Hannah Cairney was murdered. I don't understand why his hat was there but that will have its own explanation.

Billy didn't kill Hannah.

'Is this to do with the police coming last night?' Jason asks me. 'Did the police catch Billy? Did they arrest him?'

'Yes.'

'But he hasn't done anything. He's helped me. He's the one that's looked after me. You've got to believe me, Ms Crowe. He's not done anything wrong.'

'I do believe you, Jason. And you're going to have to tell the police what you told me. Billy needs you to do it.'

'But he's done nothing and I don't want to go back to the village. Please. I'm scared. I don't want what happened to Charlie to happen to me. Please, Ms Crowe.'

He's shaking like a leaf. I can't make him go back and Billy Horsburgh will be fine, for now at least. I need to know more.

'Tell me what happened when the police came onto the islands, Jason.'

'They came first last week. The day I ran. Billy heard them, just like he'd heard me. He knew they were there even before they got onto the first island and knew that they were police. He led us off the island, a way no one could ever follow in the dark, and we hid here in the cave.

'Billy said we had to stay in the cave even after they'd gone because he knew they'd be back, and he was right. More police came the next day.

'Then last night, they came back. Billy said there were more of them than before and they'd got closer this time before he heard them. He told me to go back to the cave and he'd lead them away. He made us swap coats, knowing that my yellow waterproof would stand out a mile. He gave me his coat, took mine, and told me to hurry.'

'You couldn't both get to the cave like before?'

He shakes his head sheepishly. 'They were too fast this time, and I was too slow. Billy could have got away if he'd wanted to. He knows the islands like the back of his hands. He got caught so that I would have time to get away.'

'He let them catch him?'

'Yeah.'

A silence falls between us, echoing round the cave like guilt. Jason is the only one who can break it and, finally, he has to before it crushes him.

'I wish I'd told Billy why I was here. He asked and I should have told him while I had the chance.'

I know a truth is coming.

'What would you have told him if you could have?'

'I'd have told him my pal was dead and that I ran because I was worried I'd be next.'

261

'Oh Jason …'

The boy can't look me in the eye. 'We did something stupid, me and Charlie. Something mean. To you. But we didn't …'

He looks up at the cave roof in a vain attempt to stem the tears that are beginning to stream down his face. My heart is racing in expectation at what's coming.

'Ms Crowe, I ran because Charlie had been killed and if I didn't hide then I was going to get the same.'

Even the birds in the trees of Endrick Islands are holding their breath.

'*Killed?* Charlie was killed? Not killed himself?'

Jason finally finds enough courage to look at me. He nods through the tears.

'Charlie was murdered.'

# CHAPTER 57

'You need to tell me about it, Jason. All of it. I know you want to.'

He's shaking. 'I don't know all of it.'

'Then tell me what you know. Start with this stupid thing that you did. Was this the mean thing you and Charlie McKee did to me?'

Jason's head bobs but his mouth remain closed as he wipes tears away.

'Don't worry about what you did, Jason. Worry about what might happen. Telling me is the first step to making it right.'

'I *want* to,' he sniffles. 'But I'm really scared, Ms Crowe. I don't think I can say. And what we did …'

His voice disappears and any sense of courage with it. I know I have to find strength enough for both of us. And I think it means doing it the hard way, even if it risks him choosing silence.

'I need to tell you about what happened two nights ago. The night I asked about where you and Billy were.'

'Is it bad? Like Billy thought?'

'Yes. It really is. The police found a body at the Devil's Pulpit. Someone was murdered.'

The colour drains from Jason's face. His features freeze, mouth open.

'Who …'

'Someone killed Hannah Cairney.'

He is crying. Tears for Hannah, tears for him. Tears for tears' sake.

'Jason, tell me about what happened. You must.'

He closes his eyes. Whatever it is, he can't look at me while he tells me.

'Charlie was mad at you. For telling him off. Charlie never much liked being told what to do. He wanted to get back at you. He had a plan and persuaded me ... I'm sorry. I shouldn't have let ...'

'It's okay, Jason. Go on.'

'He told me that he knew something about you. And that he knew how to drive you crazy.'

I know what's coming. I can feel it.

'He said we should make you think you'd seen him hanging. Dead. That you'd tell everyone, and they'd all think you were crazy when they found out it wasn't true. He talked me into helping him.'

'You were Auld Hangie.'

'What?'

'The devil creature. The tall beast in the branches and trees. That was you.'

He bites at his lower lip. 'Yes.'

I slow my breathing down. I have to contain it, and my anger, before I can speak again.

'Did Charlie say how he found out the thing about me?'

'Online. That was all he said. That he'd done his research.'

I massage my temples with the tips of my fingers. Try to channel calm.

'The thing he'd found out was that my son, Andrew, hanged himself. Many years ago. And that I saw it.'

Jason's eyes open. Wide. And he looks like he might vomit.

'I didn't know that. *I didn't know.* I'd never have ... Ms Crowe, I'm really ...'

My skin tingles. Cold. Everything around me seems to have slowed down. The air around my head is suffocating, clinging to me.

A rage bubbles inside, but it's directed at a dead boy. I know better than to blame victims. It's a rage with nowhere to go and I fear it might stay within me forever.

'So, Charlie McKee pretended to have hanged himself to get at me? To bring back those memories. Was I really such a terrible person to deserve that?'

Jason shakes his head, his mouth small. 'Charlie never thought things through. He was too busy trying to impress his new pals. It was wrong. Really wrong.'

'How did he do it? And how did you dress like that?'

'He'd found it on YouTube. A way to do it. He said he was sure it would work. Couldn't stop laughing about it. He got a climbing harness from the youth group and put it on under his school clothes. We stood him on a folding stool, strung a thin rope through the harness and up behind his neck and tied that over the branch above his head. Then we placed a thicker rope, a fake old-fashioned noose, round his neck for show. It was looped up over the branch but not tied. You couldn't see the thin rope behind the thick one. Not from where you were.'

It's my turn to cry. Slow, languid tears that trickle down my cheeks.

'The fake noose was at the end of a long rope. If the harness rope had broken or something went wrong, then Charlie would have just fallen to the ground, the noose rope was too long to have hanged him.

'We knew exactly when you'd be there. To within seconds. So we didn't have to have Charlie up there too long. We knew I could take the stool away and you'd be there within the minute.'

'Oh to be so predictable.' My voice is so faint I can barely hear myself.

'We used make-up to turn his face purple, stuffed his cheeks with paper hankies, put red lipstick under his eyes. It was a really terrible thing to do.'

'How did Charlie die? What happened to him?'

Jason's breathing is rapid. Uncontrolled. His hands are gesturing randomly.

'Don't know for sure. All I know is that it's probably *one* of them.'

I feel my stomach tighten.

'One of who?'

His mouth is open. His eyes wider. He's shaking.

'The Second Tier. Charlie called them Thelema.'

My mind churns with thoughts of old village tales and half-heard stories. And it chimes with fresher memories, of teenagers and pentagrams, of a voodoo doll, Twitter taunts and hashtags.

'You asked how I dressed like I did,' Jason continues. 'The devil costume. It's theirs. Thelema's. Charlie got it. We were both in the youth group, but Charlie had been elevated.'

'*Elevated?*'

'He was in Second Tier. I'm not even supposed to know there is a such a thing as Second Tier because I'm not in it, but Charlie told me. Partly he was showing off, partly he couldn't keep anything to himself. It's a group within the group. Invitation only. It's Thelema.'

Jason is gabbling. 'If you're not in it you might hear things, whispers, but that's it. No one knows unless they're in. And if you're in you say nothing. Nothing.'

'Jason, slow down, please. I'm not following. What happened? Or what do you think happened?'

'We'd done the thing with you. Saw you walk away. I got Charlie down and he was beside himself. Couldn't stop laughing. I'd seen the look on your face though and I wasn't feeling so good. Charlie was saying how he had to get the costume back or he'd be dead. That was his words. He said he wasn't kidding, that he'd be killed if they knew.'

'And didn't say who they were?'

'No.'

'So that awful costume is important to someone?'

'I'm only going by what Charlie said but yes, I'm sure it is. He told me more than he was supposed to. And he'd already got into trouble with them for it. They did ceremonies of some kind. And the costume was used in that.'

'Ceremonies?'

Jason shrugs. He doesn't know any more.

'And you're sure Charlie wasn't suicidal? He hadn't said anything would make you think that?'

'No chance, Ms Crowe. There's no way Charlie killed himself that day. No way.'

266

The boy looks confused and lost. I let him be for a few moments, sensing the enormous pressure building within him. He stares into the waterfall, perhaps seeking answers or a way out.

'Why are you here?' he asks me finally. 'I mean, I'm glad you are. *Really* glad. But you're the last person I thought might come to help.'

I give it some thought, considering it a good question.

'Like Billy, I guess I'm trying to right a wrong. Make up for not getting it right the first time. Young people make mistakes, but that's okay. That's natural. If you're lucky to live long enough to become old, then you usually don't get there without learning something. And you learn you're running out of time to do the right thing.'

He nods like he knows what I mean, but I'm not sure that he can.

'Jason, you said Billy could have got away from the police if he wanted to. But he saved you instead. Now we have to make sure that's been worthwhile.'

I take hold of his wrists, making sure that he's listening.

'We have to make sure you're safe. But we also have to make sure that whoever hurt Charlie, whoever's after you, is caught before they hurt anyone else. Jason, you can't live out here for the rest of your life. You know that, right?'

He nods tearfully.

'Who else was in the Second Tier? In Thelema?'

'I don't know for sure. And I don't know if all those in Second Tier are in Thelema.'

'But you think you might know some names?'

'Yes. Charlie said some things.'

'I need you to tell me.'

He exhales hard. 'Harris Henderson, Derek Cummings, Katie Wallace, Kai McHarg. And Hannah Cairney.'

# CHAPTER 58

*1597*

Jonet Stewart was part of a group of four women who appear to have been recognised folk healers along with Christiane Lewingstoun, Bessie Aiken and Christiane Saidler. They met, taught each other, cured for each other and generally worked together as professionals.

Andro Pennycuke urged Jonet to heal him, saying he 'begged for his health at her hand for God's sake'. She tried to heal him and failed. It was deemed unacceptable that a woman had this power of life and death over a man – particularly when she failed to save him.

Among the most heinous charges against Jonet was that she used the incantation 'The Father, the Son, and the Holy Ghost' during her healing practices. The words were deemed a blasphemous act as they were believed to have magical powers of healing but to come from the Devil.

Jonet's trial began on 15 November 1597. She was found guilty and sentenced to execution.

She was *wirriet* and *burnt*.

*2024*

Twitter

Hannah Cairney and Charlie McKee used to meet at the Crowe's cottage. She made them have sex and watched

Jason Doak was there too. All three of them at it. And her. The old witch.

She's sick

Disgusting

Evil

Burn her at the stake!

# CHAPTER 59

DC Sharma is back.

She's sitting at my kitchen table with a cup of tea in front of her, like an old friend come round for a blether. I'm pleased to see her, which in itself surprises me.

My first paranoia-driven thought when I see her on the doorstep is that she knows where I've just come from. That maybe she's followed me to Drover's Linn and knows I've met Jason. I tell myself that's unlikely, that she wouldn't be able to keep that information to herself. Now I wonder if she knows that Billy Horsburgh sent me a note via his solicitor. I think that's more likely.

I decide to test my theory by tackling it head-on.

'Soapy Moary's solicitor came to see me,' I say.

'Looking for your help?'

I shrug. 'She says he's not telling anyone much. He hasn't even told them who he is. Do you know how they caught him?'

'They got a call telling them where he'd be, sent in a team to Endrick Islands and brought him out.'

I wonder if she thinks it was me.

'Who called them?' I ask.

She's interested in why I want to know. I don't like that she can read me.

'They're not telling me that sort of stuff. But I heard from a friend that it was a man. Anonymous. That's all I know.'

'Okay.'

We're sizing each other up like boxers, warily circling the ring. I have to assume she knows more than she's letting on. Which is perhaps fair, as I do too.

'Listen, Marjorie. This village hasn't exactly been forthcoming with information. If anything, they've closed ranks further since Hannah was killed. So you're it as far as my local information goes. Are you okay with that?'

'If you're relying on the word of a crazy old woman then you must really need all the help you can get. I said I'd do anything I could to help, and I will.'

'Good. Thank you. Are you also okay with me keeping an open mind on how you seem to know the things you know?'

'So I'm to be victim, informer and suspect?'

She tilts her head to one side in thought. 'Let's just go with helping the police with their enquiries.'

'Which is a euphemism for being investigated for a crime, isn't it?'

'Okay, let's not. Will you help me, Marjorie?'

'I've said so, twice. DC Sharma, are you in danger of getting yourself into trouble with the new police investigation?'

She grins. 'Quite possibly. But it's a chance I'm prepared to take. I intend to claim ignorance if anyone calls me on it.'

There's so much I want to tell her. That I know how I was able to see Charlie an hour before he died. That Jason is alive, and I know where he is.

But I don't. I can't. Not yet.

There are things I can tell her, though.

'I have some information,' I begin.

'Go on.'

I tell her about my trip to Drymen Library and the back copies of the *Examiner*. About the Inner Circle and how Graeme Jarvie left it just as Jenni Horsburgh left the village. She's clearly interested and fires questions at me, trying to glean some more detail, and asking if the newspaper reports fit in with what I remember from the time.

She's surprised when I tell her I went to see Jarvie at the church, how he nearly fell off his ladder at seeing me there while he repaired the wall panelling. That he'd made a point of telling me that Jenni wasn't a member of the Inner Circle when I hadn't

271

suggested she was. How he'd insisted he didn't know what happened to Jenni and my feeling that he wasn't telling me the whole truth.

Sharma sits back and smiles. 'That's really helpful, Marjorie. I'm impressed.'

'There's more.'

'I'm all ears.'

'I told you and Sergeant Deacon about the talk of satanic parties at the Devil's Pulpit years ago. Well, I've spoken to someone in the youth group. That person's told me about an inner group that his friend was part of. A cult of sorts, children playing at being satanists. They describe it as being in the Second Tier. And they call themselves Thelema.'

'The same as twenty-five years ago.'

'Yes. And I was told the names of six members of Thelema.'

'Let me guess. Henderson, Cummings, McHarg, Wallace, and Hannah.'

'Yes. And Charlie McKee.'

She whistles softly. 'And you aren't going to tell me who told you this?'

'I can't say. Not for now.'

She drums her fingers lightly on the tabletop.

'Okay, I can live with that for now. Marjorie, I have a proposition for you. I'm going to talk to the Reverend Jarvie. Would you like to ride shotgun?'

I blink at her. 'I've no idea what that means.'

She seems to be doing her best not to laugh. 'I want you to come with me.'

'Why couldn't you just have said that?'

'Let's go.'

We steal into the church together, like thieves after the Sunday collection or whatever gold we can find. Reverend Jarvie's Volkswagen Beetle is parked outside in the little car park, so we know he's in the building, and want whatever element of surprise there is to be on our side.

272

Sharma's first step onto the wooden floor gives us away. It creaks and rings out, echoing through a building constructed with acoustics in mind. It's a built-in doorbell.

We stand for a moment, partly fearful of taking another raucous step, but also knowing that the alarm has been sounded, and Jarvie is now probably aware that his castle is being stormed. Instead, Sharma seems to be indulging in the moment, quietly enjoying the fact that the only people in this presbyterian stronghold are a lapsed Hindu and a witch.

The floorboard alarm works two ways. We hear footsteps coming from the left.

Jarvie isn't pleased to see us, that much is obvious. His mouth opens and quickly closes again, but we've seen it. And she'd seen the fire in his eyes before he was able to extinguish it.

'DC Sharma. How can I help you?'

She ignores the question and makes a show of continuing to look around the church as he walks towards us.

'It's a beautiful building, Mr Jarvie. Not my calling, of course, but I admire how well it was made. And how well it's looked after. Does it take a lot of maintenance to keep it like this?'

Jarvie doesn't follow her gaze; he knows his church well and keeps his eyes on her.

'It's a never-ending job, I suppose. It's like painting the Forth Bridge. As soon as you finish, it's time to start again. But it's the opposite of a thankless task. I give thanks every day for being able to do it.'

She smiles. 'You know that's not true any more?'

'*Sorry?*'

'The Forth Bridge. It *used* to be the case that when they finished painting at one end then they had to start again at the other. But then they started using some new space-age paint and now it lasts forever. Well, twenty-five years or something, but long enough. So the old saying doesn't work now. You just can't rely on anything being the same these days.'

Jarvie looks back at her, expressionless. But I can see that wheels are turning.

273

'I'd like a word with you if I could, Mr Jarvie.'

The minister exaggerates a look of surprise. 'I thought you weren't on the case any longer, DC Sharma. I was told that responsibility had been passed up the chain of command.'

'We all answer to a higher authority, Reverend, as you know. But I'm now tasked with investigating the fire-raising of Ms Crowe's cottage. Which is why I've brought her with me.'

I say nothing, as Sharma and I had agreed. My role is to make Jarvie wonder why I'm there and how much more I know. It seems to be working.

'Come through to the kitchen,' he says. 'We can talk there.'

We sit around a small wooden table, a mug and a cup waiting to be washed. The minister doesn't offer us anything to drink, presumably hoping we won't be here that long.

'Mr Jarvie,' Sharma begins, 'You're aware, of course, that some-one set fire to the cottage at Stillwater Field? And that the fire was hammered to Ms Crowe's door in the shape of a cross?'

He's clearly unhappy with the question. 'I'm obviously aware of the incident. A terrible thing, and I'm relieved that Ms Crowe escaped unharmed. I'd heard that the object nailed on Ms Crowe's door might have been cruciform, but I'm not sure what the relevance is. Are you suggesting there's a link to the church? Because that's quite a leap.'

'It's more that I'm keeping an open mind on it. And I thought you were likely to be the expert on crosses round here.'

'I suppose I might be. Do you have a point you're going to get to?'

'Yes. Yes, I do. I'd like to speak to you about other crosses.'

His reaction could be a few things. Confusion. Fluster. Annoyance. Maybe all of those.

'I think you need to be clearer, DC Sharma. I don't have time to waste on riddles. This has been a horrendous week for the village and I have much to do.'

She smiles again. 'You're absolutely right. Too many crosses for that to make sense on its own. You're familiar with Bodach Woods, Mr Jarvie?'

'Obviously.'

'I'm thinking particularly of the bit of the woods just off Spittal's Clearing. You know where I mean, right?'

'You can just take it as read that I know any part of Kilgoyne that you're likely to mention. I've lived here almost all my life.'

'Okay. Did you know there's a cross carved into a beech tree in Bodach Woods near the clearing? A proper cross, all decorative with eight points. The cross of St John.'

He doesn't blink. 'No.'

'No? It's been there for twenty-five years.'

'I said no.'

'That's surprising. Ms Crowe drew our attention to it last week. After a new cross was carved nearby.'

She's left a gap for him to step into and speak. He's choosing not to.

'That second cross seemed to have been carved at the time of Charlie McKee's death.'

He says nothing.

'Then a third appeared after Jason Doak disappeared.'

Now he speaks. 'What are these crosses and why do you think that I might know something about them?'

She smiles sadly, like she's disappointed in him.

'Well, I'd be guessing as to what their purpose is. I'd rather hear it from the person who carved them.'

No response.

'You're the expert, Mr Jarvie. Do you think the crosses are designed to act as a memorial? Maybe an act of contrition?'

He looks from Sharma to me and back. I'm guessing he's not best pleased to be asked to explain the purpose of the cross to heathens such as us.

'The cross is representative of both Christ himself and of the faith of Christians,' he says. 'In its simplest terms, it is a symbol of the crucifixion and therefore of the resurrection. It is a source of comfort and strength. It will mean whatever it meant to the person who carved it.'

'Spoken like a politician.' She smiles tightly. 'Did you know that tools are like fingerprints?' she asks.

The swift change of direction has thrown him. '*What?*'

'Tools. They're all different. Even these days, when they're all laser-cut, factory-made, they're all different. They all have microscopic variances. All have different points that make them unique. Take the chisel in your toolbox, for instance. It might look like any other bog-standard chisel in the range, but it's not. Put it under a microscope and you see all the little cuts and angles that make it unique. Like fingerprints. But sharper.'

Jarvie looks like he wants to stand, but his legs refuse to play. Instead his head rocks to the side.

'What are you suggesting?'

'Ms Crowe tells me that you double as handyman for the church. That your carpentry skills keep this place in shape. So, I'm *suggesting* that if we took the chisel from your toolbox, that we might find it to be a match to the chisel used to carve the crosses onto the tress in Bodach Woods. That's what I'm suggesting.'

He's shaking his head incredulously.

'This is ridiculous. I've no idea what you're talking about. Even if that chisel was some kind of match to these crosses you're talking about, even if carving them was some kind of crime, you still wouldn't know who used that chisel.'

Sharma is very calm. I'm impressed. And scared to move or say a word.

'You might be right, Mr Jarvie. However …'

She leaves a gap for his confidence to fall into. 'There's a fourth cross there now. It appeared after the murder of Hannah Cairney. This time, however, we were expecting it to be carved.'

I see his jawline quiver.

'So I installed a remote infrared camera on a tree opposite. A tiny little thing. So small that you wouldn't see it unless you were looking for it. And almost no chance you'd see it in the dark.'

Jarvie's eyes are strained, like he's desperately trying not to blink.

'The camera did its job. It recorded someone approaching a tree just a few feet from the others, and carving a cross of St John into the trunk. A tall man, about your height and build, wearing a dark blue parka and a hat low over his eyes.'

He says nothing but I can see his mind racing. Looking for a way out. Or an answer. Sharma doesn't give him time to think of one.

'Did you carve those crosses, Mr Jarvie?'

He hangs his head and closes his eyes.

'Yes.'

# CHAPTER 60

The minister is in a mess. He's holding his head in his hands and talking to himself. Sharma has to drag him back into the conversation.

'Tell me about the crosses, Mr Jarvie. Start with the first one.'

He looks at her for a beat, then half covers his mouth with his left hand, mumbling behind it.

'Speak clearly please, Mr Jarvie.'

'I carved that cross when Jenni Horsburgh disappeared. It was a spur of the moment decision. It just seemed the right thing to do.'

'Why?'

'I was … upset. Lots of people were. It was a traumatic thing for a small community.'

Sharma sighs. 'But lots of people didn't carve crosses onto trees. You did. *Why?* Did you have a relationship with Jenni?'

'No. *Yes*, but not the way you mean. We were friends. A bunch of us were friends.'

'Including Rowan Haldane, Adam Cummings and Lewis Dryden?'

'Including them, yes.'

Sharma studies him, seeing him sweat.

'Why did you carve the cross? What did you think it would achieve?'

'I don't …'

'Were you trying to bring Jenny back? Or did you know that she'd never left?'

'I didn't know. I … suspected. I suspected she hadn't run away as everyone else thought.'

My heart is thumping, and I realise my fists are clenched with tension. Sharma leans forward towards him.

'Mr Jarvie, why did you suspect that Jenni hadn't left? What reason did you have for thinking that?'

'I didn't know. Okay? It's important you understand that. I didn't *know*. I suspected. And yes, I should have said something about that, but I didn't. It wouldn't have changed anything.'

Sharma's voice rises in anger, taking me by surprise. 'Of course it would have changed things. Do you want to tell Jenni's mother that it wouldn't have changed anything?'

Jarvie shakes his head shamefully.

'Okay. Let's come back to that. Soon. You carved those other crosses, yes?'

'Yes.'

'Tell me why.'

'This is my village. My responsibility. The young people of Kilgoyne are my flock, whether they attend church or not. The cross is the symbol of our Lord, the power of His church and of His resurrection. I felt I had to fight the evil that has visited the village with the most powerful symbol I had. So I carved a cross after Charlie McKee took his own life. And then I couldn't stop. You must see that?'

'And yet you made those crosses secretly.'

He looks defeated. 'It wasn't a public proclamation. It was personal.'

'Did you kill Jenni Horsburgh?'

'*What*? No. No.'

'How else could you be so sure that she hadn't run away like everyone thought?'

'I wasn't sure. I told you that.'

'You were sure enough to carve a cross.'

Jarvie's stress and distress are overwhelming him. He's crumbling before our eyes. 'I *thought* something had happened to Jenni. I didn't *know*.'

Sharma is in his face. Her nose just inches from his.

'Are you making excuses to me or to yourself, Reverend? If you've spent twenty-five years convincing yourself that you didn't know about this, then I think it's about time you admitted otherwise. Don't you?'

He opens his mouth to argue, then gives it up, slumping back in his chair, eyes closed, nodding in defeat.

Sharma keeps pushing.

'I've been told that Jenni had a boyfriend. One that no one knew about. Did *you* know about him?'

'It wasn't me, if that's what you're asking. A couple of the guys were interested in her. Jenni was a good-looking girl. She hinted that she was seeing someone, but it was all a game to her. There was a … an understanding that she was seeing one of us. It was never said who, though. But it wasn't me.'

'So Haldane, Dryden or Cummings?'

'I think so. Yes.'

'Tell me about this little group of yours. What was going on behind the charity front? I *know* there was more. Do yourself a favour and tell me about it.'

His eyes scrunch closed, and he looks in pain.

'We were young. And stupid. It kicked off as a bit of a joke and got out of hand. Adam Cummings started it. He formed a group within the youth group, an inner circle to the Inner Circle. We were the best of the best, he said. And of course, we bought into that. So we bought into his stupid idea.'

'Of what?'

'A cult. A sect. Call it what you want. We messed about. Drank too much. Took drugs, although mainly just marijuana, and did all Adam's satanic Aleister Crowley stuff.'

'This was Thelema?'

Jarvie looks surprised and glares at me accusingly. 'Yes.'

'Not the kind of thing I'd have expected from a man of God,' Sharma prods.

'It's not something I'm proud of,' Jarvie snaps at her. 'But it was before I joined the church. It's a large part of *why* I became a minister. To atone. It was wrong and dumb, but it's done with.'

'Is it?' Sharma asks. 'Because looking at what's been happening in Kilgoyne this last week, I'm not too sure about that.'

'No,' Jarvie counters. 'Thelema is finished. It was part of our bargain. We walked away, stayed quiet, on the basis that everyone was done with it. There is no Thelema. There hasn't been since 1999.'

Sharma shakes her head at him. 'Maybe not a Thelema that you're part of or aware of, but it's back. And kids are dying because of it. When Hannah's body was found at the Devil's Pulpit, there was a pentagram scratched into the bank near to it. The Sigil of Baphomet.'

Jarvie looks like he's been slapped hard. His mouth is wide open.

'You need to tell me what you know, Mr Jarvie. Or tell me what you think. Start with who else was in Thelema.'

'The four of us. Jenni. Sandy and Evelyn McKee. Ricky and Julie Ferguson, before they were married.'

His mouth is tight, his eyes like a fire that has gone out.

'I don't think Jenni ran to London,' he says. 'Maybe she would have done, but she never got the chance. One of us killed her.'

# CHAPTER 61

Late March 2024
The Devil's Pulpit, Finnich Glen

*Charlie McKee was on his knees, naked, in the Carnock Burn, his pale flesh glowing alabaster white in the crimson water. Head bowed and seemingly compliant, his teenage limbs slender and long, little meat yet on his bones.*

*Five of them surrounded him, all shin-deep in the blood-coloured river. She looked at him differently from the others, she was sure. Although she'd dated him, she'd never been naked with him, not for the want of trying on his part. Now there he was, not a stitch on, cock shrivelling in the cold of the stream.*

*It was his initiation. And it was because of her. For good or for bad.*

*He'd been a pain in the arse lately. In fact, she struggled to remember a time when he hadn't been and wondered why she'd ever got involved with him. He was far more trouble than he was worth. Just a boy.*

*Spoiled. Petulant. Needy. Entitled. Throwing tantrums like a toddler.*

*He was dangerous too. Unpredictable. One minute he was threatening all sorts, next he'd say he hadn't meant it and wouldn't cause any trouble.*

*His head was pulled back by his hair and a streak of blood was drawn across his left cheekbone.*

*She knew that the trouble he could cause was off the scale. Kilgoyne would explode if Charlie pulled the pin on the grenade he was holding. In a place this size, the collateral damage would be immense.*

*She'd taken the coward's approach. The safety-first approach. Crossed her fingers and hoped he'd do nothing, say nothing. She wasn't sure that the others would be so patient. Her man knew now. He knew* about the new Thelema and was far from happy. He knew, too, that Charlie might be a problem.

A line of blood was drawn on Charlie's right cheek.

Her head was a mess of worry about actions and reactions. About truth and lies and consequences. She hadn't meant any of this.

If she'd seen it coming, she'd have sidestepped it. But it had sneaked up on her. She wasn't even sure how it had happened, when it went from some unexpected flirting, to being flattered, to being in the middle of it. To this.

To this unholy mess. To this tightrope walking, no-net nightmare.

The officiant dipped a finger in more chicken blood and drew a line across Charlie's forehead.

He'd been in the youth group for a year or so, but it was a few months ago that he'd heard whispers of the new Thelema and the old, and inevitably it appealed to his nature, to the dark within him. He wanted in. He wanted to make the move to the second tier. To Thelema.

Charlie was sly. He'd let on that he knew more than he did to get the rest out of her. He'd badgered her to vouch for him, to be his sponsor. She knew it was a bad idea, recklessly making a hostage to fortune, but she did it to keep him quiet. He'd sworn he'd shut up about what he knew if she got him in.

She hadn't been sleeping properly, jumping every time her phone rang, or the door was knocked. She was edgy, jumpy, irritable, nervous. She couldn't take any more, so she'd given in, told him she'd do it. So, there he was, words being spoken over his head, demands of fealty being made.

It was all on her.

'By the Holy Name of God Eheieh, do you swear loyalty to the Darklord?'

'I do.'

'By the most powerful Name of Elohim Gibor, do you swear on pain of death to uphold the sanctity of Thelema and never speak of it to others?'

'I do.'

283

*'By the name Tetragrammaton Elohim, I anoint you. By the Cosmos, I welcome your soul. By his unspoken Name, the greatest among Gods, I make you our brother in blood. Thelema. Thelema. Thelema.'*

*Charlie sniggered. He raised his head and burst out laughing.*

*Her heart sank. The others all looked at her. Her fault. Her mistake.*

*Charlie apologised, straightened his face, apologised again, said he'd be serious. She could feel the anger in the others though. It was done, he was in, and they'd have to deal with it, but they knew they couldn't trust him. He was just a boy.*

# CHAPTER 62

I am resuming my walks. My widdershins walks.

I've decided to take my original route every chance I get. And I'm going to walk it with a fury inside me. If I don't walk, I'll erupt. There's a volcano of rage blazing in my head and in my heart, and it might engulf this entire village.

There's rage for Hannah Cairney and Charlie McKee. Rage for Jenni Horsburgh. Rage for my Andrew. Rage for young people let down by those who were meant to protect them.

After Andrew's death, I came here to walk counter-clockwise round this village, twice a day, every day, to keep it safe. I did that for twenty-five years.

The first time I stopped, that I disrupted my route, was when things began to go wrong. A week ago, I'd been convinced my walks had been in vain because of what happened to Charlie McKee. But now I know that when I stopped, *nothing* had happened to him. It was all fake. Everything went so horribly wrong *after* I stopped.

I stopped walking and the faked event became a horrible reality.

Jarvie. Dryden. Cummings. Haldane. My fury is directed at all of them, the so-called village leaders, the little boys playing at being satanists, little boys who grew up to take charge and are guilty of a failure to protect. Worse than that, immeasurably worse than that, they collectively carried the secret of the greatest sin, knowing that one of them was culpable of it.

'*One of us killed her.*'

I'm going to walk until they give up that secret. I'm going to walk because it's the only thing I know to stop things getting worse. This evening, at 6.30 p.m., I will walk my loop. I will not stop or be stopped.

Before that, I'm going to Drover's Linn to see Jason Doak. I could take a number of routes to reach the waterfall, but I won't. I'm going straight into the heart of them to get there.

Main Street feels different. It isn't as oppressive as it has been this past week, and at first I think that maybe some of the hate has left it. Then I realise it's not the street that's different, it's me. I'm not afraid of them any more, I'm reclaiming this street. Not just for me, but for everyone in Kilgoyne who has had to suffer because of the dark fears of the few.

Some of them sense the change in me, I'm sure. I'm radiating anger rather than anxiety and they're shying away from it. Not all, of course. There are still a few cowardly catcalls, but from the safety of distance. When I turn to stare them down, they've already looked away.

My stomach still knots when I see the Endrick Arms up ahead. Standing in my way like a guard dog. This is the heart of the beast, and I'm not backing down.

When I push the door open, the sounds rush over me, raucous and intimidating. Loud voices, glasses chinking, tables moving, laughter and shouting. They're either whistling through the grave-yard, or they've already forgotten the loss of the children.

Then the noise stops. It grinds to a halt both slowly and all at once. Heads turn. Faces stare. All these familiar faces, frozen. Adam Cummings standing behind his bar. Sandy McKee and Lewis Dryden with glasses stuck halfway to their mouths. Rowan Haldane looks up from a newspaper, a glass of red wine at his side. The gang's all here. Mouths open, lips pare back, and I can see the silence will be momentary. I enjoy it while it lasts.

It caves in like a burst dam. They're all shouting at once. Not all at me; some are calling out those who are yelling at me. But the ones calling me names, demanding to know how I've the nerve to be there, saying I should be ashamed, those are the loudest. Empty vessels full of alcohol and hate.

'Get out. You've no right being in here.'

'You're evil.'

'Leave her alone. She's done nothing.'

My patience is finite today. I know that in seconds there will be a point of no return. It's the chip shop owner who throws the abuse that crosses the line.

'Have you no shame, you old witch? Three of our kids are dead and you've the cheek to walk through here like you own the place.'

The volcano erupts in me.

'You're an ignorant man. You'd be well advised to keep your mouth closed if you have no knowledge of what's coming out of it. Jason Doak isn't dead.'

That's done it. That's the match that sets the fire. There's uproar but once the words are out of my mouth there's no taking them back. I push through the Gartness doors as quickly as I can before someone can drag me by my hair to explain myself.

The doors are flung open in my wake and abuse follows me down the street. What am I talking about? How do I know that? How do I know that?

No looking back. No going back. No taking it back. It's out there now.

I walk away as fast as my old legs can carry me, eager to get off tarmac and onto dirt, to feel nature under my feet. Only then do I slow down, albeit with one ear on any sounds in my wake.

*Three of our kids are dead.* Ferguson wasn't wrong, just wrong in the three he meant. I think the person shouting out in the village hall was right when he said people here prefer to forget what happened to Jenni Horsburgh. Well, that's not going to last much longer. They'll all be thinking about her soon enough.

There's a reckoning coming to Kilgoyne. The truth will out.

Some of them may never lose their hatred of me, and that's okay if they have some left over for those who've done what they've done. If they can give up a little of their fear-based loathing of things they don't understand and instead cast blame where it lies, then I can live with that.

A twig snaps somewhere behind me.

It breaks clean and crisp, the noise sharp and unmissable. Broken like it's been stepped on.

I stop and listen. All I can hear are trees talking to each other in the wind, maybe a crow brushing through upper branches, maybe a squirrel scampering through the undergrowth. And my own heart. Beating.

Breathing out hard, I walk on. Still listening, still thinking, my imagination on overtime. It feels like they're all out here in the woods with me. Jarvie, Cummings, Dryden and Haldane. Hannah, Charlie and Andrew. All whispering, all chattering to each other.

The trees are thick here and the light is on the horizon. A distant blue that looks like safety and salvation. A voice in my head tells me to head for the light. Another voice tells me to test the situation, to see if I'm being followed.

I stop, suddenly. In the echo of my footsteps, there's another sound. Or I think there is. The tangle between reality and imagination is a twisty knot, and I can't be sure of anything. The other noise, if not a squirrel or rat or rabbit, has faded. Or stopped a moment after I did.

Maybe I can be sure of something after all. Sure that I should move faster, slip round trees and make for the light up ahead. I weave my way through the oaks, unable to hear anything above my own feet pounding on the path, and don't look back or stop till I'm beyond the trees.

Breath pours from me as I turn to look behind, and see nothing.

I hear Drover's Linn before I see it. The sound begins as a quiet rumble, then grows into a small thunder as the falling water crashes into the pool below. When it emerges into view, the arc of water flying across the curved rock above is a majestic sight. I indulge myself by taking a moment to savour its wonder, feeling a surge of reassurance that nature is stronger and more permanent than man's fleeting transgressions.

Walking to the side of the falls, I press myself close to the rock face, locate the hidden steps, and take a final look round behind me before clambering into the cave.

288

My eyes take time to adjust to the light, seeing the walls shimmer in reds and greens and dance with reflections. My echoing boots have surely signalled my arrival, but I call out to be sure.

'It's Ms Crowe. Are you here, Jason?'

He emerges as before from the same hidden recess at the back wall. The wary emergence of a boy living in fear. A fear all too justified.

'You've got food?' he asks.

I shuck my backpack off my shoulder and unzip it. 'Yes, don't worry. I've got plenty. How are you?'

'I'm okay, hungry.'

His eyes are already devouring the contents of the bag. More sandwiches, half of them egg, half roast beef, as he'd asked for. More apples, two packets of chocolate biscuits, some crisps, a wedge of cheese, a plastic tub filled with a tuna salad, and two rolls of toilet paper. 'Thanks, Ms Crowe.' He barely finishes the short sentence before ripping into the beef sandwiches, making one disappear like a magician.

'What's happened to Billy?' he asks.

I shout to make sure I'm heard above the roar of the falls. 'He's still being held by the police. He'll be okay, though. They can't put him away for something he hasn't done.'

He looks at me as if I was born yesterday and doesn't seem to share my confidence in the justice system.

'He really hasn't done anything, Ms Crowe. Other than try to help. It's not fair.'

'I think he'll be released soon,' I yell. 'When you tell them what really happened to Charlie, it will all come out.'

'When I'm safe, I'll tell them everything,' he shouts back.

'Good. Jason, I can't stay long but we're going to get you out of here as soon as possible. The police are getting close. But there's something else I wanted to ask you. About Hannah.'

'What?'

'She and Charlie McKee were dating for a while, but Hannah ended it, is that right?'

'Yes. Charlie was really unhappy about it. Said he was going to tell everyone what had happened. How it would make big trouble for someone.'

'Did he say who?'

'No. But I figured it was the guy Hannah was seeing after him. Charlie made out like it was someone who'd be in big trouble if people knew he and Hannah were together. So maybe someone who's married.'

'Okay. The police will want to know that.'

'I'll tell them anything I can,' he yells back. 'Once I'm safe.'

'If you'll let me bring the police here, you'll be safe. You can trust them.'

He shakes his head violently. 'No! I'm okay here for now. Please.'

'Okay, okay. I'm going to go now. I'll bring more food tomorrow. But you'll be home soon, Jason. I promise.'

He looks scared and for a moment I think he's going to burst into tears. I walk across quickly enough that he doesn't have time to tell me not to, and hug him. He squeezes me back and I'm glad of it.

'It's going to be okay,' I whisper.

Slipping my backpack on, I make my way to the curtain of water that is the cave's front door, descend the secreted steps and emerge out above the pool. With a deep sense of foreboding, I walk until I'm in the trees, hidden by shadow and foliage, and pause to look back at the Drover's Linn.

I stand, observing, for nearly a minute. Then I see movement by the right-hand side of the rock. A tall man, his back to me, is tracing the rock face with his hands, as if searching for an entrance.

He's confused for an age, then he finds it, follows in my recent footsteps, and makes his way into the cave.

# CHAPTER 63

M y pulse is racing as I hurry, quietly, back to the waterfall and the rock face. I can already hear raised voices within.

'Leave me alone,' Jason is yelling. 'Stay back from me.'

'I just want to talk to you,' the man is shouting back to him. 'I just want to hear what you think you know.'

'Nothing.'

'That's not what you told the old woman.'

'I was ... I ... Please leave me alone.'

My heart might burst, and I'm terrified.

'I can't do that, Jason. Not till I know. So tell me. What do you think you know?'

'I don't know anything. '

'Don't lie to me! You told her you'd tell the police everything you know. So what is it?'

'I'm scared.'

'You should have thought about that before now. You've just made things worse. You and your stupid pal. Taking things that don't belong to you. Messing with things you know nothing about.'

'You killed Charlie.'

'Don't be stupid. What is it you think you know, Jason? What do you think I did?'

Jason's angry now. Angry enough that I hear his answer loud and clear. Angry enough that he's reckless.

'You killed Charlie. And you killed Hannah Cairney.'

'That wasn't me,' the man roars. 'That was old Soapy Moary. The police have arrested him for it. They've got evidence.'

'No!' Jason screams. 'No. Billy was with me when Hannah was killed. He was with me all that night. He couldn't have done it. I'm his witness.'

Oh Jason, be careful. Don't talk yourself into the grave.

'You know Billy? You know who he is?'

Silence. Jason knows he's said too much. I don't know whether to stay where I am or go in.

'Answer me! You know who Billy is?'

'Yes, I know. Jenni's brother who lived here years ago. He's been looking after me. I know he didn't kill Hannah. You did. And just because he worked for you doesn't mean you know him. He wouldn't do that.'

*The one man who was close to Soapy Moary often enough that he had to know he was Billy Horsburgh.*

'You're the only one who knows where Billy was the night Hannah died? Is that what you're telling me, Jason?'

*The man who had the perfect chance to take and hide Billy's hat so he could use it to frame him for Hannah's murder.*

'You killed her, the same as you killed Charlie. To cover up what you'd done.'

*The married man who was scared of his affair with a teenage girl coming out.*

'I had to. I'd too much to lose.'

*The married man who was Jenni Horsburgh's secret boyfriend.*

'Let me go. Just let me go. Please. I won't say anything.'

*The man who started Thelema.*

'I can't do that. You know I can't do that.'

*Adam Cummings.*

'I've lived with this for a long time, and I've not gone through all that to lose everything now. I can't. You've got to understand that.'

*The killer of Billy's sister.*

'You killed Charlie.'

'He brought it on himself.'

*The killer of Charlie McKee.*

Jason's reply, if there is one, is muffled by the water, and the silence scares me until I hear the man shouting again.

'I killed him, but he left me no choice. He was going to talk. I'd too much to lose to let him do that.'

'That was Charlie. Not me. *Please.*'

'You should have left it alone. It's too late now. *You've* left me no choice, Jason. You see that, don't you?'

'Please.'

'You should have left things alone. Left me alone. Left the past alone. How did you get that costume?'

'Charlie got it. Derek told him about it. Please let me go.'

'Your stupid joke got him killed. The boy should never have threatened me. He set himself up for it. Died by his own rope. I just helped him.'

He's rambling now. Past any rational thinking. He's going to kill the boy.

I hear scuffling as I scramble into the step space and make my way behind the waterfall. There are voices from further back in the cave. There's shouting. Rage.

Through the cave light I see the tableau in front of me. Jason with his back flat to the wall. Deacon and Sharma, newly emerged from the hidden recess at the rear of the cave, standing in front of him, protectively.

Adam Cummings has a knife in his hand. A large-bladed weapon, the blade glistening red and green with the colours reflected from the walls.

'Put the knife down, Cummings. Do it now.' Deacon's voice is calm but urgent.

'No chance.'

Cummings swings the knife low in front of him, his eyes fixed on Deacon's. Then he lurches and makes a swishing arc through the air.

He doesn't see Sharma coming until it's too late. He begins to swing towards her, but she blocks his wrist, takes a quick step to the side and brings her instep crashing down onto the outside of his lower leg.

293

Cummings roars in agony and collapses, the knife clattering across the cave floor and out of reach.

'Leave it,' she warns him.

Cummings is breathing hard and in obvious pain. He's on one knee, propped up by an arm. As Sharma approaches, he pushes himself to his feet and half runs, half limps, careering as fast as he can to the cave edge and leaps through the waterfall and into the pool below.

Deacon and Sharma look at each other in minor shock before he mutters under his breath.

'Shit.'

They run to the hidden opening, me trailing in their wake.

When I stick my head outside, I see Cummings flailing in the water, trying to make it out while four uniformed constables wait for him to reach dry land.

Sharma and Deacon walk slowly round the Drover's Linn and are at the edge when he tries to clamber out. Sharma blocks his exit, making him tread water while she begins to read him his rights.

'Adam Cummings, I am arresting you under Section 1 of the Criminal Justice Scotland Act 2016 for the murder of Jenni Horsburgh, Charles McKee and Hannah Cairney.'

As she recites, I see Jason emerge cautiously from the cave. He blinks at the light and shyly waves towards me. A brave boy, I think to myself. A foolish, brave boy.

# CHAPTER 64

There is a small council of war at my kitchen table.

DC Sharma and DS Deacon are both in casual clothes to reinforce that they're off duty and obeying renewed instructions to keep their distance from the Major Investigation Team's case.

'I've got a pal in MIT,' Deacon is explaining. 'A mate that I used to work beside. I've heard snippets from him. He says Cummings has admitted to killing Jenni Horsburgh. He claims he lost it when she said she was going to leave the village and he demanded that she stayed. When he refused, he lashed out and hit her. Jenni responded by saying she'd tell his wife. He lost his head and killed her, but says it was an accident.

'Just like he accidentally buried her somewhere?' Sharma asks.

'Just like that. And he's refusing to say where Jenni is,' Deacon is saying. 'They think he's holding on to the information to use as a bargaining chip for a reduced sentence. Or just to prove himself an even bigger bastard.'

He hears himself. 'Apologies for the language, Marjorie.'

'None needed. Not for that man. If anyone deserves that word, it's him.'

'I've got a few more words for him,' Sharma chips in. 'I'll not share them now but if he doesn't give Jenni's mother the smallest bit of closure then I won't be able to hold my tongue.'

'There's not much they can do to drag that out of him if he doesn't want to give it up.' Deacon shakes his head wearily. 'He's the type who'll play games and string this out eternally.'

An idea is forming in a corner of my brain. My first instinct is to blurt it out, but I need to buy time to think it through.

'He admitted to Jason that he killed Charlie McKee and we have that on tape,' Deacon continues. 'But he's coughed to it officially as he'd little choice. Charlie didn't know what he was messing with. He'd mouthed off to Hannah about how he was going to spill whatever beans he knew about her and Cummings.

'I've no doubt Cummings thought it was all going to come out. Jenni, Thelema, Hannah. He found out about Charlie's stupid prank with the rope and saw his chance. He says he demanded Charlie show him how he did it. Then hanged him for real.'

Images bombard my mind with horrific effect. This is all too much.

'Sergeant, I remember on a previous visit that you were eyeing up the bottle of Ardbeg that was sitting on my worktop. I'm thinking this might be the time to indulge in a dram or two.'

They look at each other, raise eyebrows, then nod.

'Well, we're off duty, after all,' Deacon says grimly.

I fetch the bottle from the cupboard, pour three healthy measures into my best glasses and place one in front of each of us.

We all look into the whisky without reaching for it, contemplating. I pick up my glass first and draw in the deep peatiness of it, then they follow suit. I see Sharma's nose wrinkle.

'Sláinte.' I raise my glass to my mouth.

'To Jenni, Charlie and Hannah. May they rest in peace,' Deacon says. 'And to Jason, may he recover quickly.'

Sharma completes the toast, 'And may Adam Cummings rot in hell.'

The malt enflames my mouth instantly, flavours gliding over each other in symmetry. Deacon nods firmly in affirmation while Sharma's eyes widen before she breaks into a smile of surprise.

'To you, Marjorie.' She raises her glass again. 'For all the shit you had to endure.'

'I'll endure some of it for a lot longer yet,' I tell her. 'But not for as long as the parents of those poor kids will. That man Cummings is a monster.'

Sharma takes another sip. 'Sarge, do you want to tell Marjorie what else you got from your pal in MIT? She deserves to hear it.'

'She does, and it will all be public soon enough, but she should hear it now. They're going to charge Derek Cummings and Kai McHarg with fire-raising. It was them who started the blaze at your door. McHarg has admitted it and named Cummings. He says it was Harris Henderson who talked them into doing it. We'll look to charge him with incitement to commit an offence.

'That won't be the last of his charges, though. It was him who set up the fake profile on Twitter pretending to be you. It will be harder to make stick, but I hear the Fiscal is going for a hate crime charge.'

I'm not sure any of this makes me happy.

'Sergeant, has there not been enough suffering among the young people here? I've said this before but they're just children. They don't know what they're doing.'

He shakes his head. 'The law says differently, Marjorie. They're old enough. Beyond the age of responsibility. And if we let this go, then it becomes fair game for anyone to do it. Young Henderson has changed his tune though. His tough-guy act collapsed, and he cried like a bairn when he was arrested. He's confessed to all his nonsense and is going to give evidence against Cummings, so that will reduce any sentence. Henderson says they knew Adam Cummings was always flirting with Hannah, but they'd no idea she'd been seeing him in secret.'

The awfulness of that silences us all for a few moments.

'Hannah was going to tell me what she knew about Cummings. Wasn't she? She'd had enough of it.'

Deacon rubs at his eyes. 'They think so. They won't know unless Cummings tells them more. His ego might make him. They've also interviewed the rest of his group, asking why they covered for him for so long. The Fiscal will look to stick obstruction of justice charges on them. I hear Jarvie has already resigned as minister. Haldane's money will probably see him okay but he's under pressure to get out of the village, and Dryden has zero chance of being re-elected to the council. They're all claiming they didn't know that Cummings had killed Jenni.'

'But they knew someone had,' Sharma jumps in. 'They knew all this time that something terrible had happened to her.'

Deacon looks to Sharma, then to me. 'There's something else you should know, Marjorie. And this time the apology comes from Sharma and me.'

My skin tingles.

'The McKees, Sandy and Evelyn, have told MIT that their son Zak confessed that he didn't hear you tell Charlie McKee that'd he'd swing from a rope.'

'*What?*'

'It's true, Marjorie,' Sharma says, placing her hand on mine. 'Zak told his parents this a week ago, but they kept it to themselves because they thought you were to blame for what happened, so you had it coming. Zak made it up. He said it to get at you. To make trouble.'

'We just believed him,' Deacon adds. 'And we shouldn't have done.'

'Sorry, Marjorie.'

I can only close my eyes and shake my head wearily. 'As I've said many times, Sergeant, they're just children and they don't know what they're doing. I bear the boy no ill will. Nor either of you. Tell me, what are they doing with Billy Horsburgh?'

'He's been released with an apology. Adam Cummings knew who Soapy Moary was all along, getting closer to Billy than anyone else. The obvious theory is that he gave him a job to ease his conscience. But then when he thought the killing of Jenni was going to be exposed after all these years, he framed Billy for it. Billy says he lost his hat on his last shift in the pub and it looks certain that Cummings hid it from him, then placed it at the Pulpit after he killed Hannah,'

'How is he? Billy I mean. Have you heard?'

'Confused. Angry. But above all, he's in bits because he knows his sister is dead. Although he's still fighting it. Says he won't believe it till she's found. He told his solicitor that he was going straight back to Endrick Islands to put another doll up for her.'

'Poor sod,' Sharma says, knocking back more of the Ardbeg. 'He doesn't deserve this. They need to hammer Cummings till he tells them what he did with Jenni.'

'She's not far,' I tell them. 'I feel it in my bones. I always have.'

'There's still so many places he could have buried her here, though,' she argues. 'Those woods are deep. If he doesn't give up a location, then it could take months or years to find her.'

I take a deep breath and offer up my idea.

'I think there's a way.'

The words fall from me so softly that I don't think they hear me at first. Sharma asks me to repeat myself.

'I think I can find her. If she's there, and I think she is, then there might be a way.'

They look at each other, I think both hopeful and fearful all at once.

The idea that was born in the corner of my brain has grown bold enough to be spoken out loud. The confidence lasts until the words are on my lips.

'If you want to find something hidden in nature then you have to use nature to do the finding,' I begin. 'Those woods have stood there for a thousand years, and the way I know is as old as them. If Jenni has been returned to nature, then nature is the way to bring her home. Does that make sense?'

Sharma's mouth twists. Deacon remains impassive. 'Some,' she says. 'I'm having to work hard at it but it I guess it does.'

'Okay, good. Because I believe we should try dowsing.'

Sharma's mouth gets stuck halfway to closing. 'Say what?'

'Dowsing.'

'Marjorie … as in crossed sticks? As in how they find water?'

I bob my head defiantly.

'But dowsing for … a body?'

'Yes.'

'That can't work,' Sharma blurts out. Then she pauses. 'Can it?'

I make them wait for an answer, shifting my voice to project all the confidence I can find.

'Yes. Yes, I believe it can.'

Sharma swings her head to face Deacon, looking for confirmation that I'm crazy.

'It's probably the Ardbeg talking. But I'm in,' he says. 'I've read about something like this. The National Forensics Academy in the USA. Tennessee, I think. They have a body farm there in the woods and teach students to dowse for them. I don't think it's *official*, but they teach it.'

Sharma is open-mouthed. 'I'm not sure who's crazier, you or Marjorie. No offence, Marjorie.'

'None taken.'

'I'd say it's definitely me,' Deacon answers. 'It's my pension on the line if this goes wrong. Which is why I'm ordering you to do this.'

'You don't have to, I'm volunteering,' Sharma pushes back.

'I'm *ordering* you. You've got a good career ahead of you, let's keep it that way.'

'A once-promising career that I'm placing into the hands of some sticks. Have you done this before, Marjorie?'

'I have dowsed before,' I tell her. 'For water, for minerals, for lost things like jewellery or money. My grandmother taught me.'

'Okay ...'

'Apparently I showed some talent for it and had some success. It's all about belief. A sceptic can't dowse. A sceptic can only confirm their own cynicism by finding nothing. I believed because Granny Begg believed. I still do.'

'Uh huh. And you just cross the sticks and walk?'

'It doesn't have to be sticks. It can be rods or coat hangers. It can be pendulums like a penny on a wire, or keys dangling from a chain. The power isn't in the device. It merely channels the power. The power is out there, and an attuned hand and open mind can discern it.'

Sharma shakes her head and frown. 'Look, even if ... Marjorie, we have cutting-edge equipment for this sort of thing. Heat-sensor technology that can detect bodies even years after death. We really don't need to rely on ...'

'Mumbo jumbo? Hocus-pocus?'

'Right.'

'And who would search with this cutting-edge equipment? You and Sergeant Deacon? Or the new officers in town?'

Sharma begins to answer, then doesn't like what she's going to have to say. She opts for a different reply.

'I don't think I would have said this ten days ago, but Marjorie, if you say you can do this, then let's do this.'

# CHAPTER 65

The dark of Bodach Woods is a different place from the warmth of my kitchen, just as the chill of the night is a world away from the heat of the whisky. All the joking has stopped. The edge of the woods is a different reality. The prospect of Jenni Horsburgh being buried here is a sobering truth.

'Why start here?' Sharma asks. 'Why this part of the woods?'

I know her well enough by now. She knows I don't have an answer; she asks because she'd rather have one. Because she'd feel more comfortable if there was an explanation that she could get her head around. I don't have one of those.

But I try.

'You know how sometimes a place can just give you a bad feeling? That it makes your skin crawl? That you'd walk the long way round to avoid it?'

Sharma shrugs grudgingly. 'I suppose so, yes.'

'I've always felt that way about this part of the woods. I'm not sure I could tell you why. Until now. But I could *feel* it. Now? Now that I'm sure what happened to Jenni? Now, I know.'

She follows my gaze into the woods, seeing the light eaten up by the trees. We're in this and we have to do it now. It's all on me.

I stride for thirty or forty yards until I come to a halt and bend over to root through the forest floor, moving branches and easing aside flowers as I search. After a few minutes I stand and hold up my find to the fading light, judging whether it's fit for purpose.

It's a Y-shaped piece of birch twig. I turn it a few times, hold it aloft again. It will do.

They're watching me, both fascinated and sceptical. I'd never admit it, but part of me is enjoying putting on a show. I compose

302

myself, close my eyes and suck in a lungful of air, which I hold then let go in a slow, steady release.

I begin to walk in as straight a route as the woods allow, the straight line of the twig advancing in front of me, a prong held lightly in either hand. I step over and around clumps of flowers, following the line dictated by the twig.

I walk until my path is blocked by two large beech trees that defy any attempt to pass. I turn through ninety degrees, take another line of sight and begin again. This cycle repeats itself over and over; straight line to dead end, a new direction to a natural halt.

The whispers of doubt are in my ear, but I have to shut them out. This practice requires trust in the process. And it needs me to relax.

I walk for half an hour, this way and that, occasionally pausing for some sense of where I should go next, and twice shooting an apologetic glance towards Sharma.

'It's fine, Marjorie,' she reassures me. 'We've got all night. Take as much time as you need.'

It isn't true, though, and she knows it. The gloom is encircling us as the surrounding trees swallow up the light. In another half hour, we'll struggle to see the path in front of us, and half an hour after that we won't see our hands in front of our faces. In the morning, they won't be able to justify not passing what they know to the Major Investigation Team, and it's doubtful they'd use my services. It's now or never.

The secret, I think, is to be at one with the natural world. It has to flow through the birch and my blood, through the soles of my feet and the roots of the earth. There has to be a synergy between all of it, and I have to listen and feel and believe.

The twig pulls.

I stop dead in my tracks. Deacon is behind me and to the side. He must see the birch quivering.

All three of us are holding our breath. I need to know that I felt it. I take two steps backwards, forcing Sharma to dodge to the side, pause, then walk slowly forward again.

The birch tugs my hands towards the earth. I *feel* it.

'Here.'

The single word that I manage to utter is barely raised above a whisper but it echoes through Bodach Woods. There's a surge of emotion pulsing through me, toes to legs to torso, until I'm overcome with it and I'm in tears.

I feel an arm on mine. Sharma is calming me, consoling me. She's speaking softly and I can't make out words above the thrum of my senses.

Deacon has dropped to his knees and is feeling round the spot in front of my feet. He's tracing a path with his hands, shuffling along, his jeans pocked with dirt. After a while, he looks up at Sharma.

'There's a slight depression here. Consistent with a hole having been dug and filled in. The size and shape fit.'

'Holy shit,' Sharma mutters. 'Holy shit.'

My mouth is open, my breathing heavier, and I feel both hot and cold. I back away from the spot, fearful of it. My hands are shaking, and I resort to mumbling phrases under my breath.

Deacon is back on his feet, dusting his hands together. 'You're sure there's someone here, Marjorie?'

'Aren't you?'

He grimaces. 'I'm going to have to call Maitland at MIT. His reaction will be interesting. Misha, remember that I ordered you to come along. Marjorie, you heard me do it, right?'

'I did.'

'Good. I'll need to meet them at the edge of the woods. I'll shout once we're near so you can holler back and let us find you.'

Then he's gone, leaving Sharma and me in the dark, although not alone. Neither of us says anything for a while, letting the slack be taken up by the sound of the rising wind rustling against leaves and branches. Then Sharma stands in front of me, checking me over, and doing up the top button on my coat like I'm a child or an ancient relative.

'Couldn't your granny have taught you to bake cakes or to knit instead?'

I shiver inside my coat. 'Granny Begg taught me what I needed to know. Baking and knitting weren't among them. She taught me how to use what nature gave us. She taught me about the land and my people, about animals and our connection to them. She taught me about my history. She taught me well enough.'

'How does it work?' she asks. 'The dowsing.'

I shrug. 'I just know that it does.'

We find a piece of earth away from the shape, and sit and await the experts.

We fall into silence again with that, letting Bodach Woods speak to us in its ancient tongue; scurrying in the undergrowth, branches whispering as they sway, birds calling a last goodnight.

We sit there shrouded in that raucous hush, staring at the piece of ground we can no longer see, secrets at our feet, until the muffled sound of shouting breaks the spell.

'Here!' Sharma calls, repeating it twice more until the response is louder and clearer. Behind it, the boots of several men and the faint chink of metal against metal.

They emerge from the trees like ghosts, six officers clad in white, their coveralls rustling, leaves crackling below their feet. Spades are produced from a canvas holdall, lights on tripods from another, and in moments the scene is transformed. The patch of ground is illuminated, and long shadows are thrown onto the watching beech trees.

One of the six lowers his hood and glares at us. DI Tony Zebrauskas is not a happy man.

'Well, this is a shambles, isn't it? I don't for the life of me know what you idiots think you're doing. If there's nothing under that dirt except more dirt – and let's face it, that's odds-on favourite – then you, Deacon, are in deep shit. And if by some miracle there's a body in there, then the shit will be all the way over your head. I'll make sure of it.'

I see Sharma's mouth open and know she's going to argue, but before she can get a word out, Deacon's hand lands on her shoulder, squeezing it firmly. She reluctantly lets her mouth close again.

'Well, I'd say that's all stuff that can wait till morning,' Deacon answers for himself. 'Tonight, all we need to do is find out how big of an idiot I am. Let's dig.'

Zebrauskas smiles slyly. 'Have it your way.'

He turns to the other five white-clad men and tilts his head towards the site. *Do it.*

Under the artificial lights, we can see the slight depression that Deacon had traced with his hands. It was there if you wanted to see it, there if you knew where to look. It was underfoot and out of sight if you did neither, deep in the woods and long forgotten.

I'm banished to the side, along with Deacon and Sharma. We sit, quietly, and watch, a shared, impatient anxiety engulfing us. Ten minutes pass and I can stand the silence no longer, and have to break it by sharing my thought.

'Do either of you know of a poet named Robin Robertson?' I ask.

Sharma looks confused. Deacon shakes his head.

'He's a fine writer,' I explain.' A man of the Gaelic, of Scots and English. And he uses all his languages to tell what you might call modern folk tales. Of kelpies and shapeshifters. And witches.'

They say nothing.

'He writes what some call supernatural tales. Though as I say, it's all in nature. A couple of years ago, he wrote a collection of poems called *Grimoire*. Grimoire means a manual of black magic used to cast spells. One of the poems in it is called 'Of Mutadh/ Mutability'. I remember some lines of it and I think this would be the right place for them if you'll agree.'

One shrugs. One nods.

I begin. My voice low and my recitation slow.

> *Grass twists up through my hair now*
> *And my mouth is full of stones.*
> *Tell my mother and father I am coming, tell them*
> *I have not grown old.*

I let the last line drift on the wind. It snakes round trees and comes back to haunt us.

Neither of them says anything for an age and I wonder if I've filled their heads with images they'd rather not see.

'It's both beautiful and awful,' Sharma whispers. 'It says so much with so little.'

Deacon stares ahead at the patch of ground that brought us here, watching men scrape away years of dirt and secrets. I know he's thinking of grass twisting through hair and a mouth full of stones. He's thinking of Hannah too, his guilt side by side with mine.

It takes thirty minutes of careful digging, thirty minutes of anxiety and shivering in the cold. Half an hour of two men working either side of the site, digging carefully round the edges of the long rectangle, before one of them sinks to his knees and swaps his spade for a trowel. It takes another ten minutes before he turns to face Zebrauskas and nods.

The DI shakes his head in theatrical disbelief. Deacon and Sharma look at each other and at me. She mouths a silent swear word.

'Looks like it's good news, DS Deacon,' Zebrauskas snipes. 'It seems that you're only in the deepest shit now.'

Deacon stands till he's in Zebrauskas's face and holds his gaze.

'Good news? Is that what you call it in MIT when you find the buried body of a young woman? Here in the country, we call it a tragedy.'

'You should have been nowhere near this,' Zebrauskas yells.

'I was doing my job. Now why don't you do yours?'

Zebrauskas moves his head forward until the two men are nose to nose. Deacon refuses to budge.

'Why don't you two save this for another time?' Sharma shouts at them. 'There's work to be done and I want to get Ms Crowe home and out of the cold.'

They refuse to move, neither willing to back down. It's pointless male posturing. Sharma either forgets her rank or ignores it, and pushes between them, a hand firmly shoving each man.

'Have you lost your head?' Zebrauskas roars at her. 'I could have your job for that.'

'Maybe you could and maybe you couldn't,' she tells him. 'But you won't. Instead we'll all remember there's the remains of a young woman lying below our feet and act with a bit of decorum. And instead of having a pissing contest, maybe you could have the decency to thank the woman who brought an end to this, and who's given a family some closure. It wasn't your courses and modules that found Jenni, it was Ms Crowe. It wasn't your modern policing, it was something a lot older. She did this.'

I'm still sitting, tears running down my face. All eyes are now on me. Me and the forked twig that lies at my feet.

I don't know how it works. I just know that it does.

# CHAPTER 66

I close the front door of my cottage at precisely 11.30 a.m. Four seconds later, I pass through my garden gate, and click it firmly shut behind me.

After eighteen paces, I turn left onto Drymen Road, and begin the four-minute and twenty-second walk into Kilgoyne.

One minute in and I pass the war memorial on my right. He's there waiting for me as he has been twice a day, every day for the past two weeks. 11.31 a.m. and 6.31 p.m. Rain or shine, hail or wind or snow.

There's a sharp wind rising off the river, so he has his greatcoat belted tight at the waist and the new yellow beanie I bought him is pulled low over his ears.

Billy and his mother are back living in the family home in the village. He has a wardrobe of new clothes, but still has a fondness for the greatcoat. He's shaved, at least, and that's taken years off him.

Our loop takes us east to west, through and round the village, and back. At the end of Main Street, on the corner with the A81, is the Endrick Arms. The signage declares it under new ownership. It lies directly on our route, so we walk around it and in moments we're on the other side on Gartness Road.

I've closed my Twitter account, never to be reopened, but I'm told the mob have moved on, without apology, to harass someone else.

On Bodach Lane, the air is scented with bog myrtle and butterwort, while our eyes are caught by the vivid yellow-flowering broom. The bluebells are a flourishing carpet of colour, and a dotterel swoops low across them in pursuit of a breeze.

Jenni is buried in Kilgoyne churchyard now, a new headstone among the weathered grey slabs, her name freshly inscribed and clear for all to see. Her mother says she has lost a daughter but regained a son. She and Billy lay fresh flowers every week.

Billy has taken the dolls from Endrick Islands and buried them, leaving just one. He's got a way to go but he knows it, and so he's taken the hardest step.

As we walk, my mind still drifts to boys and ropes, and my grief walks with me. For Jenni, for Charlie and Hannah, above all for my Andrew. He is always with me, and always will be.

In Spittal's Clearing, the Witching Tree gleams in the sun this day, light sparkling on the odd iron pegs that stud the broken trunk. The stranger tree, the elm among beeches.

As we pass the tall elm that Charlie McKee hung from, Billy and I nod our respects as one, heads bowing as we slow but don't stop. Stopping is a chance we're not prepared to take. Instead we loop the village, wrap it in our care, and keep walking. *Widdershins*. Always widdershins.

# Acknowledgements

The research for this book took me off the beaten track to places I knew little about. Luckily, I was provided with a road map by those who know much more. In no particular order, I owe a debt of gratitude to the following. Sandra Lawrence for insights into the witch's garden; Zoey Lorne for her work on Scottish witchcraft trials; Colin Sinclair for his knowledge of birds; Alison Cross for her help with all things witchy; ex DI Aileen Sloan for her policing expertise; and Robin Robertson for the kind use of his poetry. I couldn't have written this without Robert Pitcairn's *Ancient Criminal Trials in Scotland*, John Gregorson Campbell's *Gaelic Underworld*, The University of Edinburgh's Survey of Scottish Witchcraft Database, and Janet and Stewart Farrar's *A Witches Bible*. Many thanks to Robin Robertson for allowing me to quote from his excellent *Grimoire: New Scottish Folk Tales* (Picador, 2020).

What's real and what isn't? The village of Kilgoyne exists only in my imagination, as does the Drover's Linn; the otherworldly Devil's Pulpit is real; the dolls of Endrick Islands are fictional but based on a locale and story from Mexico. The witch trials listed are, tragically, all true.

Most of this book was written far from Central Scotland, in Broad Bay near Dunedin, New Zealand. For this opportunity, I will always be grateful to Professor Liam McIlvanney and the University of Otago's Centre for Irish and Scottish Studies.

Above all, I'd like to thank my wonderful editor Phoebe Morgan for helping me make this book so much more than it was; my agent Mark Stanton for the inspiration and support; and my in-house witch – my wife, Alexandra Sokoloff – for being patient, loving, and almost always right.

# When a life ends, her work begins . . .

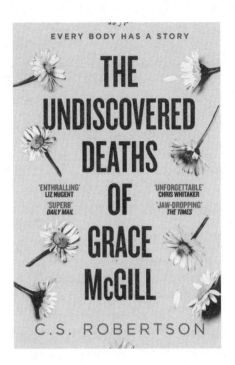

# Once you've met Grace McGill, you'll never forget her.